The School

Lisa raised the cleaver above her head and, with superhuman strength, buried it in Malcolm Hanley's skull. Her victim's face split into bloody halves and tumbled noiselessly to the floor.

She glanced knowingly at the lock on the door. The bolt clicked open smoothly. Casually, she stepped over the headmaster's corpse. Outside, the night air seemed cooler. Lisa felt the moisture that drenched her robe. *I must have gotten wet somehow,* she thought, as her fingers ran along the sticky red stains that were everywhere.

Her regal progress across the lawn was viewed with approval by the eyes that had been her companions since midnight.

The deed had been done. The contract had been sealed in blood. But the night wasn't over yet. The school had one more task for Lisa King. . . .

Skin-crawling horror
by the bestselling authors of THE BREEDER *and* MADONNA.

Other Leisure Books by Ed Kelleher & Harriette Vidal:

The Breeder
Madonna

Ed Kelleher & Harriette Vidal

THE SCHOOL

LEISURE BOOKS NEW YORK CITY

To Aggie and Sol
With Love

A LEISURE BOOK

Published by

Dorchester Publishing Co., Inc.
6 East 39th Street
New York, NY 10016

Printed in the United States of America

THE SCHOOL

"J'ai trempe dans mon esprit bleu
Les roses des essences mortes."

Maeterlinck, *Serre chaudes*

PROLOGUE

For all of her 16 years, Lisa King had been described as delicate. Pale and fragile as a child, in contrast to her three robust older brothers, she always had felt something of an outsider in a family that thrived on the basic Maine virtues of hard work, rugged competitiveness and unlimited stamina. Her porcelain complexion, slight figure and tender features mingled with a dreamy, otherworldly glow to set Lisa apart, not only in her own home but in the picturesque fishing village where she grew up. Impressionable and with a romantic nature, Lisa was referred to as "silly" by most of the boys her age and "creepy" by the girls.

Lisa's father, Edmond, a strapping six-footer who had risen to the rank of captain in the U.S. Army during World War I, returned from the front lines in Germany to pick up the reins of his family-owned paper mill, which thrived under his management even during the first, lean years of the Depression. By 1931, Lisa's brothers were already installed as apprentices at the mill, with the expectation that one day they woud take over. Lisa was another matter. As a girl, she was not expected to play any part in the business, but Edmond felt that she would never find a good husband unless she got her head out of the clouds and learned to stand on her own two feet. His wife, Anna, was less rigid. While she didn't approve of Lisa's daydreaming, she understood it and felt that her daughter's woolgathering might be channeled into some positive direction. Encouraged by her mother, Lisa began putting her fantasies down on paper, first trying her hand at poetry and then composing short stories. She began to imagine that one day she could be a famous authoress like her favorite writer, Pearl S. Buck.

Lisa kept her writings to herself, treasuring the time she spent with her pad and pencil while the other girls in town were busy learning to bake and sew. But sometimes she longed for companionship and wondered why she didn't seem to fit in with any of her schoolmates. At times like that, Anna's heart would go out to the young girl. Maybe she was set apart for a reason or destined for fame.

In the summer of her 16th birthday, Lisa immersed herself in dreams of literary glory to the point where Edmond became concerned. He decided that his daughter needed a change of scenery. He would take her out of the local high school, where her grades were mediocre, and transfer her to a private academy, where she could get strict discipline. His Army experience had taught him how a daily schedule of regimentation could make even the most listless recruit a solid, purposeful soldier. A good, stern boarding school could do the same for his daughter, away from her mother's leniency.

Lisa was terrified by the thought of leaving home. If her classmates thought she was odd here—and they had known her all her life—what would complete strangers think of her? Anna was opposed to the idea too, but Edmond was the man of the house and his word was law. He began sending away for brochures, but it was a chance remark by a Massachusetts salesman that led

Edmond King to investigate The Hanley School for Girls, a private establishment about 30 miles from Boston. Late that July, Edmond traveled to Hanley, Massachusetts, and met with the headmaster of the school, a Malcolm Hanley, who struck him as a formidable, no-nonsense type who would take Lisa's education in hand and mold her into a fit wife for some ambitious young man. Hanley's forefathers had founded the town and he embodied the New England spirit that was so important to Edmond. In fact, the headmaster had even designed the structure of the school himself, supervising every aspect of its construction down to the smallest detail. By the time Edmond King shook hands with Malcolm Hanley and agreed to entrust his daughter to his care, Lisa's father was convinced he had met a man of sterling character—and he was never wrong in his estimation of another man's worth.

Not until then.

In September, Lisa got her first glimpse of The Hanley School. She fainted as her parents' touring car turned sharply onto a winding path and suddenly the structure loomed in the distance, but Edmond and Anna dismissed her reaction as coincidence. In the car, on that same day, Lisa had started her menstrual cycle for the very first time. Her parents thought the blood and the excitement of leaving home caused her light-headedness. Lisa knew differently but kept silent. She had to. Something told her she was needed here.

Lisa's face seemed slightly out of reach as it danced in the moonlight, reflected in the glass of her second floor window at The Hanley School. Even in the dark of the night, Lisa could see the difference in that face.

That Indian summer day when her parents had brought her here seemed far removed now. Much had happened to Lisa in three months. The emotional scars she had suffered had healed, giving way to something more lasting. Lisa was a *real* woman now—thanks to

Malcolm Hanley and the school.

Lisa touched the windowpane. It was cold. She too was cold, she realized, shivering in a light dressing gown. It was just before midnight, but still she sat, not wanting to move for fear of interrupting the magic of this special night. This night belonged to Lisa.

Still flushed from the evening's success, Lisa gazed out the casement window at the neatly cropped lawn below. The grounds at the rear of the school were deserted, save for some sparrows who fluttered about, their tiny bodies making occasional dives into the water of a lavish stone birdbath. Lisa's eyes followed the movement of the rustling autumn leaves as they blew along a path toward the side lawn. Caught up in the cracked foliage, she spied what she thought was a discarded program from tonight's performance.

Lisa smiled. She could still hear the applause ringing in her ears as the heavy purple curtain came down with a final flourish. After the actors had taken their bows, Lisa stepped forward, standing timidly at first, to accept the warm ovation. The audience had loved her play, "Flowers of Darkness." With each wave of applause, Lisa had felt more self-confident, more like an author. Now, still tingling in the moonlight, Lisa ran her hand along the window seat. Her smile broadened. "You helped me do it," she said aloud.

Behind her, Lisa's roommate stirred in her sleep. Alice was a heavy sleeper, and Lisa was grateful for that. She had done all the writing of "Flowers of Darkness" during the late night hours, when everything was still. She cherished the thought of being the only one awake, the only one to feel the silent urging in the very walls of her room as she wrote, sometimes into the early hours of dawn.

Lisa heard the clock down in the foyer chiming midnight. She wasn't a bit tired. She never was—not any more. Her parents would have been astonished at her new vitality. Back home, Lisa had rarely stayed up past ten p.m., and even then her eyes would be closing. Since arriving at The Hanley School, she had become accustomed to getting by on just a few hours sleep, yet her grades were straight A's. In her letters home, Lisa had reported her improvement, and Anna had responded encouragingly, sometimes asking about her writing. Lisa had wanted to tell her mother about "Flowers of Darkness," but each time she dropped a note in the school mailbox, she realized she'd neglected to do so. When the play was chosen for production Lisa's first excited thought was to invite her parents—Anna, especially, would be so proud of her achievement—but the invitation had never been sent. Something had seen to that.

The clock finished chiming. Quietly, Lisa turned the handle on the casement window. She opened it just enough so that she could lean out, taking in the broad expanse of lawn below. To her left, where the clipped grass sloped down gently to the side lawn, she could see the single light still burning in the small white cottage that was Malcolm Hanley's home. Lisa felt a rush of warmth. How thrilling it always was to see that light, to know that she and the headmaster shared these midnight hours, together yet separate, two kindred spirits of the night.

Thinking of Malcolm Hanley had become Lisa's secret obsession. There had been so many midnights that she had leaned out the window, just like this, drawing strength from the thought that behind the shuttered doors of that cottage, he too was lost in creative solitude. She pictured him in a handsome velvet smoking jacket, his princely features intent on a volume of Keats or Byron. At other times, she imagined him composing his own sonnets—perhaps one to her.

And why not? Hadn't he taken a special interest in her from the first day she'd arrived? Didn't he give her a private smile, meant only for her, whenever they passed each other on the school grounds? Hadn't he touched her arm deliberately one day on the stairs when she was on her way to class? But, most importantly, hadn't he personally chosen "Flowers Of Darkness," her very first play, for the fall production? Dedicating a romantic poem to Lisa would be just the sort of thing she could expect next from Malcolm Hanley.

Lisa considered herself blessed. Among all her classmates, she was the only one who could see Malcolm's sensitive nature. Only Lisa could appreciate his unselfish devotion to the true aesthetics. Oh, she had heard the stories—the giggling gossip about Malcolm's reputation as a womanizer—but that was merely the chatter of immature schoolgirls who were too shallow or inept to see beyond his confident good looks to the soul that lay beneath. Lisa was above all that.

She trembled as a gust of wind blew in off the lake. Tonight really had been special. Again Lisa savored the words of praise Malcolm Hanley had spoken to her backstage minutes after the performance.

"The school is proud of you, Lisa," he had said, looking into her eyes earnestly. "You should be very pleased."

It had all been worth it, Lisa knew. Just to hear Malcolm speak to her that way had given her a sensation she had never felt before.

Now she thought back to the quiet Saturday afternoon, early in the term, when the seeds for "Flowers of Darkness" had been planted. Most of the students had been away for the weekend and Lisa was feeling homesick. She had begun to cry, huge tears running down her face, and then it had started to grow warm in her room, almost stifling. She had gone to the door to throw it open, but it appeared to be stuck. She had stared at the carved door for what seemed like hours, mesmerized by the tiny faces that were indistinguishable among flowers and small rodent-like animals. Then she had gone almost obediently to her desk and begun writing the first scene of "Flowers Of Darkness." Two short weeks later, the play was finished, and it hardly mattered that Lisa knew very well that the door to her room was smooth wood, with no faces, animals or flowers carved onto its surface.

Lisa's thoughts were interrupted by the sound of girlish laughter from the lawn below. She frowned. Someone was disturbing the silence that belonged to her and Malcolm. Ignoring the night chill, Lisa leaned further out the window, placing the palms of her hands on the peeling fire escape. Lisa spied the two young women immediately. Dressed alike, in filmy negligees, they ran skittishly across the lawn below. Lisa couldn't see their faces clearly, even when the pair stopped briefly to throw their arms around each other, huddling together for warmth and sharing a common secret. Lisa felt an inexplicable jealousy as she watched the girls separate from their embrace and continue down the slope.

Curious now, Lisa closed the window and put on her robe. Where were the two going at this hour? Probably to some clandestine meeting with the boys from the nearby Abbott School, she thought. But the Abbott School was in the other direction, across the lake. Lisa knew the boathouse was a haven for some of the girls, but that too was in the opposite direction. The girls she had just seen were heading toward the cottage, toward the house where Malcolm lived. Why would they be going there at midnight? And why were they dressed in their nightclothes? Lisa decided to investigate.

She tiptoed out the door of Room Six, padding lightly across the floor so as not to awaken Alice. Outside in the corridor, Lisa could feel the cool waxed surface beneath her naked feet. She trembled a little and pulled the robe more tightly around her slender figure. Furtively, she descended the stairs which led down to the main level of the school. The moon winked at Lisa through the small, rectangular stained-glass windows on each landing. Once on the main floor, Lisa hurried to the side exit, which had been left ajar, a large rock serving as its doorstop. Lisa knew the girls had put the stone there so as not to lock themselves out when they returned.

She hesitated. It was long after curfew. If she were caught sneaking out like this, she'd be in plenty of trouble, but in a moment of indecision, Lisa had walked through the exit, stepping over the rock to find herself outside. She moved purposefully in the direction of the cottage. Behind her, the school stood still and vigilant as the moon dipped behind clouds.

The cold grass tickled Lisa's toes at first, but as she approached the path which led to Malcolm's cottage, her feet had become numb. When she got closer to the small white house, she could make out muffled conversation, punctuated by shrill laughter. Malcolm was probably having a late night party. She must have imagined that the two girls she saw were in negligees. It must have been two of the teachers in party clothes. Lisa began to feel foolish.

But this was her night, wasn't it? Why hadn't she been invited? Tears sprang to her eyes. Once again, as she had almost all of her life, Lisa felt like an outsider. How could Malcolm do this to her?

Hurt, Lisa thought of turning back, but her face suddenly brightened with realization. Of course, she thought, it's a party for me. A surprise. I was meant to hear the two girls laughing outside my window. I was meant to follow them here. She quickened her pace, down the slope toward the cottage.

She planned to take a peek inside through the window, then run back to her room and change into one of her party dresses. The blue one, Lisa thought. Malcolm will love me in blue lace.

Suppressing an urge to giggle out loud, Lisa put her hand over her mouth and pressed her face to the windowpane. Her hand stifled the scream that threatened to tear from her throat.

At first, Lisa's innocent mind could not fully comprehend the outrage she was seeing. After a few moments, she wanted to turn and run away, but her feet were paralyzed. Nothing in her over-protected life could have prepared her for the scene that was taking place in Malcolm Hanley's bedroom. Nothing in her chaste, romantic fantasies about the headmaster came close to this defilement. Lisa had been betrayed by Malcolm. The stories, the ugly gossip had been true.

Lisa felt as though her heart would burst within her chest from the pain of this knowledge, but the pain didn't last very long. Anger took over, building to a hatred for Malcolm as deep as her love for him had once been. Still, Lisa didn't move from the window.

Inside the book-lined bedroom, oblivious to the watcher outside, Malcolm Hanley, solid citizen and headmaster of the school, sat on his bed lewdly fondling the young, naked girl who was perched on his knee. Lisa recognized Charlotte Feren, the most popular girl at the school. On the other side of the room was Charlotte's best friend Helene Ronson, still clothed and looking uncomfortable. Lisa took in the two girls but her eyes were riveted on Malcolm Hanley.

He wore only a short, silk smoking jacket and, with his legs spread slightly, Lisa could see his sex, jutting out angrily from the folds of his garment, almost like a weapon. Lisa felt sickened. Though a wave of loathing was rising in her chest, she could not take her eyes away.

Malcolm was laughing now, holding a wine decanter with one hand and continuing to caress Charlotte with the other. Some of the wine spilled onto Charlotte's thigh. Sliding the girl onto the bed, Malcolm licked at the droplets eagerly, while Helene giggled nervously.

"Come and join us, Helene," the headmaster said. Helene drew back.

"See? I told you she was shy," Charlotte said, running her fingers through Malcolm's hair.

"I'm not shy," Helene protested.

"Of course not," Malcolm said, offering her the wine. "Maybe you're thirsty."

Helene came shyly over toward the bed, while Malcolm poured wine into three glasses. Charlotte raised her glass in a toast.

"To Malcolm Hanley," she said, giggling. "Best teacher this girl ever had!"

She and Malcolm sipped from their glasses, but Helene hesitated, staring at her own glass thoughtfully. Then, with a flourish, she set it down on the night table. With a boldness that seemed to surprise her, she reached for the decanter. She raised it to her mouth and drank greedily.

"That a girl," Malcolm encouraged loudly. "Drink up!"

Helene complied. As she gulped the red wine, rivulets of the liquid trickled down from the corners of her mouth, and Charlotte clapped her hands excitedly.

"Oh, yes, Helene, isn't it lovely?" she cried.

Helene started to gag. She put the decanter down, and wiped her mouth with the back of her hand in an unladylike gesture. With mock delicacy, she reached for the strap of her negligee. Thrusting her narrow hips suggestively at Malcolm, she began a stripteaser's shimmy. Her small breasts bounced beneath the sheer fabric inches away from Malcolm's leering face.

In the window, Lisa's face was tear-stained. How could she ever have believed that Malcolm had the soul of a poet, that his secret smiles and touches on the staircase signaled a shared appreciation for everything that was sensitive and beautiful? Was the man she had looked on with such devotion the same man who was eyeing Helene with such unabashed lust? As though in answer, the headmaster's arm shot out to grab the half-naked Helene around the waist. He eased her down onto the bed next to Charlotte. His fingers hooked around the elastic of her frilly panties, sliding them down her legs.

Lisa's loathing gave way to revulsion. She had seen enough. Feeling cheated and furious, she turned away from the window and started back across the lawn. As she reached the top of the slope, she paused to stare at the dark form of the school, barely visible against the backdrop of night clouds. Lisa shivered, listening in the stillness. What she had just witnessed had turned her young life upside down, but the school itself, suddenly illuminated by moonlight, remained unchanged. Malcolm's cruelty toward her could not dent the steadfast solace that seemed to issue from the heart of the towering building. Lisa brushed away her tears and smiled.

People could hurt you with their lies and let you down and disappoint you. They could toy with your affections and leave you feeling desperate and alone, but the school would always be there, offering consolation. Now, Lisa realized, she had traded in her childhood home for the comfort of a new asylum.

From this moment on, the school would be the keeper of her secrets. Unlike people, it would never betray her. It was then that Lisa made a pact, secure in the knowledge that she would always be needed here.

While Lisa swore her peculiar allegiance, she was being watched by eyes that had made a similar contract.

With renewed strength, Lisa marched back across the lawn, heading for the school's pantry. She found her way quickly to the small room adjacent to the kitchen. Through a stained-glass window, the moonlight bathed the storage chamber with a surreal vermilion. Her eyes wide with anticipation, she gazed at one entire wall which was lined with sharp knives. Her forehead was wet with perspiration that belied her serene expression, as she approached the wall and dreamily stroked the cool, metallic edges of the blades. With detachment, she chose the most vicious-looking meat cleaver on the wall, then went out into the night once again.

The murderous instrument, clasped in her hand like a friend, swung to and fro as she strode back across the lawn. From the deepest core of the school, the unblinking eyes watched eagerly.

In seconds, Lisa was at the window again. There were

no surprises this time. The filth that awaited her on the other side of the glass was just as she had expected. Malcolm and the two girls were entwined on the bed, their drunken depravity mocking her; their naked arms and legs flailed about in a perverse sexual ballet. No, there were no surprises for Lisa. This time, the surprise would be for Malcolm Hanley.

Lisa edged along the side of the cottage to the door. She turned the knob, but the door was locked. Lisa looked questioningly back at the school. The click, as the bolt shot open, resonated in her fevered brain. An imperceptible smile touched her mouth, as the door swung open easily.

Softly, she glided through the deserted parlor to the bedroom. Her nostrils flared at the animal smell that stung the air. Balancing the cleaver in her hand, behind her back, she stood at the foot of the bed, unnoticed by the vile threesome.

"Malcolm?"

Her voice cut through the obscenity, and Malcolm looked up, startled. His eyes flashed in momentary panic. Then, taking in Lisa dressed only in her dressing gown, he relaxed and smiled.

"Lisa, what a nice surprise. Come and join us."

Charlotte and Helene burst into a fit of adolescent laughter, while Lisa looked Malcolm straight in the eye.

"I loved you," she said, accusingly.

More giggles came from the two girls, and Malcolm extended his hand toward Lisa, beckoning her. Smiling gently, she whipped the cleaver around, slashing him brutally in the shoulder. He fell back against the headboard, stunned. Like a cat, Lisa pounced on the girls, hacking at them wildly. Charlotte and Helene shrieked in pain as they tried to scramble to safety, but it was useless. The cleaver hummed through the air, silencing their frenzied cries and turning the white bedsheets a sudden crimson. Charlotte's right arm, severed neatly at the elbow, thumped to the floor. A gash in Helene's chest opened wide to her belly, and her entrails spilled out onto the carpet. *Whack. Slash. Chop.* And the girls lay dead.

Malcolm stared in disbelief. His fingers tried in vain to stem the blood that was gushing from his shoulder. He looked around dazedly. It was too late to save the girls, but he could still make a run for the door. He dove from the bed. Lisa watched with an amused smile as his naked figure stumbled into the next room.

That silly man, she thought. Where in the world does he think he's going? He's not even dressed.

Malcolm careened headlong toward the exit, which yawned promisingly. He was three feet away when the door flew shut in his face, locking at once. He tugged at the door, trying to rip it from its hinges, but it would not budge. A pathetic figure now, he fell to his knees before the oncoming Lisa.

"Lisa, please," he begged.

Lisa stood above him, cradling the blood-smeared cleaver.

"Please?" she said tauntingly.

"Please don't kill me!" Malcolm screamed.

"Oh, but I have to," she said.

Lisa raised the cleaver above her head and, with superhuman strength, buried it into Malcolm Hanley's skull. Her victim's face split into bloody halves and tumbled noiselessly to the floor.

Malcolm Hanley, the man she had worshipped from the window of her room on the second floor of the school, lay dead at her feet.

Isn't that just too bad, Lisa thought, now he'll never dedicate that romantic poem to me.

She glanced knowingly at the lock on the door. The bolt clicked open smoothly. Casually, she stepped over the headmaster's corpse. Outside, the night air seemed cooler. Lisa felt the moisture that drenched her robe. I must have gotten wet somehow, she thought, as her fingers ran along the sticky red stains that were everywhere.

Her regal progress across the lawn was viewed with approval by the eyes that had been her companions since midnight.

The deed had been done. The contract had been sealed in blood. But the night wasn't over yet. The school had one more task for Lisa King.

Part One

1

Vanessa Forbes had never felt comfortable as a passenger in any car that her mother was driving. It had been bad enough as a child before Vanessa knew that much about operating an automobile—then she had just been uneasy. But now that she was 17 and had recently received her own learner's permit, she knew exactly how bad a driver Evelyn Forbes realy was, and she was positively unnerved just sitting in the front seat beside her.

"Careful, Mom," she said, as Evelyn took another hairpin turn on the narrow, winding New England blacktop. A quick panorama of brilliant autumn foliage flashed across the windshield as Vanessa's mother jerked the steering wheel violently. The sleek, silver-gray Mercedes righted itself and shot forward with mechanical ease.

Vanessa rolled down the side window and took a deep breath of the crisp morning air. The sharp breeze caught her long, baby-fine auburn hair, whipping it around her sun-tanned face. The warm sunlight danced in the pale blue of Vanessa's eyes, which were brushed by natural, thick lashes, for years the envy of her girl friends back in Los Angeles.

Growing up in California had not prepared her for the magnificence of New England at leaf-turning time. Her anxiety at being uprooted from familiar surroundings was muted by the sheer splendor of the fall foliage in New England.

"Close that window, honey," Vanessa's mother grumbled. "You want me to freeze to death?"

Vanessa laughed. She rolled up the window and studied her mother's attractive profile as she maneuvered the car with manic glee. Evelyn Forbes looked much younger than her 40 years and delighted in the surprise on people's faces when they realized she had a daughter who was nearly of college age. Evelyn had Vanessa's finely chiseled features and full, sensuous mouth, from which a cigarette now dangled precariously.

The sign up ahead read: "Hanley. Population 5,200." Vanessa could make out a church steeple that was outlined against the stark blue sky. On either side of the road, houses began to appear, set back behind hedges and maple trees, boasting tidy, well-cared-for lawns. The blacktop was giving way to a main thoroughfare and an overhead traffic light was flashing a cautionary yellow to slow down. Evelyn kept her foot on the gas pedal as the sleepy Massachusetts hamlet rushed toward them.

"Well, this is it," Evelyn said. "Cute, huh?"

Vanessa didn't answer. Her face was pressed against the window, taking in the neat frame houses that nestled together in calm New England harmony. Near the front steps of the houses, Vanessa could see bicycles and garden hoses, everyday items that would be under lock and key back in Los Angeles. Close by the side of the road, battered tin mailboxes stood watchfully, their dented surfaces gleaming with garish colors. Overhead, a canopy of shimmering red maple leaves lined both sides of the road.

With her free hand, Evelyn extinguished her cigarette in the car's ashtray and immediately lit another. "You excited?" she asked.

Vanessa heard a screen door slam. On a porch, as they sped by, she noticed a young mother, with an infant cradled in one arm and another child tugging at her sleeve.

"A little," Vanessa admitted.

"You're scared, huh?" Mrs. Forbes said. "Hey, come on, changing schools is no big deal. California, Massachusetts, what's the difference?"

"Now you sound like Daddy."

Evelyn flicked an ash. "Don't mention your father's name," she snapped. "That son of a bitch."

Vanessa watched as the Hanley Public Library passed by on the left. It was a modest two-story building with Ionic columns in front. She decided to ignore her mother's last crack. Thinking about her father and the recent split-up was disturbing to Vanessa. She missed her father terribly. All through the trial separation, then the divorce proceedings, she had wished desperately that her parents would iron out their differences and get back together. But now that would never be. Most of Vanessa's friends' parents were divorced, failed marriages being fairly common in Beverly Hills. Still, Vanessa believed that wedding vows should be for life and she wasn't comfortable with her new status as the child of divorced parents. She hated when her mother spoke harshly of John Forbes, even though she recognized it was simply Evelyn's flippant way of covering up the hurt she must be feeling at the dissolution of her 18-year marriage. More than that, she feared being placed in the middle of her parents' differences, being forced to take sides one against the other. She thought it unfair of Evelyn to try to turn her against her father, while deep down she knew that if she ever did have to choose between them, her loyalty would be with John Forbes, who always had been a loving protector for her.

Friends and relatives who had known John and Evelyn from the beginning considered them a mismatch and marveled that they'd stuck it out as long as they had. Evelyn was a strong-willed, demanding woman who needed lots of attention. During the first few years of her marriage, she'd been the focus of John Forbes' life but as he continued to prosper in the oil business, amassing a small fortune, he'd grown increasingly distant from Evelyn and she'd reacted by turning into a clinging, nagging wife. From that point on, their break-up was assured.

Vanessa jumped as her mother hammered her fist onto the car horn. "Look at this jerk," she said angrily. "He's doing thirty. That's the kind of driver causes accidents."

Mrs. Forbes gunned the engine to pass a compact car, narrowly missing a sideswipe. The other motorist stared at her in astonishment.

"Mom," said Vanessa, "you're supposed to be doing thirty in a town. This isn't the freeway." She looked back, attempting to smile an apology to the other driver.

Evelyn eased off the gas pedal slightly. "You didn't answer my question," she said.

"What question?"

"Are you scared?"

Vanessa thought for a minute. "Sure," she confessed, "I don't know anyone at this school."

Mrs. Forbes shot her a disdainful glance. "So? You make friends. I'm going to Europe next week and I don't know anyone in Europe."

"That's different," said Vanessa quietly.

"No, it's not," insisted Evelyn. "It's a new situation and you have to meet it head on. That's your problem, Vanessa. You're too shy. You're not assertive. No matter where you go, you've got to win people over, whether it's Europe or The Hanley School. You know my motto."

"You've got a motto?" said Vanessa incredulously.

"I certainly do, young lady. All my life, I've lived by the rule—Do What You Fear."

"What does that mean?"

"Just what it says. Do what you fear. If you get thrown by a horse, get right back on that sucker and show him who's boss. If you're afraid to make friends, go up to the first person you see and introduce yourself. People will respect you and you'll feel better because you took the chance. And you know something? You'll get the upper hand. You'll build up your confidence. And that's what it's all about. Besides, you want to be an actress, and you can't do that if you're scared."

Vanessa stared ahead through the windshield. "I'm never afraid when I'm onstage," she said with conviction.

"I know that, honey, but there's a lot more to being an actress than just performing. It's not enough to just live out your fantasies in some part you're playing. First, you've got to get the part. And that means you have to be outgoing. You've got to cultivate an assertive personality. And you've got to work with other people . . ."

"Mom," interrupted Vanessa, "I'm not heading for Broadway—not yet, anyway."

"Well, you might be someday, so you'd better learn the ropes at school. God knows I'm paying a fortune for this place."

The town of Hanley was beginning to recede, as the road cut through stretches of farmland and fields dotted with grazing cows that lumbered lazily. Vanessa saw makeshift signs boasting fresh eggs, apples, corn and squash. Off in the distance, surveying acres of crops that had been placed under its charge, was an elaborate, towering scarecrow dressed in a long tattered topcoat. Vanessa smiled at the brazen phalanx of crows that perched nonchalantly across its shoulders.

Evelyn whipped the car around a curve and suddenly Vanessa felt her body grow tense. She knew that the school was only six miles from town, and at the rate her mother was driving, they'd be upon it any minute. The floor of her stomach seemed to drop away and her mouth became dry as ashes. Dense woodland shot up as if from nowhere, and all at once the road was cast in shadows.

As the vehicle roared forward, the friendly farmland seemed just a memory, giving way to a darker, more ominous landscape. Vanessa's eyes widened as she struggled to pierce an impenetrable curtain of forest that had descended on either side of the road. She knew that somewhere behind that curtain the school lay waiting.

Vanessa gripped the armrest of the front seat. She had an overpowering impulse to throw herself on the brake, forcing the car to a stop. Turn back, her mind was shouting as she squeezed her eyes shut. Vanessa felt the car negotiate a turn and bounce several times, leaving the smoothness of the blacktop for what she sensed must be a dirt road. Like a cloak being lifted from her shoulders, the fear began to subside. Vanessa opened her eyes.

The Mercedes had come to a halt outside a massive iron gate at the side of which was a bronze carved sign proclaiming: "Hanley School For Girls. Est. 1925." She gave one last shudder and the fright was gone completely.

"Well, honey," urged Evelyn. "Hop out and ring the bell. That gate isn't going to open by itself."

Vanessa approached the gate, her ankles wobbling on the dirt surface. As she stood beneath the bronze sign, it seemed to beckon her like a long-lost companion. As she pressed a circular bell that was attached to the gate-post, from somewhere far away she heard a muted jangling.

Vanessa looked through the gate, hoping to get a glimpse of the school. All she could see was a winding drive, bordered by thick foliage. In a small guard station off the entryway, a man in a dark blue uniform stood, peering through the glass at her. He came toward her, carrying a huge ring of brass keys and a clipboard.

The man waited. Vanessa stood to her full five feet, five inches, squaring her shoulders. "Vanessa Forbes," she announced, trying to sound confident.

The guard consulted his clipboard. He shook his head. "I don't see you down here."

So much for being assertive, she thought wryly. Then she got a sudden flash. "I'm not a freshman," she said quietly. "I'm a senior."

The guard flipped to another page. There was only one name on the sheet of paper. "Forbes, Vanessa. Okay," he said, nodding glumly.

Back in the car as they headed slowly up the curved driveway, Vanessa turned to her mother. "I'm the only transfer student," she said.

"That makes you special," Evelyn said.

Vanessa was leaning out of the car window as the automobile approached a sharp right turn. As the vehicle lurched, Vanessa saw a parting in the thicket of foliage and she gasped.

Her mother glanced through the window at the building that was suddenly visible.

"See, I knew you'd love it," she said. "It's just like in the brochure."

"It's like time hasn't touched it," Vanessa whispered, almost to herself. She wasn't listening to her mother anymore. Her eyes were riveted on something else.

Vanessa's first impression of the building was that it went on forever. Sunlight poured over the structure, causing the red brick to glow with a preternatural fury. The building stood boldly in its surroundings while gnarled cedars and tired oak trees pointed their branches in accusation, as if the school's presence was an assault against nature.

Vanessa let her breath escape as the sun's beams glinted fiercely on the stained-glass windows, seeming to call out in welcome. She sensed rather than heard a low hum in the air, as if from behind those crimson and violet windows ancient voices were sealing promises, sharing secrets. Just looking up at the towering four story structure made her dizzy.

The small windows, nestled among vaunted roofs and cornices, formed a strange design, jolting Vanessa's memory. She was sure she had seen that pattern somewhere before—a forgotten picture in a book perhaps, but definitely familiar.

Climbing the sides of the buliding was a tangled web of ivy which stretched to the furthest eaves, clinging to the bricks and at times threatening to obscure entire casement windows that yawned tomblike to form an opening through the mottled leaves.

Her eyes traveled upward along the sprawling succession of slate gray gables and dusky sloping mansards. She took in the high rounded turrets and tilted cupolas that jutted out toward the sky at jagged angles. Vanessa half-smiled. The school looked like an impenetrable castle. Who were they trying to keep out? she wondered. Or worse, what were they trying to keep in?

Perched on landings on either corner of the roof, their canine mouths open in malevolent snarls and their demonic eyes slyly watching, monstrous gargoyles reigned over their domain. Carved in the shapes of watchful hawks and other birds of prey, more stone figures roosted at their silent posts along the buildings upper reaches.

Vanessa trembled in fascination—and in fear. She felt like she had stepped into the setting for some kind of deranged fairy tale. Corrupt enchantment permeated the very air at The Hanley School. Something was wrong here, very wrong. She should tell her mother. Instead, Vanessa leaned back against the seat and watched wordlessly as Evelyn parked the car. By the time Vanessa got out of the automobile, the thought of telling her mother about her intuitions was nothing more than a faded memory. She took the lead as she and her mother walked across the pebbled path to the front door of the school.

Do What You Fear.

The heavy oak door was emblazoned with a bas-relief depicting a jumble of plant life, stars and winged creatures. The brass doorknob, located in the center, felt curiously warm to Vanessa's touch. She tugged at the door and it opened slowly with a heavy groan.

Vanessa inhaled deeply. The comfortable smell of a school which had been shut for summer vacation mingled with an unidentifiable aroma—nearly churchlike —which wafted toward her at once. Vanessa paused in the doorway, savoring the mustiness and a new, yet oddly aged pungency that she found almost intimate. As she stepped into the marble foyer, her face was washed in a shaft of blue light that showered down from somewhere above. Vanessa looked around uneasily.

"Gimme your hand," Mrs. Forbes said from behind her. "You shaking? What are you nervous about? You feel like you're on fire. Come on. We've got to find Mr. Hanley's office."

Evelyn's words thundered, reverberating in the cathedral-like entranceway. Vanessa looked upward, her eyes traveling along the length of the circular staircase that wound toward the second floor. Mrs. Forbes pulled at Vanessa's hand, leading her off toward the right of the stairs. Vanessa held back.

"His office is this way," she said instinctively, surprising herself.

She led her mother off in the opposite direction, down a corridor which was lined with empty classrooms. Sure enough, they soon came to a door marked with a silver plaque that read: "Matthew Hanley. Headmaster."

Vanessa knocked softly at the door.

"Come in."

Vanessa swung the door open and got her first

glimpse of Matthew Hanley. He was seated behind a huge mahogany desk. Slender yet muscular in a beautifully tailored pin-striped suit, he looked up and smiled. Vanessa flushed. Without a doubt, Matthew Hanley was the most dazzling man she had ever laid eyes on.

To call the headmaster handsome was not to do justice to his perfectly etched features—his high cheekbones, strong dimpled chin and deep set eyes of penetrating, steely gray. His perfectly formed mouth, full and disturbingly sensuous, parted slightly to reveal a row of flawlessly chiseled teeth. His nose was patrician, his forehead high. The entire face was framed by tousled layers of coal black hair that fell almost to his shoulders.

Vanessa had been staring, and she looked down self-consciously. She was relieved to hear her mother's voice behind her.

"Mr. Hanley? I'm Evelyn Forbes. This is Vanessa, my daughter." Vanessa recognized that her mother also was flustered.

Matthew stood up and came around the side of the desk, his lithe body moving with the agility and confidence of a man used to having his own way. He shook hands with Vanessa, looking deeply into her eyes.

"Oh, yes, you're the transfer student from California. Los Angeles, right?"

Vanessa was embarrassed. Her hand felt limp and moist in the headmaster's strong grip.

Mrs. Forbes extended her own hand. "Beverly Hills," she said.

Matthew Hanley pointed to a pair of leather armchairs. "Sit down, please. Did you just fly in?"

"No, we drove up from Boston," explained Evelyn. "I've taken a house there. I just signed the final papers on my divorce."

Matthew eyed Mrs. Forbes with a hint of amusement. "Well, you don't look old enough to have a teenaged daughter," he remarked.

Mrs. Forbes smoothed her skirt. "Why, thank you. I

did marry very young."

Vanessa looked over at her mother. For a brief moment, she wanted to throttle her. Ever since childhood, Vanessa had hated it when her mother acted silly around a good-looking man. She knew it was harmless but it always made her feel ill-at-ease. Still, she welcomed the exchange between Evelyn and Hanley because it gave her the chance to compose herself.

Her eyes were drawn to a large oil painting in a gilt frame that hung directly behind the headmaster's desk. Painted in brooding, somber colors, it showed an austere, quite handsome man who stared out at her with a quiet authority. She guessed from the cut of his clothes and the man's slicked back hair that the picture had been painted some years ago, perhaps in the 20's. An unsettling feeling of déjà vu came over her, forcing her to turn her eyes away from the portrait.

She glanced around the office, which was decorated with elegant efficiency. The carpet was deep and lush, its rich blue complementing the dark wood paneling which lined the room. On Matthew's desk, a lamp which Vanessa recognized as being of Tiffany design glowed warmly, illuminating a heavy crystal paperweight and sterling silver letter opener which lay nearby. Though the desk and the surrounding cabinets held a multitude of papers and files, they failed to obscure the office's overall look of luxury and masculine good taste. Vanessa's eyes returned inexorably to the huge portrait and she found herself interrupting her mother's exclamations.

"Who is that?" she asked. "You look very much like him."

Matthew Hanley's eyes followed hers to the painting. "That's my great-granduncle," he answered, a trace of pride in his voice. "He founded The Hanley School For Girls."

"He's very handsome."

Matthew leaned back with satisfaction, speaking with

an air that sounded casually rehearsed. "He was quite a remarkable man. He was the original architect of the school. Though he wasn't formally trained, he designed all the blueprints and supervised the construction down to the smallest detail. He worked closely with the bricklayers and the glaziers. I'm told that on occasion he even rolled up his sleeves and wielded a pickaxe and also personally designed stained glass and fitted it into the window fixtures. As if that wasn't enough, he helped to carve several of the gargoyles that you might have noticed on the school roof. Even most of the furnishings you'll be seeing in the classrooms and the living quarters were handpicked by Malcolm Hanley."

"That was back in the early twenties, wasn't it?" Evelyn asked.

"Exactly."

"He looks so scholarly in the painting," Mrs. Forbes went on. "Kind of sensitive." She giggled. "Not the construction worker type, if you ask me."

"Looks can be deceiving, Mrs. Forbes," Matthew said with a thin smile. "From what I understand, he worked like a man possessed. Some nights, after the building crew went home, he was still out there, working by moonlight—sometimes as late as midnight."

"Such an ambitious project for a young man," Evelyn said.

"What's more incredible," said Matthew, warming to the subject, "is the history of this property. Originally, this was farmland but no farmer could ever make it prosper. There was nothing wrong with the soil either. This is some of the most fertile land in the state . . ."

"Yes," Mrs. Forbes broke in. "We noticed all the vegetable farms on the drive over." Vanessa shot her mother a disapproving look. Why couldn't she shut up and listen to what the man was saying?

"They called in experts," the headmaster continued. "People from the Department of Agriculture, you name it. They even tried irrigating the land with special pumps, but nothing would grow here. Finally, in the 1920's, Malcolm Hanley bought the property. He got it for a song and turned it into a very successful establishment. We're very proud of The Hanley School For Girls. We have a very select student enrollment here and one of the finest faculties in the state." He paused and looked over his shoulder at the portrait. "I'm especially pleased to be carrying on in the tradition of Malcolm Hanley."

Vanessa was struggling to focus on Matthew's words but a cloud had drifted over her consciousness. Something the headmaster had just told them was drumming in her brain, something disquieting that was causing her fingers to tremble just a little.

Before she could stop herself, she spoke. "Nothing would grow here?" Vanessa asked dreamily.

Vanessa had stopped her slight trembling as she walked down the ground floor corridor of the school several paces ahead of her mother and Matthew Hanley. Again, she seemed to know exactly where she was going in her new surroundings. How could that be? she wondered. But the excitement of seeing the school auditorium for the first time quickly put to rest her vague feeling of having been here before. Behind her, Evelyn's voice rose and fell in a familiar cadence, droning on with her life story. Vanessa concentrated instead on what was on either side of her.

To her left was a succession of tapestries that hung nearly from the ceiling. Thick and detailed, and all in gloomy shades of gray and blue, they reminded Vanessa of something one might see in a monastery or perhaps in a European cathedral. But, on closer inspection, rather than depicting religious events and saintlike figures, they were cluttered with a menagerie of misshapen forms and grotesque, writhing bodies. Pretty weird artwork for a school hallway, thought Vanessa. She wondered if years ago Malcolm Hanley had selected these himself.

A square of sunlight crossed Vanessa's face, and she looked to her right. Through the window of an open classroom, the sun streamed in, illuminating the neatly lined rows of desks with a bizarre tint. Vanessa sought the source of the strange glow and found it in three small ovals of window glass stained a deep purple. She continued on down the corridor, noting that the glow from the next classroom was a peculiar green. That must take a bit of getting used to, Vanessa thought, wondering how the students reacted to that constant, odd light.

She had reached the end of the corridor. Without hesitating to look back, Vanessa turned the knob of the last door on the right. She stepped into an enormous, high-ceilinged room, filled with sloping rows of plush velvet seats and a raised proscenium stage at the far end. Matthew Hanley put his hand on her shoulder.

"This is the auditorium, Vanessa," he said. "As a drama major, you'll be spending a lot of time here."

"It's lovely," boomed Mrs. Forbes, her voice echoing in the huge room. "Just like a Broadway theatre. Isn't it lovely, Vanessa?"

The headmaster laughed. "Well, we only seat two hundred fifty, Mrs. Forbes . . ."

"I asked you to call me Evelyn."

Matthew nodded. "Fine, Evelyn. We don't compare to Broadway, but we do have a good-sized stage and some very sophisticated technical equipment. With our dramatic training, we like to think that what we do here for a student can eventually lead to Broadway."

"You hear that, honey?" Mrs. Forbes asked excitedly.

But Vanessa had moved into a pool of vermilion light, coming from a single rectangular pane of glass tucked away at the very top of the floor-length casements to the right. The brilliant red glow ran down her raised face. She shivered, her young body caught in a sudden chill.

As it swung to and fro, a hangman's noose threw a shadow across the stage. It hung from the rafters, where

Vanessa could make out a maze of theatrical lamps. She could see immediately that there was something unnatural about the tightened shape of the noose, as if it enclosed a heavy weight that was pulling it downward. Vanessa calmed herself. The noose was probably a prop or someone's idea of a grisly joke. Vanessa blinked. When she looked again, the noose was gone.

"Vanessa?" Her mother was tugging at her arm.

Vanessa squelched the hollow sensation in the pit of her stomach. "Yes, Mom?" she answered. Her voice sounded hoarse. With an effort, she stepped from the red spotlight. The air around her felt warm again.

From the side aisle of the auditorium, a woman was approaching. She appeared to be in her late 20's, trim in a modestly fashioned blouse and skirt. As she drew nearer, Vanessa saw that she had a pretty, almost angelic face topped off by thick, straight hair the color of corn silk.

"This is Karin Sayers," introduced Matthew. "She heads up the drama department and directs all the school shows. Evelyn Forbes. Vanessa Forbes."

Karin took Vanessa's hand lightly. "You come very highly recommended," she said. Her voice was deep and melodic. Vanessa liked her right away.

"She's a wonderful little actress," Mrs. Forbes said.

Karin's eyes sparkled. "Welcome to The Hanley School. I hope you'll be very happy here."

"She'll be happy," Evelyn gushed. "Won't you, darling?"

The noose. Vanessa should ask about the noose. But how could she? It wasn't there now. Instead, she looked around uneasily.

2

Karin Sayers was frightened but, for the life of her, she couldn't say why. Usually, she felt at peace at The Hanley School for Girls, especially in the fall when the new term began. As summer turned to autumn in a fiery sacrifice of red and orange and as the first cold blasts of northern air swept through the land, Karin normally felt a rebirth of excitement. But though she couldn't pinpoint the reason for her uneasiness, this year was strangely different.

Karin had been teaching at the school for five years now, and it had become home to her. She was always a little sad at the end of the term when summer vacation began. Then Karen would leave the school, a bit reluctantly, to travel abroad, but she was never as fulfilled as when she was here, teaching the young, eager girls.

As she customarily did, Karin returned to the school a week early to prepare for the fall term. The other teachers generally arrived with the students—a day or two before registration. So Karin would have five or six days to be virtually alone, getting reaccustomed to the sounds, the smells and particularly the feel of another semester. She spent lazy September mornings in her room at the rear of the third floor, organizing her lesson plan for the entire term. Afternoons were reserved for the auditorium which she had come to think of as her special province. She would sit on the stage, looking out at the empty rows of seats and imagining the students—her students, as they would be a few weeks from now as she put them through the paces of the fall production. At night, Karin walked around the grounds, happily surprised at the signs of renewed activity—the newly trimmed lawn, a fresh coat of paint on the boathouse, the carefully pruned hedges that bordered the paths. Inside, walking the dimly lit halls and staircases, she smiled at the sound of the pipes clanging in the walls, as the old plumbing protested after its summer respite. She liked the clean, reassuring scent of floor wax and furniture polish that seemed to be everywhere. The school was coming back to life—and so was she. But this year, something was slightly off kilter and Karin's euphoria was dampened with occasional flashes of a nameless fear.

Though Karin enjoyed the idea of "discovering" each day's additions and adornments during her nightly walk, she was aware that during the daylight hours when she was isolated in her room or in the auditorium the school was a quiet hub of activity. She had heard the rumble of delivery trucks bringing fresh supplies and had seen the caretakers, Mr. and Mrs. Trousdale, tramping about the premises, putting everything in readiness. In previous Septembers, Karin playfully had blocked out these interruptions so as to make her evening walk more fun, but this year she found herself welcoming each intrusion. For some reason that she couldn't explain, she valued her solitude less and felt the need to be surrounded by other people—even strangers. She found herself checking the registrar's sign-in book daily, hoping for early arrivals. But this year's ledger was just like the previous ones. No one was arriving early—except for Karin, whose name stood alone at the top of the page.

Naturally, Matthew Hanley was around but, unlike previous years, he seemed to be busy and she rarely saw him. Her colleague, Barbara Price, who taught chemistry, sometimes teased her about being at the school alone for a week with the handsome headmaster, but, in contrast to most of the females at Hanley, Karin had never been attracted to his charismatic good looks. Over the past five years, he'd made his share of passes at her, usually in a slick, well-practiced way, but she'd rebuffed him as casually as she would one of the over-sexed boys from The Abbott School across the lake. If and when Karin settled down with a man, it would certainly not be someone full of himself like Matthew Hanley. From what she had heard, anyway, he was merely a shadow of his great-granduncle Malcolm, who was at least the kind of strong, determined man she could admire.

But even that kind of man could be an imposter. Men who used their lifetime accomplishments and imposing good looks could be treacherous. Karin had heard the stories about Malcolm Hanley, telling of his manipulation of those weaker than himself and hinting of a darker side to his nature. Karin knew about men's darker sides from personal experience.

If only Natalie Sayers had lived. Karin's mother had been a ravishing beauty—that was part of the problem. When her mother died, Karin's father was constantly reminded of Natalie in Karin's thick, corn-silk colored hair, her large, clear hazel eyes, her small, naturally pouting mouth and healthy, rosy complexion. Karin had been ten that winter, just coming into her own as a natural beauty, beginning to feel comfortable with the delicate features that would mark her as a woman. Karin had been desolate at losing her mother at that age. The years ahead would be empty without Natalie there to guide her through the difficult passage of adolescence.

Karin had also been counting on her mother to exert a calming influence on Henry Sayers during those years. Karin's father had always had a mean streak in him, but Natalie, with her God-given charm, could soothe the volatile Mr. Sayers out of his often foul moods. When she died, Henry snapped, becoming more cruel—even to his lovely daughter.

No, stop, daddy, you're hurting me!

Be still, child. God wants me to do this.

Karin had not understood then, but as she got older she heard the ugly gossip circulated by the women of Valmouth, Pennsylvania, population 786. It was said by all the God-fearing ladies of Valmouth that Natalie Sayers had been carrying the child of an encyclopedia salesman who had stopped off at the Sayers' farm one morning when Henry was away. Word of this got back to Henry. Though his wife denied any wrongdoing, Henry believed the gossip to be true. The town was laughing at him—Natalie had brought shame into their house. From that day on, Henry Sayers did not utter a single word to his wife—until the day she died.

A few months later, the cold winter was suddenly jarred by a curiously balmly day. The air became sultry, punctuated by jagged streaks of heat lightning. Sometime after lunch, the lovely Natalie Sayers left the house on an errand, but, by the supper hour, she still had not returned. Growing impatient, Henry, in his shirt-sleeves, paced outside the farmhouse as Karin watched from the window. She knew that her father was seething with anger; she could see it by the stiffness of his gait as he trudged back and forth below her. The look on Henry's face was not one of concern but more of bitterness and annoyance at what he considered yet another insult. Refusing to eat, he waited until it was well past nightfall, then, carrying a large flashlight, he went out to the fields, where the corn grew to a height of more than six feet.

Karin saw the beam of the searchlight dart about in the tall, languid stalks of corn like a butterfly. Henry was several yards from the house when he heard what sounded like a wounded animal—the same noise that he and Karin had been hearing, on and off, for hours. But instead of a dog or a fox caught in a trap, he found his wife, blood pouring down her legs, in a state of feverish delirium. Rather than rush her to a nearby hospital, he brought her to the house, laid her on the kitchen table and, for three stifling hours, relentlessly prayed to God that he would be spared even more shame. Karin stood in the doorway, like an outsider, as her father raged about the evil ways of Natalie Sayers. Trembling in the thick heat, she watched while her mother's life blood streamed off the wooden table and dripped to the floor. It wasn't until dawn that she was finally dead.

Henry had been a farmer while Karin's mother was alive, working the few acres of land with his hands and some crude machinery, most of the time without any local help. Natalie had defiled their household and Henry swore he would cleanse the land, the house and the people who lived in it—or he would die trying. At first, the preaching was limited to Karin, but she was confused, not recognizing the nature of her mother's sin. She cried out in terror, seeing her father stroke the razor strap, almost lovingly, before one of his private sermons.

The seed of Satan grew in her belly. She was a fool to try to carve the wickedness from her womb.

Later, Henry converted the old barn on the property into a makeshift church. He fashioned a primitive cross out of floorboards and nailed it to the roof of the dilapidated A-frame. His new obsession led him to whitewash the walls of the barn, but the tenacious mold and mildew still seeped through in patches. And even with all the incense burning and the smell of wax from scores of store-bought candles, the smell of manure still reeked from the very seams of the barn.

When the church was ready, Henry became a self-ordained minister, forcing Karin to watch as he donned austere vestments, handsewn out of flannel and denim work clothes, and conducted a midnight ceremony as the wind whistled through the cracked walls. Before long, news of Henry Sayers' mission reached the townsfolk. Curious at first, they began showing up at the farm to hear him speak. Soon, a crowd of people shuffled into the barn every Sunday as well as a few stragglers during the week. Minister Sayers waved a ragged copy of the Bible from his pulpit but he scarcely glanced at it as he preached his brand of twisted Christianity with a vengeance. Karin didn't know which frightened her more—the private lessons with the razor strap or watching her father publicly denounce the sinfulness of women.

When Henry Sayers began drinking—sometimes as much as two quarts of whiskey a day—Karin became even more fearful. But the first time he lurched into her bedroom, grabbing her thin shoulders and calling her Natalie, she knew that the day was coming when she would have to make her escape. But that day didn't come soon enough.

The darker side of Henry Sayers, which Karin had come to know in all its hypocritical fury, was far behind her now. Her subsequent private schooling and growing devotion to the fine arts went a long way toward erasing the scars of her horrifying childhood. Now as Karin walked the deserted halls of The Hanley School For Girls, she felt as though she had found the final refuge which could protect her from the memory of everything that had gone before. But this fall when Vanessa Forbes came to the school, something was awaiting Karin that would supercede even the terrors of her past.

In the darkness of his room, Bobby Cannon sat up in bed, jolted and afraid. His eyes snapped open, but as he looked around at the familiar setting, taking in his dresser, the trunk at the foot of his bed and the posters of rock stars on the wall, it all seemed alien to him. The dream had left him struggling to climb out of some gaping pit of altered images and his limbs felt weak from the exertion. Slowly, as if he were underwater, the objects in the dorm room swam into focus and Bobby let out a long sigh of relief.

He felt the pillow behind his head. It was wet with perspiration. He looked over anxiously at his roommate, Dennis. He let out another breath. Thank God Dennis hadn't heard him scream out in fright. Maybe he didn't really scream out loud, reasoned Bobby. Maybe he just thought he had. It had been the worst nightmare he'd had since he was a little kid. He would have been embarrassed if he had awakened Dennis just because of a stupid dream.

Bobby mopped his brow and tried to fit the pieces of the dream together. Maybe he could figure out what it meant. Sometimes, a dream was just a hodgepodge of past events, strung together and not making any sense, but this nightmare had been different. It was so vivid in its brutality that Bobby was still shivering. The dream had been almost palpable. He could still feel the needle-like branches as they whipped across his face, cutting his skin as he ran through the woods trying to escape. But escape what? He couldn't remember what it was he'd been running from.

Bobby drew the blankets up around his neck. The night had grown chilly. He wanted to leap out of bed, cross the room and close the window, but the damn dream was making him afraid of getting up. This is dumb, he thought. He threw the covers off and tiptoed over to the window, careful not to disturb Dennis. Without looking outside, Bobby gently pulled the window down. Then he took a deep breath and dared look out. Across the lake stood The Hanley School, like a huge, silent soldier glaring back at him. Of course—that was it. He had dreamed about The Hanley School, or at least that had been part of the nightmare. He forced himself to gaze out at the lake. Giant, circular ripples churned from its center as if something large and unthinkable was trying to squirm up from its depths. Bobby shuddered. Boy, he thought, if the mighty Dennis Bellivin could read my mind, he'd say I'd lost all my marbles.

Bobby glanced over at Dennis who was snoring slightly. The older boy's face was turned to the wall. It was hard for some to believe that Dennis and Bobby were best friends. True, they had roomed together here at Abbott for three years—next term they both would be graduating—but they were almost a study in contrasts. While Bobby was of medium height, slender and sensitive looking, Dennis was broad and muscular. In fact, with his six foot two frame and engaging smile, Dennis Bellivin was probably the best-looking boy at The Abbott School—a real iadies man and surely the most popular senior. Dennis had the kind of good looks that put him at ease with the opposite sex. Bobby, on the other hand, had to force himself to be casual with girls, but he was easygoing. People took to his wry sense of humor and almost boyish charm, though he lacked the poise and charisma that Dennis seemed to come by naturally. Dennis was athletic and bright; though he never seemed to do any real studying, he was consistently in the top ten of his class. Bobby was smart too but he always found himself cramming before exams just to get a passing grade. If Dennis and Bobby were opposites, it had only served to strengthen their friendship.

The terror of the dream had subsided now. Bobby sat on the window ledge and watched the digital clock, flashing red numerals as it approached midnight. On the other side of the room, Dennis Bellivin's breathing was even and reassuring. Bobby grinned at the bulky lump under the covers that didn't even look like a human being. He felt lucky and privileged to have Dennis as a friend. Dennis was kind and generous and, except for his occasional moodiness and sometimes violent temper, he was the ideal roommate. When the darker side of Dennis surfaced, Bobby had been almost frightened of him at times. He would then leave his friend alone until he snapped out of it. Sometimes, Bobby would wake up in the middle of the night to see Dennis Bellivin's bed empty. He respected his roommate's privacy and never questioned him about his nightly walks. Bobby guessed that Dennis wanted to be alone with his thoughts, nothing more than that. As for his volatile behavior—well, it did take a lot to make Dennis really angry, so those times were rare.

Bobby thought back to the day last term when the Abbott School bully, John Brockum, had been picking on him, daring Bobby to fight. John had begun to get rough, shoving Bobby around and even blackening his eye. Bobby had panicked. It wasn't that he didn't know how to take care of himself. He had learned plenty growing up on the streets of Manhattan, but he was no match for Brockum, who was several inches taller and outweighed him by 50 pounds. Dennis had been at basketball practice in the gym on the other side of the school, but suddenly, almost out of nowhere, he was there, separating the two in a few swift movements. Before long, he had John Brockum on the ground, threatening to kill the boy on the spot. Even as Brockum lay on the lawn, pleading and crying for Dennis to stop, Dennis wouldn't let up on him. It took three students to pull Dennis' hands from Brockum's throat and, even then, Dennis looked as if he might still murder the bleeding boy. Bobby had been grateful to Dennis, but something about his excessive rage had shocked and alarmed him.

Bobby Cannon looked out the window of his room again. All at once, the nightmare came back to him in all its fury. The Hanley School had been chasing him across the lawn, deep into the woods. No, not the school itself, but the stone figures that lined its roof had somehow come to life and were hellbent on tearing him limb from limb. Running with every breath that was in him, Bobby had barely kept out of their clutches as they lunged for him with malevolent accuracy, no matter which way he turned. As he hurtled through the dense branches, he could hear their teeth snapping viciously just behind him. As he looked over his shoulder while still in mad flight, he could see the school itself. Behind each of those strange, stained-glass windows, a faceless horror laughed out at him in the night.

Remembering the dream, Bobby trembled. He had never felt comfortable even looking at The Hanley School For Girls. There was something peculiar about that place. Three years ago, as a freshman, he had set foot in the building for the first time and experienced a feeling of nameless apprehension. Even with all the time he'd had to spend there, rehearsing for the school plays, he had never learned to relax completely while inside the walls of The Hanley School. He wondered how the girls could handle being there all the time.

Bobby had heard all the wild stories about the school's bloody background, that kind of gossip being almost part of the curriculum at both schools. Still, Bobby, trying to be logical, preferred to think that his anxiety about The Hanley School could be traced to something that had happened to him when he was four years old. On a cold, cheerless day, his father had taken him to New York's Museum of Natural History. Bobby had been fascinated by a picture book showing dinosaurs and other extinct animals from prehistoric times, so his parents had thought he would be thrilled at seeing the museum's famed exhibit featuring dinosaur fossils. But when Bobby came face to face with the towering skeleton of a tyrannosaurus rex, gleaming white and seemingly watchful of him, he had cried out in fright and begged his father to take him home. Thinking the boy was just playing, Mr. Cannon had boosted him up on his shoulders to get a better look. The giant reptile's horrifying teeth were only inches away from

Bobby's face, and it seemed forever before his father had put him down. The memory was still vivid even now, 13 years later. With its gabled roof's ornate trimmings and echoing high-ceilinged rooms, The Hanley School had always reminded him of the Museum of Natural History. No wonder, he thought, turning back to his room, he had had that dream about snapping teeth.

But there was something unsettling about the comparison. The incident at the museum may have made Bobby fearful of vast, castle-like buildings like The Hanley School, but The Abbott School also was an immense fortress, and Bobby felt right at home here. No, his instincts were right the first time—The Hanley School was weird.

Bobby padded quietly back to his bed and slipped under the covers. The pillow still felt damp on his neck. In the other bunk, Dennis hadn't stirred. It was already after midnight—time for sleep. Bobby closed his eyes and thought about tomorrow when he would be seeing many of his friends from last term. He wondered whether the nightmare would return.

As he drifted off to sleep, the thought occurred to him that if he were ever given the choice, he would rather roam the earth with prehistoric monsters than spend one night alone in The Hanley School.

Before sleep overtook him, Bobby envisioned one last flash of a dinosaur's gnashing teeth but then relaxed. Dinosaurs were extinct, part of the past, and the past couldn't ever come back to hurt him.

Across the room, Dennis Bellivin opened his eyes and smiled.

At the edge of the water, on the Abbott School side of the lake, Dennis Bellivin and Bobby Cannon were sprawled in a patch of sunlit grass. The air was crisp and clean—"football weather," as Dennis called it, though Bobby thought of it as a classic back-to-school day. From their vantage point on the Abbott lawn, the boys had a bird's-eye view of The Hanley School, which Dennis had intensified by a pair of expensive, high-powered binoculars. He peered through the glasses at a cluster of young girls, new arrivals at Hanley, who were gathered on the side lawn. Dennis focused on a particularly well-built girl, waving good-bye to her parents who were going back out the main drive in a chauffeured limousine.

"Marie is back," he said with a grin. "I think she got bigger over the summer."

"Impossible," Bobby said. "Let me see."

He grabbed for the binoculars but Dennis held them just out of his reach.

"Patience, Bobby, everything good is worth waiting for."

After a few moments, Dennis handed the glasses over. Bobby had to adjust the focus to allow for his 20/40 vision. Dennis, of course, had perfect eyesight.

"Shit," Bobby said, finally zeroing in on the girl. "I think you're right. When you look at them tits, they look right back at you."

"*Those* tits," Bobby." Dennis corrected him with a chuckle. "We're at school now."

"Don't remind me," muttered Bobby. Looking at the statuesque Marie Kronofsky, her large, shapely breasts outlined in a tight-fitting cashmere sweater, Bobby felt a familiar pang of desire. The magnifying lenses brought Marie's voluptuous body tantalizingly close and Bobby was grateful for the chance to observe her without her knowing it.

"Bobby, you're drooling."

"I am not," Bobby said automatically, but then he realized Dennis was only kidding. He felt himself blush. The sight of Marie was exciting alright, but whenever Bobby was with her in person, his proper upbringing prevented him from staring at her chest. That usually meant he carried on a conversation with his eyes absurdly glued to her face, never daring to glance downward even for a second, lest he be thought of as just another crude, adolescent boy. Besides, Bobby knew, there was a lot more to Marie than big boobs. She was a bright, thoughtful girl, who was a little shy about her appearance and self-conscious about the inevitable jokes that the other kids made about her. Still, he realized, it sure was nice to look at those tits. These new binoculars of Dennis' were a godsend.

"You think she's still a virgin?" Bobby asked.

"'Course she's still a virgin. She's savin' it for you, Bobby."

"Yeah, I only wish!"

Sometimes, Bobby surprised himself when he talked like that. True, he was embarrassed about his lack of sexual experience—he had never made it past the heavy petting stage, though he'd gotten close a few times. He wanted desperately to make it with a girl but he was a little old-fashioned. Something inside him wanted the first time to be special. Deep down, he was nowhere near as vulgar as he sometimes sounded, but that's what the other boys expected from him—especially Dennis. At least, that's what he presumed; Dennis and he never had really talked about how he should behave.

Bobby had come from a loving family and, even at an early age, he had been taught to respect women. His mother was beautiful and refined and Bobby's father had always treated her like a lady. The same was true with his older sister, Lorraine. If someone were looking through binoculars at Lorraine this way, Bobby would want to punch him right in the mouth. Yet most of the other boys at Abbott were obsessed with sex and when you were 17 and just feeing the juices of young manhood, it wasn't easy to stick to the ideals of your parents.

Through the glasses, Bobby saw Marie turn to greet a pretty, tomboyish-looking girl who was just getting out of a car.

"There's Ingrid," Bobby said, recognizing one of his

pals.

"Good," said Dennis, "I wasn't sure she'd be coming back. Her father wanted to move to Canada. N*obody* moves to Canada."

Ingrid looked troubled as she spoke to her schoolmates, before her father came to whisk her away to register. Bobby moved the binoculars, scanning the Hanley grounds for another familiar face.

"Where's Laura Nash?" he asked with mock impatience. "How am I gonna get her this year if she doesn't even show up?"

Dennis, in his footbal jersey, was down on the lawn doing push-ups. "You shoulda got her last year," he said, a little out of breath. "Like everyone else."

"Bullshit. She was with you all term."

Dennis said something, but Bobby didn't hear what it was. The high-powered glasses had come to rest on the image of a lovely woman who looked to be about 35. Willowy, with a long mane of chestnut-colored hair, she was the kind of dazzling type Bobby dreamed of. "I think I'm in love," Bobby heard himself saying.

For a brief moment, he hoped that the beautiful woman might be a new teacher at the school, but that was too much to ask for. He could see from the way she was saying good-bye to Matthew Hanley, who had just come into his field of vision, that she must be the mother of one of the students.

"Oh, no," he begged comically. "Don't go, don't leave."

But the woman was getting into a car, a gray Mercedes, and kissing a teenaged girl good-bye.

"Isn't she something?" Bobby said. "God, is she beautiful!"

Dennis wrenched away the binoculars, fumbled with the focus and trained the glasses on The Hanley School's front lawn. He paused, taking in the mature beauty of Evelyn Forbes, then moved the glasses a fraction to the right.

"She's perfect," said Dennis.

But he was no longer looking at Mrs. Forbes. It was the vision of Vanessa that was framed in the twin circles of the binoculars.

Vanessa had promised herself she wouldn't cry but she could feel the tears well up in her eyes as she hugged her mother for the last time.

"Honey, you alright?" asked Mrs. Forbes, her hand on the door of the Mercedes.

Vanessa hesitated and brushed away a tear. "Yes, I'm okay," she said, sniffling.

Mrs. Forbes got behind the wheel of the car. Vanessa touched her mother's arm tentatively, and Evelyn smiled.

"Honey, I know it's going to be a little rough at first," she said, "but I'll only be in Europe for a few weeks. And after that, I'll be in Boston. That's not so far away."

"I know."

Evelyn's eyes swept the nearby clusters of girls chatting excitedly on the lawn. "These look like a good bunch. You'll make a lot of friends here."

"Yes, Mom," said Vanessa. "Do what you fear."

"Words to live by," Evelyn answered, gunning the car's engine to life. "I'll call you tonight when I get home."

"Drive carefully," said Vanessa. "And thanks for everything."

Evelyn shifted into reverse, preparing to make a turn. Rather than watch her drive away—that kind of farewell always made her sad—Vanessa turned back to face the school.

Just before Evelyn Forbes made the sharp turn that would put her back on the driveway leading to the gate, she glanced at the rearview mirror. Something was wrong with Vanessa, she suddenly sensed with alarm. It had to do with the way she was standing—her back stiff, almost paralyzed. For a moment, Mrs. Forbes wanted to stop the car and go back to her daughter. Vanessa looked so lost standing there, so damned alone.

Evelyn forced herself to put the idea out of her head. Vanessa would have to learn to be on her own. After all, both of them were going to start a new life now. Evelyn would be adjusting to her new status as a divorcee, and though, deep down, she was frightened, she was determined to be strong. Vanessa would have to do likewise in her new surroundings. If Evelyn turned back now, just because her daughter looked so forlorn, what would Vanessa do once her mother was too far away to comfort her?

Decisively, Mrs. Forbes raced the engine. As she drove past the stern-looking guard and through the gates, she thought of her upcoming European trip. But as Mrs. Forbes' euphoria heightened, her daughter remained riveted to the same spot she had been in when her mother had viewed her through the car mirror.

Oh, my God, the blood, screamed Vanessa's brain in shock and revulsion. A damp, pungent odor, like some invisible slimy tentacle, made its way toward her. The smell was harsh and familiar—coppery. It had to be coming from the deep, red blood that was spilling down the front steps of the school. The liquid appeared steamy, and a slight vapor hovered above it like some weird halo. The blood coursed down the steps and seeped into the ground, the earth accepting it greedily and turning the grass at Vanessa's feet a dark shade of brown. Vanessa was sickened by the sight, but her fascination as to the origin of so much blood kept her eyes glued to the macabre apparition.

Vanessa felt caught in a suffocating time warp. She watched the blood drip lazily down the steps as if in slow motion, while whispers and a faint breathing came from someplace nearby. Yet she stood alone, apart from everyone else on the lawn. More whispers—spidery voices from another dimension. A gust of fetid air brushed Vanessa's cheek, causing her to gag and grow dizzy. She squeezed her eyes shut and felt the difference immediately. Her head cleared, and when she opened her eyes once again, the blood was gone. Everything appeared normal again. The smell had disappeared, and the blades of grass and the steps of the school were clean.

Tears threatened to fall, but Vanessa checked herself. Careful, she warned, you just got here, and you're beginning to imagine things too horrible to explain. Vanessa knew she had a vivid imagination, but it wasn't like her to be envisioning a sight so grisly.

It was all Vanessa could do not to scream out a warning to Karin Sayers who was coming down the front steps of the school. There was no blood, you hallucinated it, Vanessa kept repeating to herself as Karin approached.

"Here, let me help you with those," Karin said, indicating the two large suitcases at Vanessa's feet.

"Thank you." Vanessa let the teacher take one of the bags. Picking up the other, she walked tentatively up the steps. Just before the massive ornate door swung shut behind them, Vanessa looked back over her shoulder. The steps and surrounding area were gleaming clean.

Vanessa followed Karin upstairs and down the long corridor on the second floor where the first block of students' quarters was located. As on the main floor, the walls were adorned with heavy, brooding tapestries. Vanessa noticed the difference in the wall hangings as she stopped to study one up close. These tapestries were abstract and minimalist in design, depicting none of the misshapen forms that hung on the ones on the floor below. And, unlike those, these woven wall hangings were in shades of red rather than blue. Vanessa gave an involuntary shudder, reminded of the deep, crimson liquid that she had imagined pouring down the steps just minutes before. She looked at the sun streaming through the small, stained-glass window above her head. It seemed to make the design on the tapestry almost three-dimensional—like a hologram. But when Vanessa moved further to one side, blocking the light, the design became flat and dull.

Karin had stopped a few feet away. She studied the girl for a moment. "I especially like that one too," Karin remarked.

Vanessa smiled. She found the tapestry disturbing but shook her head in agreement. "Do you know what period those are from?" she asked.

"They're really quite old."

"They seem strangely modern."

"Yes, they do, but I've been told that the school founder picked out all the furnishings personally."

"I know. Mr. Hanley gave my mother and me a brief history of this place," Vanessa said, once again following Karin down the hallway.

"Oh?"

For a split second, Vanessa saw a shadow of concern creep across the teacher's face, but it was gone before Vanessa could ask if something was wrong.

"Here's your room," Karin said, putting down her valise. They had stopped in front of the next to last door on the second floor. "It's number six."

She stepped aside and let Vanessa push open the door to what would be her new home.

Vanessa felt a momentary twinge of apprehension as the door swung wide. The feeling evaporated as soon as she stepped inside. Sunlight beamed in from the large casement window, and the sudden movement from the door sent dust motes dancing crazily in the rays of light. Above the casement that was framed with frilly, lace curtains, the small, blue stained-glass window nestled like an omnipresent eye, winking at Vanessa as if alive.

Two medium-sized beds, each draped with a lovely floral comforter, were separated by a mahogany night table which supported a long-stemmed, goose-necked lamp. The room had twin dressers, one on either side, with a large, beveled glass mirror above each. Vanessa walked across to the bed nearest the window and set her suitcase down.

"It's beautiful," she said dreamily, admiring the intricate carvings on the woodwork of the room.

"Isn't it?" Karin said, bringing Vanessa her other bag. "The furniture is from the 1920's and 30's, but my guess is that some date back even earlier."

Vanessa sat on the bed. The mattress was thick and comfortable. She gazed out the window. Through the sheer fabric of the curtains she could make out a large gray building across the lake.

"That's the Abbott Boys' Academy. We do all our school plays with the students from Abbott."

"I see." Vanessa hoped Karin would leave. She wanted to inspect her new quarters alone, but she didn't want to be impolite to her new teacher. She'd only just met Karin, but Vanessa had taken an immediate liking to the older woman.

"Have you decided on the fall play yet?" Vanessa asked.

Karin sat down on the opposite bed. "Yes, we're doing 'Twelfth Night.' "

"Or 'What You Will.' "

Karin smiled at the girl. "I think you'll be very comfortable here, Vanessa. I've learned to think of Hanley as my home. I hope you'll come to love it here as much as I do."

Vanessa felt a sudden flood of warmth for her new drama teacher. She was glad she'd be spending a lot of time with Karin Sayers. Karin looked almost proper, but Vanessa sensed that she was a kind, generous person. Maybe Vanessa's life at Hanley would be fine after all.

Her thoughts turned to Shakespeare's "Twelfth Night." The play had some wonderful roles for women—Olivia, the rich countess; Maria, the serving wench; and her favorite, Viola, who disguises herself as a man. Vanessa knew which part *she* wanted.

Sensing that the girl wanted to be alone, Karin got to

her feet. "I'll leave you to unpack and settle in. By the way, you'll be sharing this room with Laura Nash. She hasn't registered yet, but if Laura is running true to form, she'll be the last one to arrive. She's a very bright student and has a beautiful singing voice. She also has a mind of her own—with a real stubborn streak." Karin paused at the door. "I'm sure Laura will show you the ropes soon enough. In the meantime, if you need anything, you know where to find me."

"Thanks."

Karin Sayers left Room Six and closed the door softly behind her. Karin liked the new student. There was something vulnerable, even fragile, that appealed to the teacher. It was also going to be nice working with a new actress. She hoped the girl was talented and that she wouldn't be as shy and quiet in class as she was today. Karin grinned at the thought of Vanessa's roommate. If anyone could bring Vanessa around, Laura Nash could.

Karin headed down the stairs to the auditorium. The feeling of dread she'd had yesterday was almost gone. She could feel the school coming to life with the arrival of the returning students. Yet, there was still some anxiety, some nagging suspicion that all was not as it should be. As she passed the wall hangings on the main level, hundreds of eyes stared out at her in unearthly shades of blue, voicing silent agreement.

3

"Operator? I'd like to make a collect call to Beverly Hills, California."

Vanessa was in the old-fashioned, wooden phone booth at the end of the second floor corridor. As she waited for the operator to put her call through, she admired the flawless condition of the booth, a remnant from the past that reminded her of something she'd seen in old movies. The booth even had an overhead light that came on automatically when you closed the door and a small fan which could be activated by a metal switch. Vanessa smiled as she thought about the phones back home—open call boxes that were generally blanketed with graffiti. In all the years that this booth had been here—and judging from the look, it dated back to the pre-war period—no one had ever dared to write or carve on its shining surface.

"Go ahead, please," the operator said.

"Daddy, it's Vanessa."

At the other end of the country, John Forbes was seated in a deck chair at the edge of a kidney-shaped swimming pool. Though he was attired only in a bathing suit, John looked the part of a successful Los Angeles executive. Handsome, in his early 40's, he exuded self-confidence, wearing his corporate prosperity like a second suit of skin. His even California tan, his toned muscles fresh from a morning on the tennis court, his perfectly manicured fingernails, his immaculately styled hair, going slightly gray at the temples—all attested to John Forbes' image as a self-made oil tycoon.

Forbes pressed the receiver to his ear and strained to hear above the din of the poolside cocktail party that was going on all around him. Only a few feet away, a bartender was mixing a tumbler of martinis and a reggae band on the patio was offering a deafening rendition of "Feelings." A pair of bikini-clad actresses had just dived noisily into the water and were splashing about wildly.

"Speak up, honey, I can't hear a damned thing."

He waved at the band's lead singer to quiet down, but the man shook his unruly hair in the other direction, oblivious to John's request.

"Hold that down for a minute," Forbes called out impatiently. "It's my daughter."

Getting no response, John got up and went over to the glass partition of his eight room, split-level house. Sliding the glass open, he stepped into his sunken living room and closed the door behind him, shutting out the sound. The air conditioning was a relief and Forbes smiled, hearing his daughter's voice.

"I'm in Hanley, Massachusetts. I'm at the school."

A butler approached, carrying a tray of champagne glasses. John grabbed one and took a sip of the bubbly liquid.

"That's good, honey. How is it back there? How's school?"

Forbes glanced around the living room. People were sprawled on the sofas and the floors. He frowned, seeing a bearded record producer who was laying out cocaine lines on the mirrored surface of his coffee table. He noticed overflowing ashtrays and cigarette butts everywhere. John hated to throw these parties but recognized his obligation to entertain visiting clients with the kind of bash they expected at a Hollywood get-together.

"It's fine, Daddy," Vanessa answered, then hesitated. "Well, I don't know, I just got here. I met the principal, only here they call him the headmaster. I met the woman in charge of the drama department, and she's real nice. I miss you, Daddy. I miss you a lot."

"I miss you too, darling. I wish I could be there but I got a corporation to run. What's the school like, honey? In the brochure, it looked like one of those haunted castles from Edgar Allan Poe."

Vanessa laughed nervously. "That's not too far off."

"Well, why shouldn't you have a castle? You've always been my little princess. Maybe you'll meet your Prince Charming there, huh?"

"I don't know, Daddy. It's an all-girls school, remember? There's a boys academy but I haven't met anyone from there yet. The school is beautiful alright, but to tell you the truth, it's a little weird."

"Don't worry, darling. You'll get used to it."

Noticing a young girl coming down the corridor, Vanessa turned her head to face the wall of the booth and lowered her voice.

"Daddy, could I ask you a question?"

"Sure, honey."

"Just in case I don't like it here, let's say by the end of the term, do you think it would be alright if I came to live with you and changed schools?"

John Forbes could hear the plaintiveness in his daughter's voice but he also knew the custody terms he had agreed to in the divorce. He took a deep breath.

"Vanessa, take it easy. Things have a way of working out. You'll probably learn to love that place in a couple of months."

"But what if I don't, Daddy?"

"Let's see what happens. It's a new experience.

You've only been there for one day, right? If you're still not happy by Christmas, maybe I can talk to your mother."

"Oh, I'm happy, Daddy," said Vanessa quickly. "I didn't mean to worry you."

"See? You're just nervous. I was the same way when I was your age."

Vanessa recognized the lie but it comforted her. She doubted her father had ever been frightened of anything. She glanced around. The girl from down the hall had taken a seat on an Edwardian divan a few feet from the phone booth. She was a pretty girl with dark, straight hair and wide eyes which were focused on a paperback novel.

"Did your mother wreck the car yet?" Vanessa knew her father's changing-the-subject tone, but she didn't mind.

"Not yet," she said, laughing.

"She will," John said, not unkindly. "And I'm sure I'll get the bill for it."

Vanessa laughed again. It was a good sound to John Forbes. He was glad she had called; all she had needed was a little pick-up from her father. Across the living room, he noticed Barbara, his secretary, was motioning at a flashing light on one of the other phones. He hoped it was that call from Brussels he was expecting.

"You need anything? Need any money?" he asked hurriedly.

"No, Daddy, Mom took care of me."

Barbara had picked up the phone and was holding the receiver out. He saw her mouth the words: "It's Belgium."

"Call me anytime. If you need me, I'm just a phone call away. Bye, sweetheart. Take care of yourself, okay?"

"I will, Daddy. Bye."

As Vanessa hung up the receiver, the elated feeling she'd had a moment before when speaking with her father gave way to a sudden, hollow ache of loneliness in the pit of her stomach. She made a conscious effort not to cry, remembering her father's words of encouragement. Besides, the girl on the couch was peering at her curiously over the top of her book.

Vanessa eased open the folding door of the phone booth. She nodded at the girl apologetically.

"Sorry, I didn't mean to take so long. It was long distance."

"No prob," the girl said with a friendly smile. She offered her hand. "My name's Ingrid Strummer."

"Hi, I'm Vanessa Forbes."

"You're new here, aren't you?"

"Yeah, I'm the transfer student. The only one."

Ingrid reached for the door of the phone booth. "Hey, don't look so sad. The fun's just beginning."

"My parents are divorced too," Ingrid said thoughtfully.

She and her new friend, Vanessa Forbes, were perched on a stone bench just off to the side of the main entrance. On the lawn there was a flurry of activity. Many of the students had arrived for registration and they huddled in groups, getting reacquainted, catching up on what they'd done over the summer and comparing notes on courses to take and teachers to avoid. The early afternoon sun cut through the chill in the air and more than a few girls had taken off jackets and sweaters, which were strewn about on the grass. The school was beginning to take on an autumnal lived-in look.

"Divorce is a little rough at first, but you get used to it," Ingrid lied.

"I hope so," Vanessa said.

Ingrid waved at several of her classmates across the lawn. She knew they wanted her to join them, but she was enjoying her conversation. Ingrid relished the novelty of playing the "I've-Been-Through-It-All" girl, delighting in Vanessa's eagerness to absorb her knowledge about the pitfalls of a broken home.

"My mother was screwed up," Ingrid said, almost proudly. "Still is. She would walk around the house like a zombie. Every time I turned around, she was sneaking a drink. Sometimes she fell down in a stupor at the end of the day."

"Oh, my God."

Seeing that Vanessa was impressed, Ingrid decided to embellish. "That's not all. She used to pop Valiums. Her medicine chest was Drug City."

"Where'd she get all the drugs?"

"My Dad's a doctor. He'd give her anything to shut her up." Ingrid couldn't believe she was playing with the truth like this but she was flattered by Vanessa's attention, feeling a certain bond with this delicate wisp of a girl. "What's your father do?" she asked.

Vanessa looked apologetic. "He's in the oil business."

Ingrid grinned. "Hey, don't feel bad. Capitalism is in these days. Let's face it. All of our parents are loaded. Otherwise, we couldn't afford to go to this place." She rolled her eyes comically. "God, why couldn't I have been born dirt poor so I could go to a good public school!"

"Being rich isn't so bad. Besides, Daddy gives a lot of money away. You know, charities, the arts. He's very generous. It's gonna be weird being here when he's way out there in California."

Ingrid gave her a conspiratorial pat on the arm. "I got news for you, Vanessa. It's weird being here anyway."

Vanessa laughed but found her eyes moving involuntarily to the front steps of the school. No blood.

"Speaking of weird," Ingrid said, indicating a thin, almost mousy teenager who was scurrying toward them with nervous, jerky steps.

"Who's that?"

"That's Rickie Webster," Ingrid answered, waving at the girl who was fast approaching. "She's a sophomore. The lights are on but nobody's home. You know what I mean?" Ingrid threw her head back crazily.

"Hi, I'm back," Rickie announced, tugging at one of her braids anxiously. She reminded Vanessa of a timid deer caught in the headlights of a car—all eyes, frightened and astonished.

When Rickie reached the two of them, she hesitated. She shifted her gangly legs in an uneasy fashion. Vanessa could tell that the girl was uncomfortable about how to greet her schoolmate. Ingrid made no motion to hug her, giving an offhand introduction instead.

"Hi, Rick. Vanessa Forbes. Rickie Webster. Vanessa's a senior."

"Hi," Rickie said, shly. She pulled at her other braid almost as though she were trying to straighten her head out.

Vanessa did her best to smile a warm hello. Seeing Rickie fidget made Vanessa feel self-conscious for the girl. Rickie seemed to wear her young neuroses like a badge. Not wanting to stare or give away her feelings, Vanessa let her eyes wander, resisting the impulse to look back at the front steps. Instead, she looked up, but that was a mistake.

Sound became muffled. As though looking through the lens of a camera, precise and focused, her eyes zoomed in on a dog-like carving at the edge of the roof. Its mouth fierce and cavernous, its sharp teeth threatening, the gargoyle seemed to lock eyes with Vanessa almost malevolently. She was aware that a conversation between Ingrid and Rickie was going on just a few feet away from her, yet she couldn't distinguish the words. As she gazed upward, the stone beast seemed to gnash its angry fangs at her, dripping saliva and working its teeth as if it were chewing on something bloody and long dead. She could almost smell the decay coming from its mouth. The monster's eyes, deep set and scowling, flashed back at her as though it were measuring its next victim. More saliva dripped, mingled with blood and remnants of chewed flesh. Vanessa tried to blink but her eye muscles were paralyzed. She had the dark, unsettling feeling that she would not be able to look away until the vicious, stone mongrel released her from their hellish connection.

Vanessa's eyes teared, and a shadow passed over her vision. From somewhere in the muted, cottony wad that was her hearing came a persistent blare of noise. Her body relaxed, she was able to blink her eyes, and sound came roaring back to her with a rush of relief. The fiendish canine on the roof top was once again nothing more than a stone sculpture—cold and unmoving. She now recognied the relentless noise to be that of a car horn.

First, the noose in the auditorium, then the blood on the front steps—now this! Was it all just some obscene fluke of the light? Vanessa looked at the stained-glass windows, gleaming every shade of the rainbow. Yes, the colored glass and the bright sun could have played tricks with her vision—but only in the auditorium. How could she explain the two grotesque hallucinations she experienced outside the school? Surely, the stained glass couldn't be acting as some kind of reflector. Or could it? No. Nerves. It has to be my nerves, thought Vanessa. What else could it be?

"Hey, Vanessa? You alright?" Ingrid was asking with concern.

Vanessa noticed the girl staring at her and knew she must look pale and frightened. She forced a smile to her lips.

"I'm fine. I just got a bit dizzy looking up. I'm okay now." Vanessa was trying to convince herself as well as Ingrid.

Rickie hadn't noticed anything unusual. She was absorbed in twisting a piece of jewelry that hung on a chain from her knobby neck.

Ingrid pointed to the source of the loud honking. "I think your mother is a little out of control," she said to Rickie.

Mrs. Marion Webster, a stick of a woman, was leaning on a green station wagon, one hand waving frantically for Rickie to join her, the other pressing heavily on the car horn.

"I'll see you later," said Rickie in a soft voice. "My mom's going nuts." She tried hard to smile, but it came out so lopsided she almost looked as if she were grimacing. Rickie padded off before Vanessa could even say good-bye.

"She's not the only one going nuts," Ingrid observed, shaking her head at Rickie's slight figure as she rejoined her mother and struggled to pick up an overstuffed suitcase nearly as big as she was. The girl started carrying it up the steps with her mother, bird-thin, following close behind.

Vanessa blanched. *Oh, my God, Rickie!*

"Hey, there you go again. You look like you just saw a ghost."

Get a grip on yourself, Vanessa thought. "No, really, I'm fine. I think I have a headache, that's all. Probably why I'm getting dizzy."

Ingrid didn't believe Vanessa for a second but didn't want to press. Instead, she grinned. "Well, Rickie does have that effect on people."

"I don't know. Rickie seems okay."

"Yeah, Richard Nixon seemed okay too, didn't he?"

Vanessa's eyes went once more to the edge of the roof. Ingrid followed Vanessa's line of vision to the carved dog-like gargoyles that were perched there and suppressed a shudder. "Oh, you've met Rover. We've become buddies—you know, man's best friend and all that."

Vanessa laughed in spite of herself. She marveled at Ingrid's offhand sense of humor and thought she would like to be friends with this girl. Laughing at the gargoyle put things back into perspective. It was just a statue—nothing more. *But what about Rickie?*

"What room are you in?" asked Ingrid.

"Six. I'm rooming with a girl named Laura Nash. Do you know her?"

Ingrid grinned amiably. "Oh, yes, I know Laura Nash. Everyone knows Laura Nash." The girl paused for emphasis. "You'll meet Laura soon enough. No way is she here this early. She never shows up a minute before she absolutely has to. She's your roommate, huh? Well, I've got a sleeping bag. I guess you'll be bunking with me a lot."

"Why is that?"

Ingrid looked thoughtful for a moment. "How shall I put it? This is a girl's school . . . but Laura has been doing her best to change that."

"She brings boys into the room?"

"They should be paying tuition."

"You mean to sleep over?" Vanessa asked incredulously.

Ingrid nodded. "I'll give the girl credit. She brings in only the best-looking boys. She's got good taste. Of course, there are nights when I wish she'd keep it down a bit. See, I'm right next door in Room Seven."

"Then we're neighbors," Vanessa said, pleased with the thought.

"Yeah. You won't have to go very far when Laura kicks you out."

"Isn't she afraid of getting caught?" Vanessa asked, amused at the idea.

"I don't think Laura Nash is afraid of anything," Ingrid said with a trace of awe.

Vanessa felt a little better now. Having Laura Nash as a roommate would probably provide the needed diversion to get her mind off her own problems. Also, it was comforting to know that Ingrid would be right next door, should Vanessa need her. Vanessa knew that friends would be important if she were to survive in this new place. Maybe in time, those grisly visions she had seen would fade from her thoughts. If it happened again, she could try to be more rational. All she had to do was close her eyes and the horrifying scene would disappear. But that wasn't quite true, she thought with a stab of reality. She had struggled to shut her eyes with the stone carving, but the dog-beast would not allow it. Still, that was nothing more than a hallucination, some perverse extension of her overactive mind. If these phenomena continued to appear once she got settled in her new surroundings, she promised herself to seek help.

In her mind, she examined the pattern. First, sound became muted or conversation seemed to cease. Then reality slipped away as the hallucination took over. But, she thought with alarm, that was not what happened a few moments before with Rickie Webster. Sound had not been distorted. How could Vanessa explain what she had seen after Rickie had rejoined her mother at the station wagon? The bleeding skeleton that was holding the oversized suitcase was revolting. And as it walked up the steps of the school a rotting corpse that should have been Rickie Webster had turned to Vanessa and blown a kiss across the lawn. Thirty yards away, Vanessa could feel the pure evil emanating from the vision. Thirty yards away, Vanessa had felt the putrid, cold breath of the kiss as it had lightly caressed her lips.

As Vanessa and Ingrid sat on the bench getting acquainted, they were being watched. Dennis Bellivin pursed his lips as he scrutinized Vanessa's lovely face through the binoculars, taking in her every movement.

"She is the lucky one," Dennis murmured.

"Huh?" Bobby Cannon asked. He had gotten bored with the high-powered glasses and was thumbing through a copy of Mad Magazine.

"Yes, I have decided," Dennis said solemnly.

"Oh, *you* have decided? Doesn't she have anything to say about this?"

"Of course not," Dennis said smugly.

Bobby put down the magazine. "Who are we talking

about anyway?"

Dennis gave him the glasses. "The new girl. The one talking to Ingrid. You missed her before. You were too busy salivating over her mother. I want that girl, Bobby. And I'll have her too. How can she resist me?"

Bobby adjusted the focus. "Others have," he remarked dryly.

"Yeah? Name one."

Bobby made no reply. He looked with appreciation at the slender gracefulness that was Vanessa Forbes. She was pretty alright, he decided after taking a careful inventory of her attributes, but not really Dennis Bellivin's type.

"Isn't she a bit slim for you?" Bobby asked, careful not to offend his friend. "She's not exactly the cheerleader type."

Dennis turned to him with irritation. "Bobby, how well do you know me? What makes you think you know what kind of girl I want?"

Bobby was surprised at Dennis' tone. "Hey," he said, trying to be casual, "I'm just going by your past record. She's not what you usually go for." The last thing Bobby needed was an argument with Dennis.

His friend took back the binoculars. "Don't try to classify me, Bobby," he warned. "I'm a lot more complicated than you think."

"Sorry, I didn't mean anything by it."

Dennis' voice softened. "That girl is special. Bobby, did you ever see somebody for the first time and feel like you've known them all your life?"

"Yeah, I guess so." Bobby was relieved that Dennis' flash of anger had dissipated as quickly as it had flared up.

"I just had that feeling," Dennis said strangely. "That girl belongs with me."

Bobby got up, rolled up the magazine and stuck it in his back pocket. "I'm gonna go over there and say hello to Ingrid. You coming?"

"Sure, I'll take a little stroll." Dennis put the glasses to his eyes for one final look at Vanessa. She had left the stone bench and was going inside the school.

"Ready?" Bobby asked, brushing the grass from his trousers.

Dennis put down the glasses. "No, I changed my mind, Bobby. You go by yourself."

Walking the lakeside path leading to The Hanley School, Bobby reflected on Dennis Bellivin's change of attitude. In all the time he had known Dennis, the other boy had never indicated any depth of feeling about anyone or anything unless it was sports or Playboy centerfolds. In three years of friendship Dennis had never come down so heavily on Bobby for an innocent remark. There had been something almost threatening about the way Dennis had reprimanded him. True, Bobby had witnessed Dennis' fiery temper and bouts of moodiness, but they had never been directed at him. Though Dennis didn't look it to Bobby, maybe he really was complex. Maybe when he went for his nighttime walks, he was brooding over something he couldn't share with Bobby. Was it possible that Bobby, so grateful for Dennis Bellivin's friendship, was overlooking a deeper part of his personality? But, on the other hand, maybe Dennis' quick flare-up was just an overreaction. Bobby hoped so. He didn't want to start the senior year on a bad footing with Dennis.

He passed by the boathouse, noticing that the shambling structure had a fresh coat of white paint. Bobby wondered if this year he would see more of the inside of the boathouse, meeting for late night rendezvous with the likes of Laura Nash or Marie Kronofsky. He peeked through the window. Nobody in there now—but the place would get a real workout during the year when Hanley girls and Abbot boys had make-out sessions. He could just discern the battered hurricane lamp that the kids used as a signal when they wanted to be alone for some midnight meeting. Bobby hoped that one night soon he'd be leading Laura or Marie through that door, six-pack in hand, lighting the wick on that lamp and hanging it in the window to assure them privacy. God, how he wanted to get laid!

Bobby Cannon's optimistic thoughts were suddenly dampened by this year's first close-up view of Hanley. The gabled edifice loomed with a melancholy presence as he drew nearer. Wherever the dappled autumn sunlight caught its glass surfaces, they sparkled—an army of intricate crystals that was almost blinding. Bobby tucked his head down, keeping his eyes diverted from the stone figures that he knew were up there. He didn't want to have nightmares tonight.

He heard a cry of excitement from across the lawn. Ingrid was racing toward him, her arms outstretched. In seconds, she was embracing him affectionately.

"You son of a bitch, I've been trying to call you," she exclaimed.

"You were?" That made him feel good. "I was out by the lake with Dennis."

Ingrid gave him a knowing smile. "Did you two have the old binoculars out again? Checking out the girls, huh? You know, Bobby, you and Dennis are going to get arrested some day as Peeping Toms. I'm glad we've got stained glass in the shower room."

"No, you're not," countered Bobby. "You hate that colored glass as much as I do."

"Oh, God, Bobby, don't remind me. I thought I'd be out of here this term."

"Well, I know you hate it, but I'm glad you're back. Besides, it's the last year for both of us. After next May, we'll never have to see this place again."

"I guess you saw the new girl—Vanessa Forbes. What do you think?"

"Is that her name? I suppose I'd better tell you right now. Dennis has his eyes on her."

"Really?" Ingrid said, surprised. "That's not like him. Vanessa isn't really his type."

"God, don't let Dennis hear you say that. I told him the same thing five minutes ago and he nearly bit my fucking head off."

Ingrid took Bobby's arm and led him over toward a group of girls that included Marie Kronofsky. Bobby felt his face redden as he tried to look away from Marie's breasts.

Before they got within hearing range of the others, Ingrid turned to Bobby seriously. "You mean it? Is Dennis really interested in Vanessa?"

"I would say he's hooked. As a matter of fact, I've never seen him go this apeshit for a girl he hasn't even met."

Ingrid stopped on the lawn. She looked at Bobby. "I don't know," Ingrid said. "Maybe it's just a hunch but I have this weird feeling about Vanessa. I think if Dennis tries to get something started with her, he's going to have his hands full."

Inside Room Six, Vanessa was perplexed. A gust of cool air was coming from somewhere, strong enough to sweep her hair back from her face, but, with the casement windows closed, the source of the breeze was a puzzle. Vanessa even stood on a chair to examine the crimson stained glass above, running her hand along the edge of the window in search of a crack which might be letting in an outside draft. She found nothing.

Vanessa stepped down. This was silly, she told herself. It didn't matter where the air was coming from. It was an old building and there were probably lots of cracks in the walls. The blast of air could even be coming from the space under the door and ricocheting off the walls to give the illusion that it was originating somewhere else. It might bother her in the winter, she knew, but right now it was kind of pleasant. Besides, she had unpacking to do. Almost as soon as she had this thought, the breeze ceased.

But Vanessa hardly noticed that. Instead, she was concentrating on something that was far more demanding—a low murmur that was just below the level of normal sound. It crept insistently just under the babble of the girls downstairs on the lawn, the branches blowing against the window, the chirping of birds, the rumbling of the old pipes—like a barely audible, faraway radio station.

Vanessa! She strained to hear. Was some kind of voice, buried in a whisper of sound, breathing her name? She listened. It was almost like eavesdropping on another dimension. *Vanessa!*

There it was again, slightly louder and more pronounced, but still immersed in an impenetrable wave of noise. Vanessa had the oddest feeling that, whatever this was, she should not be listening to it. But she was too frightened to ignore this greeting that seemed to come from some dark, limitless plane.

Vanessa! But as the fathomless whisper embraced her for the third time, she knew with a curious assurance it would be its final salutation. Vanessa leaned forward, craning her neck to hear the wheezy expulsion of breath that signaled the last communication from places unknown.

Normal sound returned, and the everyday noises of the school seemed a notch louder now, as if to make up for the brief period of distortion. Vanessa eased herself down onto her bed. Was she going mad? Weren't the bizarre hallucinations she had been experiencing bad enough? Was she now going to be subjected to hearing imaginary voices? First seeing things, then hearing things—what would be next?

High-pitched laughter from the lawn below helped to calm Vanessa's nerves. This was a girls' high school, she reasoned—nothing more sinister than that. Wasn't it just a little too coincidental that these grotesque sights and noises, unlike anything she had ever known before, had commenced as soon as her mother's car had driven off, leaving her on her own? Wasn't she merely looking for an excuse to call her parents so that ultimately she could go back home to California and go to school there? Vanessa had read a couple of psychology books last year, enough to surmise her current state of mind.

Then the question wasn't whether she was going mad. Rather it was whether she was trying to delude herself into thinking she was crazy—which, in turn, would convince her parents that she didn't belong here. Vanessa was acting spoiled and immature—and she knew it.

Do What You Fear.

This time the words came from her own consciousness and she moved off the bed as if in reply. Okay, this was a strange place, and yes, she missed Los Angeles. If she got lonely for her father, there was a phone at the end of the hall, and she could call him every day. Meanwhile, she thought with determination, she was going to move into her new home and that meant getting her bags unpacked and her things put away.

Vanessa opened her two valises and couldn't believe all the junk she'd crammed in there—all the vestiges of California, she realized. Glancing at the closet near her bed, she suspected there wouldn't be much room. The antique dresser wasn't very big either. She wondered if her roommate would have as much stuff as she did. Maybe Laura Nash would let her have a bit of space in her closet. No way, thought Vanessa. From what she'd heard about Laura, she had to be the kind of girl who would be asking *her* for some extra room. Oh, well, she would make do with what she had—apparently all the other girls at Hanley did.

Vanessa spotted her overnight case on the floor. She knew just what she needed. The small suitcase contained her silver tray, make-up and pretty perfume bottles along with a framed photo of her father taken earlier that year. Once she got the dresser adorned with these much loved possessions, she'd have put her personal stamp on these unfamiliar surroundings.

She blew some dust off the dresser and carefully placed her mother's tray upon it. Vanessa unpacked the three small, antique atomizers that she had received from her grandmother on her 16th birthday. They had been Granny Flo's when she was a teenager, back in the early 1940's, and were considered quite rare and valuable. Next to her delicately shaped vials, Vanessa placed her comb and brush set, and on the far edge of the bureau she set the photograph of John Forbes. Her father was grinning engagingly out at the camera and holding onto Vanessa; both were seated atop a large, muscular palomino. Father and daughter looked happy and tanned. Vanessa touched the frame lightly before returning to the overnight bag.

Next was a round lace doily, upon which she arranged her makeup cases and creams. Vanessa didn't like messy bottles, so she had replaced them with porcelain containers. She even had a heart-shaped dish for hairpins—though she thought with a smile that she had never had cause to use them, allowing her long, auburn hair to hang loosely to her shoulders.

There! Vanessa stood back and admired the top of the dresser. Only her jewelry box remained. She lined it up in the center and took from it several chains, draping them decoratively on the small box along with a few rings. That's much better, Vanessa observed. She turned and moved back several steps to get a view of her handiwork from the other side of the room. She never saw her black pearl ring, a present from her mother, jar itself loose from the cluster of jewelry to tumble behind the bureau. Nor did she notice the perfume churn in the bottles, ever so slightly, as she stood there, feeling so much better about the school.

Now it was time to tackle the closet. Vanessa surveyed the suitcase which contained her skirts and dresses. Taking out some velvet and lace items, she laid them gently on the bed, then went to the closet. V*anessa*! Her heart pumped faster. She listened. Nothing.

It was only her imagination. She put her hand on the closet doorknob. Perspiration broke out on her forehead and just above her upper lip. She could feel the moisture under her arms, clammy and irritating. I'm being an idiot, Vanessa thought. It's just a closet. But she wished she had opened it before, when she had first entered the room with Karin Sayers. It would now be ajar and she would see that nothing was in it—hiding behind the door and waiting to strike out at her. Okay, Vanessa scolded herself, you can either put your clothes away like a normal person, or you can stand here sweating till your roommate shows up—and then tell her you're afraid of closets and look like a jerk!

But she wasn't afraid of closets. She was afraid of *this* closet. She pulled open the door. The metal hangers jangled against one another as Vanessa took a small step back from the unexpected noise. Smiling slightly now at her foolishness, she poked her head into the closet. Empty. Just a small, empty cubicle.

She began hanging up her clothes. On the top shelf of the closet, she tucked away some lavender sachets, then lifted her valise up to place it beside them. Vanessa went back to the other suitcase, which held her underwear, sweaters and T-shirts. She laid all the garments on the bed and then stored the bag in the closet with the other one. The shelf was too high for Vanessa to notice the small clump of green mold in the corner of the closet that was festering there—minute particles of life growing in the warm, damp atmosphere.

Vanessa shut the closet door. Thinking better, she opened it a crack. Turning to the antique dresser, she placed her bras, panties and T-shirts in the top drawer. She arranged some potpourri in its corners and went to gather an armload of sweaters from the bed. She put her neatly-folded blue turtleneck on the bottom of the drawer. Then the remaining sweaters dropped from her suddenly limp arms to the floor, and the scream froze in her throat.

In the corner of the open drawer, next to the sweet-smelling sachet, lay a bloodied, severed arm, its painted nails a bright pink, its fingers moving pleadingly. Silence replaced sound, like someone had turned off a valve in her head, and an electric current of fright traveled up her spine to the back of her neck, threatening to choke her. Somewhere underneath this horror, Vanessa struggled to tell herself she was imagining the disgusting filth in her dresser drawer.

Vanessa recoiled in terror at the blood-drenched apparition. The sweaters lay in a pile at her feet. *Touch it, Vanessa.* The words came to her as if down a long column of steel in her brain. Some evil presence at the very core of her mind was suggesting the unthinkable. I can't touch it, she nearly said aloud. But she knew at the same time that if she didn't reach for the arm, it would be admitting that it really existed. But how could she bring herself to touch the throbbing, blue-veined appendage, the palm of which opened and closed like a desperate vise?

Yes, she would touch it. That was the only way to prove it wasn't there. Tentatively, Vanessa brought her hand forward. The bloody stump moved in anticipation. It's beckoning me, Vanessa thought with revulsion. She extended her fingers, trying to keep them from quaking. They were only inches away from the drawer now—but it was too late. Like a fish on a hook, flapping frantically, the rotting hand jerked upward from the bottom of the drawer. Snapping wildly, it reached out to grasp her own fingers in a maniacal handshake. The decayed fingernails clawed at the edge of the drawer, trying to propel themselves outward. With a burst of strength, Vanessa slammed the drawer violently, shutting the dead thing inside.

Almost at once, her head reeled with a whooshing roar of noise, like an escaping rush of fetid breath. Vanessa knew, in the second before she spun to race to the door, that the sighing—vile and ear-splitting—came from the closed dresser drawer. She flung herself over the bed and tore open the door of Room Six.

"Oh, my God!"

Hovering in the doorway, her huge feet planted squarely on the polished oak floor, her muscular arms folded across her strapping body, was one of the most peculiar-looking women Vanessa had ever seen in her life.

"Is that the way you answer the door?" asked the woman in a husky voice.

With a tank-like thrust forward, the burly woman pushed her way into the room. Vanessa saw that she was carrying a bundle of sheets and blankets. Gray-haired and elderly, the woman scowled at Vanessa in disapproval. Still badly shaken, Vanessa tried to stammer a reply, but her eyes kept going to the dresser. The deafening sighs were gone and normal everyday sound had returned. Vanessa peered at the intruder gratefully. The old woman was angry but Vanessa didn't care, just relieved to have someone else in the room.

The woman dumped the blankets and linen on the bed. "Almost sixty years I've been working at this school, and every year the girls are getting stranger. What happened here? You look awful." The old woman glanced down at the floor. "Is that where you keep your sweaters? Nice."

Embarrassed, Vanessa picked up the sweaters. Instinctively, she started toward the dresser to put them away, but stopped. The elderly woman noticed her reluctance to approach the bureau. Vanessa was still sweating and had never ceased trembling.

"You afraid of something?" the woman asked accusingly. "Did you see something in there? What was it, a mouse? I thought we got rid of all the mice."

Vanessa was still too shaken to reply.

Matter-of-factly, the old woman opened the dresser drawer, the same one that moments earlier had harbored the amputated limb. Vanessa forced herself to look inside, even though she knew what she would see. There was no arm.

The woman tugged open the other drawers. "Well, if there was a mouse in here, he's gone now."

Vanessa was barely listening. The relief she felt at not seeing the sickening arm was diminished by the realization that there was something drastically wrong with her mind. It was one thing to need an excuse to call home, but how could she explain the awful clarity of these visions?

The old woman was appraising her. "You're the new one, aren't you?" she asked with the slightest trace of disdain. Or was Vanessa just imagining her attitude?

"I'm Vanessa Forbes."

The woman did not offer to shake hands. "Blanche Trousdale. My husband and I are the caretakers. You'll get used to us."

4

Night hung over the school like a waiting shroud. Each evening, in those few minutes before the light slipped into inexorable darkness, The Hanley School was suffused with a preternatural glow from which it could draw sustenance. The tricks of light that accompanied dusk, that eerie shimmering as all of nature drew in its breath for the oncoming night, fluttered over the building in a cloud of evil confidentiality. This veritable fortress, armed with all its stone, slate and marble, sucked in its daylight charm and waited, poised for the blanket that was night.

Phantom footsteps padded through the corridors, restless, taking ghostly inventory, reminiscing of days long ago, thrilling in anticipation of what was still to come. Violent impulses throbbed in the hallways like blood pumping through an athlete's veins. And for the few, the very few, the muffled whispers could be heard—the tittering, conspiratorial voices that made promises to the damned that could only be kept at night.

Karin Sayers could not yet hear these whispers. On this night, a full moon, dangling low in the sky, glorified the school, immersing it in sparkling gold. Backstage at the auditorium, Karin sat at her desk, making notes as she went over the principal roles for "Twelfth Night," the play she had chosen for the fall production.

Karin was tense and could feel the muscles in the lower part of her back tightening. Karin sat up straight in the high-backed chair and stretched her spine. There, that's better, she thought. She rubbed her eyes with the backs of her index fingers to relieve the pinched feeling at the bridge of her nose. From the floor-to-ceiling window nearest to her desk, the glow from the moonlight made the auditorium seem warm. She closed her eyes and let the light rinse over her like a healing solution. When she opened them, the light had grown brighter.

Karin squinted from the new brilliance. *The window was aflame. The blinding light turned a sickly orange as a ragged sheet of fire streaked skyward. Karin could feel the flames searing the hair on her body.* Daddy! *The heat radiated through the old barn's windows, the glass imploding, some jagged particles tearing into Karin's flesh. She could see her father through the wall of flames, lying like a sacrifice on the makeshift altar, his body limp like a weathered scarecrow. Thwaack!* No! *Don't think about that.* Daddy! *Karin watched in childish fascination as something took shape next to* Henry Sayers' *body. The man-thing, unquestionably evil, was being born from the flames.* It's *Daddy's mouth!* He *must still be alive.* It's *moving.* No! *The floating mouth belonged to no human being.* Its *jaw reached up high through the blaze, swirling through the inferno, coming toward* Karin. *Its lips, ravaged with burns, moved robot-like. You'll listen and be a good girl like your father tells you or you'll wind up like your mother.* Daddy, *please don't.*

The tongues of flame vanished. Once again through the window, Karin could see the moon suspended above the treetops. There was no fire, no scorching death. God, it had seemed so real. Karin's face still felt hot from the flames. Why now? Why was Karin thinking about the past now? She had been so good at mentally locking that door. She wasn't ready to see it open.

letting the nightmarish memories slide through. She knew if she kept up dredging her childhood, she would plunge into a crippling depression.

Karin glanced down at her notes and the opened volume of Shakespeare. I have to keep busy, she resolved. Determinedly, she reached for the metal box of index cards she'd been using. Empty. She would have to go to the supply room for some more. Karin stood, but made no effort to move. Instead, her eyes sought the window. It's okay, she thought. No fire, no burning church. Karin knew she would have to face her past at some point. She'd have to confront the fire and what had happened to her that awful evening, but this wasn't the time. She had "Twelfth Night" and the new school year to look forward to. As she moved across the stage, she vowed to say an extra prayer tonight for her father's tortured soul.

Karin reached the door to the backstage supply room. Turning on the overhead light, she froze at a sudden sound. The chill that ran down the length of Karin's back was icy, and she looked at the light chain. Of course, she sighed. The chain had made the noise. *Your father is a very sick man, young lady. Right on the edge.* Karin concentrated, calming herself. She looked around the small cubicle. Its walls were lined with shelves, almost to the ceiling. Each shelf was crammed to capacity, with some threatening to spill the precariously balanced school supplies to the floor.

Karin eyed the reams of paper, pads, notebooks, pencils, pens and assorted mimeographed school forms. Great, she thought. Everything but index cards. After a minute, Karin spotted the familiar metal box of colored index cards on a shelf near the floor. Bending down to pick up the box, she heard a strange sound. She leaned closer to the floorboards and listened. She recognized the noise of running water. It must be the maintenance man downstairs, she thought. No, not at this hour. He probably was down there this afternoon and forgot to turn off the faucet. She would have to find him and get him to turn off the dripping water. It wasn't a good idea to let the faucet run all night—these pipes were old, there could be a flood. No, it was stupid to go looking for Walter Cox. She would go down and turn off the water herself.

Karin reached for one of the flashlights on the top shelf. Testing it, she saw the beam of light was steady. Good, the batteries were fresh. She switched off the overhead light, heading for the side stairwell near the auditorium.

Karin never used this staircase. It frightened her. These stairs supposedly were to be used in emergency situations only. Of course, the handyman went up and down them all the time, and Karin guessed that anyone wanting access to the sub-basement would have to go down them, too. She felt a little comforted at the thought that the Trousdales probably used these stairs all the time, since their quarters were on the first level of the cellar.

She descended the staircase, holding out the flashlight in front of her. The steps here were steeper, irregular. Karin had to hold tightly to the bannister so as not to trip in her high heels. The stairwell was only dimly lit from a low wattage bulb overhead. Karin was glad she had brought the flashlight, its strong beam cutting through the semi-darkness. She passed the door which she suspected led to the Trousdales' quarters and kept going downward. The sound of the dripping faucet grew louder.

Below, Karin began to make out a musty, confined space containing a furnace, a boiler and a sink. Karin went carefully down the last few steps and went over to the faucet. She turned off the spigot, and the flow of water stopped. All at once, there was silence in the gloomy, damp room. Above the stained and cracked porcelain sink, Karin found a light switch. She pressed it and a small light came on, illuminating the area like a rusty halo and throwing the rest of the room into dancing shadows.

When Karin would think about the incident later in her room, she would not be able to remember which came first—the silky whispers, suggestive, almost obscene, or the breathing, raspy and brittle with age. But by the following day, Karin would scarcely be able to recall hearing them at all.

Karin listened to the ghostly voices. Oddly enough, they didn't frighten her. Instead, Karin embraced these intrusions like some skilled lover, allowing them to take charge, letting them guide her to the ultimate goal. She felt strangely aroused and on the brink of something thrilling.

Moving slowly around the claustrophobic space, Karin used the flashlight to illuminate the corners of the room. Brushing aside clinging cobwebs, she noticed several large metal containers, the kind used for storage. She let the light play over them quickly. The whispers grew in volume, more impelling, prodding Karin. The beam from the flashlight came to rest on a small, wooden trunk tucked away in a corner of the room. Karin could see there was also a door that led somewhere, with a heavy padlock affixed to it. But it wasn't the door that held her interest; it was the trunk.

Mindless of the dusty floor, Karin knelt down in front of the small container. She could smell the mildew, but the pungency was pleasing. No lock. Karin's excitement grew. She opened the trunk. Inside, an old-fashioned frame lay on top. As Karin carefully lifted it up for a closer look, she realized that it was a group photograph of 25 girls, wearing school blazers and pleated skirts, smiling out at her. The girls stood in three rows in the customary school class pose. Beneath them, in the middle of the first row stood the placard that read: "Hanley School, Class of 1933."

Karin's eyes were drawn to the girl in the second row on the left. There was something different about the girl's stiff posture and the vacant sadness in her expression. Karin felt a momentary stab of sorrow for the girl, who looked so much more vulnerable than her grinning classmates. But the feeling passed as Karin again heard the whispers, this time more clearly. It was a rushing sound, as of distant waterfalls, limitless and insistent like a thousand muted screams of madness. Karin set the photograph down beside her and explored the trunk again.

There was only one other item in the box. Karin blew the dust off the leather-bound folder. She opened it to the title page. "Flowers of Darkness, A Play by Lisa King," Karin read aloud. As if someone were standing directly behind Karin, she heard a sigh of contentment. Karin's senses prickled. She whirled around. She was still alone. The whispering had ceased, taking with it the breathing.

Karin turned her attention once more to the old folder. The binding was worn and the pages threatened to loosen to her touch. The script felt comfortable in her hands, like an old acquaintance. Karin turned to page one and began reading.

A half hour later, curled up on the cement floor, the muscles in her legs taut from the uncomfortable position, her eyes watery and strained from squinting, Karin Sayers was still reading. Behind the padlocked door, long forgotten by Karin, an eager vigil was being kept.

The school's dining room on the ground floor was small but comfortable. The art deco design, a holdover from the 1930's, featured large black and white squares of linoleum, an assortment of brass fixtures and, along one entire wall, a glass and chrome counter on which food was displayed cafeteria-style. An added luxury was the hulking antique jukebox that squatted in a corner.

Vanessa paid for her dinner at the turn of the century gold-plated cash register and carried her tray across the nearly empty room to where Ingrid and Rickie were seated. Ingrid cast an appraising glance at Vanessa's selection of dessert and nodded approvingly.

"Good choice," she commented. "There's not much they can do to fruit salad."

Rickie nodded gravely. "Don't ever eat the jello here. I got sick once from the jello."

Ingrid laughed. "No one gets sick from jello, but Rickie . . ." She jerked her thumb at her friend in feigned disbelief.

"Where is everybody?" asked Vanessa.

"It's always like this the first few days," Ingrid explained. "The food is so bad in this place, most of the kids bring stuff from home that lasts 'em a week."

"Oh, I thought maybe it was almost curfew."

"Curfew is later," Ingrid explained. "School nights, we're supposed to be in our rooms by ten."

"What about lights?"

"They like 'em off by eleven," Ingrid said. "Unless you've got a good excuse."

Rickie played with her food, some remnants of leathery meat loaf. "Like if you've got a test and you want to study."

"There's not much to do around here," Ingrid said, sipping milk through a straw. "It's like a morgue. Except in a morgue, people are dead. We're just terminally bored. Of course, there is Mrs. Trousdale. I think she passed away in 1929, but she doesn't have the good sense to lay down."

Vanessa speared a chunk of pineapple and took a tentative bite. "Oh, I don't know," she said. "I met her today, and she looked pretty alive to me. Strong as an ox."

"You know those gargoyles up on the roof?" Ingrid said. "I think she posed for them."

"There's a game room," Rickie said vaguely.

"Huh?"

"But no games." Rickie looked lost in space.

"That's not true, Rick. We've got some wonderful games here. All the current stuff. Pinochle, Chinese Checkers, Parcheesi. Believe it or not, there's even a mah jong set in there."

"We don't go in the game room very often," Rickie said solemnly.

"Are you kidding?" Ingrid laughed. "No one's been in there since World War II."

"Except for the ghosts," Rickie said in a voice barely above a whisper.

"Ghosts?" asked Vanessa. "What are you talking about?"

"Rickie thinks this place is haunted."

"So do you," Rickie said, accusingly.

"Do you, Ingrid?"

Ingrid looked thoughtful for a moment. "I don't know if I believe in ghosts, but sometimes in the middle of the night, I hear weird noises. I get the feeling that there's something else here besides people."

"What do you mean?"

"I'm not sure. Everybody says its an old building so you have to expect strange sounds. But I've been in old places before and I never got scared."

Vanessa had an impulse to tell the two girls about the frightening events of the past few hours, but just as quickly, she thought better of it. It was one thing to talk about odd noises in the night, but quite another to bring up the grisly sights she had recently experienced. She decided to change the subject.

"What about the town?" Vanessa asked. "It looked lovely on the way in."

Ingrid shrugged. "Sure, it's nice to look at, but so's a postcard."

"It's dull," Rickie said. "It doesn't even have a shopping mall."

"It barely has a five-and-ten," Ingrid said.

Vanessa noticed that Rickie was looking at her curiously, as though she was trying to get up the nerve to ask her something. There was a long pause, then Rickie spoke.

"What did you think of Matthew Hanley?"

"He's young. I thought he'd be older."

Rickie leaned forward. "You think he's good-looking?"

"Yes, he's very attractive."

Ingrid crumpled up her empty milk carton. "He knows it too, the bastard. Thinks he's God's gift to women."

Rickie was staring at Vanessa with big brown eyes. "Some of the girls have crushes on him. I don't, but some of the girls do."

Ingrid chuckled. "Yeah, like ninety-eight percent. We're the two percent that doesn't."

"Ingrid's lying," Rickie said, a little too vehemently. "She's got the hots for him."

"I do not," squealed Ingrid, her face reddening. Then she broke into a grin. "Well, maybe a little."

"Yeah, maybe a lot," Rickie said, sarcastically.

"When you met him, Vanessa, did he come on to you?"

Now it was Vanessa's turn to blush. "I think my mother was flirting with him."

"They say he fools around with the girls," Rickie said, earnestly.

"They say?" Ingrid laughed. "We know it's true. I could name five girls he had just last semester."

Rickie lowered her voice conspiratorially. "Four years ago, one of the juniors got pregnant, and they said it was Matthew Hanley's child. She had to leave the school and everything."

"He got away with it?" Vanessa asked, incredulously. "Didn't they do anything?"

"No one could prove anything," Rickie said. "The whole thing was hushed up."

"What about the parents? Didn't they report it?"

"Report it to who?" Ingrid said. "The son of a bitch owns the school. And the town, in case you forgot, is called Hanley. Get my point? Besides, he probably slipped them some money."

"But the other parents . . . wouldn't they pull their kids out of the school once they found out?"

Ingrid gave Vanessa a look that was gently ironic. "Yeah? What would they do with them then? God forbid they'd have to look around for another good school. That would mean they'd have to fly home from the Riviera or Aspen or wherever the hell they are. Let's face it—we're all in this place because our parents dumped us here."

"I don't think that's true about my folks," Vanessa said, defensively. But she knew that Ingrid had touched a nerve.

"Then you're the exception. It's true of most of the girls at Hanley, and just about all the boys at Abbott, too."

"What's the story with the Abbott School?"

"There's some nice boys over there," Rickie replied.

Ingrid laughed. "Young and inexperienced, but nice."

"Listen to her."

"You'll meet them," Ingrid promised. "I'll introduce you to the good ones."

"Thanks."

"No problem. Stick with me, kid, and pretty soon you'll be as miserable as the rest of us."

"Yeah," Rickie complained. "Nothing ever happens in this place."

"Phone call for Vanessa Forbes." A woman's dry, impersonal voice came onto the school p.a. system.

Vanessa looked at the two girls. "Where do I go?"

"You can take it in there," Ingrid said. "There's a house phone on every floor."

"I think I'll take it upstairs. I'll meet up with you two later."

Vanessa went up to the second floor. On a table, near her room, was the beige house phone. Vanessa picked up the receiver and heard her mother's voice.

"Honey, is that you?"

"Yeah, Mom, it's me. Where are you?"

"I'm back in Boston. I made it in record time. How's it going? Have you made any friends yet?"

"A couple. Karin Sayers is really nice, Mom. We're doing 'Twelfth Night.' God, would I love to play Viola!"

"You will, darling, whoever that is. What else is going on?"

"I called Daddy. He asked about you."

"Yeah, he probably wanted to know if I was arrested for speeding."

Vanessa grinned. "Something like that. Listen, have a good time in Europe. Send me a postcard, okay?"

"Send you a card? I'm sending you a whole wardrobe. I think about you all the time, Vanessa. I love you, honey. Tell me honestly, are you alright?"

Vanessa could hear the concern in her mother's voice. For a brief moment, Vanessa thought about telling her mother everything—the blood, the severed arm—but she stopped herself. This wasn't the time—not on the phone—to alarm Mrs. Forbes with talk about hallucinations. She would not act like a spoiled kid. She would not use those visions as an excuse to go back to California or to prevent her mother from taking a well-deserved vacation.

"I'm fine, Mom. Just a little tired."

Evelyn Forbes sensed deception in her daughter's voice and wondered whether she should mention the odd sense of misgiving she'd had when she had left Vanessa alone at the school. But she decided against it—no need to add to the girl's stress. A few new friends and the discipline of the fall term would work wonders.

"Promise me something, darling. Are you listening?"

"Yes, Mom."

"If anything goes wrong, or if you're unhappy for any reason at all, you'll call me. You can always track me down in Europe through American Express. And if you can't, don't hesitate to call your father."

"I promise."

"Well, I'll say goodnight then. Take care of yourself, honey. You're in a good school. Make the best of it."

"I will."

"Oh," Mrs. Forbes added, excitedly, "did I tell you I may be going to Italy? The Vatican? St. Peter's? I'll tell the Pope you said hello."

At that moment, Vanessa felt very much alone. "Say a prayer for me."

Outside on the front lawn, Dennis Bellivin was passing around a pint bottle of cognac.

"Here, suck on some of this," he suggested to Ingrid.

Above, the golden moon floated high in the sky now, sending its light wafting down to fuse with the unnatural glow from the scattered, iron-encrusted lampposts on the front grounds. The chilly air foretold of the cold nights of autumn that were to come.

Ingrid drank greedily from the bottle. "Hmm. Cognac. Coming up in the world, Dennis."

"Well, I made it to senior year. That's pretty amazing."

"I'd say it's a goddamn miracle," Bobby Cannon said, joking.

Ingrid passed the pint of cognac to Rickie, who shook her head, refusing. "No thank you."

Dennis looked at her teasingly. "How about a quaalude?"

"I don't take drugs either. You know that, Dennis."

"That's your problem, Rickie. You're trying to cope with this place straight."

"You got ludes?" Ingrid asked in disbelief.

Dennis fished in his shirt pocket. He handed her a pill. "Here, knock yourself out."

"Thank you. I will." Ingrid grabbed for the cognac again and washed down the pill.

Dennis waited until Ingrid handed him back the bottle. He looked at her with a cocky air. "There's a new girl here," he began.

"Here it comes," Bobby said.

"Dark hair, very pretty," Dennis went on. "Drove up in a gray Mercedes."

"Shit," Ingrid said, "you don't waste any time, do you?'

"You know who I mean?"

Ingrid nodded. "I just had dinner with her."

"Yeah, yeah, go on," Dennis prompted.

Ingrid glanced over at Bobby, remembering their conversation of this afternoon. "Her name's Vanessa Forbes. She's a senior and she's not for you, Dennis."

Dennis looked annoyed. "That's the second time I've heard that today. Look, I just want to meet her."

"And I suppose you want me to arrange it."

Dennis shook his head. "No, thank you, Ingrid. I'll take care of it."

"Mr. Cool strikes again."

"That's right, Ingrid. Once Vanessa and I have met, the girl doesn't stand a chance."

Karin's room at the rear of the third story was exactly one floor above Room Six. The small chamber was a monument to Karin's longtime interest in the performing arts. Theatrical posters, playbills and photographs of her favorite actors and dancers adorned the walls in stylish frames. Karin's brass bed was covered with a lovely patchwork quilt, a legacy of her grandmother, and Karin had embellished it with her own touch, a pair of circular, embroidered lace pillows she had found at a flea market in Stockbridge. An oak rolltop desk from the turn of the century was her work space. Next to it, along the wall by the window, was a steamer trunk, covered with picturesque stickers from hotels and theaters around the world.

Seated in a white wicker rocker beneath a huge photograph of John Barrymore as Rasputin, Karin Sayers was reading the last scene of "Flowers Of Darkness." Beside her on the gold leafed night table next to her bed was her copy of the King James Bible, prominently displayed. It was the only item of her father's Karin still possessed; miraculously, it had escaped the fire that devoured his makeshift church. Though Henry Sayers' religious fanaticism had frightened and revolted Karin, old ways were hard to abandon and she still read from the Scriptures every night before she went to sleep.

The play was drawing to an end, and Karin was moved by the author's fervor. Though the plot was simple, "Flowers Of Darkness" demanded Karin's complete concentration, which she readily gave. The characters, figments from the imagination of someone named Lisa King, came to life for Karin in a hazy dream world—not quite real, yet not entirely make-believe.

Karin read the last word—"Curtain"—sighed, closed the manuscript and laid it gently on the bed. The script was a superb piece of writing—beautiful, evocative and haunting. Though some of the characters were grotesque, they swam before Karin's eyes now like people she knew, people she had just talked to today.

The whispers were back.

Karin had been so engrossed in the play that she hadn't realized, not until they had grown in rank volume and had become strangely insistent, that they were back. But Karin felt no fear now, just a mild curiosity.

Karin's hair trembled with the passing of a soft breeze. She looked at the window but knew she would find it closed. This wind was not from nature. Playfully, suggestively, the breeze slid up and down the length of Karin's body in a silky, unnatural, but expertly executed rhythm. The wind kissed the intimate parts of Karin teasingly. All at once, the air was still. The breeze had vanished, and there were no more whispers.

Karin glanced around the room, her eyes coming to rest for a moment on the Bible that lay on her night table. *The Good Lord wants me to do this, Karin. It will drive the demons from you.* Karin blinked her eyes. Seeing the familiar volume gave her an instant of uneasiness. She felt an odd shiver of anticipation dancing in her stomach. Her flesh felt slightly cold now, as if someone had been stroking it with a thin finger of glass. Her thinking had become incredibly lucid. Karin knew what she had to do.

She smiled to herself and laid her head back against the rocker. She never saw the water in the goldfish bowl across the room begin churning of its own accord. The two goldfish peered out at her through the thick glass, their bulbous eyes staring at their owner mournfully, their oval mouths opening and closing as if they were trying to call out a warning.

Karin got into bed and fell into a deep sleep that would last until morning. That night, for the first time in many years, the King James Bible on the night table would remain unopened.

5

Laura Nash was angry with herself. Here she was just a few hours away from having to walk through the front gates of Hanley and already she was annoyed and bored. It was bad enough that for the next ten months of the school term she would be bored to death, but to spend her last remaining hours of vacation feeling this listless was unthinkable. Thank God, she thought, this was her senior year at the Hanley hellhole. In less than a year she would never have to see that dungeon again.

This was the one bright thought Laura had as she sat in the late night gloom of the smoke-filled roadside bar just outside the town of Hanley waiting for Fred what's-his-name to buy her another round. She watched through the grime-encrusted window as the pink and orange neon sign, almost obscene in its clashing colors, flashed on and off, proclaiming The Bull's Pit Bar & Grill. Noticing the last word, Laura shuddered. God, she thought, this dump actually serves food. Laura was revolted, knowing she would rather die than eat a meal here.

She took another sip of her gin and tonic and tried to

ignore what looked like grease floating around in the glass. Fred's reflection in the window seemed to be signaling something to her. He was pointing to a pay phone at the end of the bar. Good, he was going to make a phone call. That would keep him away a little longer. She nodded her head and forced a tentative smile to her lips. She had to be nice to Fred if she wanted that lift he had promised her.

Last year when she had decided to hitch to Hanley, it had taken her six or seven rides to get all the way to the school. This time she had been lucky with Fred. He had picked her up in Manhattan and she'd been delighted to learn that he was driving all the way to Boston. One look at Laura's legs as she'd gotten into the car—she'd given him a generous flash of thigh deliberately—and he'd quickly agreed to drive the 30 miles out of his way to Hanley. Of course, poor Fred had no idea when Laura asked for a ride to her place that the place would turn out to be an all-girls school. Laura had to stifle a giggle at the thought of what Fred's face would look like when they approached the gates of Hanley. She knew that he was dying to get into her pants, and she had done nothing to make him think otherwise. On the other hand, she never actually agreed to sleep with him tonight. Laura Nash played this kind of game well. For a young girl, she was already a master of deception. She had an instinct for knowing just what people wanted from her—whether it be sex or something else—and the ability to make them think they were going to get it even if, as was usually the case, they wouldn't. This, coupled with startling good looks, almost always got her what she wanted. In this case, it was simply a ride to Hanley and she was almost there.

Laura knew that hitching a ride with a stranger could be dangerous, but she also knew that though Fred was a jerk, he was basically harmless. She would charm him out of his anger later at the school—and if that failed, she would put on her little girl act. That always worked.

There would be nothing he could do at that point. Laura bet that he would even ask to see her again. Men! They were so predictable.

Laura had learned at an early age how to manipulate a situation. She had the best teacher in the world—Amanda Nash, her mother. She had watched her mother manipulate and pull her father's strings all her life.

Laura was so lost in thought that she was hardly aware of the man as he came over to her booth and slid in opposite her.

"Penny for your thoughts."

Fucking original, thought Laura as she glanced up at Fred, who placed a fresh gin and tonic in front of her. Laura smiled sweetly at him, but suddenly she wanted to be away from Fred what's-his-name and far away from the Bull's Pit Bar & Grill. Even school seemed more appealing right now. She fingered her purse. What she really needed now was some cocaine.

"I'll be right back," said Laura, gathering her pocketbook and heading toward the ladies room. On the way, she passed a handsome young trucker type at the end of the bar, who was ordering some coffee for the road. The driver smiled at her, and Laura winked back. She had an idea.

The rest room was little more than a cubicle, stuffy and unclean. Laura bolted the door and stood in front of the grease-caked mirror.

"Jesus," she mumbled, giving herself the once-over in the glass. In the harsh glow of a bare light bulb, Laura's face seemed to age 20 years. The cracks and smudges on the mirror transposed themselves onto her youthful skin, giving her a twisted image of what she might look like in middle age. Her skin looked haggard and almost jaundiced, her hair limp and colorless. Laura laughed to spite the reflection.

She took the cocaine vial from her purse and measured out a hefty spoonful of the drug. Expertly, she snorted the white powder into each nostril, careful not to spill a single flake. The metallic taste of the narcotic trickled down her throat and Laura gave an involuntary gag. That cold sensation on the back of her tongue was the one drawback of coke snorting she would never get used to.

There, thought Laura, that was better. She could feel the drug's euphoria almost at once. She threw back her shoulders confidently. Getting her luggage would be easy. She'd simply tell Fred she had to retrieve something from her bags. Step two would be dealing with the trucker. That would be no problem either. Laura grinned and took another quick hit of coke. Too bad it was so late. None of the girls would be up to see her arrive at the front gates in the cab of a tractor trailer.

Vanessa lay in a troubled sleep. Bad dreams, unremembered, already had awakened her twice in the night. Now as she tossed fitfully, she once again kicked off the blankets, exposing herself to an uncanny chill, not as if someone had turned off the heat but rather as though the room had always been devoid of warmth from the beginning. Across the room, where Vanessa had placed it earlier, a tiny five watt nightlamp burned, casting a shard of light into the closet, which was slightly ajar for her comfort. In the timeworn walls, pipes jangled and thumped, their abrupt noises mingling with the measured, even breathing of the students who slept unawares. Like a thin layer of sound, another murmur rose and fell consumptively, there for those who might dare to listen but unheard by those who preferred to sleep.

Footsteps were clicking upstairs from the ground level, then advancing along the corridor of the second floor. A pause outside the door of Room Six was followed by the sudden loud turning of a key in the lock. The door to the room flew open. There was a glare of light. Vanessa gave a violent turn in her sleep and sat up in bed, her eyes snapping open.

"Jesus Christ! You scared the hell out of me," Laura Nash said accusingly, her hand still on the light switch by the door. She kicked the door shut with her foot, nearly stumbling over her luggage.

"Who are you?" Vanessa asked, rubbing her eyes. She gathered the blankets up from the floor and wrapped herself in them for warmth.

"If this is number six, I'm Laura Nash. Your cellmate." She gave Vanessa a mock salute.

"What time is it?"

Laura shrugged. "Who knows? It's dark out. Does that help?" Laura slipped out of her coat and sank down on the other bed. "What's your name?"

"I'm Vanessa Forbes."

"Hi, Vanessa. Do you know you're sleeping in my bed?"

"I am?"

"No one told you, huh?" Laura laughed. "I always get the bed by the window. It's kind of a school tradition."

Vanessa got up, still sleepy, taking the blankets with her. "Oh, I'm sorry. I'll move."

"Nah, it can wait till morning. I'm not expecting anyone tonight."

"You're kidding, aren't you?"

"No, I'm serious. Sometimes a guy has to make a quick getaway. I don't want him climbing over beds if he has to get to the fire escape. Don't look so shocked. I don't do it that often, no matter what anyone says, and I'll always give you fair warning."

Laura took a makeup kit out of her overnight bag, opened a compact and spread some cocaine onto its tiny mirror. Taking a single-edged razor blade, she began chopping chunks of the drug into powder.

"I just spent four hours in some bar on the other side of town, stuck with this guy, Fred something, who gave me a ride from New York. I was so bored I was playing Pac-Man with some kid who I thought was a dwarf. I need a new razor blade. You got one?"

"Huh?"

"Razor blade. This one's dull. Can't chop a damn thing with this." Laura opened the casement window and tossed the blade out onto the lawn as Vanessa watched in amazement. Laura found another blade in her purse.

"Never mind. I got one. Anyway, I got a ride from this guy who told me he was a record producer. Just some jerk driving a Toyota. Halfway through Connecticut, I open my mouth and sing two notes. Suddenly, this guy's a record producer. I guess he thought I never heard that one before. Anyway, I played along, right? I needed the lift. He got me as far as Hanley but then he was really getting on my nerves. I ditched him in The Bull's Pit Bar & Grill, do you believe that name? Typical Hanley dive, right? I spotted this really good-looking trucker, and he took me the rest of the way. Fred's probably still waiting for me back at the bar, but I'm long gone. History. Record Producer. Yeah, on the Asshole label. Boy, that dirt road is a bitch on your kidneys when you're riding in a semi. Have some coke? It'll wake you up."

She shoved the mirror under Vanessa's nose, but Vanessa shook her head and smiled politely. "No thanks."

"You don't want coke?" Laura rolled her eyes. "They put me in a room with a girl who doesn't do drugs? Oh, well, more for me." Laura quickly snorted her lines and then the ones she had laid out for her roommate.

"So how do you like this place? Did you meet any of the teachers?"

Vanessa had to grin. It was hard to get a word in. "I met Karin Sayers."

"You a drama major? Me, too. I'm really a singer. A goddamned good one, too. People are always trying to compare me to Pat Benatar but I got my own style. Personally, I think I sound like Billie Holiday only more rock 'n' roll. Karin's okay. Kinda straight. Her father's a minister. He's dead now. Burned to death in a fire. I think he was one of those crackpot evangelists. Maybe he lit himself up as a human sacrifice, who knows? I guess you met Matthew Hanley, huh? Not bad, huh? He can bang his eraser on my blackboard any time."

Vanessa laughed out loud, enjoying her roommate's non-stop monologue. Laura might be high but it was a pleasure for Vanessa not to feel obligated to even join in the conversation. The tension and anxiety she'd been feeling all day seemed to evaporate in the flood of energy that Laura Nash was exuding. Vanessa felt excited. In many ways, the two girls might be opposite personalities but how could Vanessa feel frightened at this school when she had a roommate so full of life?

"Yeah," Laura continued with a devilish grin, "Matthew can keep me after school any day."

"That seems to be the general opinion around here."

Laura nodded. "Yeah, everybody wants to get it on with Matthew. He was after me all last year. I thought about it over the summer. This year I think I'll let him have what he wants."

"I heard he fools around with the girls, but it's hard to believe."

"Are you kidding? He's a lech. A good-looking lech, but still he's a lech. It's the Hanley name. Every man in that family is a goddamn horny bastard. The guy who founded this school—a perv."

"Really?"

"I guess no one told you about what happened to him. His untimely demise, shall we say. It was quite a scandal." Laura leaned forward, obviously relishing the chance to tell the story. "Seems old Malcolm was in the sack one night, matriculating with a couple of foxy young students. This was a million years ago—1920 or something. Happened at the cottage down the other side of the lawn." Laura waved at the window vaguely and took a deep breath. "There was this girl who had a crush on him. She was a real weirdo. I think she also was a drama major. Anyway, she was jealous. In the dead of night, she went downstairs to the kitchen and got a meat cleaver. The rack is still there where it used to hang. I mean you can see it and everything. So she snuck down to the cottage, looked through the window and almost shit. Malcolm was in bed with the two girls. So what does she do? She goes inside and hacks the three of them to pieces."

"Oh, my God, how horrible."

"Yeah, they don't put it in the school brochure, do they? But I'll tell you what's really horrible. They closed down the school but only for a little while. The Hanley name is big enough around these parts to cover up a scandal and even get away with murder."

"What happened to the girl? The one who did it?"

"She was whacko. Suicide."

For a brief second, a phrase came back to Vanessa from her meeting that morning in the headmaster's office. "Nothing would grow here," she said under her breath.

"What did you say?" asked Laura.

"Nothing."

Dreams would not be remembered by those who slept soundly this night. The moon, like a sinister orb of light, hung over the school, not bright enough to illuminate its darkened corners so that the building resembled a giant box-like creature that had taken root in the soil. There was no definition to the structure this night, only a mass of twisted shapes all joined together in grotesque harmony.

For those who didn't sleep during the darkest hours, an unearthly, contented sighing seemed to issue from the bowels of the building. But the few who were awake wouldn't dare acknowledge this sound—to their friends or even to themselves—not even when the night was finally over. To do so would be an admission that something was wrong at Hanley—very wrong. This was the first night of school, so excuses were easily fashioned, and the phantom breathing was attributed to the old plumbing making odd noises.

Walter Cox knew better, but he had come to a silent agreement with the school many years before when he had first come to work there. He was 15 years younger then, and the steady diet of hard liquor had yet to put weathered creases on his gaunt face and disturb his nervous system so that often he could not control a slight shaking in his hands. He had taken the job as maintenance man with the intention of only staying at it for a year. Now, at age 55, Walter was still vowing that this year would be his last. He had good reason. The school gave him the willies, with all that God-awful pounding that Walter could swear was someone breathing into the very pipes, not to mention that nerve-racking gibberish in the walls. Was it really people whispering? Walter would strain his ears but in 15 years he had not been able to solve the mystery. This year, though, he thought he was closer—the whisperings had grown louder. By next summer, he'd be gone, he told himself. But then he'd said that every year, hadn't he?

Sometimes, Walter Cox rationalized his unwillingness to leave with the thought that his job really wasn't so bad. Even though the building was old, it rarely needed repairs, almost as though it was able to maintain itself. Of course, that was a notion Walter didn't want to dwell on too much. He liked to think he was just fortunate that no one knew how little work he actually had to do. There wasn't much supervision of his activities, and though the hours could sometimes be long, there were seldom enough duties to fill up his day. In his long tenure at the school, Walter had devised an elaborate system of hiding out, utilizing numerous back stairways and alcoves to wile away the idle hours with his favorite pastimes—drinking, napping, and spying on the unsuspecting young girls.

Whenever the strangeness threatened to get to Walter, he consoled himself with the thought that this was a pretty cushy job. Sure, the money could be better, but where else could an aging hopeless drunk find employment where he could sip from a whiskey bottle at any hour of the day and, more important, where there were so many juicy opportunities of feasting his eyes on delectable teenage pussy?

That last delightful prospect was uppermost on Walter's mind the next morning at 7:30, as he lumbered across the lawn, his face ruddy from the previous night's excesses. He really had tied one on last night—the night before school started was always an occasion—and his head rattled with a throbbing pain that even three extra-strength aspirins hadn't diminished. Walter rubbed his forehead, the pumping of blood in his veins pounding like a hydraulic drill inside his skull. He patted the pint bottle of rye in his overalls' pocket. Hair of the dog—that would fix him right up.

Another beautiful sunny day. Walter cursed the weather under his breath. Though the sun had just cleared the tops of the red maples on the side lawn, its piercing rays were already enough to make Walter wince. His eyes, perpetually bloodshot and oversensitive to light, grew moist with tears. Walter muttered to himself again—six fuckin' days without rain. He would have to water the lawns again and that would cut into his sleeping time, goddamn it. Angrily, Walter kicked at the grass with his battered engineer boots, nearly losing his footing.

As he reached the side drive, Walter looked up at a window on the second floor and grinned crookedly. The girls would be coming into the shower room soon, and he could hardly wait. It had been a long barren summer and Walter had had to be content with his girlie magazines. But those were just pictures. A connoisseur always preferred the real thing. To Walter's disappointment, a few of the choice lookers had graduated but with a new semester came new girls, and he hungered to get a look at the latest crop. Well, it was just one flight up, he thought to himself. Maybe today wouldn't be such a bad day after all.

The school was beginning to stir with morning sounds —water bubbling through pipes, doors closing, windows being throw open to let in the biting autumn air, the many sounds of a new day.

Karin Sayers had been fully awake by 6 a.m. She had a strange feeling of satiation, as if she had made love for hours with an intimate companion. She felt cared for, even loved. Usually, the first day of classes was invigorating for Karin, but this other feeling seemed to overpower any desire to move from her bed.

Karin forced herself to sit up, and something fell to the floor as she disrupted the covers. The script. She had been so tired last night when she had finished reading "Flowers of Darkness" that she had just fallen asleep with the manuscript on the blanket beside her.

Karin looked at the pale yellow stained-glass window just above the casement. When it was overcast, the yellow of the window became muted. If the sunlight beamed through, the color was enhanced and became a bright spot in the room. Karin could tell today was going to be a clear day. 7:30. Had she been daydreaming for over an hour? Karin picked up the small digital clock on the nightstand. She smiled to herself. Yes. She had no memory of where the past hour had gone, yet, somehow, she felt rejuvenated.

After running a bath full of steamy water, Karin relaxed in the tub. She paid no real attention to the water in the bath as it churned slightly, even though she remained perfectly still. Soon, Karin gave in to the rush of pleasure that was washing over her body along with the swirling bathwater. In her bedroom, the rocker had begun to move back and forth, in and out of the pool of light shining through the pale yellow oval window.

Ingrid was in a foul mood and was glad she was alone. At least, she didn't have to face a roommate. Her room, once designed as a storage space but finally converted into living quarters, was not nearly as large as those along the hallway, but she didn't mind the compact quarters. It was a small sacrifice for the luxury of not having to share the space.

Ingrid looked around the room. The walls were devoid of decor—that was the way she preferred them. Even the cork bulletin board near the door, which the other girls covered with snapshots of their boy friends and posters of their favorite rock stars, was completely bare. Ingrid had kept it that way for three years, and it would remain so until the day she left the school. She felt that as long as she made no effort to impose her personality on the room, she could keep a distance from the school itself and not slip into even a tacit alliance with this building she had come to loathe.

God, she thought, first morning here and already I wish I were someplace else—anywhere. Ten months, Ingrid, and you're out of here. She comforted herself with that thought. Still, this was no way to be feeling on the very first day. She'd be nuts before September was over if she let depression take over now.

Ingrid threw off the blankets. The room was unusually warm today, and that annoying stained glass window didn't help. The room took on the red tint of the window, which made it seem aglow with heat. Ingrid resisted an impulse to throw something at the oval glass, breaking it once and for all. God, Malcolm Hanley must have been tripping on magic mushrooms when he designed this fucking place.

Sliding off the bed, Ingrid got to her knees and retrieved the small suitcase from under it. Her hands went to the flask nestled in the secret compartment on the bottom. She unscrewed the top and took a gulp. The alcohol burned her throat all the way down to the pit of her stomach. She welcomed the stinging sensation; it was like medicine that was bad tasting but would heal you in the long run. Another swallow. Ingrid could feel her sour mood giving way to indifference. She would be able to face people in a little while—not quite yet, but soon. She started to put the flask back, thought better of it and placed it on the bed. She decided she would need it with her at all times in this, her final year at Hanley.

Down the corridor, Marie Kronofsky was shaking her roommate, Rickie Webster.

"Hey, Rickie, wake up. You're dreaming."

As Rickie blinked her eyes, the image of Marie swam before her. Rickie had been having a nightmare—a bad one. She had been crying in her sleep.

"I'm okay," Rickie said. "I'm okay, really." She could see the concern on her roommate's face. "This is scary. I had this really horrible dream, but now I can't remember the first thing about it."

"You're not used to being here yet," Marie said, brushing her dark hair up into a shower cap. "You know it takes a little while to get used to a different bed."

"Yeah, I guess," Rickie said, not looking convinced.

"I didn't sleep so hot myself. I kept hearing noises."

"What kind of noises?"

"I don't know. Like people whispering. I thought it was outside the door, but sometimes it sounded like it was in the walls."

"Stop it, Marie," Rickie snapped. "That's just stupid."

Surprised at Rickie's vehemence, Marie put down her hairbrush. "It's not stupid, Rickie. We've all heard the noises. But it's an old building and plays tricks on you. It was probably someone talking in the basement. You know how sound travels."

"You know what? I bet I could hear those noises in my sleep. I bet they were part of my dream."

"Do you remember any of it?"

"No, I told you I couldn't. Are you deaf?"

Marie looked offended. "Hey, take it easy. I was only trying to help."

"Help? I'm not the one who needs help. You're the

one who heard people in the walls. You're the one who's crazy. Not me."

"Rickie, no one's talking about being crazy. What's the matter with you anyway?"

Tears suddenly came to Rickie's eyes, and her voice took on a faraway tone. "Everybody always wants to help, but they only make things worse. How can anyone know what I'm feeling inside, when I don't even know myself?"

Marie stepped back, uncomfortable. She wanted to put her arm around the younger girl, but something told her not to. "I'm sorry if I said anything. I didn't mean to upset you."

Rickie half-smiled. "I got a bad feeling about this year. Real bad."

"What do you mean?"

Rickie didn't answer. She turned away to face the wall.

"Rickie?"

When she finally spoke, Rickie's voice was barely audible. "If only I could remember that dream . . ."

Down the corridor in Room Six, Laura Nash hadn't dreamt at all. She hadn't even been to sleep. On the top of her dresser, her cocaine supply had noticeably dwindled but the drug's effects were undeniable. During the night, while Vanessa slept, Laura had quietly, but with great energy, moved her roommate's belongings to the other side of the room, making way for her own clothes, which she had unpacked. Finished with hanging up and putting away all her things, Laura had excitedly gotten down to what she'd really been looking forward to—transforming Room Six into the kind of place a girl could be proud to call home.

Now with the casement wide open, Laura sat cross-legged in the window seat, meticulously applying a coat of blushing pink polish to her fingernails. She'd been perched there for a few minutes, savoring the crisp clarity of a New England autumn morning. Generally

Laura was a late sleeper, often just making her first class as the bell was ringing, but on those occasions when she stayed up all night, she could appreciate the quiet drama of a sunrise. Not that Laura was a sentimentalist—how could she be when the melodious sound of birds chirping had just been interrupted by a vulgar, resounding belch from Walter Cox as he trudged across the lawn? Some things never change, thought Laura with a half-grin, but maybe that old degenerate had the right idea—stay pickled all the time and you can cope with anything.

To each his own—that was Laura's philosophy. She turned away from the window and leaned over toward her dresser to snort two more hefty lines of coke. She glanced over at Vanessa, still sleeping. Give her five more minutes, Laura decided generously, and then it would be time for some loud rock 'n' roll. All through the night, Laura had been listening to cassettes on her Walkman, but there was nothing like a little Bruce Springsteen at top volume to let all the girls know that Laura Nash was back. Besides, she was providing a service by giving them a musical education.

Vanessa's head moved on the pillow. She opened her eyes slowly and then stared dumbfounded. Laura had completely taken over one entire side of the room, arranging her paraphernalia—from floppy hats to tape cassettes to feathered boas to a staggering array of perfumes, lipsticks and compacts—to establish an instant lived-in atmosphere that would have taken Vanessa months to achieve. And it didn't stop there. Laura had taken to the walls, decorating two sides of the room with lobby-sized movie posters of "Casablanca" and "A Star Is Born," along with a rich assortment of art reproductions—everything from Frank Frazetta to Maxfield Parrish—plus, situated incongruously in their midst, large glossy photos of film and rock stars, all of them male and most of them naked to the waist. Even the ceiling had not been spared. As Vanessa looked up, she stared into the eyes of Richard Gere.

"My God," said Vanessa, taking it all in.

"Jesus, I thought you'd never wake up." Laura waved her hand around the room grandly. "Good job, huh? You think I could be an interior decorator?"

Vanessa laughed. "I don't believe this. Did you stay up all night?"

Laura nodded at the cocaine. "Who could sleep? I was going to repaint the closets. I even thought about waxing the hallway. I couldn't wait for you to get up so I can make your bed."

"It's your bed now, isn't it?" Vanessa said, remembering Laura's remark from the previous night.

"Well, it is from now on. But I didn't want to disturb you. I can't believe I stood on your pillow to hang up Richard Gere and you didn't even hear me."

"That's surprising. I'm usually a very light sleeper."

"You don't want to be a light sleeper around here. You'd never get any rest."

Vanessa's eyes were still roving along the walls, noticing the broad spectrum of Laura's interests. "You certainly have taste that's—what's the word?—eclectic."

"Is that anything like electric? Does that mean you don't like it?"

"No, it's great," Vanessa said, beginning to get used to the room's new look.

"Like I told you last night, I'm big on tradition. The way I look at it, this place is musty, like a museum. It's never going to be like home, but at least I can make it look like someone lives here. Like I live here. Doing all this decorating, it's like a ritual for me. No matter what time I get into Hanley, it's always the first thing I do. It makes me feel like no matter how weird things get around here, I've always got one little niche where I can feel comfortable."

"What do you mean . . . weird?"

"Vanessa, you must have noticed this place looks like a mausoleum. It's a dungeon. The outside looks like some castle out of 'Grimm's Fairy Tales.' The only thing they're missing is a moat. I mean, the roof has gargoyles, for God's sake. And what about the caretakers? Have you met the Trousdales? I call them the Munsters. Jesus, this place is nuts."

Vanessa smiled at her roommate's outburst. But looking at the mirror on the dresser, she could tell where some of it was coming from. "You did a lot of that coke, didn't you?" she asked.

"There's still half a gram left. You want some?"

"No, that's alright."

Laura looked at her with disbelief. "You don't do coke at all?"

"Well, maybe for studying."

"Shit." Laura laughed. "Why waste it?"

Again, Vanessa found herself laughing. Her first impression of Laura Nash had been correct. This vivacious, carefree girl was just the kind of person Vanessa needed to be around. And Laura had the right idea about the room. She might not be homesick like Vanessa, but the trick of surrounding yourself with familiar objects made sense. Any shocks Vanessa might conjure up about the school would be deflected, once she had replaced the cold, impersonal setting with possessions she could closely identify with. Vanessa scanned her side of the room which, in comparison to Laura's, looked comically empty. Already, she was picturing the changes she would make with just one shopping trip into town. She could pick up duplicates of the rock star posters that decorated her bedroom back in California. And once her mother returned from Europe, Vanessa could send for her collection of stuffed animals that would take up almost one wall by itself. Laura's way of coping was a revelation. She might not be able to match her new roommate for variety and extravagance, but goddamn it, she was sure going to try.

"What are you smiling at, Vanessa?"

"You. I'm really glad you're here."

Laura smiled back. Despite the drugs, she seemed so healthy, so much in charge of her own life. Laura had been at the school for three years and looked no worse for wear. True, she didn't know her very well, and the girl might be heavily dependent on cocaine, but, to Vanessa's eyes anyway, she appeared to be living proof that, with the right attitude, Hanley could be a breeze. And Vanessa had only one year to go.

She glanced at Laura's dresser. Yesterday, Vanessa had seen a bloody arm in there. Now, with the top of the dresser spilling over with Laura's scarves and magazines, it seemed ridiculous that anything loathsome could ever have been there. Vanessa's eyes moved involuntarily to the handles of the second drawer. Despite her newfound confidence, she knew she could never open that drawer again.

Walter Cox's knobby fingers shook with anticipation. Parked on a small stepladder in the second floor utility room, he could hear the sound of running water from the girls' shower facilities on the other side of the wall. Beads of perspiration stood out on his furrowed brow. It was like this every first morning of a new school year. Relishing the splatter of water, his lips drew back to reveal his tobacco-stained teeth. Good, he thought, one of the little whores was in there prancing around naked and wet under the spray.

Walter moved his hand along the wall, feeling for the familiar patch of plaster. When his fingers found it, he eagerly began to dig the loose rubble from his peep hole in the wall that separated the closet from the showers.

He was very proud of his spying technique. No one could hear him if he was very quiet, and when he was finished, he would just stuff the plaster back in the wall, and nobody was the wiser. He had first devised his secret spying method shortly after coming to the school and had been watching the girls undetected ever since.

Boy, their parents would be pissed off if they knew old Walt was looking at their daughters' titties bouncing around. Serves the tramps right.

He pressed his wrinkled face against the wall and looked through the peephole. Immediately, a naked body came into view. Shit, Walter swore. It's that skinny little one. Hardly any tits, no ass to speak of, even her bush wasn't worth looking at. Well, he would just be patient. Others would be coming in soon enough. Walter double-checked to be sure the closet door was locked, then he reached for his bottle, took a long drink, opened his zipper and waited.

Rickie Webster always felt a bit queasy the first day of school, but this was different. The undisclosed nightmare had stayed with her like a bitter taste in her mouth, and her whole body ached. She hoped she wasn't getting her period. That meant cramps—bad ones. If so, the timing couldn't be worse. What she didn't need was pain on the first day of school if she was to keep her resolution for the new semester.

Rickie had promised herself that this year she was going to be more outgoing, less nervous about herself. Well, she decided, as she soaped herself under the spray of the shower, if the cramps got too much for her, maybe she would take something for them. If she took drugs now and then with the other girls, maybe she would be more popular. She knew her schoolmates thought she was strange, but, worse than that, she knew they felt sorry for her. Rickie resented people pitying her; she wished they would just take her as an equal.

Maybe this year she could change all that. Be more personable. Stop being afraid of her own shadow. If she kept acting so straight, she would never fit in here. She vowed that the next time she was offered a drink, she would not refuse. Maybe she could pretend to swallow the liquor, even though the taste made her gag. And if she was at a party and a joint was being passed around, what was the harm in taking a little puff? Rickie hoped this year she at least would be invited to a party.

Rickie liked to get to the showers before the other girls. If she really rushed, she could be washed, dried and dressed before they even came in. She was embarrassed by her underdeveloped chest and her almost transluscent skin, stretched over her rib cage, causing it to stand out. Quickly, she lathered her body and began to shampoo her hair. She didn't hear Laura Nash step into the shower room.

Rickie jumped back at the sudden intrusion and had to lean against the wall to regain her footing. So much for not being afraid this year, she thought forlornly.

"Rick the Stick! How the hell are you?" Even in a loose-fitting terry cloth robe, Laura looked sexy. If I had a body like that, Rickie thought, it wouldn't matter so much that I'm high-strung.

Laura smiled at Rickie. "So how was your summer?" Laura slipped out of her robe and hung it on a hook near the door. She came over to the shower next to Rickie.

The younger girl's face grew flushed. She couldn't take her eyes from Laura's voluptuous body, now completely nude, and had to force herself to look away.

"Uh, my summer was, uh, really great," she stammered. "I spent two months at my grandmother's farm. She grows, uh, asparagus."

Rickie turned her back to Laura and busied herself by sponging cool water over her body. She made up her mind to just stand like this until Laura left, then she wouldn't have to face her. But that was stupid. She was already finished with her shower. She couldn't just stand there for five minutes like an idiot. All she had to do was turn around, get her towel and leave. Her feet were rooted to the tiles.

"Asparagus, huh? Sounds thrilling." Laura gave a little chuckle to let Rickie know that she was only kidding, but Rickie felt foolish. Why was she always coming out with things that made her seem as dull as she really was?

Rickie dared a peek over her shoulder. Good. Laura's back was toward her and she was shampooing her hair. That meant Laura's eyes would be closed for awhile—enough time for Rickie to get out of there.

Rickie turned off the shower and reached for her towel. She wrapped it tightly around her thin body. Her hair hung in wet strings down her back, but she would dry it later before twisting it into her customary braids. She took a few steps backward, toward the shower room door but then she could go no further. Something wouldn't let her move.

Something magnetic was drawing Rickie into Laura's circle like a delicate finger of desire, summoning up a sexuality Rickie could scarcely recognize. Despite the cool shower, she began to feel hot, dirty. How could she be attracted to Laura? This was wrong. Rickie had never wanted to be with any woman—not *that* way. Rickie couldn't even remember feeling this way about a boy.

Rickie watched as Laura, completely unaware of the younger girl's eyes on her, moved under the silky spray of the shower. Laura began to sing a popular rock song in a husky voice, but Rickie couldn't follow the words. She was too disoriented to concentrate. She wondered what it would be like to stroke Laura's flawless skin and became terrified at the thought.

Rickie continued to look on in an odd mixture of awe and fear as Laura turned around, eyes still closed, to let the water rinse her long blonde hair free of soap. The bottle of shampoo slipped from Laura's fingers and landed in front of Rickie. Her mouth slighly parted, Rickie stood gaping at Laura. If only she could touch her, just for a moment.

"Hey, Rick, grab that for me, will ya?"

Trembling, Rickie reached for the shampoo. Her fingers closed around the plastic bottle. She hoped Laura wouldn't open her eyes and see her hand shaking. She imagined she felt the heat from Laura's body as she leaned closer. Her nostrils filled with the smell of Laura, a blend of muskiness and soap. Rickie went to hand the shampoo to Laura, who was now looking right at her.

Laura studied the girl for a minute and then took the shampoo. As Rickie gave her the bottle, she couldn't resist brushing her palm against Laura's skin, cool from the shower. Rickie jumped back as if she had been burned over an open fire.

Rickie knew if she didn't rush from the room this instant she would be violently sick. Holding her hand over her mouth, she turned and ran toward the door, praying that Laura hadn't noticed her behavior. She could hear Laura calling out to her, asking if anything was wrong, but Rickie didn't stop to answer.

She slammed the shower room door as if to shut out Laura forever. It wasn't until Rickie was almost back in her own room that she realized she had been running down the school corridor wrapped in a towel, her hair dripping wet, her small, bony feet making a slapping suction noise as she padded toward safety.

When Laura Nash had taken off her robe, Walter Cox had nearly broken his neck, tumbling off his small stepladder in excitement. The sight of her nude body had so thrilled him that even as he scrambled to his feet, he was panting like a dog. Thirstily, he had gulped from his pint bottle, then returned to the business of spying.

Laura sure was a piece of ass. She had been a special favorite of Walter's from the first day he had laid eyes on her. She had the kind of figure that could put the broads in the girlie magazines to shame. Laura even could turn him on fully dressed. Naked as a jaybird in the shower, she was enough to make his old heart pump like a piston.

Too bad she hadn't been alone this morning. Looking at that jumpy kid next to her was a turn-off. Damn that skinny cunt. She had ruined it for him today, he thought, as he fingered his still limp penis. Running out of there like some crazy bitch. Probably ashamed on account of she had no tits.

Walter grinned lewdly, saliva caked at the corners of his thin, angry mouth. He had seen the way the nervous one had looked at the blonde. Walter knew that look. But there was something else about that girl. She had acted like she was in some kind of a trance. Probably some drug the bitch took. Walter knew that almost all the girls fooled around with drugs. He had found enough half-smoked marijuana cigarettes and empty pill bottles to know that. He didn't blame the girls. Goddamn place could drive anyone batty. Look at what it had done to him.

Laura was still scrubbing herself in the shower but Walter could hear people in the hallways now. It was getting late. He had better haul his ass out of here and see what work had to be done today. He would have all year to watch the blonde. Maybe next time he'd be able to make it happen, he thought sadly, zipping up his pants.

6

A small, heavy door separated the furnace room from the living quarters of Blanche and Desmond Trousdale. For more than half a century, the Trousdales inhabited this makeshift apartment, carrying out their duties as caretakers of The Hanley School.

The compact, three room railroad flat was a haven for bric-a-brac, the clutter of a married couple who didn't believe in throwing anything out. Yet for all the accumulated junk, the apartment was spotless. Very little dust got in, as there were only two tiny windows, both located at the rear. But even with the occasional bright spots of various antiques, the cheerless gloom of a cellar hung over the quarters.

The heavily paneled rooms and dark furnishings added a touch of melancholy, as though the Trousdales were trying to conceal any pleasure in their surroundings. The joy in the old couple's lives was their fierce, protective love for the school, a job for which they had been hand-picked by Malcolm Hanley himself.

The Trousdales' apartment was off-limits to the students. That was one rule the Hanley girls never broke, though it was more from fear of the old pair—and of the basement itself—than respect for the Trousdales' wishes.

Blanche Trousdale, though five-ten and 180 pounds, looked dwarfed next to her husband, Desmond, an imposing giant of a man, who stood well over six feet. An unruly crop of thick, snow white hair topped off Desmond's unnaturally large head. His hawk-like nose looked as though it had been nailed onto his beefy face, the pale cheeks of which hung down like bull-dogs' jowls.

A little after eight o'clock on this first day of classes, Blanche's bulk was draped over the kitchen table, as she sipped noisily from a soupbowl full of coffee. On the other side of the room, Desmond sat beside a small cage which contained his pet tarantula. One at a time, he fed squirming lizards to the spider with one hand, while eating oatmeal with the other.

"Walter's drinking again," said Blanche between slurps of coffee. "I saw a bottle in his pants."

Desmond didn't bother to look up. He coaxed the tarantula, waving a lizard in front of it. "Come on, baby, eat your breakfast."

"Did you hear what I said?"

"Walter's drinking again. I'm not surprised. The man's a hopeless alcoholic."

"I think you ought to have a talk with him. You know how clumsy he gets when he's drunk. You wouldn't want him to have an accident."

Desmond's attention was still on the spider, which had ripped the lizard from his hand. "That's a good girl. Eat it all up."

"We don't need Walter having an accident," Blanche went on. "Not this year. Not when everything's going so well."

Demond glanced across the kitchen table. "Walter's been drinking for as long as I've known him. He won't have an accident. But I'll talk to him."

Satisfied, Blanche buttered some toast. "The Nash girl woke me up last night, sneaking in at all hours. I don't suppose you heard her."

"I heard her. I'm not deaf yet."

"I hate that little bitch," Blanche said, folding the slice of toast and cramming it into her mouth intact. "She's so cocky. Thinks she's better than everybody else. Thinks she can step out of line and nothing will happen to her."

Desmond reached for another lizard. "That could change."

"You mean that? You think she'll be one of them?"

"Why not? She's got all the makings."

"I hope so. The school has waited a long time. I want everything to be perfect."

"Stop worrying, Blanche. It will be perfect. Whoever's picked, they'll get what they deserve."

Desmond smiled approvingly as the helpless lizard was sucked into the mouth of the tarantula.

Karin knocked on the door of Matthew Hanley's first floor office.

"Come in."

Matthew was standing beneath the portrait of his great-granduncle. He smiled at his visitor. The headmaster, looking the picture of authority in his perfectly tailored blue corduroy suit selected especially for the first day of school, knew that he cut an impressive figure. His eyes swept over Karin briefly. She looked stunning, as usual. He hoped that her extra eye makeup had been applied just for his benefit. Maybe this would be the year she broke down and went out with him.

"Can I see you for a minute?" she asked.

"Of course." He waved her to a chair, glad to see the blush that crossed her face at the sight of him.

"It's about the fall play. I don't want to do 'Twelfth Night.' I want to do something else. I want to do this."

Proudly, she handed him the manuscript of "Flowers Of Darkness." Noticing the title page, Matthew frowned.

"Where in the world did you find this, Karin?"

"In the basement. It was tucked away in a trunk."

"What were you doing in the basement?"

Karin hesitated. "I was looking for supplies." Her eyes lowered, avoiding the headmaster's look.

" 'Flowers Of Darkness by Lisa King,' " Matthew read. "I thought all the copies were destroyed."

"Destroyed? Whatever for?"

Matthew took a seat behind his desk. "Do you know the story of what happened to Malcolm Hanley, my great-granduncle?"

Karin shifted uncomfortably in her chair. "Yes. You know how people talk. It's part of the school history."

"Do you know who Lisa King is?"

"No."

Matthew lit a cigarette. "Lisa King is the student who murdered Malcolm Hanley."

"Oh, my God."

" 'Flowers Of Darkness' is the play that was performed that night."

"I'm sorry."

"There was a public outrage about the killings. Apparently, there were some sexual overtones. From what I understand, the play was a little strange, and even though it had nothing to do with what happened, out of respect for the Hanley name, the town council confiscated all the scripts." Matthew nodded at the bound volume. "All but this one, I guess."

"But how could they do that?"

"Well, it made the school pretty notorious for awhile. Even the Boston papers came out to cover the story. I think the town council wanted to eradicate every trace of what took place that night. That's the way some people think. By seizing copies of the play, they thought they could erase everything so the whole episode would be forgotten."

"The play really isn't so strange," Karin said, thoughtfully. "In fact, it's a very good piece of writing."

"You know," Matthew confessed, "I'd be curious to read it. I've heard so much about 'Flowers Of Darkness.' It's a bit exciting having a copy of it in my hand."

"There are some marvelous parts in there. I think the kids would really enjoy doing it."

"It's a far cry from 'Twelfth Night.' I've got to think about the school board, the parents . . ."

"But it's been over fifty years," Karin interrupted. "Who would remember?"

"In this town," Matthew said, pointedly, "they'd remember. Sometimes I think they've got nothing better to do. Besides, even the best eraser can't obliterate everything."

"Why don't you read it?" Karin suggested. "And then tell me what you think."

"Fair enough. I'll read it tonight."

"Thank you," Karin said, getting up to go. Matthew accompanied her to the door. Karin looked at him directly. "You're not just promising to read this for my sake, are you? I mean, you really will consider it for the fall production? You know I'd never have brought this script in here if I knew about its history. I would never offend you and your family. I realize doing the play could be controversial, and I don't want you to take a stand on something if it's going to cause problems."

"Stop right there, Karin," Matthew said, putting an arm around her shoulder. "I'm not like other people. I'm not afraid of controversy. I'm the headmaster here at Hanley and if I say the play will be done, you can count on it."

"I just love this play," Karin said, simply. "I know it's the right thing to do."

"Well, that's what we both want, isn't it, Karin?" Matthew said, squeezing her shoulder. "What's right for the school."

It was Vanessa's luck to be assigned a desk in her home room that placed her squarely in the path of the morning sun's rays which blazed brightly through a rainbow-hued circle of glass at the top of the casement windows. At first, she felt pleased at the prospect of starting the morning drenched in nature's colors, but after a few minutes of filling out school registration forms, the varegated light became disturbing and she developed a dull ache just behind her eyes.

Vanessa tried to stay calm but she couldn't help remembering what had happened to her the day before when she stood in a pool of light in the auditorium—the noose—but that was different. The twisted strand of rope was a hallucination, brought on by nerves and insecurity about being away from home. That would not happen again. She wouldn't allow it.

Her home room teacher, Mrs. Price, a plump redhead, droned on about school regulations as Vanessa strained to concentrate. She found herself squinting from the light and shaded her face with her hand. This was absurd, thought Vanessa. Her desk was the only one that was caught in a blinding shaft of light. She simply would raise her hand and ask Mrs. Price if she could sit somewhere else. Just then, the sun seemed to move a fraction of an inch in the heavens, and the prism of light became nothing more than a decorative rainbow.

Vanessa leaned back, feeling vaguely suspicious. The coincidence had been almost too precise. She thought she was beginning to detect a pattern in the school's way of dealing with her panic. She had been about to tell her mother about the noose in the auditorium, but something had failed her. She had lost the moment. The same thing happened when she saw the blood streaming down the front steps, Rickie's skeleton, the severed arm. Each time there was just enough momentary horror, real or imaginary, to make Vanessa too frightened to speak. Then the horror would vanish and something would furnish her with an excuse not to be afraid. The pattern even extended to something harmless but annoying like being the only student in the class to be discomforted by a beam of colored light. And again, just as she was about to complain, the moment dissipated. It was as though she were being teased.

Wait a minute, she reprimanded herself. What was she doing anyway? Talking about the school like it was a living thing, with a fixed system of behavior. How could it be responsible for decisions that she made in her own mind or excuses she used to justify them? The school was merely a building—four walls and a roof—so how could it control the sun's movement in the sky? Wasn't Vanessa being a little melodramatic?

She leaned forward again. She would have to put all of this nonsense out of her mind. She hadn't heard a word Mrs. Price had said in the last five minutes, and she'd never get through the term if she didn't pay attention. After all, she was here to learn. She looked around the classroom. The other students, though bored, were listening carefully to the teacher. Vanessa hoped she hadn't missed anything important. She didn't want to start the year off badly.

To her relief, Mrs. Price was only reminding the girls about the locations of the emergency fire exits, and after another moment, Vanessa's attention began to wander. She ran her hand along the surface of her oak desk, feeling the carved indentations of initials and slogans that students had left over the years. Little pieces of their lives, tiny tributes, had been etched into the wood to remain immortal long after they were gone. Idly, Vanessa read what were once profound inscriptions.

"Daisy Loves Tom." "Abbott Boys Are Gross." "Cindy & Chuck 4-Ever." "Walter Is A Perv." As her eyes scanned the wood, they were drawn toward a dark knot near the corner of the desk. Around the imperfection in the wood, someone had painstakingly carved the outline of a flower, with delicate petals shooting out on all sides. The effect was of a black rose, so vivid and detailed as to appear almost lifelike. Beneath it, carved in elaborate curlicues stood the initials "L.K."

Vanessa smiled. She was charmed by the perfection of the flower's design, its intricate web of chiseled lines. Someone in the past had created that dark rose with a care and devotion that Vanessa could admire—someone with the initials "L.K."

Vanessa felt heartened. Whoever "L.K." was, she had sat at this desk in the same shaft of sunlight, filtered through the rainbow glass. She must have been an unusual girl to fashion something so lovely. Vanessa looked up once again at the stained-glass window. The distorted colors must have irritated "L.K." too, but, still, she took the time and effort to make something so artistic. She must have been a survivor. Well, Vanessa decided, she could be a survivor, too.

Ingrid Strummer lay on her bed in a half-stupor, listening vaguely to the noise of the girls on the lawn outside. Though she had sworn to herself to ease up on the alcohol, she had sat through the entire home room period that morning, dying for a drink. She'd hoped she would be assigned to Mrs. Price's class—everyone at Hanley knew she was a breeze—but instead she'd gotten that awful old bitch, Mrs. Dyer, who talked a mile a minute and was always giving surprise quizzes. Two minutes after the bell rang, Ingrid was in her room, mixing up a batch of Bloody Marys.

Her glass had been filled and emptied several times, and Ingrid was feeling the results. She was light-headed but the rest of her body felt sluggish and uncoordinated. All her friends were downstairs and she was too sloshed to join them. She would be missed. For her first three years at Hanley, she had pretty much kept her excessive drinking a secret, but a few of the girls suspected—particularly Laura, who didn't miss a trick. And if Ingrid didn't show up to compare notes with the other students after the first home room session, there might be talk.

Even Laura, who with her own lifestyle could not afford to be that judgmental, might let loose with some innuendoes, especially if she was on coke, when she couldn't keep her mouth shut about anything.

Ingrid sat up, feeling dizzy. If she went downstairs right this minute, she could tell the others she had been busy unpacking some things. She knew she wouldn't be steady on her feet and might even slur a word or two, but she could always say she'd dropped a lude. She wanted to be with the other girls and maybe see Bobby if he came over from Abbott. That would be better than being inside the school where, for the first time she could remember, the liquor wasn't even calming her. If anything, it was having the opposite effect—enhancing her apprehension.

She was troubled by the thought that alcohol might not be the same crutch for her this semester that it had been before. How could she ever cope for an entire year if she didn't dull her senses somehow? Hanley had a way of creeping under Ingrid's skin once she let her guard down. Without alcohol to shield her, she might succumb to the school's eerie presence and let it have whatever it was after. Improbable as the thought might be to an outsider, Ingrid had lived there long enough to know that if she were unprotected the school might hurt her.

Resolutely, Ingrid struggled to her feet. Her body wavered, but with an effort, she managed to stand straight. She would throw icy water on her face, rinse the smell of alcohol from her breath with mouthwash and go down to the cafeteria for a cup of mud-like black coffee. She would comb her hair and make herself presentable. The school might do its best to overwhelm her during the year, but today, at least, she was going to get the better of it.

Filled with good intentions, Ingrid took a step forward. That was as far as she got. Her eyes were closing even as she toppled back onto the bed.

When Ingrid awoke, hours later, she would have only the dimmest memory of a cooing sound, seeming to emanate from the walls of her room, like a mother's gentle voice, coaxing an infant to sleep.

"Why do I have to put down my birthday?" Laura muttered. "Don't they have that from last year?"

She and Vanessa were sprawled on the front lawn, filling out yet more registration papers. Not too far away, the rhythmic chopping of hedgecutters punctuated the sound of students talking. Walter Cox's face looked ravaged from his morning drinks and his hands shook as he tried to round out the uneven hedges. He had one ear cocked, hoping to pick up some juicy sex talk from the girls, but today it was just the babble of boring school shit. Once in awhile, Walter looked up from his pruning to see if any of the bitches were watching him, but they didn't seem to know he existed.

Vanessa studied her registration card. "Allergies. What am I allergic to?" she asked.

Laura jerked her finger at the building. "Probably this place. I know I am. They ought to give us vaccination shots. Is there one for boredom?"

Vanessa drew a line through the question about allergies. She glanced around the lawn. "I don't see Ingrid," she said.

Laura snickered. "She's probably passed out in her room."

"What do you mean?"

Laura lifted an imaginary bottle to her mouth and pretended to guzzle. "Ingrid likes her booze. In fact, she looked a little glassy-eyed in home room."

"I had no idea. She drinks this early in the day?"

"Ingrid doesn't know what time it is." Laura laughed. "She's a drunk."

"You mean she's got a problem."

Laura turned serious for a moment. "Ingrid's a secret drinker. She thinks no one knows what she's doing, but she can't fool me. I've got a sixth sense about things like that."

"But that's terrible."

"Not really. Everyone's gotta deal with this place in their own way. To each his own, I say. Ingrid's own happens to be hundred proof vodka. Me, I like to drink too, as long as it doesn't interfere with my drugs."

"Shhh," Vanessa cautioned, looking across the lawn. "I think that gardener can hear you."

"Who? Walter Cox? He's a bigger drunk than Ingrid. He doesn't care what I'm saying. He's too busy looking up the girls' skirts." She turned and gave the old man a mock salute. "How's it hanging, Walter?" she shouted.

Walter scowled. He spit ceremoniously on the grass and made an ominous gesture with the hedge clippers.

Vanessa blushed. She lowered her voice. "God, Laura, everybody at the school is either on drugs or liquor. I'm not a prude, but I can't see myself getting into either of those. Not the way you're talking anyway. What's going to happen to me? How am I going to cope?"

Laura shrugged her shoulders. "Maybe you'll be okay. You might not need anything. Maybe you'll come to love the school." She giggled. "But in case you don't, I know a good dealer in town."

"I'll remember that. It might be fun to get high some night just for the hell of it."

Laura waved her finger at her and laughed. "Uh-uh, that's how it starts. The school's gonna get you."

Vanessa leaned back on her elbows and put her face toward the sun. It felt good, comforting. The air was bracing and Vanessa luxuriated for a moment in the autumnal radiance. Her stay at the school—only a little more than 24 hours now—had been a series of intense sensations, some of them horrifying, but moments like this, serene and clear, were revitalizing. Vanessa had read about manic depression—how a person's moods could shift dramatically from joy to despair and back again. Incredibly enough, The Hanley School somehow seemed to embody this mental disorder. Vanessa enjoyed the feeling of calm that had just come over her, as though nothing could harm her, but she dreaded what was at the other end of the spectrum, those gruesome hallucinations that were like dark threads in an emerging pattern. If only Vanessa could find the middle ground, she would sacrifice the moments of elation to be spared the depths of sickening fear.

Vanessa moved her head slowly in a circular motion, savoring the release of any lingering tension in her neck muscles. Her eyes came to rest on the massive, hawk-like gargoyle that had startled her yesterday. Roosting on its stony nest, the carved bird's bulging eyes bore into hers. Vanessa dismissed her momentary stab of alarm; she would not let some tasteless stone monument interfere with her feeling of well-being. But she could not look away. Something had changed. The bird, that had resembled a hawk or falcon the previous day, now with its exaggerated predatory stance, voluminous folded wings and grotesquely plucked neck, was recognizable for what it was—a vulture.

It was only her imagination, Vanessa forced herself to believe. And then it moved! Crouched on its powerful talons, the bird flapped its colossal wings, blotting out the sun. The sound of the unfolding wings was like the roar of hundreds of birds taking off in flight. Just as quickly, before Vanessa could wrench her eyes away, the wings slapped back down against the creature's bulk with an ear-splitting crack. Vanessa was buffeted by a malodorous gust of air so overwhelming that she could feel her scalp prickle at the sheer force of it.

Vanessa swiveled in panic toward Laura, whose attention was completely focused on the handsome Matthew Hanley who was standing before them. My God, thought Vanessa, how could a hallucination make me feel a blast of wind like that? But was it something her mind had conjured up? Vanessa stole a fearful glance back up at the roof's edge. The hawk was rigidly posed, unmoving, no more threatening than before—all vestiges of the vulture had disappeared.

Vanessa stared at Matthew Hanley. She wondered how long he had been there. Had he and Laura noticed anything about her? But Matthew had just arrived, and she listened with relief at what was obviously a greeting.

"Well, Miss Nash, how nice of you to honor us with your presence." Matthew's tone was teasing and even a little flirtatious.

Still shaken, Vanessa reached up to smooth her hair back into place. But, of course, every strand was intact, just as before.

"Oh, it's great to be back," Laura countered, with just a trace of sarcasm. "I've been looking forward to this all summer." Boldly, Laura ran her eyes up and down Matthew's muscular body.

Matthew acknowledged her interest with a wry smile. "I hear you came in a bit late last night. I hope you managed to get some sleep."

"If I'm having a good time, Mr. Hanley, I don't think about sleep."

"I wouldn't want to stand in the way of your having a good time, Laura, but you are here to get an education."

"I'm always ready to be educated," Laura said, playfully. She stared pointedly at the headmaster. Matthew looked away and seemed to notice Vanessa for the first time.

"And how about you, Vanessa? Are you all settled in? Everything alright, any problems?"

"Not so far," Vanessa said. The words sounded funny, so untrue.

"She'll be fine, Mr. Hanley," Laura said. "I'm showing her the ropes."

Matthew laughed. "I'm sure you are, Laura." He looked back at Vanessa. "Remember, if you need anything, my door is always open."

"So is mine, Matthew," Laura said under her breath as the headmaster continued on toward the school. "Drop by anytime."

"Uh oh," Vanessa kidded, beginning to feel more like herself again. "Does that mean I'll have to spend the night in Ingrid's room?"

"Nah, Matthew would never come to my room. He's horny, but not suicidal. That would be too dangerous. Besides, his cottage is right over there behind the school."

"You really think he's interested in you?"

"Are you crazy? Didn't you see him flirting with me? He was practically drooling on my foot."

Vanessa had to laugh. "I guess he was pretty friendly."

Laura nodded. "He's always been friendly. This year he's going to get to do something about it."

Vanessa hesitated for a moment. "Laura, did you notice anything funny—before Mr. Hanley came over?"

"What do you mean, funny?"

"I don't know how to put it. Did I look strange to you for a minute there?"

Vanessa could tell by Laura's expression that she didn't have a clue as to what she was talking about. Vanessa wished she hadn't brought the matter up, but the other girl looked thoughtful.

"To tell you the truth, I wasn't really looking at you. Why? Is anything the matter?"

"No, not really. Never mind."

"Are you sure?"

"Yes. Positive."

"You know, Vanessa, I really meant what I said before—about showing you the ropes. I know my way around here pretty good. Not just at the school, but in town, too. I'm plugged into what's going on. I keep my eyes open. My ears, too. I generally know what's happening around this morgue. You know something else? People trust me. They tell me things because they know I won't repeat them. So if anything's ever bothering you, just tell me—it'll go no further. I know how to keep my mouth shut."

"Thanks, Laura. I'll remember that."

"By the way," Laura said, suddenly animated, "I had an interesting experience in the shower this morning. Did you meet Rickie Webster?"

"I met her yesterday."

"Well," Laura went on, "Rickie's never been packed too tight, if you know what I mean. But this morning she tried to cop a feel off of me in the shower."

"You're kidding."

"It happened real fast. I pretended not to notice. She kinda ran her hand along my arm but I got the feeling she wanted to go further."

"Maybe it was just an accident."

"I doubt it. She was gawking at me for five minutes before she worked up the nerve. After it happened, she ran out of the shower like she was gonna puke. She didn't even put her robe on. You know, I kinda felt sorry for her. Rick the Stick. Jesus!"

"Do you think she's a lesbian?"

"No," Laura said, thoughtfully. "That's just it. I don't kow what made her do it. It was like something came over her."

"What are you going to do? Are you going to talk to her?"

"No. I'll let it slide. It's no big deal." Laura's face broke into a grin. "Oh, my God, look who's here."

She scrambled to her feet and raced across the lawn toward Dennis and Bobby, who had just come into view from around the corner. Laura gave Dennis a big hug, then planted a polite kiss on Bobby's cheek. She led the two boys back over to Vanessa.

"You gotta meet these guys," Laura said, excitedly. "Vanessa Forbes. This is Dennis Bellivin. Around here we call him 'The Hunk.' And Bobby Cannon, Abbott School's answer to William F. Buckley."

"Not really," Bobby said, taking Vanessa's hand shyly. He shot a sidelong glance at Dennis, who was looking at Vanessa with that combination of confidence and intensity he had seen before. Bobby could tell Dennis wasn't kidding—he was pulling out all the stops for this one.

"Nice to meet you, Dennis," Vanessa said.

"My pleasure," Dennis said huskily, flashing her his best smile.

Dennis squeezed Vanessa's hand, then held onto it lingeringly. His eyes connected with Vanessa's, then seemed to search deeper. Immediately, Laura sensed the electricity of their meeting. There was something primitive in Dennis' hungry gaze, while Vanessa reminded her of an all too willing prey—frightened and vulnerable, but captivated.

"Jesus," Laura said, "you two want to be alone?" At least, she had cut the awkward tension with an offhand remark.

Vanessa blushed, and Dennis released her hand. It was as though they were emerging from some private circle of Dennis' design.

When Dennis spoke again, his voice was more casual. "I hear you're from California, Vanessa. I spent a summer in Malibu."

"Dennis was looking for the perfect wave," Laura said.

Dennis glanced at Laura and gave her a half-smile, but his eyes returned to Vanessa meaningfully.

"I'm always looking for perfection," he said.

Bobby felt unsettled and a little embarrassed. Why was Dennis making such a deliberate show of coming onto a girl? Usually, he made a play so effortlessly. Sometimes just a crooked smile and a couple of funny lines were enough to get a girl interested. Vanessa seemed so taken with him already—why get so heavy? Still, Dennis must know what he was doing. He'd made such a point of telling Bobby he was going to get Vanessa. He certainly wouldn't blow that chance by coming on too strong at a first meeting. And judging from Vanessa's reaction, Dennis wasn't going overboard at all. Maybe Dennis had been right. Vanessa might be his type after all.

Up in her room, Rickie sat on her bed, clutching a pillow to her breasts. She smelled the tangy odor of nervous perspiration coming from the damp spots underneath her arms. She had been perspiring heavily all morning and had hoped none of the other girls in home room could tell. It was bad enough they thought that she was weird, she didn't want them to think she was dirty. But that was how Rickie felt now—stained.

The morning, filled with its routine of registration and first day jitters, had been terrifying for Rickie. She couldn't quite understand why. Normally, Rickie liked routine; it was one of the few things that made her feel stable. But today, she had hardly responded in class and barely nodded when the other girls greeted her. All summer, she'd been looking forward to the first day of class. Now registration was over and she'd had no fun at all.

Rickie could hear her classmates out on the lawn, talking, probably exchanging summer gossip, not knowing how she felt. Not that it would have mattered if they did know how miserable she was, Rickie thought with a jab of self-pity. No one cared anyway. Not really. The laughter outside shot through her head like daggers. Why couldn't she be happy, too? The walls of her room seemed to be moving in on her, and Rickie felt an oppression so strong that it threatened to stifle her if she didn't escape.

But that wouldn't be easy. How was she going to face the other kids? They'd been socializing on the lawn for more than an hour. What if Laura had noticed what Rickie did this morning in the shower and what if she told the other girls? They might be making fun of her right now. Yes, of course, that was what they were laughing at, Rickie thought, feeling ashamed. All morning, she had been trying to figure out what had compelled her to make that feeble pass at Laura, but just when she thought she could excuse her behavior or dismiss the incident entirely her thoughts became a mass of confusion.

Rickie struggled to get a grip on herself. She had to go outside. She couldn't avoid the other students for the rest of the term. She got up slowly, testing her legs, almost daring them to hold the rest of her body. She was still very nervous and took a few tentative steps toward the window. The sun was warm and soothing on her face. She could feel her hands grow still, and the sadness she felt just a moment ago began to ebb, taking her fear along with it.

The red stained-glass window, up near the ceiling, acted like a reflector, soaking Rickie in the sun's rays. Suddenly, Rickie felt purged. She stood there, in that isolated red spot of color and warmth, and held her arms out, as if by doing so she could gather in all the comfort she needed and feed it into her body. A smile began to form on her face, and even her mousy hair seemed vibrant in the light.

Rickie couldn't tell for sure, but she thought her sudden sense of well-being was connected to the sounds that had started up in her room. She felt the intimation of someone—no, *something*—murmuring next to her, insisting that she calm down, rationalizing her behavior, granting her the needed excuses that had eluded her all morning.

The sound, like brush strokes on a canvas, urged her on. Rickie found herself turning to walk toward the door. She was feeling good about herself now, trusting her instincts, and those instincts, which had usually proved to be wrong in the past, were telling her to join her friends. She needed to be with the kids now, and she wouldn't be afraid to see Laura.

After all, Rickie thought, as she closed the door behind her, she hadn't done anything really bad this morning. But as she walked down the corridor toward the stairs, her hands trembled once more, and the start of a headache pounded in her temples.

Rickie sniffed. She looked at her blouse. It was soiled from perspiration. She couldn't go downstairs like this.

What she needed was a hot bath and a change of clothes. She paused for a moment, her hand on the banister, and imagined how cleaned and refreshed she would be in a little while.

Back in Rickie's room, the whispering which danced around the red spot of sun had changed to a low-pitched, demonic snarl, drawing the warmth from the light and turning it bone-chillingly cold.

7

Walter's hands, stained from the grass and sweaty, tore the crusts from the white bread of a bologna sandwich. His arms and shoulders ached from the strain of clipping the hedges, one of his least favorite chores because of the concentration it required. It wasn't like raking leaves or mowing the lawn which he could perform no matter how drunk or hungover he was. Last spring when he'd cut the hedges unevenly because he'd had a bitch of a headache, he'd caught hell from Desmond Trousdale, and the evidence of his carelessness was pretty difficult to refute. This morning, he'd done a better job but it was still one big pain in the ass. He was relieved it was lunchtime so he could concentrate on something more to his liking—a bologna on white with lots of ketchup, a pint of liquor and the magazine he'd received in a plain brown wrapper the other day.

Walter stretched his legs out and put them up onto the stone bench. He liked it over here on the side lawn, away from the main entrance. There was less noise; it was shady and more private. Walter didn't want any interruptions while he was in the middle of a good story, and the "Spanking Corner" of *Naughty Nymphettes* magazine had some interesting articles this month. Walter had pawed over the glossy color photographs the night before, feasting his eyes on the pictures of adolescent girls with their legs spread, but he liked to save the literature portion for daylight hours.

With mounting excitement, Walter read about the punishment inflicted on a helpless teenage girl who had disobeyed her boy friend. Serves her right, he thought, those bitches just don't know their place these days. Relishing the girl's flogging, in-between bits of his bologna sandwich, Walter daydreamed that he was meting out the same discipline to some of the girls at Hanley. That blonde tramp, for instance—what was her name, Nash? She'd had the nerve to mock him this morning with her smartass remarks about drinking. She thought he wasn't onto her but he was. The next time she asked him how it was hanging, he might just open his pants and show her. Sometimes Walter wished he could be headmaster of Hanley for a day, so he could pound some good manners into these girls.

The old janitor was so engrossed in his fantasy that Desmond Trousdale had turned the corner of the school and spied the magazine before Walter had a chance to stuff it in his back pocket. The caretaker approached him, and Walter could tell by Desmond's stern look this was not going to be a friendly chat.

"Are you drinking again?" Desmond asked, accusingly. "My wife says she saw you with a bottle."

"Not me, sir," Walter lied. "I been dry for two weeks now." Trying to appear nonchalant, he shoved the pint of whiskey deeper into his overalls' pocket.

"You're lying, you worthless drunk."

"Oh, no sir, it's the truth, swear to God."

Desmond glared at the copy of *Naughty Nymphettes*, which was still clutched in Walter's hand. "What's that magazine? Didn't I warn you about that? Keep that stuff in your room where it belongs."

"They're just pictures."

"It doesn't belong out in the open. There's girls walking around. Kids. You oughta be ashamed of yourself."

Walter gestured scornfully at a few of the Hanley students nearby. "Ah, they don't pay me no mind," he said.

"Yeah, but you pay them some mind, don't you? I've seen the way you look at those girls, undressing them with your eyes."

"Ain't no law against looking," Walter muttered.

"Make sure looking's all you do."

Walter glanced back at the girls. "Ah, they like it when I look. You see the way they parade around? Tight pants. No bras. It's not decent."

"What would you know about decent?" Desmond said, his voice rising angrily. "Get back to work. Lunch hour's over."

The caretaker marched off across the lawn. Walter watched contemptuously, then, just for spite, snuck a quick nip from his bottle. He belched loudly.

"Filthy bastard!" he swore.

By midafternoon, the day had turned unusually warm, almost summer-like. Vanessa took advantage of the brilliant sunlight to wander down by the lake, paperback novel in hand. She spread out a blanket on the grass and stared out at the placid, sun-dappled water. It was good to be by herself again.

Dennis, Bobby and Laura had gone into town in search of some beer and pizza. Though Dennis had pressured her to go along, Vanessa had resisted, saying she would wait for them at the lake. It seemed a perfect day for a picnic.

Vanessa was vaguely puzzled at Dennis Bellivin's aggressive attention toward her which she found a little overbearing. She knew she was pretty and she was used to guys making a fuss over her, but there was something blatantly manipulative about the way Dennis had behaved earlier, going far beyond anything Vanessa had ever experienced. He had been self-assured, even cocky, and their initial meeting had signaled a possessiveness that was unexpected, coming from a 17 year old boy, even a mature one, as Dennis appeared to be.

What was more surprising, however, was her own reaction to his attitude. Dennis was really handsome and she liked a boy who could take charge of a situation; it showed maturity. But with anyone else, she would resent that kind of attitude, as if he alone were making the choice as to what their relationship would be and she had no say in the matter. Presumption like that, on the part of any boy, was a turn-off, yet one deep look into Dennis' eyes and Vanessa had gone right along with what he was orchestrating.

Sudddenly, a hand touched her on the shoulder. Startled, Vanessa whirled around.

"God, you frightened me!"

Dennis eased himself down onto the blanket next to Vanessa. He handed her a beer which was concealed in a paper bag. Vanessa looked around nervously. Across the lawn, she could see Bobby and Laura removing the box of pizza and several packages from Dennis' car.

"You startled me," Vanessa said. "You shouldn't scare people like that."

Dennis trained his eyes on her and smiled. "Oh, were you scared?"

"A little."

"Do you get scared a lot?" Something in Dennis' tone was unnerving.

"Sometimes."

"What scares you?"

"What scares me? That's a funny question." Off in the distance, Bobby and Laura seemed to be coming across the lawn in slow motion, as if in a dream.

"What scares you?" Dennis repeated.

Vanessa thought for a moment. She really didn't want to answer this question, but she felt a little helpless under Dennis' fixed stare. "I don't know," she said hesitantly. "Being alone. The dark. Sometimes I get scared for no reason."

"What about the school? Does the school scare you?"

Vanessa looked up at the dark red building which seemed to loom closer, threateningly. "What do you mean?"

Dennis put his arm around her shoulder, and she did not pull away. "You must have heard about the history. The mass murders. It's a strange place. Sometimes I look over at it from the other side of the lake—you know, at night—and the moonlight is reflecting off those stained-glass windows. The school looks almost alive."

"Alive?"

"Like it's breathing. Like it's a living thing and nothing's changed. I feel like I could go back in time." Dennis paused. "I feel like it could be 1931."

Vanessa was becoming uncomfortable. "Next you'll be teling me it's haunted."

"It might be haunted," Dennis said quietly.

"I don't believe that. I don't believe in ghosts. It's the living that'll hurt you, not the dead."

Dennis laughed. "Are you sure?"

Vanessa made no reply. Dennis was really bothering her. What a strange way for a guy to be talking. Couldn't he see that the subject made her nervous? She had hoped this afternoon would be free of dark thoughts and now Dennis had stirred them all up again. Well, Bobby and Laura would be there in a minute and that would be the end of Dennis' bizarre interrogation.

As he approached the lake with Laura, Bobby could tell that Dennis was laying it on thick with Vanessa. He wasn't even acknowledging that they were almost on top of them, carrying the pizza. Bobby had to smile at the corny way Dennis was gazing into Vanessa's eyes again.

"I think Vanessa is smitten," Laura whispered.

"The son of a bitch has charm," Bobby admitted. "I'll say that for him." But when Vanessa looked up at the two of them, Bobby couldn't miss her signal—as if she were welcoming the intrusion.

"Yeah, he's got charm," Laura agreed. "I went out with him all last year, remember?"

Bobby looked at Laura hopefully. He grinned. "What about this year?"

Laura gave him a playful tap on the arm. "You never know, Bobby," she teased.

Rickie Webster came out the side door and squinted into the bright sunlight. She felt better now. The warm bath had helped and she had changed into a fresh shirt and a pair of cut-offs. She had brushed her hair loose instead of wearing it in braids, and it hung down limply to her shoulders.

Almost at once, she spotted Laura Nash over by the lake. Turn around—that was her first impulse. Rickie took a step backward and leaned against the brick wall. Her bare legs brushed against the rough surface and her skinny limbs tingled. Without a second thought, she moved forward. She was nearly to the lake before she realized she had even started walking.

"Are you alright? You look like shit," Laura said between mouthfuls of mushroom pizza.

"I had to get out of that place," Rickie said, her words running together. "I felt like the walls were closing in on me."

"Jesus, first day of school and we're off and running. Here, you want some pizza."

"No, thank you. I'm not hungry."

Rickie slumped down next to Bobby, who looked at her critically. "God, you really do look awful. Maybe you should lie down."

"You want a Valium?" Laura offered. "I got some in my bag."

Rickie's heart was sinking. Why were they hurting her feelings like this? She had just seen herself in the mirror and had thought she looked pretty good. She struggled to keep up her confidence. Maybe a Valium was a good idea. It might calm her and, besides, she'd already made up her mind to do some drugs with the kids now and then if it would help to make them accept her. "Okay, I'll have one."

Bobby jumped up. "I'll get 'em."

He went over to Laura's purse, which was on the blanket next to Vanessa and Dennis, who silently were drinking beer. Suddenly, Rickie realized she was alone with Laura. She shivered slightly. An unfamiliar thrill of sexual anticipation crept over her. This was different from this morning in the shower when she just had wanted to touch Laura. Now she wanted something much more. Rickie watched the rise and fall of Laura's breasts beneath the tight cotton fabric of her shirt. Her body looked so inviting, so soft. Rickie could feel her own nipples hardening as she continued to stare at the outline of the other girl's breasts. If Laura would let her —just for a moment—Rickie could make her feel so good, excited just like her.

Laura blocked her move in midair. "Uh-uh," she snapped. "Don't touch me, okay? I didn't say anything in the shower, but I don't go that way. You like girls? Fine. Do your own thing. Just don't do it with me."

Laura's eyes were blazing, and Rickie withered before her. She wanted to run across the lawn in shame, to run out of the gates of Hanley and never come back. She struggled to be brave, to get out the words that would placate Laura and make everything alright.

"I swear to you, Laura. I know what you're thinking. I'm not like that. I don't know why I did it . . ."

Laura looked skeptical, but despite what Rickie had done, she saw a naked honesty in the girl's desperate explanation.

Bobby had returned with the purse. Laura took out the

Valium bottle. "I think we'd better give her two, Bobby," she said with a dismissive laugh.

Laura decided to say nothing about the incident to anyone. It wasn't her nature to keep her mouth shut about something like that, but Rickie had seemed so pathetic, so lost, that Laura sensed somehow that it would crush the girl if word got around. But more than that, Laura suspected that Rickie was being truthful. She might be neurotic and high-strung, but no way was the girl a lesbian. Lonely and confused maybe, but not sexually attracted to women.

That evening, Laura joined Vanessa in the cafeteria for dinner. She was curious to hear what her roommate thought about Dennis Bellivin. Laura had had fun with Dennis the previous year, and especially liked his sense of adventure. Dennis wasn't afraid of anything. He could have gotten expelled from Abbott if he'd ever gotten caught sneaking into her room at night. For that matter, Laura could have been kicked out of Hanley. But neither one of them had given it a second thought. Half the fun was in the danger anyhow, and after that had worn off, it was inevitable that she and Dennis would grow a bit bored with each other. That was exactly what had happened and neither of them had any regrets. Looking back on it, Dennis had been a fantastic lover and Laura had even learned a few tricks from him. But now she was content just to have him as a friend, something that didn't happen often with her ex-lovers.

Laura and Dennis had been two of a kind—daring, impulsive and nonconformist. Vanessa Forbes, with none of those characteristics, seemed an odd choice for Dennis' attention. Laura wanted to know what the hell was going on between those two.

"You like him, don't you?" she began.

"Yeah, he's alright," Vanessa said in a noncommital tone.

"He's more than alright, honey. I speak from

experience."

Vanessa looked down at her plate. She cut off a piece of minute steak. "He asked me to go to the movies Sunday night."

Laura smiled. "Great. Go for it."

"Are you sure? I mean, you did go out with him. Do you still care about Dennis?"

"Absolutely. We're great friends. We finished being a hot item last June. I told you, this year I'm stalking bigger game. I'm going all the way to the top—Matthew Hanley."

Vanessa took a bite of steak. "You're gonna get in trouble. They'll bounce you out of here."

Laura shrugged. "I should be so lucky. Who's gonna do the bouncing? Matthew?"

The laugh froze in Vanessa's throat.

Blood! A throbbing, living heart pumped blood onto her plate. The steak was gone, replaced by this pulpy organ, its valves opening and closing in a grotesque parody of a life-giving force. Nausea swept over Vanessa. Her fork clattered to the floor with a deafening noise. She gaped at the palpitating heart, which was submerging her dinner tray in a sea of bubbling blood. Vanessa gasped and recoiled in fright.

"My God, Vanessa, what's the matter?" Laura asked in alarm.

Vanessa covered her eyes with her hands. She knew before she took them away that the heart would be gone and the minute steak would be back on her plate.

"I thought I saw something," she said, aware of how foolish she sounded.

"What?"

"Nothing." She reached down to pick up her fork. "It must have been the light."

Vanessa looked around the cafeteria. Even with the early moonlight shining through the windows, there was no way to believe that this was anything except a hallucination brought on by her own mind.

"Yeah," Laura said, "the light gets weird here sometimes. Whoever put those stained-glass windows in must have been on acid."

Vanessa smiled and relaxed a bit. She could feel herself returning to normal. But looking at the flat slab of steak on her plate, she knew that her appetite had disappeared. Unable to take another bite, Vanessa pushed the dinner tray away.

The sky, dark and swollen with clouds, wrapped the school in a blackness so dense it seemed to be protecting the structure so as not to let in even the smallest amount of moonlight. The night had always been an emphatic companion to the school, watching it grow on the blood that had been shed there. The ground on which the building stood had been desecrated more than 100 years before. The land had waited patiently for the formation of the school, this malevolent monument which now gave testimony to unimaginable evil. In the 1920's, Malcolm Hanley had done well obeying the obscene commands he had received from the greatest evil of all.

An owl hooted in the darkness, nesting in one of the tall elms near the side lawn, not far from Matthew Hanley's cottage. Though the headmaster's house stood only yards away from the main building, it shared none of that structure's fortress-like adornments. The cheerful, one-story bungalow was painted white, with natural wood shutters covering the windows. The only splashes of color on the cottage were the single red stained-glass window high up near the roof and an abundance of ivy which climbed up the sides of the house.

Matthew Hanley stood in his book-lined study, looking out the window at the school. Eyesore was always the word that came to mind when he gazed out at the nearby building. Here, in the privacy of his quarters, there was no need for Matthew to pretend that he felt pride about The Hanley School. His great-granduncle Malcolm must have been completely mad to design such a gloomy structure. The building was downright ugly, definitely an eyesore.

When Matthew had taken over at Hanley, several years back, he had wasted no time redecorating the cottage to his liking. Finding the interior drab and colorless, he had wallpapered it with bright patterns. Keeping many of the beautiful antique pieces, he had embellished the look of the house with some contemporary furnishings and modern objets d'art which offset the mahogany bookshelves and woodwork. With some thick, intricately designed Persian rugs as the final touch, he had managed to change the bungalow's appearance drastically. From then on, Matthew felt at home there.

Though he tried to make himself comfortable at the school, Matthew never really felt like he belonged there. True, he was proud of Malcolm Hanley and what the man had done almost single-handedly, but secretly Matthew thought his predecessor a fool. To have been killed by some deranged, lovesick girl in such an embarrassing, shameful way was beyond comprehension—especially for a man of Malcolm's stature. Matthew's ancestor may have been a dynamic innovator, but ultimately he was a fool.

Matthew had it made—and he was no fool. The school and the land had all been handed down to him. In a few years he'd sell all of it, and he'd make a bundle, too. Then he would be able to leave the country and travel to all the exotic places he had always promised himself he would visit—Japan, Egypt, the South Seas—preferably in the company of some gorgeous young woman.

Matthew knew his reputation as a ladies' man was widespread, but at least as far as the running of The Hanley School was concerned, he felt he had succeeded in deceiving everyone. He cultivated his image as a serious educator, and when it came to questions of school policy, he had the Hanley board of trustees firmly in his back pocket. But the truth of the matter was that Matthew Hanley couldn't care less about the school. To him, it was an outmoded institution, and he wasn't about to spend the rest of his life in a tomb like that. Ten months out of every year was just too much to give to the school. Thank God for the girls. At least they provided some diversion.

Of course, Matthew had to be very cautious with the girls from now on. That business a while back with that starry-eyed junior had caused something of a stir. It was a good thing she had a history of being unstable. The little jerk had accused him of getting her pregnant, but fortunately her parents didn't want to make a big case out of it. They were loaded anyway—a quick abortion and the girl was transferred to another school. It had never been proven that Matthew was the father, though he knew the girl was a virgin before he touched her. It had all been her fault anyway. She had lied to him and said she was on the pill, but Matthew had been less angry with the girl than he had been with himself. Out of all the students at Hanley, he had to pick a girl who was a hysterical liar. He had been very careful since that incident.

Matthew refilled his glass of Scotch. He thought of Karin Sayers. Karin was no girl. She was a desirable young woman, one of the few who didn't fall all over when Matthew was around. The headmaster thought of Karin as a challenge and had made several subtle passes at her, all of which she expertly rebuffed. If only she would let herself go. Of course, he knew about her strict upbringing and had heard some pretty nasty rumors about her father, but that was a long time ago. The problem with Karin was her obsession with being a good teacher. Matthew knew about women like her—uptight, unable to relax. But once they did, they were usually the best bed partners. Matthew smiled at the thought of Karin, naked and writhing underneath him, begging for him. Maybe he could get to her yet.

Matthew looked at the script of "Flowers of Darkness," which he had finished reading a few minutes earlier. Pretty strong stuff for high school kids. He wondered why the prim Karin Sayers was so worked up about doing this play. A story about witches and selling one's soul—with a strong sexual undertone—was not something he'd have thought Karin would have chosen. Still, the play was skillfully written, enough so for Matthew to read it in one sitting. He smiled. The students would probably love doing something this unconventional. Matthew himself thrilled at the thought of going against the grain and putting on this play. It was risky, but, if the truth were known, Matthew was bored.

He took a long drink of Scotch and made his decision. He would let Karin do "Flowers Of Darkness" this fall. It would be provocative, even shocking. It would be just what the school needed. Matthew set down his glass and looked back out at the bleak outline of the school once more. He felt a sharp twist of uneasiness. He could have sworn he saw the building pulsate for a moment. He shook off the feeling. Instead he grinned, thinking of the fall production. Old Malcolm would probably turn over in his grave.

Alone in her room, Karin had been reading from her Bible a passage from the Book Of Revelations:

"And in those days men will seek death and will not find it; they will long to die and death will fly from them . . ."

She was in the midst of that prophecy when Matthew Hanley's call came. Karin had been ecstatic that he had agreed to do "Flowers Of Darkness." The headmaster had imposed only two conditions. The title of the play would have to be changed, and Lisa King's name would never be mentioned. Karin suggested they rename the play "The Dark"—the title had just popped into her mind—and she'd promised Matthew no one would ever find out who wrote the play. Karin smiled at the hesitation in Matthew's normally self-assured voice when he ended the phone conversation by saying, "I hope to God nobody remembers this thing."

Karin tried to go back to her reading but kept staring at the same page without really seeing the words. She thought of the headmaster. She hadn't expected that he would permit her to do this play. Maybe Matthew was made of stronger stuff; maybe she had misjudged him. *Stop! Please, Daddy, stop! You're hurting me. What are you doing? No. Oh, please don't. Daddy, you're tearing me apart. Oh, God, no!* Karin forced the painful memory from her consciousness. But something wouldn't let her forget. Karin felt faint. *You're an evil man. Sinful. Oh, God, why did Mommy go?*

Karin walked across to the small bathroom and threw some water on her face. That helped a little. She changed into her nightgown and got into bed. Again she tried to read her Bible, but the intruding memories kept coming back like blinding flashes of insight. There was nothing she could put her finger on—only thoughts that were just out of reach.

The whispers were back. Karin felt almost joyful at the familiar sound. The murmuring erased remnants of the past. It was provocative, playful. The sound wove in and out of Karin's mind. The volume, at first loud, then soft, was alluring. Soon, Karin felt lulled. Reminders of the past retreated into alcoves, hidden in layers of protective covering inside her brain. The Bible, which she had laid across her breasts, became strangely heated and heavy. She removed it and placed it on her night table. *Hide it.* Why? What was telling her to hide the book that had given her comfort almost every night of her life? No. She was just overtired, still a little stimulated from the first day of classes. Karin switched off the light. The whispers wouldn't let her sleep. *Get rid of it.* Karin fidgeted with the blankets. It felt like something was pulling the covers off her body. *Now!*

Karin got up but didn't put the light on. From under

her bed, she took a large suitcase where she stored extra sweaters. She buried the Bible at the bottom of the case, locked the valise and shoved it back under the bed.

Karin slid back under the covers and listened for the whispers. They were still there, more comforting than before. Karin nestled her head into the pillow. Within moments, she was enveloped in the arms of a deep, dreamless sleep.

8

The next afternoon, when Vanessa filed into the school auditorium with the rest of the drama students, she felt a momentary apprehension as she hesitantly looked above the stage. There was no noose hanging from the rafters. She had known there wouldn't be. She didn't even know why she looked.

Vanessa took a seat in the third row, next to Laura and Bobby.

"Do you see what I see?" Laura asked.

Vanessa looked around. "What?"

Laura pointed to a folding table, stacked high with newly-bound scripts. "That doesn't look like 'Twelfth Night.' Whenever we do Shakespeare, it's usually just little paperbacks."

Dennis sauntered down the aisle and sat down just behind Vanessa. "I thought I was gonna be late. I just got back from the garage. Had a new muffler installed."

"Great," Bobby said, "but how am I going to hear you coming?"

"No problem, Bobby, the engine still rattles." Dennis ran his hand along Vanessa's shoulder. "The old heap will be in great shape for Sunday."

Vanessa turned around. "Did you find out what's playing?"

"There's only one movie in this town," Dennis said with a laugh. "I hope you haven't seen it. It's a revival. 'Night Of The Living Dead.' "

"For a theater in Hanley, that's appropriate," Laura said, dryly.

Karin Sayers emerged from the wings and walked across the stage to a podium. Vanessa noticed at once that there was something awry about Karin's appearance, even in the way she held herself. Coquettish—that was the word that came to Vanessa's mind. There was a slight air of female vanity, bordering on the seductive, in the way Karin had strode to center stage, hips swaying more than necessary in contrast to her normal straightforward gait. Unlike the other day when Karin had been dressed rather primly, she now wore a tight skirt and sweater that accentuated her curvy body. Vanessa looked around at the other kids who were staring at the teacher with typically blank expressions. Maybe I'm wrong, thought Vanessa. Maybe this was the way Karin generally looked and her proper appearance two days ago was the exception. But just then, Vanessa heard some titters from the back of the auditorium. She wasn't the only one who had picked up on Karin's different, somewhat tantalizing, image.

The drama instructor leaned forward on the podium. Her voice rang out in the auditorium, clear but with a throaty undertone. "You may have heard we're doing 'Twelfth Night' this year," she said, "but there's been a change."

Laura poked Vanessa in the arm. "See? I told you something was up."

"Instead," Karin continued, "we'll be doing a play by an anonymous author. It's called 'The Dark.' "

An inexplicable tingle of fear crept up Vanessa's spine. Deep inside her mind, a small vein of memory had been tapped, unleashing a quick flare of déjà vu that vanished in its own brightness.

"It's a wonderful script, very challenging. This is a play that has a strong sense of history, a story of passion and forbidden love. It tells us something about the human spirit, the risks lovers will take to be with each other against all odds."

Vanessa was studying the drama teacher. She was speaking with intense fervor, with a kind of missionary zeal approaching fanaticism. Odd. In her previous encounters with Karin Sayers, the woman had been so reserved, almost soft-spoken. Now her eyes blazed with a surprising conviction.

Bobby Cannon nudged Vanessa. "Sounds pretty sexy," he whispered. "I've never seen Sayers so worked up."

Laura interrupted the teacher. "Miss Sayers? Any singing parts?"

Karin paused. She looked at Laura reproachfully. "No, I'm afraid not," she said with an edge of sarcasm in her voice, "but there was only one singing role in 'Twelfth Night' and that was The Fool. Were you planning to go up for that one?"

There was a ripple of laughter in the auditorium, but some of the students looked uncomfortable. Vanessa could see that Karin's cutting reply had stung Laura. Vanessa patted Laura's hand, but, after a moment, her roommate just shrugged and slumped down into her seat.

Vanessa put her head back as the drama instructor went on excitedly about the virtues of "The Dark." More than a tale of tradition and undying love, it was a drama with precise structure and a depth of characterization. Vanessa found her eyes shifting toward the vermilion rectangle of glass at the top of the casement windows on the side of the auditorium. For the first time since she had been sitting there, she noticed that there was no shaft of sunlight coming through, but that wasn't surprising. It had been drizzling all day. Vanessa watched lazily as rivulets of water ran down the dark red pane of glass. She felt curiously empty. Could it be she missed the pinpoint of light which had previously seemed aimed directly at her? Moreover, Vanessa couldn't believe it had been raining all day and she had scarcely been aware of it.

"Once you read this script," Karin concluded, "I think you'll agree this is a play whose time has come."

Karin's voice filled the room, her determination to present "The Dark" washing across the students like a powerful wave. The teacher's enthusiasm was hitting its mark, and there was a contagious stirring in the seats as the young people responded to her impassioned delivery. At the rear of the hall, unnoticed by the students, Desmond and Blanche Trousdale also heard the fire in Karin's voice and they glowed approvingly.

Laura Nash usually enjoyed being with people. She loved their reaction to her, and she loved performing for them, both on and off stage. But not this evening. Right now, Laura wanted to be alone. Vanessa was shaping up as a good roommate, easy enough to get along with and not the type to initiate a conversation if she sensed that the other person didn't want to talk. Tonight Laura didn't feel like being with anyone else. Perhaps a bit later, but now she was restless and needed some fresh air. Maybe a walk down by the lake.

Jesus, thought Laura as she closed the side door of the school behind her. It's only my second night here and I'm bored stiff already. At this rate, I should really be nuts by next month. Laura took a deep breath; the smell of newly fallen rain was everywhere. Alongside the building's entrance, a squat forsythia was glistening, its green leaves beaded with moisture. Laura loved a fall day after it had rained, and today there had been a good, steady downpour. She caught her breath at the invigorating beauty of the New England night, taking the wool sweater that she had draped around her shoulders and slipping her arms into the sleeves. She pulled up the bulky knit collar against the evening chill and started off toward the lake. Maybe she would take a closer look at the boathouse. She had noticed the day before that someone had repainted it and cleaned it up.

Laura spun around as she felt something brush against her shoulder. Nothing. She hadn't reached the trees, so the feather-light touch couldn't be blamed on a low branch. Her deep blue eyes scanned the lawn. No one was there. A short distance away, an old weeping willow hung sadly with the weight of a thousand raindrops. Laura continued on.

Even before she heard it she sensed the derisive laughter coming from someplace very close to her.

Laura stopped, planting her feet firmly in the wet grass. "Okay, you son of a bitch," she said with annoyance, "come out right now where I can see you."

Still nothing.

Laura heard it again. Now the faint chuckling seemed to be coming from above. She turned to look up at the school. Even in the dim twilight, she could see there wasn't anyone standing in the windows. Still, there was no denying the sibilant laughter she had heard. She peered more intently at the building. Pearls of light danced in the stained-glass windows. Along the walls, the sinuous ivy clung tenaciously in the half-light, reminding Laura of writhing black serpents. Suddenly, Laura smelled the choking stench of sulphur. Before she could raise her hand to her mouth to avoid gagging, the odor was gone.

Laura took an involuntary step backward. Oh, good, Nash—next you'll be imagining the devil himself strolling down the steps of Hanley, tail swinging in the breeze. Laura laughed aloud at the image, and her laughter seemed to echo back at her. She listened for a moment. Silent. Shit, she thought, this damn place plays tricks on you—especially at night.

Laura turned once more and hurried off in the direction of the lake. She dug a half-crumpled pack of cigarettes out of her pocket and stopped to light one. *Laura.* The wind carried the sound of her name, and she shook her head. Uh-oh, I'm not letting this place get to me. Laura inhaled deeply on the cigarette, then looked out at the lake. It resembled a large, black pit, shining in the early night—calm on top but buried within it ancient mysteries too horrible to dwell on. Laura knew at once she didn't want to be here by herself. Nothing about the school had ever really scared her before, but tonight she found herself surrendering to an irrational fear.

No way could Laura go down to the lake now. She'd really spooked herself. But still wanting some air, she looked off in the other direction—toward Matthew Hanley's cottage. With a half-smile, she turned left and started down the gentle slope, away from the lake, away from the school. As she moved down the lawn, Laura resisted the temptation to turn around and try to spot what was looking at her. She could feel eyes, cold and malicious, boring into her back.

Moments later, Laura found herself in the vicinity of Matthew's cottage. Laura thought he probably was great in bed, and he ought to be, she thought, laughing to herself. He certainly had enough experience. She drew closer to the small white cottage. Now that she was so near, she felt hesitant. How would it look if she were caught snooping around where Matthew lived? But she wasn't snooping at all—she was merely out for a walk in the cool night air. Yet there was something seductive, even thrilling, about being this close to Matthew Hanley's bedroom. God, he sure was sexy.

Laura was surprised at the way she was thinking. Sure, Matthew was a great-looking guy, but Laura could have been with him last year. What was there about this semester that suddenly made him seem so desirable?

Almost on tiptoe, Laura approached the window that she knew looked into his bedroom. Cautious at first, she purposefully leaned closer to the glass and peered in. She barely stifled the scream as she felt a firm hand grasping her shoulder. Laura whirled around.

"Good evening, Miss Nash."

"Oh, shit, Mr. Hanley! What are you doing here?"

The headmaster looked amused. "What am I doing here? I happen to live here. Didn't you know that?"

Laura struggled to regain her composure. In the near darkness, Matthew looked dangerously handsome. "Yes, of course, I know that."

"Were you looking for me?"

"No. Should I be? You know, you really shouldn't come up behind a girl like that. If I was like some girls, I might have screamed."

"You don't look like the kind that screams."

Laura eyed him up and down. "Oh, what kind is that?"

"You know, timid girls. Afraid of their own shadows. Afraid of their own feelings. Afraid to take a chance."

Laura smiled provocatively and shook her head. "Uh-uh. I'm not one of those."

"No, I didn't think you were."

Without even realizing, Laura had moved closer to Matthew, near enough to feel the heat radiating from his body. God, she wished he would touch her.

Matthew's eyes slid over her body. He reached out and brushed his fingers against Laura's face. Involuntarily, Laura closed her eyes and waited for his kiss. When it came, soft and silky, she was jolted by the electricity. Their lips met for only the slightest instant, leaving her hungry for what his eyes promised.

Sitting cross-legged on the window ledge of his room, Bobby Cannon squinted through his high-powered binoculars at the two shadowy figures down by Matthew's cottage. He had been closely following Laura's rambling walk and had watched with great interest as she'd met up with another person, whose identity he could not be sure of. He guessed that Laura's brief encounter was with Matthew Hanley but the night shadows and drooping branches prevented him from getting a clear look at whoever it was who had just kissed her. Bobby put down the glasses. It had to be Matthew, he reasoned. Who else would be down near the bungalow wearing a suit at this time of night?

Bobby smiled. He hoped it was Matthew. He knew that every year the headmaster staked out his conquests from among the young girls. Bobby disapproved of his behavior. The man in charge of a girls school should set an example, especially when he was old enough to be their father. But it wasn't just a sense of conventional morality that made Bobby frown on such conduct. No, when it came right down to it, he was jealous of Matthew's success. It grated on him that Matthew didn't even use his position as headmaster to seduce the young women. On the contrary, they seemed to fall all over him. Bobby couldn't help being envious, expecially since he himself was a virgin. At least if Matthew had zeroed in on Laura Nash, he would have his hands full. Last year when he'd made passes at her, Laura didn't bite. She'd rejected him in favor of Dennis. This semester, if she gave in, it would be her choice and Matthew would have met his match.

But where did that leave Bobby? He didn't even have the nerve to ask her out on a date. For three years, they'd been just buddies and this year wasn't shaping up to be any different if she was going to start going out with Matthew. Oh, well, it would be a long year. Matthew's flings usually didn't last that long, so maybe Bobby could catch her on the rebound. And, who knows, maybe that wasn't Matthew down by the cottage after all.

Bobby recapped the binoculars and tossed them onto the bed. There would be nothing more to see outside tonight and zooming in on the school itself was not his idea of entertainment. Neither was "The Dark," the script that lay next to the binoculars on Bobby's pillow.

He'd managed to read only half of the play before giving up on it as one of the strangest dramatic works he'd ever come across. There was such an underlying tone of sexuality—not something like *Playboy* but darker and more disturbing. He wondered what had possessed the normally reserved Karin Sayers to be so daring as to pass up Shakespeare in favor of something this weird. Bobby recognized that the script was skillfully written and there were some very good parts for actors but the story was so bizarre and grim, Bobby had taken to his binoculars just for the diversion. The upcoming auditions ought to be interesting. Bobby hoped he'd land the role of a warlock.

Bobby glanced over at the empty bunk across the room. Dennis had gone into town after reading "The Dark." He had loved the play.

Vanessa wasn't sure how she felt about "The Dark." She was still in the midst of reading Act Two, and she was curiously touched by the drama's poignant love scenes. Her romantic nature was stimulated by the hero's devotion, his willingness to die for the woman he loved. But the sequences involving witchcraft were disturbing, and the author's fanatical obsession with the supernatural made Vanessa nervous. This was not just a play that touched on the occult. It was drenched in it, with an authenticity Vanessa suspected was not the work of some novice, but rather of a writer schooled in the intricacies of the dark arts. Whoever had created "The Dark" was a person Vanessa would not like to encounter in real life. The playwright seemed too close to the core of sorcery and black magic, not that Vanessa was an expert in these matters. It was more likely she was unnerved because the drama unfolded in a rural New England setting not unlike this one. Though it took place centuries ago, "The Dark" felt as real as the quilt she had just thrown over her legs to ward off the chill that seemed to come through the walls into Room Six.

Vanessa shivered and went back to her reading. On the dresser across the room, an antique vial of perfume vibrated slightly on the smooth mahogany surface. Absorbed in the script, Vanessa failed to notice the amber colored perfume begin to change shades, darkening as if from an instantaneous aging. In seconds, the once clear liquid had turned the color of wet earth, a muddy brown. Vanessa never saw the vial as it began to noiselessly slide along the dresser top, as though propelled by invisible fingers. The tiny bottle of perfume reached the edge of the bureau, teetering there for a moment, before it toppled to the floor. Vanessa looked up, startled at the crash of glass, as the room was permeated with a sickly sweet stench of rotted flowers.

Puzzled, Vanessa jumped up. She looked at the shattered glass. The spilled perfume formed a small puddle which was ugly and congealed. Kneeling down to touch it, Vanessa thought the liquid felt sticky and repulsive. It took her a moment even to realize what it was, then she was confused. What had happened to the perfume to transform it into this foreign substance? She stared sadly at the remnants of her grandmother's vial, smashed to the floor for no reason. She picked up a shard of broken glass. Mesmerized, she ran her index finger along the sharp edge, drawing a bright red bubble of blood. She brought her hand up to her mouth and licked off the blood, grimacing from the medicinal taste of the perfume's residue.

The door to Room Six was flung open, startling Vanessa.

"Jesus, what crawled up and died in here?" Ingrid Strummer was standing in the doorway, a copy of "The Dark" in her hand, her face screwed up in distaste at the pungent aroma that filled the room.

Vanessa was jolted back to reality. She reached for some tissues and began mopping up the viscous brown puddle, gingerly picking the glass from its midst. "It's perfume. The bottle just broke."

"Smells like a skunk," Ingrid said, flopping down on Laura's bed. She waved the script at Vanessa. "Did you read this? Pretty strange. What happened to your hand?"

"Nothing. I was just . . . it's nothing."

"God, it smells awful in here."

"I'm mopping it up, aren't I?" Vanessa snapped. "What do you want me to do?"

"I never saw perfume like that," Ingrid muttered. "It must have got spoiled."

"There was nothing wrong with it a few minutes ago," Vanessa said, annoyed. She picked up the last remaining splinters of glass and emptied them into a wastebasket, then pushed open the casement window to let some air in.

"That's impossible. It couldn't go bad just like that. Look at the tissues. It's barely soaking through." Vanessa noticed for the first time that Ingrid's words were a little slurred.

"Okay, Ingrid, if you're such an expert, you tell me—what happened?"

Ingrid drew back. "Hey, I'm sorry. If that perfume was okay just a while ago, how could it get like that?" There was a touch of fear in Ingrid's voice.

"I don't know. It was a present. It was one of my favorite things in the world."

The two girls exchanged looks, caught up in memories of lost treasures. Just then, Laura Nash burst into the room, a broad smile on her face.

"Guess who can't wait to get his little paws on me," she gushed.

Ingrid looked over from the bed. "Matthew Hanley," she said knowingly.

"Yeah, I'd be under the sheets with him now if he didn't have to go to town. Hey, what's going on here? This place smells like a fucking sewer."

"Vanessa broke a bottle."

"I didn't break it. It broke by itself. I was just sitting

here and it fell off the dresser."

"You must have done something," Ingrid said in a low voice. "Maybe you hit the dresser with your foot."

"I didn't hit it with anything. I was over here."

"Hey, calm down," Laura interjected. "What was in the bottle? Embalming fluid?"

Vanessa shook her head. "Perfume."

Laura laughed. "You mean toilet water? Christ, it sure smells like something from the toilet."

"It just broke, all by itself," Vanessa repeated.

Laura pushed the window further open. "Well, believe it or not, that's happened to me. It's something about this room. It's kind of on an angle. I think the architect, when he designed this room, forgot to bring his slide rule."

Vanessa looked relieved. "It's happened to you?"

"Sure. Things move around in this room. I forgot to tell you. It's a little added feature. Another way this school has of making you nuts."

Ingrid's expression was skeptical. "I never noticed anything. It happens just in here?"

"I don't know. I call it 'Room Six Madness.' "

"Speaking of madness," Ingrid said, picking up the script, "have you looked at this?"

"I didn't get to it yet," Laura admitted.

"Check this out."

Ingrid thumbed through the play, selected a passage and handed the manuscript to Laura. She read for a moment, then flashed a wicked smile at the other two girls.

"Pretty hot stuff."

Ingrid bounced on the bed excitedly. "Yeah, there's witches fucking around with warlocks. Black magic. Evil spells. You name it."

Laura tossed the script back to her. "Karin Sayers picked that? Minister's daughter, huh? So much for religion." She glanced across at Vanessa. "Did you read it?"

"I'm almost finished."

"Well, what do you think?"

Vanessa's eyes met her reflection in the dresser mirror. "It's a love story," she said quietly. "I think it's kind of beautiful."

Even as she spoke the words, she caught her own surprised expression in the glass. The lie had come so effortlessly—yet she had no idea why she had given that reply.

After midnight. A blustery autumn wind, born of an icy Canadian air mass, rattled the windows of the school. It wrenched the leaves, some of them barely turned from their summer's green, off the branches of the nearby trees, sending them scattering in a frenzy of nocturnal whirlwinds. High in the cold September sky, the moon tugged at a somber blanket of clouds, trying to break through to illuminate the ground below. But the clouds were unyielding and The Hanley School remained cloaked in darkness.

From the front driveway, the school resembled an oblong of black on black. At the rear of the building was the only beacon of light emanating from the dark structure. It was a tiny pinpoint of brightness coming from the window of Room Six, where Vanessa sat in her robe reading the last page of "The Dark" with the aid of a flashlight.

Behind her, on the bed near the window, Laura Nash was buried underneath a mountain of covers; her breathing, deep and even, was the only sound in the room. Vanessa had been careful, turning the final pages of the script, not to waken her roommate. The tranquility of the midnight setting was in marked contrast to the building excitement—even the tingling trepidation—of the play's second act. As she read each line of dialogue by the glow of her small light, her anticipation of the drama's final outcome grew stronger. Though she eagerly awaited the conclusion, she had almost a sense of dejection at the realization that soon the play would be over. Vanessa may have had mixed emotions about the script's subject matter and its undertone of evil, but she knew this much—she didn't want it to end.

She turned the last page. The final words of "The Dark" burned into her brain, searing her senses. The play's epilogue ignited a flame in Vanessa's memory, struggling to the forefront of her mind. Breathlessly, she read the words: "And from that day on, nothing would grow there."

In her room upstairs, Karin stirred. Just like the night before, her sleep had been deep and without dreams, but tonight something had awakened her. She listened to the wind pounding against the building with a shrill keening wail. Normally, it took Karin a few minutes to gather her senses upon awakening, but tonight she felt unexpectedly alert.

She rose from the bed, wrapping herself in her robe. The room was cold, almost unnaturally so. The heat in the building was never turned on until the end of September, and though the sound of clanging in the steampipes often annoyed her, tonight she would have welcomed their persistent noise. Anything was better than this chill.

Karin glanced at the clock. It was nearly one. The sensible thing to do would be to crawl back into bed but she felt too restless. She would rather pace around than stay in one position. Maybe she could put the energy to good use, so she switched on her bedside lamp.

Her eyes adjusted instantly to the brightness. That too was unusual. Karin was sensitive to sudden changes of light but now she didn't even squint as the room was illuminated. What would she do? She was wide-awake. She sat down at her desk and decided to do a little work, some preparations on her lessons.

Karin looked out onto the lawn. The square of light from her window was the only bright spot on the grass, and she wondered if she were the only person awake in the school. She took a childlike delight in pretending this was so. She reached into her briefcase for the lesson plan and spread it out on the desk. But her eyes drifted over to the mirror.

Karin frowned at her reflection. Dressed in the robe, with her hair tied back, she looked so severe—like the classic image of a schoolmarm. She loosened the folds of the robe, slipping it from her shoulders to expose her firm, naked breasts. She undid her hair, letting it fall to her shoulders in a rush. Karin smiled. The schoolmarm image was gone.

The wind outside seemed to be mingling with another sound. Breathing. The whispers. Were they back again? No matter. They had comforted her before. In fact, they were a pleasant change from the constant barrage of gusts against the window.

It didn't occur to Karin to question why the soft murmurings could be heard against the fierce backdrop of the powerful blasts of wind.

Karin pushed the lesson plan aside. She had another idea. She would make a list of things to buy in town the next day. She ran her hand sensuously over her breast and decided that the image of a prim schoolteacher would have to go.

9

"The scene is a witches' training ground. Adrian, the warlock, declares his love for Emily."

At the podium in the auditorium, Karin wore a new outfit she had picked up at lunch hour on her shopping excursion. Her formfitting gray woolen slacks were tucked into a pair of high-heeled, calf-length leather boots, black and shiny. Above a silver belt, barely touching it, was a soft woolen sweater, the top three buttons of which were unfastened. Unlike the previous day, when the drama teacher had looked like she had purposely dressed up, she now gave the impression of a woman totally at home in a style that had never before been her own. Her cornsilk hair flowed freely down her neck, topped off by a metal barrette nestled in its folds.

Karin surveyed her auditioning students who were arranged in the first four rows of the hall. She pointed to Dennis Bellivin. He got to his feet, stepped over Bobby and walked determinedly up to the stage. He held out his script to Karin, who indicated where he was to begin. Confidently, Dennis took center stage and began to read in a deep resonant voice.

"I the dog and she the bitch. I the handle and she the axe. I the cock and she the hen. As my will, so must it be."

There was scattered laughter from the students, and Dennis looked around uneasily. In the first row, Laura was giggling into her hand.

"Go on, Dennis," Karin urged.

Dennis hesitated, then continued with a surprising surge of conviction. "Lord Cernunnos, I ask of thee, let Emily no pleasure, sleep, nor solace see, till heart and loins be joined to me. As my will, so must it be!"

In the front row of the theatre, listening intently and following along in her script, Vanessa mouthed the words of Dennis' final line.

"Let my flower of darkness come to me."

After Dennis had finished, drawing an appreciative nod from Karin Sayers, a succession of would-be Adrians trooped up onstage. They were followed by several Hanley girls who were auditioning for the role of the leader of the witches' coven. Laura Nash was among them. She smiled grimly at the text and then began to read.

"It is not my hand which does this deed but that of The Horned One. As blade pierces heart, so shall the loins of Demian burn with lust for Emily."

Bobby stuck an elbow in Dennis' ribs. "My loins burn with lust for you, Laura," he whispered toward the stage.

"I know, Horny One," Dennis said, laughing. He passed Bobby a silver flask. Bobby ducked behind the seat and took a hearty swig of bourbon.

"I think Laura's a shoo-in," Dennis said. "She's got a lock on the Chief Priestess."

"Either that or the Sabbatic Goat."

Bobby handed back the flask. His interest perked up further at the calling of Marie Kronofski's name. The well-developed young girl hurried up from the audience.

Bobby was almost drooling. "Look at those knockers,

Dennis. Bring back the casting couch!"

The afternoon dragged on. Karin had rolled a blackboard onto the stage, marking off with chalk the roles that had already been filled. Dennis had landed the part of Adrian, the male lead. True to Dennis' prediction, Laura had gotten the role of the Chief Priestess. Bobby would play Hector, a hapless apprentice warlock, and Ingrid was listed as the stage manager. Rickie, Marie and several other students had been cast in supporting roles. Now it was Vanessa's turn to try out for the part of Emily, the beautiful young witch sentenced to burn at the stake.

"Vanessa, would you like to begin?" Karin asked from the podium.

Vanessa's hands trembled. She had been on edge since the auditions had begun, but even though her fingers tightly gripped the manuscript to steady her nerves, she knew from past experience that once she started speaking the lines, her tension would dissolve and a certain professional self-assure would take over.

"By the mysteries of the deep," she began, feeling the expected wave of confidence gratefully, "by the flames of The Devil's hearth, by the power of the east, by the silence of the night . . ."

Vanessa could tell by the unusual hush that had fallen on the auditorium that she was giving a good reading. She was tempted to steal a glance at Dennis in the second row, just to get his reaction. If she had, she would have noticed he was hanging on her every word, his lips moving noiselessly with hers, staring at her intently.

"And by the holy rites of Hecate, I call Adrian, by the ties of love, to stroke my flesh, to lay with me in a field of stone, to submerge himself in a Flower Of Darkness . . ."

A few feet away from her, Karin's eyes blazed with satisfaction. She bit her lip excitedly.

"I call Adrian," Vanessa implored, her voice crying out

in the auditorium. "Warm seed, warm heart; let us never be apart."

Vanessa went on, delivering Emily's impassioned speech with such clarity and conviction that it would be impossible for any other girl to get the part. Dennis continued to stare at her, smiling knowingly.

Out in the foyer afterwards, Bobby and some of the Hanley girls were discussing the auditions.

"I don't believe they're letting us do this play," Rickie Webster said, glumly.

"Hey, it's better than 'Twelfth Night,' " Bobby replied.

"My mother's going to die when she sees this," Marie predicted with a laugh.

"I think it's gross," Ingrid said.

"What's gross about it?" Bobby asked, playfully. "I think it's art."

"Yeah?" Rickie challenged. "So how come the playwright took his name off of it?"

"Don't knock Anonymous," Bobby said. "He wrote a lot of good shit."

The doors to the auditorium opened, and Vanessa walked out with Dennis.

"Hey, Adrian!" Bobby greeted his roommate.

"Hey, Hector!" Dennis came over and shook the boys hand. "Congratulations."

"What are you guys up to?" Bobby asked.

Dennis grinned. "I don't know. Go into town, burn someone at the stake, have a cold beer, sacrifice some virgins . . ."

Bobby went over to Vanessa, who was smiling shyly at the others. "You're going to be a great Emily," he said.

"Thank you."

Dennis slapped Bobby on the back. "Let's get a drink. I'll drive." He turned to Vanessa. "You'll come with me, right?"

"Sure."

Vanessa reached into the sleeve of her jacket for her

scarf. It wasn't there. "I left something inside. I'll be right back."

"We'll mix up some devil incense while you're gone," Bobby said.

Vanessa felt disoriented as soon as she stepped into the now deserted auditorium. The hall was in darkness except for the dim glow from a bulb which hung somewhere in the stage area. Just a few minutes ago, the auditorium had been lit up, alive with the sounds and laughter of the kids. Now there was a silence so dense that Vanessa could almost feel it touching her skin like a clammy, unclean rag. *Get out now!* This room was filthy with vile memories and secrets, ready to seep into her brain if she let down her guard for even the slightest instant.

Vanessa paused and waited for her eyes to get used to the darkness. Strangely, they didn't. Vanessa felt along the wall for the light switch. She turned it on. The setting she found herself in was enough to make Vanessa think her eyes were playing tricks on her. She rubbed them hard with the backs of her hands, but it didn't help. The auditorium seats, which had been upholstered in a dark green minutes before, were now covered in a rich purple material matching the thick velvet curtain which was drawn across the stage. The walls were a light gray instead of the lime green; the carpet was now a plush burgundy tweed.

Strewn about on the empty seats and in the aisles were discarded programs boasting the name of a play. The hall seemed to embrace its mementos of the past in silent reminiscence. Vanessa felt as if she'd been hurled through some porthole of time and was now caught in a time warp, seeing the school as it had once been. The atmosphere was musty and heavy and surrounded Vanessa like a smothering blanket.

Vanessa gripped the back of one of the seats. It's my imagination, she tried to convince herself. Like before, I'm hallucinating. Her eyes went back to the programs.

She knew there would be a date on them. She wanted to pick up a program and read it, but she was afraid of what she might find there. *Run. Get out of here.* Vanessa hesitated. How could she race out of there? What if she ran through the large doors and her friends weren't there? What if she really had stepped into some other dimension and she couldn't get back? Vanessa shook her head. Impossible. It's just your mind playing tricks on you again. Pick up the program. *Yes, Vanessa, pick up the program.*

Vanessa leaned over to pick up the program but before she could get a good look at the cover, she heard a sudden noise from the stage. The thick curtain was slowly going up. Vanessa watched wide-eyed at what was gradually revealed behind the purple drape.

A straight-back chair was lying on its side as if someone had just kicked it over. A few feet above it, dangling in midair, were the ghostly white legs of a girl. The curtain flew upward. Into full view came the body of a young girl convulsing violently on a thick twisting rope which was tightly knotted around her frail neck. The girl's tongue hung from her mouth like a bloated slice of meat. The features on her porcelain-like face were now contorted into a deathly grimace. Clothed only in a sheer nightgown that was torn, the girl was drenched in a red, sticky substance. Vanessa knew at once it must be blood.

A flood of emotions swept over Vanessa—fear, revulsion, confusion—but these were dwarfed by an overwhelming sadness which seemed to emanate from the corpse that now rocked gently to and fro above the stage. Vanessa could feel the torment that had once surrounded the girl's life. The accompanying terror that Vanessa felt was not from the grotesque vision itself but from the realization that she understood the girl's total despair. The onslaught of horror, when it finally came, reached into the depths of Vanessa's being, gripping her stomach in a vise, driving her backward, forcing her to gag and struggle for breath.

Vanessa. She could hear the girl's voice inside her head, the sound reaching out over lost years, pleading, seductive. The lilt in the girl's voice was profoundly evil.

"Vanessa."

Vanessa cocked her head and tried to concentrate on the figure that was slowly approaching from the stage area. She watched incredulously as the auditorium seemed to waver for an instant, as if a strong gust of hot air was blowing through. Then all was back to what should have been, like a movie frame coming into focus. The furnishings were as Vanessa had left them after the auditions. The stage was empty. No dead girl dangled from a noose. The voice Vanessa had heard calling out to her a second ago came from Karin Sayers, who was just a few feet away now, a look of concern on her pretty face.

"Vanessa? Are you alright?"

Vanessa caught her breath. Her heart was racing. For an instant, she couldn't remember why she had gone back into the auditorium. Then she recalled.

"I was looking for my scarf," she stammered.

"Is this it?" Karin asked, taking something from behind her back.

"Yes, thank you."

Karin handed her the scarf, her eyes searching Vanessa's face curiously.

Vanessa looked away. "I gotta go," she blurted. She dashed out through the heavy doors, still not absolutely certain her friends would be waiting for her in the hall, and she sighed with relief when she saw them.

Dennis came forward. "You okay? You look white."

"Yeah, I'm okay." She leaned against the wall, trying to regain her composure. "Why don't you go on without me, Dennis? I've changed my mind. I'm a little tired. I think I'll go to my room."

"Did something just happen?"

"No, nothing happened. I'll see you tomorrow."

Before Dennis could answer, Vanessa brushed past him on her way to the stairs. Dennis watched as she took the steps two at a time. He glanced back at the others and shrugged.

"Was it something I said?" he asked, laughing.

On the second floor landing, Vanessa began gathering herself. What had just happened was no hallucination—she was certain of that. No longer did she think that any of those past visions were hallucinations either. There could only be two possible explanations. Someone was trying to drive her mad by staging elaborate illusions or—and this, she admitted, was becoming more likely—there was a supernatural force of some kind that was aimed directly at her. That second possibility was just too awful to consider.

Vanessa remembered the promise she had made to herself—to seek professional help if the visions continued. But who could she go to? The school counselor? A psychiatrist? They might be helpful if Vanessa still believed she was bringing on these visions because she wanted to go home. But how could she tell them of these new suspicions? They would probably diagnose her as paranoid. She'd go home alright, but that would be admitting defeat. Vanessa wanted something more than that; she wanted to find out the truth. Life here might be disturbing, but if Vanessa could persevere and get to the bottom of these terrifying apparitions, then soon she'd be able to go home—but on her terms.

Feeling a new resolve now, Vanessa examined the first possibility—that someone was playing carefully orchestrated pranks on her. Immediately, the image of a solicitous Karin Sayers crossed her mind. Was it a coincidence that both times Vanessa had seen something in the school auditorium Karin Sayers had appeared on the scene a moment later? Maybe Karin was connected to the strange events. But, Vanessa reasoned, the drama teacher had been nowhere in sight when she saw that vision of blood on the front steps of the school or the severed arm in the privacy of her own room.

Vanessa headed down the corridor to Room Six. Maybe she really did need some rest.

The only movie theatre in town was called Dreamland. It was aptly named, since with its 1920's elegance, it evoked an era when movie palaces flourished and the films they showed—with stars like Garbo, Chaplin and Valentino—were the stuff that dreams were made of. Slightly tarnished through the ravages of time, Dreamland still had echoes of its former glory, though they often went unnoticed by the filmgoers of today.

Dennis and Vanessa came out of the Sunday night showing of "Night Of The Living Dead," blinking their eyes in the harsh light of the marquee. Dennis put his arm around Vanessa, and they walked toward his car in the unusually balmly evening.

"That was fun," Dennis said. "Would you like to see it again some time when you're not hiding under the seat?"

"Oh, yeah, Dennis? I believe I saw you jump a few times."

"Yeah, but I didn't spill a root beer all over the kid next to me."

"Are you kidding? He was so stoned he didn't even notice."

"Lucky for you."

As they got into Dennis' car, Vanessa was quiet for a moment, thinking of the zombie movie they had just seen. She turned to Dennis. "I know that was just a horror film, but do you think anything like that could actually happen in real life?"

"You mean people eating human flesh?" Dennis asked, his eyes brightening. He dove across the front seat and playfully bit Vanessa on the neck. She drew back instinctively.

"Dennis, you scared me."

"Did I? That's the second time this week."

"I know. And I wish you wouldn't do it."

"I'm sorry," Dennis said, starting the car, "but maybe you scare too easily."

"I never used to till I came to this place."

"Well, I know some of the teachers are a little ghoulish, but I hope you're not implying there are any zombies around."

Vanessa stared out the window as they drove down Main Street. "It's just that after seeing a movie like that, with the school being so weird and everything, I wonder where people get their ideas."

"What do you mean?"

"The people who made that picture. Do you think they based it on something that actually happened?"

"Jesus Christ, I hope not. I'd hate to think there were cannibals running around." He looked at Vanessa. "But don't you think that movie was a little far-fetched?"

"I would have if I'd seen it a week ago. Now I'm not so sure what's far-fetched anymore."

"What happened a week ago?"

"I arrived at Hanley."

"Vanessa, why don't you tell me what you're getting at?"

"Not now, Dennis. I'd rather talk about something else."

"Something less scary?"

"That's right."

A few minutes later, Vanessa and Dennis were back on the school grounds. It was a little after nine p.m. and the front lawn was alive with activity. A girl Vanessa recognized from gym class was playing a guitar for a cluster of friends, and a touch football game was in clumsy progress, lit only by the moon. Vanessa spotted Bobby Cannon in the huddle. He waved a hello.

"Come on," Dennis said, taking Vanessa by the arm. "I know a place that's a little more private."

Vanessa waved back at Bobby, who watched

knowingly as Dennis steered her down the slope in the direction of the lake. The sounds from the lawn died away and the two of them were suddenly alone, approaching the boathouse. On the water, moondrops flickered in hundreds of tiny reflections.

Dennis pried open the door to the newly painted building, and they went inside. Though the light within was dim, Dennis knew his way around. He went immediately to the window ledge and lit a kerosene lantern which bathed the small room in a friendly orange glow.

Looking around, Vanessa felt comfortable. With its thick throw pillows and its simple wicker furniture, the place had a homey quality which reminded Vanessa of secret clubhouses from her childhood.

"Very cozy, Dennis," she said, nodding approvingly. "Laura told me about this place."

Dennis' face split open in a grin. "Laura should know."

Vanessa sank down onto one of the oversized cushions. Dennis adjusted the wick on the lantern, bringing it down to a romantic half-light.

Vanessa smiled. "Is that for lost sailors?"

"It's so we won't be disturbed."

"I get it. You think of everything, don't you?"

Dennis joined her on the cushion. "Around here, we call this place the Abbott School Annex."

Dennis studied her.

"Are you scared?" he asked.

Vanessa was hesitant. "No. Not now."

"But something's wrong. You're not still thinking about that movie, are you?"

Vanessa shook her head. "No, it's something else, but it's just as horrible."

"Want to tell me what it is?"

"I don't know. You'll think I'm crazy."

"I don't care. Everyone's a little nuts."

"Are you sure you won't laugh?"

Dennis drew her closer. "Try me."

Vanessa thought for a moment, choosing her words

carefully. "Do you ever see things that aren't there?"

"You mean hallucinate? I once did some blotter acid and saw about a million cats flying over Cape Cod Bay."

"No, I don't mean that," Vanessa said, earnestly. "I mean when you're straight. No drugs."

"What kind of things?"

"Horrible things. Blood. Dead bodies. But not from the present. Like something out of the past."

"Where did you see these things?"

"In the school. It's never happened to me before, but the day I came here it started."

"It only happens at the school? Is that what happened to you the other day? In the auditorium?"

Vanessa's voice took on a dreamy tone. "I went back to get my scarf and the room looked different. It was like I was standing in another time period. God, Dennis, it's just what you were talking about. Remember? You said the school made you feel like you could go back in time?"

"Like it was 1931 again," Dennis whispered.

"Exactly. But I don't think you ever saw anything like what I saw in that auditorium." Tears came to Vanessa's eyes. She inhaled deeply.

"Go on," urged Dennis.

Vanessa gripped his hand. "I saw a dead girl hanging from the rafters right over the stage. Her face was all twisted and her body was covered with blood. She couldn't have been more than sixteen years old."

"Jesus Christ!"

"Dennis, the way that girl looked was horrible, just awful, but that wasn't the worst part. I don't know how to put this but I was picking up on what that girl was feeling. I don't mean the pain she was going through by dying. I'm talking about something that came before that. Dennis, this girl suffered. I'm not sure why but she went through some terrible ordeal before she hung herself. Something happened to her, some grief, that was really more than she could handle. It might have been connected with violence. I almost felt I could identify with her—not just a normal feeling of sympathy but as if she were communicating with me, warning me, reaching out to me from beyond the grave."

"Did you tell anybody?"

"No, but Karin Sayers was there. I think she could tell that something was wrong. Do you believe me?"

Dennis shifted his weight on the pillow. "Yes. I believe you *think* you saw something."

Vanessa was downcast. "You think I imagined it."

"Well, what else could it be? Nobody reported a hanging in the school the other day."

"Dennis, this hanging didn't happen the other day. It happened a long time ago. I told you everything in the auditorium had changed—like it was some other time period—but that didn't make it less real."

"It disappeared, though, didn't it? I mean it didn't stay there."

Vanessa nodded. Her voice sounded faraway. "When I looked again, everything was gone. But I know what I saw."

Dennis pressed her closer to him. "I think you should try to forget about it. But promise you'll tell me if something like that happens again."

"I will."

"You haven't had any problems since then, have you?"

"No," Vanessa admitted.

"Well, look around you. You don't see anything here that could harm you. The boathouse is off-limits to anything scary."

Vanessa leaned into him. "I know. I must be spoiling your evening with all this weird stuff."

"The evening's not over," Dennis said, huskily. His lips nuzzled her face, coming to rest on her mouth. They locked together in a lingering kiss. With his free hand, Dennis reached down to unfasten the top button of Vanessa's blouse. She sighed as his hand touched her bare breast.

Dennis took Vanessa's blouse completely off. He ran his tongue around the contours of her mouth, tracing a pattern down to her neck, then continuing further to her breasts. Vanessa's nipple grew hard to the touch of Dennis' tongue. She leaned back savoring his gentle caress. Vanessa reached out to lock her arms tightly around Dennis' back, and he pressed himself against her. She could feel him hardening. Expertly he ran his hand under her skirt, along her smooth thigh, up to her panties. He could feel her getting wet through the sheer material. Vanessa was growing excited now. She wanted Dennis but her mind was racing. Something was holding her back. She couldn't let herself go, not completely. She didn't know what it was.

A moment later she did.

The scream caught in Vanessa's throat, so intense in its fury, she thought it would rip her tongue from her mouth. Before her disbelieving eyes, the face of Dennis Bellivin had fallen away. In its place, resting monstrously on his broad shoulders, caked blood embedded in its features, was a face Vanessa had seen once before—in a portrait. But this visage of Malcolm Hanley was not looking out at her confidently. Instead, it had been split in half by a gleaming meat cleaver that was still buried deep in its skull. The eyes of the grisly head bulged out at odd angles as if on stalks. The bottom half of the cracked faced was twisted in a macabre snarl. One entire piece of Malcolm Hanley's jaw flapped down, dangling bizarrely from a few bloody tendons. The cry of terror that forced its way past Vanessa's clenched teeth left her weak and sobbing on the pillow.

"What the fuck?" Dennis cried out, looking around frantically. Vanessa had crawled into a ball on the cushion, her shoulders heaving with oncoming hysteria. Dennis turned back and tried to comfort her, but she kept her eyes averted from him.

"Vanessa, what's wrong? What did you see?"

Vanessa dug herself deeper into the pillow, trying to make herself as small as possible—anything so she would never have to see that face again. Dennis cradled her head in his hands, attempting to pry her free of the cushion.

"Vanessa, look at me."

"I can't," she moaned. Vanessa kept her eyes squeezed tight.

"Yes, you can!" Dennis tugged her by the hair, forcing her to face him. Recognizing the signs of hysterical behavior, he slapped Vanessa, not hard but just enough to stun her. It worked. Her eyes shot open.

It took Vanessa a moment to focus, to realize that the ghastly vision of The Hanley School's founder was gone. Instead, she was staring at Dennis' concerned face. Vanessa crumpled into his arms. Her tears continued to flow freely but the hysteria had subsided.

"I don't know what's happening to me," she said, sobbing.

"You're okay now. Just calm down."

Dennis had Vanessa under control. She had dried her eyes and put her blouse back on again. Dennis hovered near her patiently. When she gave him a half-smile, he was relieved. The panic was over.

"Do you want to tell me what happened?" he asked gently. "What did you see?"

Vanessa bit her lip. "I can't tell you."

"Was it like in the auditorium?"

"In a way. But this was worse. Get me out of here, Dennis. I just want to go to sleep."

Rickie Webster was in her room, hunched over in front of her dresser, peering at herself in the mirror. The young girl with large eyes, red and puffy from crying, who stared back at her, didn't look like a teenager. The frown lines, the ashen, dry complexion, the aura of discontent—all were of an old woman who had lived her life in misery. The turmoil that churned inside of Rickie made her feel aged, like a stranger wearing some else's skin.

Rickie was too young and confused to sort out her emotions. And lately, her already fragile psyche was crowded with thoughts of Laura Nash. Every time Rickie tried to rationalize what had prompted her to make a pass at Laura, she would draw a blank. Then she would be overcome by a longing for Laura so acute that she felt as if she were drowning in a sexual sea of emotion.

Yet underneath the peculiar desire, an embarrassment burned her conscience. Rickie was ashamed of herself. She remembered a time when she was a child, perhaps ten years old, and she had dreamt about one of her teachers. She awoke to find her mother standing over her and felt a rain of blows on her face. *Stop it. You stop it at once, Rickie Webster. That is a disgusting, dirty thing to do. Nice girls don't do filthy things like that to themselves.* Rickie had felt humiliated then, though she didn't understand what she had done to make her mother so upset. Years later, of course, she knew—but that only added to her shame.

Rickie wasn't a very happy girl, but these past few days she was so depressed that tears threatened to spill at the slightest provocation. She simply had to snap out of it—but how? Well, she could start by getting away from the mirror. Looking at her reflection only made things worse. Rickie went across the room and sat down on the bed.

Suddenly, the room fell unnaturally silent. Gone were the sounds of the old plumbing in the walls, the ticking of the clock on Rickie's bedside table, even Rickie's heartbeat. She couldn't hear any of it. And with the uncanny quiet, a mass of swirling hot air spun around the room playfully, dancing around the corners and coming to rest on the bed with Rickie. At once, Rickie relaxed. The warm breeze soothed her and seemed to drain away the stress of the last week. Rickie lay back on the bed, sinking into the essence of the strange gust of air. She slipped effortlessly into its scorching embrace.

When Rickie Webster opened her eyes a few minutes later, all was back to normal. The pipes played their rusty music in the walls, the clock ticked away and Rickie could hear her muted heartbeat deep within her chest. The breeze had disappeared, leaving behind it a slightly fetid smell of spoiled meat.

Rickie stood up. Her legs felt strong and resilient, and she ran her hands through her hair boldly. Without hesitation, she walked to the door and went out into the hallway. It was cooler there but Rickie walked in her own cloud of warm air. She continued down the hallway toward Room Six. For the first time in days, something made Rickie Webster smile.

"Come on in. It's open."

Rickie let herself into Room Six. Laura sat in the corner of the room before a makeshift dressing table. Rickie stood at the door, watching in fascination as Laura, a marijuana cigarette dangling from the corner of her mouth, deftly applied her eye makeup. In a tight red sweater and a straight black skirt slit at the side, Laura looked scintillating.

Laura glanced up. "Oh, hi," she said coolly. God, she thought, Rickie looks terrible, worse than ever. Her goddamned hair looks like she combed it with a blender.

Laura turned back to the mirror. "You looking for Vanessa? She went to the movies."

Rickie didn't answer. She began to tremble. Laura noticed and hoped there wasn't going to be another scene. Maybe she could distract Rickie with some girl talk. She fastened a barrette to her hair.

"What do you think, Rickie? Makes me look innocent?"

Rickie came closer. Laura tried to ignore the pleading look in the young girl's eyes.

"On the other hand," Laura went on, trying to sound nonchalant, "I don't want to look *too* innocent."

Rickie was right next to her now. She leaned over and kissed Laura's neck. Laura threw her arms back, shoving

Rickie away, the joint flying out of her mouth.

"Goddamn it, I warned you about that! I don't want you touching me. You got some fucking nerve. I think there's something wrong with you." Laura had all she could do not to slap Rickie senseless.

Rickie recoiled. She stared at Laura, her large eyes struggling to comprehend what was going on.

"I didn't mean it. I . . ."

Laura pushed her again, furiously. "You didn't *mean* it?"

Tears were flowing down Rickie's face. She cowered in the corner. "I don't know. I'm mixed up . . ."

Laura regarded her with pity, yet spoke through clenched teeth. "Yeah, I'll say you're mixed up. You're fucked up! This is the third time you've done this. I'm getting real tired of you coming onto me. You told me you don't like girls and I believed you. But if that's true, then what the fuck is this all about? Answer me. I asked you a question."

"I can't. I don't know . . ."

Laura picked up the joint and took an angry drag on it. Rickie looked so puny, so totally bewildered, it was hard for Laura to sustain her rage. But she couldn't let her off with forgiveness—not again.

"I think you need some kind of help, Rickie, and I mean fast. You come in here in a goddamn trance and do something like that. Then when I scream at you, it's like you wake up and you don't know why you did it. Well, you better find out why you did it. You better get some shrink to tell you why. And until you do, you stay away from me, you got that?"

"Yes," Rickie mumbled, unable to meet Laura's eyes.

Laura turned away from her. She didn't know what else to say. Just as before, there was a niggling thought in her mind that the girl was telling the truth. She really wasn't a lesbian and really didn't know what she was doing. When she came into the room, Rickie looked like a sleepwalker. Now she looked wide-awake and sorry.

Suddenly, Laura felt creepy. If Rickie really couldn't help herself, what was it that was making her behave like this?

Laura glanced back at Rickie. She wanted her out of the room. There was something unhealthy about being around her, like a madness that Laura wanted no part of.

"Okay, Rickie," Laura said, quietly but firmly, "get yourself together and leave. I don't want you near me. Not tonight. Not anytime. If you ever try that again, I'll put you through a wall. Understand?"

Rickie bolted from the room in tears, slamming the door after her. Laura dragged again on her joint, feeling relieved and just a trifle sad. She sat back down at the makeup table. Her eyes grew wide with amazement as she watched a full jar of cold cream uproot itself from its place on the table, roll a few inches to the edge, then topple onto the floor. Laura stared down at the jar in disbelief. She stubbed out her marijuana cigarette and threw back her head in exasperation.

"This place is a nuthouse," she said aloud.

Vanessa had never seen The Hanley School from the other side of the lake. She and Dennis had walked there from the boathouse at Vanessa's insistence. After she had calmed down, Dennis had reminded her that it was nearly curfew, but Vanessa couldn't bring herself to go back into the building that she knew was the source of her anxiety. Now, surveying it from across the water, the school looked no less malevolent despite the distance she had placed between it and herself. In fact, with its evil gargoyles glaring out into the night, it seemed even more threatening as if, at any moment, it could rear up from its moorings and bound across the lake to smother her in a stony caress.

"Doesn't it look beautiful?" Dennis said, idly stroking Vanessa's hair.

"No, it looks evil. I can't believe they designed that place as a school."

"Well, you know what they say about best-laid plans.

Maybe it turned into something else."

Vanessa shuddered. "What do you mean?"

"From what I hear, Malcolm Hanley was a pretty weird guy. Who knows what he had in mind?"

"Did you know he carved some of those gargoyles himself?"

"Really? Who told you that?"

"Matthew. He said Malcolm Hanley worked like a man possessed. I wonder why he carved them. They're so vicious—so ugly."

"They have to be," Dennis said. "Don't you know that? The whole idea of putting gargoyles on a building is to ward off evil spirits."

Vanessa gave a half-laugh. "Well, they're not doing a very good job, Dennis."

"Come on," Dennis said. They had passed the halfway mark now and were walking back toward the school. "I know you've seen some pretty horrible stuff since you've been here, and I know that you've been scared. But just because something scares you, doesn't mean it's evil. Sometimes being scared serves as a warning."

Vanessa slowed her pace, eyeing the approaching building. She was tempted to tell Dennis that one of her visions was of a dog-like gargoyle spouting blood and chewed flesh, gnashing its teeth at her fiendishly. She wondered if that was one of the stone figures Malcolm Hanley had personally carved. Maybe Dennis was right. Maybe what she saw that first day of school *was* a warning.

And then there was the strange feeling of empathy with the hanging girl in the auditorium. Could that also have been a warning? But a warning against what? The school itself? Some inherent evil in the building? Or was it some malignant force from outside that had chosen Hanley as a breeding ground for whatever horror it was working?

Vanessa looked over at Dennis' handsome face outlined in the moonlight. As she studied his features, she was convinced of one thing—what she had seen in the boathouse earlier could not have been an elaborate trick. She had been too close to Dennis—she had been about to make love to him—for anyone to have staged that sudden grisly transformation without her having felt or seen something. That left only one possible explanation for the visions—the supernatural. Was it something from beyond the grave and, if so, what did it want with Vanessa? She was almost afraid to find out.

"Hey, who's that?" Dennis pointed across the lawn.

Vanessa recognized her roommate hurrying away from the school. "It's Laura."

Dennis grinned. "Where do you suppose she's going dressed like that?"

"I think I know, Dennis. There's only one place she could be going."

Laura didn't see the couple approaching from the lake as she made her way down the slope of the lawn toward Matthew Hanley's cottage. She felt a little light-headed from the grass, having smoked a second joint after Rickie left just to calm herself down, but she walked with quick, purposeful steps. Though it was late, there still might be some kids out on the grounds, and Laura did not want to be seen.

As she neared Matthew's house, she had a sudden urge to look back at the school, remembering the other night—that laughter and the stench of sulphur. She wanted to turn around to reassure herself that nothing was watching her, but she resisted the impulse. And she knew, though she was ashamed to admit it, it was out of fear.

I've had enough aggravation for one night, Laura thought. If I never see Rickie Webster again, that would be too soon for me.

The next morning Laura Nash would regret that she ever harbored that thought.

"Surprised?" Laura said playfully as Matthew let her into his cottage. "Didn't think I'd come, did you?"

Matthew took Laura's shawl from her shoulders. He stepped back, his eyes traveling appreciatively down her body. "You look great," he said.

Laura kicked off her shoes and sat down on the sofa, arranging her slit skirt provocatively. I'll bet he's a leg man, she thought. This should give him an eyeful.

"I've got a very nice 1972 rosé," Matthew said. "Would you like some?"

"Of course."

Matthew popped the cork on the wine bottle and poured them each a glass.

"I hear you're playing a priestess." He sat down across from her, giving himself the most advantageous view of her legs.

"Yeah, an evil temptress. Right up my alley."

Matthew handed her the wine glass. "Taste this. It's from a little town near the German border."

Laura took a sip and licked her lips. "I like wine with bubbles. It's sexy."

Matthew stood up. He moved over to the couch beside her and put his arm around her shoulder. "Does anyone know you're down here?"

"Yeah, I took out a billboard downtown."

"No, I'm serious. You didn't tell anyone?"

Laura reached over and began unbuttoning his shirt. "You're safe. My lips are sealed."

Matthew drew near to kiss her. "We'll see about that."

Laura's first thought as Matthew brought his mouth down hard on hers was that this guy really knew his way around women. Usually it took her a while to feel turned on, but in just a few moments Laura felt the excitement building in her.

He sucked at her lips, drawing them into his mouth, hinting at what was to come later. He licked at her ear and brought his lips down along her neck. Laura pressed against him and breathed in his scent—masculine, musky like an animal.

Matthew began tugging at Laura's sweater, easing it

up over her naked breasts.

"No. Stop, Matthew. I'll do that."

Laura stood up. Seductively, she stripped off the sweater and threw it on the floor. She unfastened her skirt, letting it slide down her legs, and stepped out of it. She wore no panties underneath.

She eased back down onto the sofa. "Isn't that better?" she asked coaxingly. She reached for the light switch.

"No," Matthew whispered. "I want to see you."

"That's not fair. You're still dressed." She pulled at Matthew's T-shirt and, with one muscular motion, he tore it off. Laura unbuckled his jeans and brought them down his hips. Quickly, he took off his briefs. They were both naked now. Laura felt wicked and that was part of the excitement.

Matthew touched Laura's breasts, playfully, teasingly. He massaged her nipples with slow, circular motions. He sucked at one, then the other, and she could feel his erection growing harder, more insistent.

Matthew's hands went to the soft flesh of Laura's inner thighs. His fingers opened her, probing inside the wetness. He moved his fingers up and down her sensitive skin as she sighed eagerly. Matthew brought his head down to rest between her parted thighs, as she opened her legs further. He entered her with his tongue, at the same time using his fingers to heighten the pleasure. She cradled his head and pushed hard against his mouth. Expertly, Matthew made Laura come, with a suddenness she had never experienced before. She cried out loud as the spasms shook her.

Soon, his mouth was on hers, his tongue darting in and out. She could taste herself on his lips. The pleasure he was giving her was almost painful.

"You're beautiful," he whispered.

"I'll bet you say that to all the girls at Hanley."

Matthew laughed. "Yes, but usually I'm lying."

"You know, you're as good as they say you are."

"I'm not finished yet."

He took Laura gently in his arms. They were both perspiring, the moisture of their naked bodies mingling. Laura breathed in deeply, loving the smell of his sweat mixed with her own sweetness. She took hold of his hard cock, sliding her hand up and down, making him groan. Her breath began to quicken once more. They were both on the floor now, locked in a passionate embrace.

Laura had to have him that moment. She opened her legs invitingly and guided him into her. He held back for a second, causing her to moan in anticipation, then pushed up inside her as far as he could go. Laura arched her hips to take his entire length. They moved as one as he plunged deeply. Laura cried out in pain, raised her back off the floor and met his thrust. Matthew's strong hands gripped her buttocks urgently. With one easy motion, he rolled her over so that she was on top of him. He cupped her breasts as she straddled him, working her hips back and forth.

"Now," Laura begged. "Now!"

Matthew's lithe body lifted clear off the floor as he drove upward. They came together, her pounding heart matching his. She thought she would explode with the intensity. Laura collapsed on top of him, struggling to catch her breath as he enveloped her in his embrace.

Minutes later, as the two of them slipped into an exhausted half-sleep, their breathing quieted. But there was an added breathing in the room now—a stale exhalation of breath. Its origin was not of passion. Rather, it stemmed from the decay of a lifeless tomb. Outside the window, a sultry rusting was in the air. The torrid gust, oppressive and suffocating, carried the scent of sulphur along as it touched the autumn foliage and glided over the lawn toward the school. The breeze danced almost carnally around the school's darkened corners, brushing the red brick lovingly. The gust visited the sleeping inhabitants through their opened windows.

Its mass, an amalgam of malevolent memories and carnage, swept over the sleeping forms, leaving an aura of evil in its wake. It forced its way through the cracks in Matthew Hanley's office, lifting papers from the desk and whirling them wildly in midair. From above, the handsome face of the school's founder watched. As the breeze spun around the portrait of Malcolm Hanley one final time, the painting stirred slightly as if the dead headmaster were nodding in approval.

Rickie Webster pressed her face against the casement window, curious as to why the wind should look so black. Even against the dark sky, she could see the density of the whirlwind, looking like a streak of dirt on the night. It had an odd smell, too—that's what had gotten her out of a deep sleep. That and the voices. Even as she'd sat up in bed, fully awake, it had taken her a few moments to realize that the whispers were in her head. The sound had reverberated in her brain like a thousand miniscule wings flapping against her ears, like phantoms trying to get out.

Riickiieee. There it was again. The murmur was sibilant and thin, but not weak. Rickie knew there was strength in that voice. If only it would tell her why she was feeling so drained and what she could do to make the hurt go away. Rickie's pain came from deep within. Shame and remorse were making her fragile body ache as if she were running a high fever.

She was so confused—the only thing she could be certain of was that she was sick. Only pain seemed real to her. Hot, salty tears ran down the translucent skin of her face, and she could taste them as they slid into her mouth. Blood was salty too, thought Rickie. She arched her body and felt the strain of her tired muscles. She was debilitated and had to lie down.

Back in bed, Rickie wrapped her frail arms around her body, drawing her legs up to her stomach to retreat into her smallness. She lay there and waited for the whispers.

Outside, a cloud passed in front of the moon, slicing it in two. Rickie watched the shadows change patterns, the glow from the stained-glass windows flooding over her. It was at this moment that fear came to her. She had the sensation that the walls were beginning to pulsate as if they were about to close in on her, and she could hear the room breathing. Suddenly she blacked out, her eyes fluttering closed like two fallen butterflies.

Riickiieee. Her eyes darted open. This time the voice was not in her head. Something in the room had called her name. Fearfully, Rickie looked around. Thank God, she thought, the walls were still now—no moving or breathing could be heard. *Relax, little girl. You don't have to be afraid any more. You need to sleep, Riickiieee. You'll feel so much better if you sleeeep.* Yes, Rickie thought, I don't have to think about anything if I sleep. I won't feel ashamed and useless if I just go to sleep.

Once again, she shut her eyes. *No! Not that way, Riickiieee.* Rickie smiled. The whispers were back and they were helping her now. She could tell they meant her no harm. They had made the walls stop closing in on her and taken the nasty breathing away. Soon the voices would make her feel good again.

Slowly, the tension eased. Rickie uncurled herself and stood up. The murmuring was more insistent now, and there was more than one voice. It didn't matter. Rickie was comforted by them. Humming tunelessly, Rickie began to make her bed, taking care to get it just right. She didn't want anyone saying she wasn't always a neat person. She smoothed the blankets, then stood back to admire her handiwork. Perfect. Rickie went to the dresser and removed her makeup case. Putting aside the untouched powder, blush and lipstick, she found the item she needed. She held it up and watched the light from the window catch the handle, gleaming out a welcome. Rickie replaced the cosmetics case in the dresser. She was almost ready now.

Quickly, she slipped out of her nightgown. She had to

be naked for what she was about to do. She opened the door and stepped into the corridor. The warm rush of air was waiting for her, shielding her from the night chill. The whispers were multiplying now, crowding her fevered brain with a roar of encouragement. Rickie padded off down the hall, a scrawny wraith in the squares of moonlight.

The tile floor of the shower room was slippery and cold but, within seconds, it seemed to warm beneath Rickie's bare feet. She turned on the shower spigot and adjusted the spray so that the temperature of the water was just right. She stepped into the stream of water, letting it rinse over her skinny body luxuriously. The freezing gush from the shower faucet melded with the primitive whispered cadence in Rickie's mind to make her tingle. Rickie grimaced, but only for the slightest second, then watched in fascination as the water swirled—deep red, suddenly—toward the engulfing drain.

She cut the other wrist open. She let the razor fall from her hand. It clattered to the tiles like the cackling laughter that echoed in Rickie's brain. The voices had helped and had showed her what to do. Rickie could never have ended her unhappy life without them. Now they were taunting her, making a mockery of her obedience, but Rickie Webster was too far gone to care.

As her life's blood ebbed from her veins, pouring in a rush toward the shower drain, Rickie's limp body slid down the tiled wall toward extinction. So hopelessly scrawny, never really developed into a woman, she appeared to the figure in the doorway as if she herself might slip away, disappearing into the shower drain forever. Mrs. Trousdale smiled at the pathetically comic sight. The image of that vicious smile—the last thing Rickie ever saw—would be imprinted on her soul for eternity.

10

"I'll just be a minute, Matthew. I'm going to take a quick shower."

Laura Nash climbed over the inert lump on the bed next to her. It wasn't until she was standing that she realized that the lump wasn't even breathing. Alarmed, she pulled back the blankets. Matthew Hanley wasn't even there.

Laura smiled and walked unsteadily into the bathroom. God, what a hangover, she moaned to herself. She and the headmaster had polished off two bottles of wine the night before. That plus the weed she had smoked back at school had put Laura way over the edge. Thank God I didn't do any coke, thought Laura. I'd probably be dead today. Shit, I wish I had a couple of lines right now. That would wake me up. Too bad it's back in my room. Oh, well, a cold shower will have to do.

As Laura lifted her leg to get into the tub, she stifled a groan. The insides of her thighs ached. Jesus, she thought, that was some workout last night. Good old Matthew was a nonstop fucking machine. After they had collapsed in each other's arms. Laura had assumed that they would be out for the night, but an amorous Matthew had woken her up at two a.m. for another round of lovemaking. It was then that they had broken open the second bottle of rosé. Laura wasn't absolutely sure if she had a hangover now or if she was still drunk.

Laura turned on the water and began soaping her body. She stood under the nozzle, letting the spray wash over her. She wondered where Matthew was—it was only 7:30. Shit, she thought, I must have been unconscious. I didn't even hear him get up. Then vaguely she remembered the ringing of a telephone. It had been sometime during the night and, for a second, she thought she had dreamed it. No, that was it. Someone had called and Matthew had to go somewhere. Laura hoped nothing was wrong.

She felt satisfied at the way things had gone last night. Even with his reputation as a ladies' man, Matthew had surprised her with his eagerness to get her between the sheets. Correction, we were screwing right on the floor. She was glad she had waited until she was a senior before sleeping with him. This way an otherwise boring year could pass by very nicely, even excitingly, and Matthew wasn't like some starry-eyed boy who would put pressure on her and start talking about love. They could shake hands at graduation and be happy with the memory of many hot nights in the sack.

Laura could feel herself reviving in the spray of the water. She closed her eyes and put her head back, allowing the water to rinse over her face and hair. Suddenly, she tensed. The water smelled odd—metallic, almost rusty. And there was something different about its consistency. It was slick and oily. Laura's eyes flew open in fear. Her face twisted in revulsion. Gushers of blood were raining down in her. Laura's entire body was awash in a nauseating crimson foam. She jumped from the tub and ran screaming from the room.

A special assembly was called for noon that day in the auditorium. Word of Rickie's death had spread through the student body like a brushfire. Now the girls sat stunned as Matthew Hanley addressed them in somber tones.

Laura Nash sat in the very last row of seats, as close to the door as possible. Her face was ashen and she trembled a little, but she sat up straight. Whatever insanity had prompted Rickie to take her own life, Laura knew that she herself had to be strong or that madness might threaten her. The guilt that she felt at the way she had treated Rickie was somehow lessened by the suspicion that something more powerful than any of them had driven Rickie to actions that were totally uncharacteristic of her. Rickie had always been a troubled girl, but she didn't make passes at Laura because she was a lesbian. She hadn't slashed her wrists because Laura had rebuked her. Some alien force had persuaded Rickie to end her life. Laura recalled the other night when she had gotten the creeps crossing the lawn—and she was a strong, rational girl. If Rickie had experienced similar sensations, she might have been too fragile and vulnerable to withstand them. Laura knew she had to be strong and watchful or she might be in trouble, too.

"Early this morning," Matthew said in a subdued voice from the stage, "I was awakened by a phone call. It was a very distressed Mrs. Trousdale, the caretaker of our school, informing me that she had found the body of someone we were genuinely fond of here at Hanley. I'm speaking of Regina Webster . . . many of you knew her as Rickie . . ."

Laura glanced down a few rows. Ingrid Strummer was signaling to her with a silver flask. "You look terrible, Laura," she whispered. "Want a slug?"

Laura shook her head. The last thing she needed right now was alcohol. She was still trying to clear the cobwebs from her brain.

Ingrid turned to Marie, who was sitting beside her. Marie took a pull on the flask gratefully. Unlike Laura, who hadn't been able to shed a tear, both girls' eyes were red from crying.

"There's more where that came from," Ingrid said, taking back the flask. "I have a feeling we're going to need it today."

Marie looked wistful. "I think we're going to need it all year."

"Rickie was an exceptional student," Matthew went on, "but she also had her share of emotional problems. As headmaster of Hanley, I only wish that we could have seen the signs of anxiety. Perhaps we could have helped her . . ."

In the fifth row, Barbara Price, the chemistry teacher, wiped a tear from her eye. Two seats over sat Karin Sayers, looking hard and indifferent. The drama teacher's hair hung loosely to her shoulders, and her mouth was set in stern lines, accentuated by a scarlet gash of lipstick. She seemed not to hear a single word Matthew was saying.

"Rickie is gone," he continued. "We will all miss her, but it's the beginning of the school term. We have a long year ahead of us. We mustn't let this tragedy weigh upon our minds and cause us to lose faith with one another."

Vanessa studied Matthew intently from the first row, only a few feet away from him. A new awareness was dawning in her eyes. Maybe it was the way the headmaster filled out his navy blue suit or the way he spoke with such a calm, authoritative tone. Matthew sounded so caring when he talked about the loss of Rickie. How could Vanessa never have noticed before what a striking, sensitive man he was? And now he was taking command in such a difficult situation. Even though he spoke to the audience as an entirety, he seemed to be reaching out to each one of them as individuals. He certainly had caught Vanessa's eye more than once from the podium. She had a sudden thrilling thought. What if he was singling her out from all the others? And if so, what did that mean?

Vanessa felt a surge of hope. If Matthew Hanley cared about her—and his quick, darting glances indicated that he might—then perhaps she could confide in him about the supernatural occurrences that had dogged her ever since she'd come to Hanley. If the horrific visions were some kind of warning—if that poor girl hanging in the auditorium had been struggling to communicate with her—then maybe Matthew Hanley, who knew this school better than any man alive, could shed some light on it. For all Vanessa knew, something like what she was going through might have happened to another girl before. Maybe she wasn't the first victim.

Suddenly, with a yearning that surprised her, she missed Rickie Webster very much.

Over at The Abbott School, Bobby Cannon kept glancing at his watch. A few more minutes and World History would be over. The teacher was rattling on about the Peloponnesian War, and Bobby had no idea what he was saying. There was a lengthy pause. Bobby saw a few hands shoot up around him. Oh shit, he thought, Mr. Palance had just asked a question. The old teacher had a habit of calling on kids who didn't raise their hand. Bobby had to think quickly. He lifted his arm, but just barely. The history teacher scanned the rows of students and then called on Dennis Bellivin, who was waving his hand confidently.

Bobby didn't even have to listen to know that Dennis was giving the correct answer. Dennis always did. His voice rang out and Bobby caught the words "Sparta," "Athens" and "The Peace of Nicias." He still didn't have a clue what his friend was talking about. He looked at his watch again.

Dennis was amplifying his answer now. That was another trick of his to impress the teachers, always throwing in extra information that hadn't been asked for. Bobby felt himself growing annoyed. How could Dennis be taking the trouble to brown-nose the teacher when just a few hours earlier he and Bobby had watched from their window through binoculars as the police had carted Rickie Webster's lifeless body away in a rubber bag with as much feeling as if they were hauling a sack of potatoes? Dennis might be Bobby's best friend but sometimes his behavior was astonishing.

Dennis had shown almost no reaction this morning when they'd learned of Rickie's suicide. To Bobby, he had seemed strangely indifferent. True, Bobby and Dennis had never been really close to Rickie, but how could you remain aloof about such a young girl who had killed herself in such a terrible way? Even kids at Abbott who had never met Rickie Webster were shocked and saddened by her death. The whole school was buzzing about what had happened, yet Dennis acted as if it were no big deal.

That night, Bobby would awaken to the roar of rain pounding on the window. In a cold sweat from yet another unremembered nightmare, he would look across the room and see that the bed opposite him was empty. Dennis had gotten up from sleep sometime during the night and was out there somewhere, brooding in the downpour. Bobby's first thought would be that Dennis did care—he must be upset about Rickie. Bobby wanted to believe that.

Dennis Bellivin sat in the boathouse looking out at The Hanley School through the rain. He was deep in thought. But Rickie Webster was the furthest thing from his mind.

Part Two

11

During the ensuing weeks, the memory of Rickie Webster faded like the colors of the autumn leaves. The initial shock which had buffeted Hanley and Abbott gave way as September slipped into October and the attention of the students was diverted to thoughts of football games, the Harvester Dance and the fall play. Laura Nash continued to see Matthew on the sly, though the headmaser was away for several weekends in Connecticut, investigating job offers from some other private schools. Dennis Bellivin led the Abbott football team to three consecutive victories and was elected president of the student government. Ingrid Strummer no longer made a secret of her heavy drinking; she was missing classes on occasion and was already in danger of failing biology. Bobby Cannon realized his dream of going out with Marie; there was no romance yet but the other Abbott boys began to look at him in a different light when he would escort her back from cheerleader practice. Karin Sayers conducted rehearsals of "The Dark" with a fervor that, at times, was a little frightening. True to her word, Evelyn Forbes had returned to

Boston, furnishing Vanessa with a complete fall wardrobe from Paris. Vanessa left the clothes, with their tags still on them, in a trunk. More than anything, she wished the visions would go away.

One morning in mid-October, Vanessa was gathering her books for class. Across the room, Laura, half-asleep, was drying her hair.

"I didn't hear you last night," Vanessa said. "What time did you get in?"

"I didn't. I got in this morning. Half an hour ago."

"You'd better watch it. Some of the kids were talking about you and Matthew. Ingrid saw you coming out of the cottage the other day."

Laura looked up, a bit annoyed. "So? Ingrid knows what's going on."

"That's not the point. She could have been anybody. What if she had been Mrs. Trousdale?"

"You mean The Hulk? Jesus, if Ingrid was Mrs. Trousdale, she'd *really* have an excuse to be fucked up."

"I'm serious, Laura. I just don't want you to have a problem."

Laura turned off the dryer and began rolling her prebreakfast joint. "Uh-uh, it's not my problem. It's Matthew's. He's taking a lot bigger risk than I am." She batted her eyelashes in mock innocence. "I'm just the underage girl who's being taken advantage of."

"Just try to be careful, okay?"

"Yeah, yeah," Laura said, waving her hand dismissively. "So what did you do last night?"

"Dennis took me bowling."

Laura smiled. "Bowling? Is that all? You still haven't slept with him?"

"I told you I don't want to talk about that."

"I never thought of Dennis as the patient type. He certainly wasn't that way with me. He must really like you."

Vanessa finished collecting her books. "I think he does. Relationships aren't just jumping in and out of bed, you know."

"Mine usually are."

Vanessa sat down across from Laura. She didn't have much time before her first class, but her roommate had just given her a perfect opening to pursue something that had been nagging at her for weeks. "Don't you and Matthew ever talk about anything?"

Laura puffed on her joint. "Oh, sure, we talk all the time. Are we going to do it on the bed or standing up? Should we have white wine? Should we drink a six-pack? And then there's always should we leave the lights on?"

Vanessa smiled briefly, but went on. "But Matthew strikes me as the kind of guy who'd be a good listener. Like he would understand."

"Understand what?"

"I don't know," Vanessa said, hesitantly. "Any problems you might be having."

"I'm not sure that I have any problems—not the kind that I would tell him about."

"Do you ever talk to Matthew about the school?"

"What are you getting at?"

"The weird stuff that goes on here. The crazy angles in the rooms. The light. The feeling of being watched . . ." Vanessa's voice trailed off.

Laura blew smoke into the air. "Are you kidding? I could never talk to Matthew about that stuff. He's a Hanley. His people built this place."

"Yeah, but that's exactly why he might understand."

Laura shook her head. "I don't think so."

"Why not?" Vanessa asked, her voice rising with conviction. "Maybe it's also happened to him. He's spent more time in this school than any of us."

Laura thought that over for a minute. "Yeah, but if none of that funny stuff happened to him, he'll think we're all nuts."

"Did he think when you saw blood in the shower that you were nuts then?"

"I never told him," Laura said in a small voice.

"Why not?"

"I'm not sure he would have believed me," Laura admitted, "and I guess I didn't want him thinking I'm just some hysterical girl."

Vanessa's hopes were sinking. Laura was a strong person, and if she were afraid to tell Matthew about a traumatic experience, how could Vanessa ever hope to get up enough courage to confide in him? Maybe Laura was right. The headmaster *was* a Hanley. How could she suggest to him that the school might be controlled by a supernatural force? Besides, Vanessa had not been harmed by any of her strange visions, at least not physically. Maybe the thing to do was simply make it through senior year and then be rid of this place forever.

Laura seemed to read her last thought. "You know, Vanessa, graduation isn't that far away. If we both stick together, and we don't make waves, we can get through this. Next June, we'll walk out that front gate for the last time and we'll give this whole fucking place the finger."

Vanessa laughed and felt a certain relief. But on her way to class, something troubled her. It wasn't like Laura not to make waves. Vanessa wondered if her roommate was just as scared as she was.

A thin line of perspiration beaded Karin Sayer's upper lip as she hurried down the backstairs that afternoon on her way to four o'clock rehearsal. Lines from "The Dark" echoed inside her brain. Today was the day they were going to rehearse the stake burning scene. Karin could hardly wait and had been in a near frenzy since early morning.

This scene had to be perfect, and that was why Karin didn't have a minute to spare. The backstairs led right into the makeup room, where the drama teacher would be able to get ready. It wasn't enough just to tell the students how to play witches. After all, they were just kids. Today Karin Sayers would have to show them.

Karin sat at the makeup table and switched on the

fluorescent lit mirror. From the nearby stage area she could hear the conversation of the students who were waiting for her and recognized the voice of the Forbes girl. Vanessa already had showed some promise, but she was only an adequate actress. She would need a mentor like Karin in order to fully immerse herself in her character.

Karin laughed in childish delight, picturing the images of the students when she performed the part of the beautiful Emily—part witch, part seductress and, with Karin as the tutor, all woman. The drama teacher had even dressed for the role of Emily today. She wanted everything to be perfect.

A sharp pain shot through Karin's head, like a thin sliver of metal her pierced her brain. She grew dizzy and had to close her eyes for fear of falling off the chair. As quickly as the pain had come, it dissipated. Karin opened her eyes and glanced up at her reflection. The woman who stared back at her appeared haunted, but that was not what made Karin catch her breath in alarm. The person in the mirror seemed a stranger to her. It had something to do with the way she was dressed. The low-cut peasant blouse, caught up tightly at the waist, made Karin's breasts appear fuller than they were. Her black skirt was so tight Karin wondered how she had ever gotten into it. Then there was her skin. Even with the heavy makeup she had applied, it looked ghostly white, making her eyes appear as if they were about to bulge from their sockets. My God, thought Karin. I look worse than a witch. I look positively demented. *Sinner! Clean your face off, girl. You'll be following your tramp mother to an early grave if I see you looking like that again. Daddy, stop, you're hurting me. The rough washcloth rubbed hard on Karin's soft young skin as her father scrubbed her face until it almost bled. I'll drive the devil from you yet, girl, or I'll see you dead.* Karin shook her head violently back and forth. No, not now. Don't think about that. She had to prepare. She forced the unpleasant memories away, but they threatened to creep back, like the tendrils of damp hair that clung to her neck.

A warm current of air rushed to her aid, creating a vacuum of heat that seemed to draw the tension from Karin. The white haze of warmth blanketed her, soothing and familiar. She felt grateful for the balmy air that was starting to feel like an old companion.

Just then, the soft, comforting aura was disturbed by the scent of something pungent. A face was pressed close to hers seeming to have come out of nowhere, and Karin detected the unmistakable smell of alcohol. She turned and faced Ingrid Strummer.

"Miss Sayers," the stage manager said, "everyone's ready."

"Are they?" Karin said, vaguely. She made a mental note to talk to Ingrid sometime soon about her drinking. Karin had noticed it before, and there were very strict rules about that sort of behavior. Karin stood and adjusted the elastic on her blouse so as to accentuate her cleavage, her action not unnoticed by Ingrid.

Karin strutted onto the stage, basking in the immediate attention that her appearance elicited from the students. The girls stared open-mouthed at Karin's provocative, almost indecent, outfit, and from the boys came an irreverent whistle of appreciation. At the side of the stage, Bobby Cannon turned to Dennis and raised an eyebrow. "Jesus Christ," he said, "she looks just like a whore."

After the flurry of excitement died down, Karin began the rehearsal, putting the students through their paces with a vigor even more pronounced than before. The drama teacher was everywhere, her eyes sparkling as she exhorted the young actors to a higher intensity. Breathless at times, she offered constant admonishments, teasing the students and egging them on to match her own zeal. Some of the weaker students threatened to cave in under her continuing pressure, but others, like Dennis Bellivin, seemed to thrive on it.

Before an hour was up, the Hanley and Abbott actors were rehearsing at a new fever pitch, and Karin had guided them so adroitly that they had reached this higher level without even realizing what was happening. The young people were unaware how easily they were slipping into their characters. Stalking the stage like a seductive bird of prey, Karin Sayers was directing with a fury.

A ten minute break was long overdue but Karin had no intention of stopping the momentum. She called Vanessa and Dennis to center stage for the pivotal burning at the stake scene. In the wings, Laura Nash moaned with annoyance and nudged Ingrid for another sip from her flask.

"God," Laura complained, "at this rate, we'll be here all night."

Karin fixed Dennis and Vanessa with a commanding stare. "Now listen, you two, this is a scene of absolute passion. I want to see sexuality. I want you to make love to each other with every word you speak."

Vanessa looked uneasy, but Dennis smiled with self-assurance. Karin took a seat downstage and waited for them to begin.

Vanessa addressed Dennis, speaking haltingly. "And by the holy rites of Hecate, I call Adrian, by the ties of love, to stroke my flesh, to lay with me . . ."

Karin jumped up, waving her arms. "Passion, Vanessa," she shouted. "You want him to ravage you!"

Vanessa nodded uncertainly. She cleared her throat and started again. "And by the holy rites of Hecate, I call Adrian . . ."

Karin moved forward, took Vanessa by the shoulders and edged her aside. "Not like that, Vanessa," she said gently. "Like this."

She stood a few feet from Dennis. Her eyes went out to him imploringly. The audience of students grew hushed as the drama teacher leaned forward, speaking in a breathy voice, barely above a whisper.

"And by the holy rites of Hecate, I call Adrian, by the ties of love, to stroke my flesh, to lay with me in a field of stone . . ."

Dennis could feel his stomach muscles tightening. Karin's eyes, heavy-lidded and alluring, were having a disturbing effect on him. He felt himself magnetized, as if he were being drawn into her very being. At the same time, Dennis could feel himself growing aroused. It was hard to believe that this drama teacher was merely playing a role. This seemed like much more.

". . . to submerge himself in a Flower of Darkness . . ."

Karin had cupped her palms and was running them enticingly over her full breasts. Dennis nervously watched her, increasingly excited. She moved her hands lower to her hips, letting them linger there, and shifted so that her legs were slightly apart. In her tight black skirt, with the upper part of her body arched, she seemed to be beckoning to him. God, he thought, this woman is hot.

". . . to entwine our limbs, to let your heat come into my body . . ."

Bobby Cannon had come up to stand beside Laura. "Something's wrong with Vanessa," he whispered.

"Vanessa? Something's wrong with Sayers. Check her out."

"No, I'm serious. She looks scared to death."

Laura glanced over at Vanessa. She could see that the girl was pale and trembling slightly. But Laura's attention reverted to the drama teacher. She had never seen her like this.

Karin drew nearer to Dennis, pressing her body sensuously against his. "I call you, Adrian, warm seed, warm heart; let us never be apart."

There was a drunken titter from Ingrid Strummer which broke the spell that Karin Sayers had created. One could almost hear the students let out their collective breath, hoping that the intensity of Karin's performance was over. Vanessa Forbes did not look relieved. No one had noticed she had inched away from Karin and Dennis. No one paid attention to the look of abject horror on her face.

"Do you want to talk about it?" Bobby asked Vanessa as they watched the sun set on the lake.

"Talk about what?"

"When Sayers was doing her speech, I was watching you. You looked terrified."

Vanessa looked dreamily out at the orange glow on the water. She felt reluctant to tell Bobby about all the thoughts that were churning in her mind. She had already confided in Dennis and told Laura about some of her fears. Bobby might be just one more person that would tell her it was simply her imagination. Vanessa felt defeated, but what did she have to lose? Besides, there was always the chance Bobby would understand.

"I've been seeing things," she began slowly, "ever since I came to Hanley. I've been hearing things, too. Dennis says it's all in my mind, but it isn't. I think it's the school."

Vanessa stole a glance at Bobby. She had half-expected him to be looking at her skeptically. Instead, his expression was sympathetic. Oddly, he looked somewhat relieved. Had Vanessa touched a nerve in him?

"Go on, Vanessa," he urged softly..

For the next half hour, Vanessa poured out to Bobby all the horrors she had experienced since coming to the school. Bobby listened attentively—he didn't interrupt even once—and Vanessa sensed a growing rapport between them. The sun was well below the horizon when she finally finished, and Vanessa felt purged.

"I've gone through all of this, Bobby," she concluded, "and I don't think I'm the only one either. All the girls I've talked to say there's something wrong here even if they haven't seen all the stuff I've seen. And I know of one case that's just as crazy as anything that's happened to me. Laura was taking a shower one day and she swears that blood came out of the nozzle. Not just blood, Bobby, gushers of it." She looked at Bobby hopefully. "What do you think?"

"Well," Bobby said, "if you think you're nuts, then I must be nuts, too. I didn't see any of the shit you saw, but I know what you mean. I know that feeling of being watched, and you won't catch me walking around the Hanley grounds after dark—not by myself anyway."

Vanessa reached out to Bobby and hugged him gratefully. She had a sudden thought since night was falling rapidly. "You're not scared being here right now, are you? I mean just the two of us?"

Bobby gave her a half-grin. "Well, I wasn't till you mentioned it."

"Maybe you should go soon."

Bobby nodded. "Not until you tell me what happened to you today."

"You mean in the auditorium?" Vanessa looked alarmed. "Did everybody see how scared I was?"

"If you're talking about Dennis, the only thing he was looking at was Karin Sayers' breasts."

"I know, Bobby, but he didn't see what I saw. I'm sure nobody did. When Miss Sayers started to do the part, I saw her turn into a witch. I mean a real witch from a long time ago, slowly, bit by bit. The longer she talked the uglier she got. She turned into one of those horrible old crones like you see on Halloween."

"Jesus, this place is fucked."

Vanessa got to her feet. "You know, I never told anybody this before tonight but I trust you, Bobby, and I think you believe me."

Bobby stood up and squeezed her hand. "I do believe you."

"I think Rickie Webster's death was no suicide. I think something drove her to do that."

"I don't know, Vanessa. Rickie always was a little strange."

"A lot of people are strange but they don't kill themselves. When I saw that girl hanging from the noose in the auditorium, I felt like she was giving me a warning. Rickie's death was another warning. Did you ever hear about the history of this place?"

"About the murders? Everybody's heard that."

"No, I mean before that. This place was barren land. Nothing would grow here."

Slow recognition on Bobby's face. "The last line of 'The Dark.' "

Karin Sayers had dreamt about her father again last night. This morning she remembered the dream because the whispers in her room had told her she could. Karin had tried to put the memories out of her mind, but the murmuring had grown stronger, even angry.

In her black satin nightgown, Karin lay very still on her bed. The room was stifling this morning, but she did not want to disturb the stillness by getting up to open a window. A lazy, sticky warmth grazed Karin's body, mixing with her own heat.

Oh, God. He's burning up in there. Daddy! Help. Someone help him.

The breath of the fiery blast roared in the young girl's ears. I didn't mean it. I've killed him. Oh, God, he's going to burn up and die and I won't have anyone.

The girl stood and watched the scorching flames dissolve her father's flesh. Like a wax figure, Henry Sayers was melting into his own altar. Karin choked on the smell of his death. The sickeningly sweet odor of charred human meat fused with the stench of the gasoline that soaked her pale blue dress. I'm sorry, Daddy. You shouldn't have hurt me so much. You made me do bad things. Now you have to die. The young Karin Sayers was going into shock. Spittle dribbled down her dirt-streaked chin and a demented snicker erupted from her throat. She began to dance in a circle, the red haze of the flames her companion. It was Karin's celebration. Just Karin and the night knew what really happened. For years, the night had been Karin's enemy. As darkness crept up on her, it would bring her father into the room where she slept. Towering above her, his breath a foul stench of whiskey, Henry Sayers waved The Discipliner. And then, with his other hand, he touched her down there. But that was only the beginning. He did horrible things to her—hurting her, spreading her open. Now the night was Karin's friend, shielding her in a blanket of silky ebony, hiding her. Only the night phantoms were witness to the murder. And each soulless form, whirling in the flames, told another the story. Karin had heard the night creatures whispering about her. She didn't care anymore. As the windows of the crude wooden church shattered, raining shards of glass on Karin, blood flowed with the young girl's perspiration. Karin smiled as she rubbed at her body, feeling the places where her hair had been singed. The fires of hell were consuming her father in the very church he had built, where he had preached the word of God. Hypocrite. Child molester. Rapist. Karin danced in an endless circle. Not until her thin legs threatened to give out—not until her heart was hammering so hard she thought it would burst from her chest—not until she saw the orange glow from the rising sun did she finally sink down to rest. In the morning, when the townspeople found her, Karin lay curled in a ball next to the ruined church. There wasn't a mark on her. No blood. No scratches. No scorched flesh. She lay sleeping like a baby. She had thought she heard the neighbors saying she looked so much like her mother. It had given one of the God-fearing ladies quite a scare.

The heat in Karin's room intensified as the sun seeped through the stained-glass window. Suddenly, Karin felt certain that she was not alone in her room. Before, she had just heard and sensed the whispers. Now she sensed something more. Something unknown was slithering along the floor in an invisible world of unmistakable evil. Karin's fear mixed with an odd feeling of honor. She knew that she was being let in on a secret, that the presence was giving her a hint of its mystery. Intuitively, she knew that in the past only a few chosen people had been aware of it. Now Karin felt she might be alone in her grasp of its existence. Though she felt privileged, her fear was stronger and self-preservation made her leap from the bed. The rush of truth that assaulted her was chilling even in the oppressive heat of her room. My God, she thought, I'm losing my mind. The presence mocked her as she ran to the bathroom, slamming the door as if a thin plank of wood could shut out the disembodied creature in the next room.

Karin turned on the bathroom light and watched as the bulb seemed to explode into prisms of colored illumination, casting daggers about the room. Momentarily blinded by the brilliance, Karin closed her eyes briefly, then opened them. She looked into the mirror, trying to block out the fear by concentrating on her image. Karin's eye shadow was smeared from the day before; ringlets of hair shimmered wildly like thousands of snakes about her face.

What's happening to me? Karin ran her fingers through her hair to straighten some of the tangle. What have I been doing to myself? I'm not even sure who I am anymore. And those ungodly whispers! Karin's eyes darted to the bathroom door. What was in her bedroom? What was in The Hanley School? Karin knew that something was wrong at Hanley this year. She had sensed it from the first day of the term. Her uneasiness had not been her imagination. But why now, after all these years? Karin fought back the tears. She didn't believe in ghosts but there was something about Hanley this semester that was haunted. Still, it wasn't some spirit that was making Karin look so drawn and haggard. No ghost was controlling her behavior. The conclusion was evident: she was having some kind of nervous breakdown. Guilt. She had lived with so much of it all this time. Why was she dressing like a whore? Why was she making up her face to disguise her natural beauty with a look that was so grotesque? Karin guessed that she was behaving this way as a means of escape. I'm changing my appearance so I can become somebody else, Karin rationalized, so I don't have to face who I really am. That was the answer. Karin *hoped* it was the answer.

Hands touched her head. No, leave me alone! *We've missed you, Karin*. Was that her mother's voice amidst the murmuring? Daddy? The heat slid in under the bathroom door and licked at her feet, knowing and understanding her. Karin and the warm breeze were sisters. Theirs was a mutual dependence. I'm not losing my mind, Karin insisted, I'm not. The mist seemed to cloak her brain in a strange cover of darkness. *Welcome back, Karin. We'll take care of you now. You have nothing to fear*. A chorus of voices reassured her. Karin's knuckles grew white as she clutched the edge of the sink. No, please don't let them take me, she pleaded inwardly. Out loud she shouted, "What do you want from me?"

Karin stood motionless. She struggled to hold onto sanity and reality, but it was too late. Something dreadful had happened. Something final. The world had changed. The unknown had entered Karin Sayers' life. Karin's lips drew back and parted. From then came peal after peal of maniacal laughter.

The sun was strong, but the first nip of winter was in the air. Walter Cox didn't need the cold weather as an excuse to take a few extra swigs from his bourbon flask this morning. Hell, Walter didn't need an excuse to do anything. He was his own man. He had to be, surrounded by all the pussies in this school.

Entering the utility room, Walter could already hear the sound of girls cavorting on the other side of the wall. He adjusted the stepladder and eased his gaunt frame up to its usual perch. Quickly, he gouged out the plaster from the peephole, positioning his bloodshot eye to the tiny aperture. He grinned. There were four girls there, all naked as jaybirds.

Walter salivated. The Polish twat with the big jugs was soaping herself only a few feet away. The handyman wasted no time going for his zipper. He hadn't seen the Kronofsky girl in the shower for a couple of weeks and she was one of his favorites. The last time he'd spotted her, she'd managed to work him up real good. Walter had gotten half-hard that day and things might have gotten better but Marie had left the shower room too quickly. Walter needed time to get his juices flowing since he wasn't as young as he used to be. This morning Marie was shampooing her hair. That meant she'd stick around for a little bit, giving Walter the extra few minutes he needed—if it was going to happen at all.

He squinted through the peephole, pumping away at himself with his right hand. Marie was joined in the shower by Ingrid Strummer. She stepped out of her bathrobe and Walter threw her a quick glance. Ingrid wasn't much to look at—her tits were average and she had no ass to speak of—but Walter liked her. A few days ago, he'd caught her taking a nip from a can of beer between classes. He had smiled at her knowingly, and she'd winked back at him. Ever since then, Walter had entertained the possibility that maybe she fancied him. He'd get naked with her in a minute, but that was just fantasy. Whacking off to Marie was real.

Walter paused in mid-stroke. He had heard something —a peculiar knocking in the pipes. The school's plumbing was antiquated and he was used to its constant clanging and thumping, but this noise was different—a piercing whine that went right through Walter's nervous system, making him wince. He wondered if the pressure was building up in the pipes. Walter made a mental note to check on it later. Right now he was too busy. His attention was riveted to Marie's body which was having the desired effect. Walter was going rigid with excitement.

Just then there was another noise, more immediate than the squealing pipes. It made the blood freeze in Walter Cox's old veins. "Oh, shit," Walter said aloud as he saw the doorknob to the utility room turn slowly. Someone was coming in from the landing. Walter had forgotten to lock the door. He cursed his luck and fumbled with his pants, desperately trying to stuff his erection back into his boxer shorts. As he tugged at his zipper frantically, he was caught in a thin sliver of light. The door was opening. "Jesus Christ," Walter spat. His pants were still open, and he would never be able to get the plaster back in the wall.

Suddenly, the room was flooded with light. A figure was outlined in the doorway. What Walter saw made his heart leap, and he shook with panic. He had really fucked up this time. This could cost him his job.

"I wasn't doing anything," Walter protested. "I was just looking for a broom. I wasn't doing anything, honest!"

Walter stopped. Something told him there was no need to go on making excuses. He could tell by the seductive pose of the intruder—firm, round hips wrapped enticingly in leather and jutting forward to outline her crotch—that snitching on him for spying on the girls was hardly on her mind. The sheer, see-through blouse with a low-cut lace bra made Karin Sayers look like a $25 whore Walter had seen one time in an alley in Boston.

Karin pushed the door closed with the stiletto heel of her shoe, then shot the bolt on the door. She and Walter Cox were alone now in the dark, cramped quarters. Karin began unbuttoning her blouse. His open trousers forgotten now, Walter brought his hand to his throat in astonishment as Karin Sayers' luscious breasts were exposed. In a matter of moments, she stood nude before him. Walter gaped at her, cowering in the corner.

Walter's mind was buzzing. This wasn't something from the pages of *Naughty Nymphettes*, and this wasn't some girl on the other side of the shower room wall. This was Miss Sayers, a minister's daughter. She was a girl brought up as a good Christian. What was she doing here in a dingy, damp backstairs room, running her hand along her pussy like she expected him to do something, for Christ's sake? Oh, he'd been watching this crazy broad lately. He'd seen how she changed from Miss

Prim-and-Proper-Tightass the last few weeks into a real cockteaser. Everyone at the school was talking about it. If they only could see her now—naked with the janitor. This was too nuts to be true. She must have really gone over the edge.

Karin moistened her lips with the tip of her tongue. The way she looked at him, with her tits thrown forward like that, was making it hard for Walter to remain still. He felt dizzy. Walter had a sudden thought. What if this was a come-on, a trick? She was looking at him with those big eyes but he could just see himself making a move on her. She was acting so crazy lately. What if she was the kind of hysterical bitch that would scream "Rape!" the minute he put his hands on her. Walter might lose his job after all.

For the first time in years, Walter wished he wasn't such a drunkard. If only he could think clearly. He should never have had that bourbon. Karin Sayers was just standing there, looking so goddamn sure of what he was going to do. Walter wished he knew what he was going to do. He knew he should bolt out of the room, get the hell out of there, or he'd really be up shit's creek. But Karin had her hands on her lovely hips now and had lifted one leg slightly, resting it on a toolbox nearby. Walter stared at the dark patch of hair between her legs. It looked like it was his for the taking. Wait a minute, he thought. Who was the crazy one anyway? This was pussy being handed to him on a silver platter. If he passed up a shot like this, Walter would hate himself for the rest of his natural life.

He put his hand to his still opened trousers. With a mischievous grin, he realized that he was more than ready for her. Still, he remained in the corner, feeling awkward. It had been a long time—too long to remember. Stupid as it seemed, he wasn't sure how to make the first move, but he didn't have to. Karin Sayers made it for him.

As Karin brought her face down between his legs,

Walter felt a twinge of remorse. He wished he didn't have on these Army surplus drawers, but his one pair of briefs—the sexy red ones with the hearts on them—was tucked away in his bureau for special occasions.

"Well, what sort of outfit do you think Sayers will have on this morning?" Laura Nash smiled at Vanessa across their cafeteria breakfast trays, as the morning sun cast bright pockets of light over the room.

Vanessa buttered her toast. "I don't know. something from Frederick's of Hollywood?"

"Maybe today's the day she'll go topless."

Vanessa giggled. "You know, it wouldn't surprise me. She's certainly changed a lot in one month. She never even used to wear makeup."

"Yeah, and now she lays it on with a fucking roller. You think she's got a kinky boy friend in town?"

Vanessa looked serious. "I think it's the school. It changes people."

"Hey, it hasn't changed me," Laura said. "It hasn't changed Ingrid."

"It's changed me," Vanessa said quietly. "And it has so changed Ingrid. She's drinking so much that she doesn't care who knows it."

"So? She's just being more honest. The girl's an alcoholic. She had a drinking problem before she even came here. Now she just falls down in public—that's the only difference."

"It's not funny."

Laura folded her arms and looked at Vanessa challengingly. "Okay, how has the school changed you?"

"I'm not sure. These things I've been seeing . . .I'm afraid. It's like my feelings aren't my own. I've been frightened before but this is something from inside. I can't explain it."

"Try."

"I don't know. Didn't you feel different after you saw

the blood come out of the shower that time?"

Laura considered this. "Sure, I admit it. Now when I take a shower, I don't get under the water right away. I stand back for a couple of seconds. Who knows what the fuck's going to come out? But that's not really changing. That's just being careful. Let's face it, this whole place spooks both of us. Maybe we do get scared more now, but we're still the same people. We still dress the same, and we're not shoveling on makeup." Laura paused. "We're still behaving the way we always did."

"Maybe it's just me then, Laura. Sometimes I feel like my own emotions are being dictated from somewhere else. You haven't felt that, have you?"

"No," Laura admitted. "I'm not even sure what the hell that means."

Vanessa wanted to answer but stopped herself. Laura was having an affair with Matthew Hanley. How could Vanessa possibly tell her of the inexplicable, almost overwhelming attraction she'd been feeling for the headmaster ever since the day of Rickie Webster's death? It had come over her so abruptly and had seemed so foreign her that Vanessa felt it bordered on the abnormal. That morning during the eulogy for Rickie, Vanessa had pondered about confiding to Matthew all her fears and insecurities regarding the school, but so far she hadn't been able to do so. If she couldn't bring herself to unburden herself to the headmaster, how could she tell the girl he was sleeping with? That would amount to the same thing. She had never even told Laura about the visions—not really—but what she felt for Matthew Hanley, this powerful magnetic draw, was not a vision. It came from within Vanessa, but how did it get inside there? And why was it growing stronger every day? It wasn't like some vision where you could close your eyes for a second and it would go away. Vanessa looked across at Laura, who was still waiting for a reply. No, she couldn't tell her. It was better to remain silent until she could sort all these things out clearly in her mind.

"Maybe you're right," Vanessa conceded. "Maybe we really haven't changed."

Her sentence was punctuated by the shrill ringing of the school bell. Vanessa and Laura jumped at the sudden sound.

Laura looked embarrassed and laughed nervously. "I'm not so sure about that."

In the early 1950's, at the time of the Korean conflict, Walter Cox, as a young draftee in basic training, was ordered to run a mile, burdened with the weight of his full Army field gear, including M-1 rifle, back pack and ammunition belt. When he crossed the finish line, he'd collapsed in a heap, feeling so physically depleted that he thought he would never move again. In the intervening years, most of them spent in drunken laziness, he had often recalled that day in the mud at Fort Bliss, telling anyone who would listen that it was the most exhausted he had ever been in his life. He'd vowed that never again would he allow himself to be reduced to such a state of weakness and fatigue. This morning, after half an hour with Karin Sayers, his vow had gone down the shitter and Walter felt like he'd just run five miles and been flattened by an armored personnel carrier.

He lay on the cold floor of the utility room in the same position Karin had left him in five minutes before. He could barely move a muscle. His back ached from the rough wall he'd been jammed up against while they were doing it standing up. Twin charley horses gripped the insides of his thighs—he should never have wrapped his legs around Karin when they were on the floor—but those pains were nothing compared to the burning sensation in his groin. That girl had a mouth on her like a goddamn vise.

Walter looked at his pants, which were still tangled around his ankles. He was too tired even to reach down and pull them up. For the moment, it was so much nicer just to lie on his stomach, his sweaty face pressed to the cool tiled floor. Walter was certain he didn't ever want to get up again, but that was stupid. It was already time for him to be at work. The Trousdales, those goddamn slave drivers, would be looking for him. What if they found him, half-naked, passed out here? Walter would have a lot of explaining to do and he'd need all his strength to go looking for a new job.

He'd need his strength anyway. Karin would probably be back for more this time tomorrow since it was obvious that she had fallen for him. And why not? He had porked her within an inch of her life. He'd surprised himself with the tricks his withered old rod had been capable of, but, Jesus, he was paying the price now. Maybe at lunch time, instead of drinking, he should soak in a tub of warm water and load up on Vitamin E like he'd read in the advice column of *Stud Forum* magazine.

Walter thanked his lucky stars that whatever had driven Karin nuts—and there was no doubt in his mind that she had flipped out—had also driven her into his arms. Walter ran his palm along the stubble on his chin. Tomorrow would be different. He would shave and maybe put on some cologne. He felt like a new man. She might be a nutcase but Karin Sayers was one hell of a real woman.

For the first time since Karin had appeared in the doorway, Walter became aware that the utility room had grown unusually quiet—no laughing and shouting from the shower room, no sound at all from the pipes. It must be really late, Walter reasoned. He fumbled for his watch. It had stopped. He wound the timepiece and listened for its ticking. Instead he heard something else.

Squeeeak.

Whooooosh.

Something was making strange slurping noises deep within the school. Walter cocked an ear. It sounded like someone was working a squeegee down below. Walter was baffled. The sound was faint but distinct. If someone was removing water from one of the floors downstairs, the sound shouldn't have traveled this far. Of course Walter knew that in an old building like this one, sounds could play tricks on you, but he'd never heard anything quite like this. Damn it, he would have to investigate.

Walter got to his feet, nearly toppling over from the pants that were twisted around his ankles. He pulled up his trousers and tucked in his shirt. His legs wobbled unsteadily as he trudged painfully from the room. Out on the landing leading to the back stairway, Walter felt distracted. It was odd not knowing how long he had been in the utility room. Walter seemed to have completely lost track of time. Even the steps and the bannister seemed alien to him. He continued downstairs, supporting himself on one wall. Jesus, I'm like a fucking cripple, he thought.

One flight down, Walter came to the door marked "Auditorium." There was a mirror hanging there and the janitor caught a glimpse of his reflection. He looked stooped and unkempt, about ten years older than he had earlier that morning. "Oh, God, look at this," he said aloud, inspecting his neck. A purplish bruise on his rubbery skin peeped over the collar line of his shirt. "Christ, that's all I need," Walter muttered. "That bitch gave me a hickey." But as he groped his way downstairs, the handyman was secretly pleased at this badge of his reawakened sexuality.

The next landing led to the stage level of the auditorium. *Squeeeak*. *Whoooosh*. There were the noises again, only this time louder.

A few feet away was the backstage storeroom. Walter unlocked the door. Inside the musty room, the noises were closer, almost palpitating. Walter picked up a flashlight from one of the shelves and headed for the winding flight of stairs at the back of the storeroom. The noises were at least one level further down.

Walter descended the claustrophobic stairway and found himself in the furnace room. This was a familiar area to him, his work often taking him down here. He let the ray from the flashlight play along the walls, pausing at the large, metal-plated door that dominated one side of the room. Walter had never been certain exactly where that door led to. When he had first started working at Hanley and Desmond Trousdale took him on a tour of the building, the old caretaker had pronounced that door off-limits. Walter had never been issued a key to the padlock that always hung there. Now he squinted in the dim light and saw that the padlock was gone and the metal-plated door stood slightly ajar.

Walter hesitated a few feet from the door. The palpitating sounds were coming from somewhere downstairs and this door must lead there. Walter recalled Desmond's warning. "Stay away from this door. It doesn't concern you." That had been fine with Walter. It was one less key he had to carry around on the chain that dangled from his belt. But what if there was something wrong downstairs? What if someone was in trouble and that was the reason for the strange, pumping noises? If there were a problem anywhere in the school, that had to concern Walter, didn't it?

Walter brightened as he realized that he was legitimately investigating an unusual sound on the premises. That was his job, and if anyone had been looking for him earlier, while he was with Karin Sayers, he now had the perfect alibi. He'd been scouting around downstairs, trying to find out what the hell was going on. The metal-plated door yawned open, and Walter was curious to know what lay behind it. *Squeeeak. Whooosh. Sluurrp.* The noises seemed to be calling him. Maybe he should go for help. Maybe he should get Desmond. But Walter was a new man now. No, he would investigate this himself.

There was just enough room for Walter to slide his wiry body through the door's opening. Immediately, he found himself on a small landing and trained his flashlight downward. Light was flickering from some kind of chamber below. On the wall of the landing, tied to a metal clamp, Walter noticed a rope ladder. He unhooked it, dropping it down into the semi-darkness. The noises had grown in volume, but that wasn't what disturbed Walter most. It was the nature of the sounds—sucking, chewing, gulping. Christ, thought Walter, it sounds like there's some animal down there having a feast.

Maybe it was rats, Walter guessed. No, the noise was much too loud. Some kind of wild dog? If so, Walter hoped the goddamn thing was chained up. And then he heard it, with just the faintest hint of urgency. *Walter.* Someone or something was calling him. *Walter.* It wasn't just one caller. It was a multitude, and all of them sounded vaguely like Karin Sayers.

"What the fuck?" Walter said under his breath. He looked at his hands. They were moist and shaking. He wondered if all the boozing he had done over the years had finally caught up with him. Maybe he was having the d.t.'s. He steadied himself. *Come. Walter.*

Walter felt compelled. He swung his body onto the rope ladder and climbed briskly down. As Walter's foot touched the hard, stone floor, it seemed to trigger a deathly silence. The whooshing, chomping noises had ceased. No one was calling his name.

Nervously, Walter looked around the small, low-ceilinged chamber. Lit by a profusion of candles, the room smelled of decay but was surprisingly immaculate. One side of the chamber was comprised of a stone slab resembling an ancient altar. A black cloth was stretched across it. On the fabric, Walter could recognize a strange design that seemed disturbingly familiar. He couldn't place exacctly what it was, though he suspected it was something he saw every day.

Above the alter hung an inverted cross. Walter knew that was some kind of symbol but had no idea what it meant. Nearby was an ornate stone stand on which a huge black volume rested. Walter tiptoed across the room. He felt intimidated, like some trespasser on sacred ground. He opened the massive book.

On the title page, etched inside a rectangle of scowling satyrs, mutant flowers and sharp-fanged rodents, were the words "The Book Of Necromancy."

A frown creased Walter's brow. He wasn't much for big words, but he didn't like the look of this one. And the drawings on the pages were nasty. He ran his fingers along the gold trim of the pages. What was this book doing here? What was this room all about? Who lit the candles? Who kept the place so spotless? How come the door upstairs was open like that when all this time it had been padlocked? Walter felt this small, forbidding chamber had been purposefully revealed to him and that someone might be watching his every move.

Something black and furry came into Walter's line of vision. He spun around just as feather-like feet brushed against his neck. Stumbling back, Walter hacked at the air frantically.

"Christ on a crutch," he exclaimed. "You scared the shit out of me."

Walter watched as the Trousdales' tarantula scurried off into the darkness.

The sudden presence of the spider was enough to convince Walter it was time to get out of there. Whoever's room this was—whether it was the Trousdales' or someone else's—Walter had no business down here. He'd better haul ass up that rope ladder and ask questions later, from the safety of the upper floors.

He started for the ladder. *Walter.*

The janitor tensed, then slowly relaxed. This had to be some kind of joke. Someone was hiding behind the wall or else the place was wired. Maybe there was a tape recorder on that other stone slab. Walter went over to it and lifted some black garments from the slab. There was nothing hidden there. Curious, Walter unfolded one of the items of clothing. It was the kind of robe that priests wore. He held the black garment up to his body and felt an instantaneous chill. The same inverted cross covered one whole side of the robe, embroidered in fine gold stitches. Walter put it back with the other garments.

Next to them on the stone, carved deeply into its core, was a five-pointed star with a circle in the center. Walter took a deep breath. He'd seen a few horror movies in his time and that sure looked like one of those pentagrams they were always talking about, but Walter couldn't remember what it was used for. Didn't it have something to do with sacrificial rites?

Tentatively, he reached out to touch the stone. *Sluurrp.* He jumped back. The stone had moved, but that was crazy. The fucking thing weighed a ton. And what was that sound? The noises were starting up again.

Walter reached for the rope ladder. This room was too goddamn spooky. *Squeeeak. Whooooosh.* The ladder dropped from the upper landing and fell into a useless coil at his feet.

Walter looked around. His eyes must be playing tricks on him again. The room had gotten smaller. He stared at the nearby wall, measuring its crevices to see if there was a way he could scale its surface up to the landing. He nodded with satisfaction. There were enough indentations in the stone wall—if he climbed carefully, he could make it.

The janitor reconsidered. What if he got halfway up and then fell? He could hurt himself badly, maybe break his back. Wouldn't it be better to just call out for help? Jesus, thought Walter, that's not the answer. Who's gong to hear me? Probably one of the Trousdales, and then I'll catch hell for being down here in the first place. They'll never believe I heard something down here. They'll just think I was drunk and snooping.

A terrifying thought hit Walter. What *had* he heard down here? He didn't have to wait long to find out.

Whooooosh. Deafening this time. Crashing in Walter's ears. Some unknown beast that inhabited and engulfed the room was drawing in its breath and gurgling in its bottomless throat. It sounded like some dreadful monster was about to devour him. So why couldn't Walter see it? Becoming completely sober in an instant, Walter moved quickly this time toward the wall. But he needn't have bothered. The wall, undulating, moved toward him.

Its crevices eaten away by age—those imperfections that before had promised Walter footholds to safety—were all growing smooth before his stunned eyes, creating a glassy, slippery surface to which it would be impossible to cling. *Pssshh*. Walter heard another noise—rustling, burbling. He spun around.

The wall behind him was closing in, contracting its chiseled features, becoming flawless and pristine. "Oh, God, help me," Walter pleaded. The walls roared back their dismissal. They inched forward. *Squeeeak*. *Sluurrp*. Walter struggled to breathe. The air was becoming thick, and he could feel the gritty smell of stone and decay clogging his lungs, choking feeble coughs from his fear-ravaged chest. Knowing it was hopeless, Walter still made a leap for the wall, his battered sneakers flailing out for traction. It was no use. The wall, still moving, would not give him a grip. Walter fell backward, bashing his head against the other wall, only inches away now.

Somehow the walls had become tubular like writhing intestines. Walter's bladder let loose. Through the narrow tunnel that was all that remained between the two converging walls, the janitor spied the altar-like slab at the far end of the room. It was his only possible means of escape. If he could squeeze through and heft himself up onto the altar, he could be saved. The walls would have to crush the heavy stone of the slab to get at him. *Squuuush*. No sooner had he reached the opening, wedging himself a few feet into its narrow confines, then he felt the surface of the walls changing, turning soft and pliable. A hundred yawning mouths, miniscule at first, were appearing on either side of him—lips, steel-like jaws, gaping throats. The lips puckered, offering deadly kisses. The jaws gnashed ravenously. The gaping throats, empty, awaited their sustenance.

The core of The Hanley School, never more alive, was about to wolf down its victim. Just before Walter Cox disappeared into the bowels of the school, his arthritic arm grasped the black altar cloth he had examined before. His last terrified thought was a sudden realization—the pattern on the fabric he had found so oddly familiar was the silhouette of the stained-glass windows throughout the entire school.

12

When Matthew Hanley strode across the lawn from his cottage that morning, shortly after nine o'clock, he kept his head down. It was a habit he had gotten into recently. Seeing the school this early in the day never failed to bring out a mixture of distaste and depression that could stay with him for hours. If he didn't look up at the eyesore, maybe it wouldn't get to him today.

Matthew had changed his timetable for leaving Hanley. He hoped that in one more year he could turn his back on this place and not have to wait any longer. Relaxing on a beach in the South Seas—or for that matter, anywhere but here—was not something he should postpone. The new term was little more than a month old, but already just setting foot inside the school was enough to knot his stomach.

As he approached the front steps, Matthew broke from habit and stole a quick glance up at the rectangular structure that squatted before him. He was instantly sorry. Against the drab outline of nearly bare autumn limbs, the building looked like some primitive beast, licking its chops, ready to pounce on some unsuspecting prey.

Matthew hurried inside. There was a mountain of paperwork on his desk, but the headmaster would welcome the monotony of a task he usually loathed. There were administrative reports to plough through and quite a bit of correspondence to catch up on, but he remembered he also had some travel brochures that had arrived in the mail the other day. At least, they would provide a distraction.

On the way to his office, Matthew spotted Laura Nash disappearing into a classroom. Late as usual, he noted. Matthew knew he should be annoyed, but when it came right down to it, he couldn't care less. Laura was beginning to bore him these days. He was still having sex with her two or three nights a week, and though she had proved herself inventive and even daring in bed, the excitement of a new conquest had died down for him. Their lovemaking was becoming mechanical now. Besides, after they were finished, there was nothing to talk about since they had very little in common. As a very young man, Matthew had overlooked a bed partner's inability to carry on a conversation—whether from lack of knowledge of shyness, it didn't matter—but now that he was older, he hated to admit it but he needed something with more substance than just a roll in the hay. Laura wasn't stupid or even shy, but she was only 17—what could they really hope to share with each other?

It was true though that the last few times they had been together, Laura had seemed on the verge of bringing up something that was weighing on her mind. In each case, she had started to speak, then thought better of it. Matthew had wished she would go on—anything was better than the inane chatter or, worse, the silence that inevitably followed intercourse—but Matthew had hesitated to prod her. In the past, he'd had his share of lovestruck teenaged girls declaring their devotion. What if Laura had just been working herself up to pouring her heart out about their future relationship? Matthew didn't think he'd be able to sit through that without laughing. Still, the thought nagged at him that Laura was skirting some other issue. She would get so apprehensive just before she changed the subject, almost as if she were afraid of something and didn't trust Matthew enough to confide in him. It was a slight blow to the headmaster's vanity, but maybe he was better off not knowing what was on her mind. The bottom line, Matthew told himself, was that Laura was just a kid. It all amounted to game-playing. What he needed was a real woman.

Someone like Karin Sayers. Now there was a woman to be stranded on a tropical island with. Matthew Hanley wasn't blind. For the past few weeks, he had been an avid witness to her sexy transformation. A beautiful woman to begin with, Karin had evolved into a genuine knockout and the object of Matthew's lust. Of late, Matthew conceded, she'd been going overboard on the cosmetics and her wardrobe was bordering on the grotesque. At time, there also was a frenetic madness in her eyes and some of her mannerisms. It was precisely this paradox—a minister's daughter looking like a tart—that stirred up Matthew's excitement. She had become a welcomed intruder in his fantasy world. And on recent occasions when he'd been making love to Laura Nash, Matthew had closed his eyes and imagined it was Karin Sayers. He knew, of course, that if he could get Karin in hand—and God, how he'd love to do just that—he could rein her in a little and persuade her to dress a bit more conventionally, at least in public. The way she would fix herself up in his bedroom—with leather, slit-skirts, garter belts—would be another story. And Karin Sayers was a woman he could talk to in bed with pleasure.

As Matthew thumbed through the teachers' reports on his desk, he looked instinctively for the file marked "Karin Sayers." There wasn't any. He wondered about that. In all the years she'd been teaching at Hanley she had never failed to hand in her reports on time. This was quite unlike her, and he made a note to talk to her about it. Maybe they could do it in town over a cocktail.

His thoughts were interrupted by a light rapping on his office door. Matthew looked up to see the caretaker, Desmond Trousdale, carrying a small, metal cashbox in one hand.

"Mr. Hanley, can I see you a minute?"

"What is it, Desmond? Come on in."

Matthew glowered at the old man as he padded across the carpet, his crepe soles crunching as he went. Matthew nodded at an armchair, but Desmond ignored the offer, preferring to stand, towering over the desk like a giant oak. Matthew continued to look at him with irritation. He didn't like the Trousdales. In his mind, they were an eyesore, just like the school itself. He didn't care for their attitude, the way they strutted around Hanley like they owned the place. The Trousdales' devotion to the school was almost like a religious fervor, but they were just caretakers. They had nothing to do with the way this place was run. That was Matthew's job. He wished the old couple would learn to know their place. On more than one occasion, Matthew had wanted to send them packing just on general principle, but the Trousdales were such a fixture there that dismissing them would be like closing off an entire floor of the building.

Matthew waited for Desmond to state his business. He didn't appreciate the old man's psychological ploy of standing there, making the headmaster look up to him. It was goddamned rude and gave Matthew a crick in his neck. He likes the idea of looking down on me, smirking like that, thought Matthew. He thinks because my great-granduncle hired him, he can treat me like I'm still a kid.

"Well?" Matthew said impatiently.

Desmond leaned a bony hand on Matthew's desk. "It's about Walter Cox. I'm afraid a crime has been committed."

"What are you talking about?"

"Walter's disappeared. This is my petty cashbox. Someone broke into it and took all the money. About $150."

"Are you sure it was Walter? How do you know he's not sleeping off a drunk somewhere? It wouldn't be the first time."

Desmond Trousdale shifted his weight. "I went to Walter's locker. All his stuff is gone."

Matthew frowned at the old caretaker. "This is hard to believe. Walter's been here a long time. He might be an alcoholic, but I don't think he's a thief."

"He's gone, isn't he? The money's gone, too. All the evidence points to Walter."

"Did you try calling him at home?"

"His phone's been disconnected," Desmond said, lying.

Matthew could feel his annoyance growing. He hated the smug, judgmental air Desmond was giving off. Still, he had to admit things did not look good for Walter Cox.

"Walter was my responsibility," Desmond continued. "He was one of my employees. He let us down. He let the school down. I think we should keep this nasty little episode under wraps, if you know what I mean. I'm sure we both agree that the good name of the school is our number one priority." Desmond's shrewd eyes gleamed wickedly. "The last thing we need is another slur on Hanley."

Matthew stood up. Goddamn this son of a bitch! He was right, of course—the school didn't need any more bad publicity—but he resented the barely veiled insinuation in Desmond's tone. The public image of the school was Matthew's problem, not some caretaker's. He wondered if Desmond knew about that girl's pregnancy a couple of years ago. Of course, he did. The Trousdales knew everything. Matthew paced behind the desk.

As if reading his thoughts, Desmond went on. "I think the most important thing, Mr. Hanley, is that we don't involve the police."

This brought Matthew up short. "No, don't call the police. Not for $150. He wasn't much of a handyman anyhow. We had enough of the police after the Webster girl's suicide." Matthew sank back down into his chair. "I'll put an ad in the paper, and we'll get a new handyman."

"Fine. Just let me know when you want me to do the interviews."

Matthew glared at him. "*I'll* do the interviews."

"Whoever we get has got to be an improvement."

"Maybe so, but you hired Walter. Don't forget that."

"Yes, sir," Desmond said with a thin smile.

"That will be all, Desmond."

The caretaker didn't move. "Sir, about the $150 . . ."

"I'll write you a check."

Desmond held up the metal box. "I'll need another ten for a new lock."

"I'll add it on," Matthew said evenly. He opened a leather book on his desk and scribbled a check. "Here. Let's not mention this to anyone, alright?"

"I already told the missus."

"Naturally. Just see that it goes no further."

Desmond folded the check and stuffed it into his pocket. "You know us, Mr. Hanley. We've always been loyal to the school."

Like Matthew Hanley, Vanessa felt that the school looked particularly malignant that day, like a savage entity, cunning and ominous. There was an evil charge of electricity in the air which had been bothering her all afternoon. During English class, Vanessa had felt stifled, as if the air itself was pressing down on her. Feeling faint, she had asked to be excused. But going out on the front lawn, rather than reviving her, had only heightened her anxiety as she walked into the lengthening shadow of the building's grim facade.

Now it was a few hours later. Rehearsal was over. Dusk

was falling rapidly. In the netherlight of approaching darkness, the school always looked its meanest. The oval stained-glass windows, in the semi-darkness, twinkled vicious, little winks as testament to the school's inherent slyness, visible to anyone who wasn't afraid to admit that they were in the presence of something abnormal and unhealthy. Vanessa knew she was no longer alone in suspecting that the school was evil, even threatening. At times like this, she almost wished she could drag every one of the girls out of their rooms to gaze up at the building's prison-like walls, the incongruous stained-glass eyes, and, over it all, the sprawling mansards and turrets housing a stone jungle of barbaric carved predators. It was truly a blatant facade of evil.

But why couldn't everyone see it? Why were so many of the girls afraid even to look? Or were they just uncaring and oblivious to everything but their selfish preoccupations—boy friends, clothes, money, whatever? Life seemed to muddle on at Hanley, despite the strange occurrences and catastrophes. Sometimes Vanessa wished she could close her eyes to what was really going on, like so many of the others, but she couldn't. Something had chosen her. She was different. She was meant to see.

Without looking back, Vanessa hurried down the side lawn, away from the school. She caught movement from the corner of her eye and realized someone was moving down the slope toward the bushes. She recognized his confident walk. It was Matthew Hanley. He must be on his way to the cottage, Vanessa thought. Her entire body tingled, and Vanessa had the immediate impulse to follow him. Her urge to be with him was so overwhelming, she had to catch herself. She almost switched direction in mid-step to run after him. This uncanny obsession for the headmaster that was eating away at her had to stop. It was almost as mad and inexplicable as the visions that the school had forced upon her. As Matthew faded into the foliage, Vanessa continued on in her original direction.

The lantern in the boathouse window was unlit. Grateful and still troubled by what had just happened, Vanessa pushed open the door. She heard a quick intake of breath. God, there was someone in here. A match flickered and she saw the surprised face of Ingrid Strummer.

"Ingrid? What are you doing here?"

The other girl fumbled with the lantern. "Didn't you know? This is community property. Or did you think you and Dennis had exclusive rights to this place?"

Vanessa came inside. As the light came on, she looked around. There was no one else there. "I was supposed to meet Dennis," she said. "What are you doing here in the dark, all by yourself?"

Ingrid rubbed her eyes. "I was watching the sunset. I guess I fell asleep. I come down here sometimes after school. It's calm being on the water."

Vanessa curled up on a cushion. "I just saw Matthew Hanley," she said. God, she even relished the sound of his name on her lips.

"So?" Ingrid yawned. "I see him all the time." She reached for something on the floor and put it into her tote bag. Vanessa recognized the glint of Ingrid's flask.

"No, this was different. Something came over me. I felt like running across the lawn and throwing myself on him." Vanessa could have bitten her tongue. Why had she just made that ridiculous confession? The words had just poured out of her mouth.

"Join the club, honey." Ingrid laughed, and her words were slightly slurred.

"I felt like ripping his clothes off," Vanessa blurted out. "That's not like me. I don't even want him."

"Sounds to me like you do."

"But I swear I don't." Vanessa shook her head. "I'm sitting here talking to you right now and I don't have any desire for Matthew Hanley, but I think about him at the strangest times. He just pops into my head. I pass him by on the lawn and I just turn to mush."

"It's the school, Vanessa. Nothing surprises me about this place. You know something? I believe you. You tell me you don't want Matthew, but you go apeshit when you see him. That's just the kind of weird crap that goes on around here all the time."

"Yet we stay here," Vanessa said, quietly. "How come we don't do something?"

"Some of us do." Ingrid retrieved her flask. "Here," she said. "It doesn't explain things but it sure helps you live with it."

"No thanks, Ingrid, that's not the answer. You can do what you want, but I'd rather have all my wits about me in this place."

Ingrid looked challenging. "I can do what I want? No lecture? You're not one of the girls who disapproves? I've been catching shit from almost everybody. That's why I come down here after school." She took a drink. "Fuck the sunset."

"Well, if you really want the truth, Ingrid, I think you're overdoing it. But since I'm screwed up myself, I'm the last person in the world who should pass judgment."

Ingrid looked out the window. "Here comes Dennis. I presume you're not going to tell him about Matthew."

Vanessa smoothed her hair. "Oh, I would never tell Dennis. He'd be furious."

Ingrid put away the flask, got up and buttoned her jacket. For some reason, Vanessa didn't want her to leave.

"You know what was the weirdest part?" she asked. "When I was standing on the lawn just now, I never wanted Matthew to have any other woman but me. I was jealous. I don't think I've ever felt like that in my life."

Ingrid giggled. "Well, if you want Matthew all to yourself, that's going to be a little tough. He's been screwing Laura and God knows how many other girls at the school."

Vanessa felt a nervous twinge. "What about you?" she

asked. "You're not one of them, are you?"

"No. He hasn't got around to me yet."

"But you've thought about it?"

"Sure," Ingrid admitted. "Who hasn't? He's a great-looking guy. Maybe I just don't have the guts."

They could hear Dennis approaching on the wooden planks outside. Ingrid put a comforting hand on Vanessa's shoulder.

"Want some advice before I go?" Ingrid asked. "Forget about Matthew. You've got something better."

Vanessa nodded and felt a rush of warmth for her friend. Nonetheless, she wished that the footsteps outside belonged not to Dennis Bellivin but to Matthew Hanley.

Karin Sayers had been in a fog all day. She'd had a full schedule of classes, then after school there had been a rehearsal of "The Dark." In the auditorium with the students she could barely remember a time when coaching and directing them gave her pleasure. Recently, unless she was on stage herself and enacting a role, rehearsals were tedious and distracting. Karin had more important, more exciting things on her mind. Today, for instance, she impatiently had checked her watch dozens of times, not even caring if the kids saw her. Karin wanted only to be back in her room, alone with the soothing voices.

Karin had enjoyed a secret thrill all day. The scent of lovemaking with the old man had clung to her, sticky and animal-like, nestling in her panties. Her skin was alive with the musky smells of sweat and sex. A few times on the stairs, between classes, in the crush of students, she had gotten a whiff of the pungent odor she must be giving off. Several of the girls had cast quick, puzzled glances at her. Were they just looking at her because of the way she was dressed? Or, could they detect on her the aroma of sex with Walter Cox? Karin hoped it was the latter. The mere thought of that made her skin tingle.

Back in her room at last that evening, Karin took a shower. The voices wanted her to be clean now. It was their special time to be together. Karin looked at the clock. Six p.m. All day she had been imagining the hands on her watch standing straight up like that. It was a trick she had taught herself as a child to make time pass more quickly. She had forgotten about it all these years, but the voices had made her remember.

You are one of us now, Karin. We have a world of secrets to share with you. There is no more past. You have closed the door on all that. You must help us open the door to your future.

The whispers were particularly comforting tonight. Karin knew they were mollified by her obedience that day. She longed to explore the secrets of the school and ached to open that door they spoke of—but she was confused. How could she help them? It was she who needed their guidance. Karin sensed she would always need their guidance.

After her shower, Karin slipped into some silk lounging pajamas. Her face, scrubbed clean from the hot water, gave off an innocent, almost virginal glow. Still slightly damp, her hair hung in modest folds to her shoulders. Surveying her chaste image in the mirror, Karin shook her head disapprovingly. This would never do.

After generously applying makeup, she stepped back to admire herself in the full-length mirror behind the door. Very sexy. Karin was ready.

Karin started for the bedroom, but she had forgotten something—a daub of her favorite perfume behind her ears, between her breasts, between her legs. Karin felt silky, like the whispers she knew were waiting for her in the next room.

Karin felt it immediately. The room vibrated with a loving presence. It was around her, on her, all over her. She settled down comfortably onto the bed and smiled, anticipating. This morning, in the utility room, Karin had been the seducer. Tonight, in her own room, she would be the seduced. She knew what was expected of her and shivered willingly at the thought of what was to come.

The room filled with the scent of her desire. Something hovered in the air. *Karriinn. Sooo niice. Sooo sofftt.* Karin's nipples strained against the sheer fabric of her pajamas. She unbuttoned her top. Her fingers seemed to be aided by a warm gush of air which slipped under the garment to surround her arms. *Faster, Karin.*

Perspiration beaded like pearls all over Karin's body. She licked the salty substance from the edges of her mouth, savoring its tang. She squeezed her breasts, naked now, burning in the sudden red glow of the room. The stained-glass window, the ever-present eye, watched over her approvingly. More whispers like hundreds of small, audible hands weaved a web of sexual desire over her. Their demands were like the rustling of paper in a mounting fire. Her nipples hard now, she wet her fingers and began to massage them. Her hands traveled up and down her body, smoothing a pathway for phantom kisses from the lips of an invisible lover. Karin felt her entire body acquiesce. The sultry breeze was taking over, lightly brushing her submissive skin.

Karin lay back on the pillows. She raised her hips, sliding the pajama bottoms from her legs. Instantly, she could feel the heat accelerate—insistent, sticky, supple. *Goood, Karin. You feeel sooo goood.* Karin took her fingers and began rubbing the sensitive flesh between her legs. She opened herself to her touch, but felt a stronger, more urgent presence there, waiting to gain entry. She fingered her clitoris, spreading herself further apart, wet and heated. *That's right, Karriinn. Now!*

Karin felt a cry well up in her throat. Shock. Surprise. Delight. A weight had eased itself onto her naked flesh like a second skin. She could feel it teasing her clitoris, replacing her groping fingers with its gossamer touch. The voices were growing now in volume—obscene, corrupt, not to be denied, but scintillating in their sordid authority. Karin stifled a scream of rapture. She felt it enter her then, thick and icy. She arched her body upward to meet the ramming motion of the formless entity. Vaguely, Karin had the impression of an outline above her, straddling her. For a second, she thought she saw the imprint of haunted eyes. The presence was filling her now, and even the heat of her body, which seemed to be coming off in waves, couldn't warm the biting coldness inside her. As Karin rode up and down on the bed, her rhythmic breathing was matched by an ancient panting that emanated from the school itself, that had lived there in its own timeless current. Its scorching breath, fetid and dense, blew in puffs against her mouth. This desecration lifted Karin to a plane, where for a moment her substance melted away, replaced by an all-consuming oneness with infinite evil.

The breathing was growing raspy, more urgent now. Her thighs tensed in anticipation. It ejaculated—icy, sharp, cold bursts of demonic seed. Karin's own spasms erupted to greet it. She threw back her head on the pillow, moaning in pleasure. It wasn't until her own passion had subsided, that she realized the vile entity that had lured her so lovingly was gone. The icicle-like sting had evaporated. The stench in the air had been extinguished. The panting against her lips had abated. The presence had vanished.

As she lay there quivering in aftershock, Karin foundered in delirious madness, too far gone to feel the fear that was buried deep within. Like a sad reminder of the innocent, God-fearing Karin, Henry Sayers' Bible, trapped in the valise under her bed, began to smolder, its gilt-edged pages charring in remorse.

"Matthew!"

Vanessa's cry of passion echoed through the boat-house. Lying beneath Dennis, their clothes in a heap on the floor, she never saw the knowing half-smile on his lips. She only heard the abrupt anger in his voice.

"You know something, Vanessa? You sure have a way of boosting a guy's ego."

Embarrassment flushed Vanessa's face to a bright red. Dennis raised his naked body from her. "I'm sorry," Vanessa protested. "I don't know what made me say that. Come back, Dennis."

Dennis was already halfway across the room, reaching for his jeans. "No, I don't feel like it," he said simply. He put his shirt on, tucking it into his trousers. There was a long silence. Finally, Dennis came over and sat across from her. Vanessa wrapped a blanket around her. The night air, whistling through the boards of the boathouse, was suddenly very chilling.

"Matthew Hanley," Dennis said, accusingly. "Jesus, you too, huh? Every girl in the school has got a thing for him."

"I don't have a thing for him . . ." Vanessa began.

Dennis waved a hand at her to be quiet. His smirk was one of taunting disbelief. "Oh, but I think you do, Vanessa. Here we are making love. You're not on drugs and you're not drunk. But you call out Matthew Hanley's name. If that isn't having a thing for him, I'd like to know what is."

"Look, I said I was sorry."

"Being sorry doesn't help. Last time we were here, you got hysterical. I never did find out what the hell that was about. Now you're yelling out 'Matthew!' like a goddamn jerk. You know what I think? They're just excuses. Why don't you come right out and say it? You just don't want to fuck me."

"Dennis, please try to understand," Vanessa said meekly, "I don't know what's happening to me. I couldn't tell you about the last time. It was too horrible."

"That's what you say. Okay, forget about the last time. What about this time? You were fantasizing Matthew Hanley while you were making love to me. Admit it."

Vanessa shook her head. "I don't even like him. I

wasn't picturing him or anything. I told you I don't know what made me say his name."

"What an odd choice of words, Vanesa. Something *made* you say it?"

"Remember how I told you the school is doing weird things to me? Well, now it's making me think about Matthew Hanley."

"Jesus Christ, Vanessa, do you expect me to believe that? First the school is making you see things. And now it's putting words in your mouth." Dennis lit a cigarette. He looked at her, amused. "Sounds to me like the school's really fucking up your mind, huh?"

Vanessa tucked her head into the blanket. She couldn't see Dennis' cruel smile. "It's not just me," she said almost defiantly. She clenched her fists. Did she really believe that? Vanessa knew that if the other girls at Hanley were going through the same things it would make it more bearable for her—even if it was she who was getting the brunt of the school's psychic assault. But what had made Vanessa special? What was there in her character or background that had singled her out for the school's most abrasive madness? She forced herself to peer out of the blanket at Dennis, who was looking at her skeptically, still waiting for an explanation.

"Go on, Vanessa."

"Look at Karin Sayers. Do you see the way she's dressing lately? Haven't you seen her at rehearsals? She's acting like she's crazy. It's like she's on the make for every boy in the room. She's a minister's daughter! What about Rickie? I'm convinced something drove her to suicide. She didn't kill herself—she was murdered!"

"Oh, for fuck's sake," Dennis muttered. "Who killed her. The school?"

Vanessa hated the glint of amusement in Dennis' eye. And there was something else about his look that was off-kilter. Vanessa wished she could put her finger on what it was. She felt disheartened. She should have known she wouldn't be able to reach Dennis with her private fears, certainly not after the humiliation she had just caused him while they were making love. Moreover, for the first time, she was beginning to see a cruel, almost uncaring streak in Dennis she had never noticed before. Still, since she had come this far, she might as well continue.

"Dennis, I think the school is evil."

"Oh, you do?" Dennis waited until her eyes met his. "What do you really know about evil?" he asked softly.

"I know I don't want to be around it."

Dennis blew a perfect smoke ring into the air. "You're around evil all the time. It's not confined to one place."

"It's in the school. I'm certain of that. I want to get out of here as soon as I can. I've had just about enough of this place."

"Where are you going to go?"

"I don't know. Back home. My father will get me into some other school."

"Aren't you forgetting something? What about us? I found you. Do you think I'm just going to let you go?"

"Come with me," Vanessa offered. "I think you ought to get out of here, too."

Dennis stubbed out his cigarette on the boathouse floor. He gave Vanessa an odd smile. "Why? I like this place. I feel right at home here."

Their lips parted. Vanessa said good night to Dennis on the front steps of the school. She watched him trudge back across the lawn. Their walk from the boathouse had been in silence, and Vanessa had concentrated on the smell of rain in the air. Just before Dennis had leaned down to kiss her, she'd had an impulse to pull back, but she didn't. Still, there was a coldness to Dennis tonight that went far beyond his anger at what Vanessa did in the boathouse. She had hurt him by calling out Matthew's name, but the subsequent exchange between them had been fraught with cynical innuendo. For the first time since they'd met, Vanessa didn't feel right about the very basis of their relationship.

The school didn't feel right to Vanessa tonight either. Inside, in the foyer, she stood at the bottom of the stairs leading up to the second floor, touched by an indefinable dread. She supported herself against the curve of the bannister. This was absurd, being afraid to walk usptairs to her own room.

She steeled herself. *Do What You Fear, Vanessa*. Her mother's advice. Vanessa hunched her shoulders, then bolted up the steps, two at a time. When she reached the second floor landing, she gave a nervous laugh. It echoed in the deserted stairwell derisively and seemed to follow Vanessa all the way back to her room.

That night, in the darkest hours, the evil that had dwelled at The Hanley School found new strength and cloaked itself thickly over the surrounding countryside like a poisonous net, making all hope impossible. A violent rainstorm had driven itself against the school in a senseless fury and then, suddenly, stopped in the dead of night. The crashing of thunder could still be heard, like a muted cannon growling somewhere in the distance. The ominous clouds squeezed out their final drops of water like so many tears, leaving the sky a dismal gray. The quiet was punctuated by occasional drips and gurglings as the rain washed off the surfaces of the school.

Alone in Room Six, Vanessa had tossed fitfully for the better part of the night. She had been possessed by strange dreams which now, as she walked the floor nervously, she could not remember. She looked over at Laura's empty bed and wished her roommate would come home soon. Vanessa would welcome the company, but she knew Laura's pattern. If it got to be this late, then Laura would be spending the night at Matthew Hanley's cottage. She would be back in time to shower and not before.

Vanessa considered knocking on Ingrid's door and

asking if she could spend the night with her, but as uncomfortable as Vanessa felt in her room, the thought of going out in the hall was frightening. The floorboards beneath her feet creaked, unnaturally loud, as Vanessa paced. Everything seemed intensified—the echo of her laugh on the stairs earlier, the rivulets of rain that gushed in the drainpipe near her window, the very floor itself. Vanessa had the odd sensation that the school was somehow passing a judgment on her, heightening its customary noises, subtly turning up the volume on its critical wavelength. She came to a halt by the door and heard a shifting, rubbery movement. The walls of Room Six seemed to be deviating into a disapproving frown. The room itself was scowling at her. The word "traitor" careened around in her head. Vanessa felt as if she had broken some unearthly confidence that the school had entrusted only to her.

At once, the room was alive with an irreconcilable anger. Vanessa stumbled backwards from the force of the hostility which she knew was aimed directly at her. But why? Was it because she had made up her mind to leave the school? Was it because she was turning her back on Hanley when she knew it had chosen her for something?

Whispers now. *Vaanesssa. You belong heeere.* "No! I won't listen! I won't stay here!" Vanessa swore out loud in her room. "You won't make me! You won't make me filthy like you!" Laughter now—gleeful, disembodied, soiled. It sneered at her. The cackling was pervasive, whistling down the corridors outside, permeating the room, like the sound of miniature demons on a rampage of insane revenge. *You belong, you belong, you belong.* Proudly, triumphantly, it sang out her commitment. A whirlwind of steamy air flared around the room, tearing wildly at the bed covers and nearly ripping Vanessa's nightgown from her body. The stained-glass window seemed to stretch its oval opening, mutating into a large, bloody cavity in the wall of the room. Vanessa could smell the acrid scent of sulphur in the air. Her last thought, before her knees buckled and she slumped to the floor, was that the smell of sulphur was associated in Christian belief with the presence of Satan.

Over at The Abbott School, Dennis hadn't slept well either—but for a different reason. He was excited, overstimulated from the events of that evening. When the pounding rain had awakened Bobby Cannon, Dennis had pretended to be asleep. He was in no mood for conversation with Bobby. He preferred to be alone with his thoughts, content with the knowledge that promises made to him years before were soon to be fulfilled.

The rain had let up now, and Bobby had gone back to sleep. Dennis listened to his roommate's even breathing as he sat by the window in his underwear, looking out at the building that had changed his life—The Hanley School. A dark outline against the brooding rainclouds, the school looked vibrant, alive with expectation, and Dennis tingled with the realization that he was inexorably tied to its past, present and—best of all—its future.

Immediately, he thought of Vanessa. Now the union was complete. Tonight's conversation in the boathouse had confirmed that. Dennis had to laugh at how apologetic she had gotten after calling out Matthew's name. Did she really think it mattered? Did she really think he cared? If only she hadn't been so flustered and preoccupied with her feeble explanations, she might have caught a quick glimpse of his quiet exhilaration. Dennis was glad she hadn't noticed—it could have ruined everything. He recalled their little squabble in the boathouse. Dennis knew he had instigated it, and he had laid the sarcasm on really thick. And why not? It had been mind-fucking time. He enjoyed it. In the future, though, he would have to be more careful. Fucking her brain over was fun, but at this point, it was pretty much easy pickings. Besides, there was too much at stake now.

Vanessa's declaration that she was going to leave the school was something Dennis had expected. She had certainly given enough indications before that she was finding life at Hanley intolerable. Of course, Dennis would have to prevent any attempt on Vanessa's part to quit school. That was his responsibility and he welcomed it. He wondered if, in the boathouse, Vanessa had believed him when he expressed his reluctance to let her go. He would have to reinforce his so-called dedication to her in the coming weeks. That would mean more declarations of love, some talk of their future together, and letting up on those cryptic little remarks that only added to Vanessa's already mounting fear of the school. Dennis would have to keep a check on himself. It wouldn't be easy, but maybe he'd have a little help.

Bobby Cannon coughed in his sleep. Dennis glanced across the room, prepared to scramble back into bed at any sign of Bobby's waking up, but the other boy resumed his regular breathing. On the table between the two bunks rested Dennis' football helmet. There was a big game this Saturday against the county champions. Dennis had barely thought about it. Why get worked up about a game? He knew that Abbot would win and it was he who would lead them to victory. Dennis remembered he had a Chemistry exam the next day. He hadn't opened a book to study, but he would breeze through that test in the morning, probably pulling down a 90 at least. This was just the way things were, and they would only get better in years to come. Dennis took one final look out the window at The Hanley School. He was a winner. He would always be a winner. The school would see to that.

13

A week passed and Vanessa did not leave the school. She made a few half-hearted attempts to call her mother, but always during hours when she knew Evelyn Forbes was not likely to be home. Vanessa even went into town and picked up a train schedule, but after circling a few departure times, she simply put the schedule in a drawer. When she looked for it later, it was gone. Vanessa never went back to town for another.

Dennis had been a sweetheart lately, and that had been another factor. He got her a seat on the 50 yard line for his miraculous come-from-behind victory against the county champions, during which Dennis scored the winning touchdown on a quarterback sneak. At the victory party afterwards, Dennis had been more than attentive, toasting their future with champagne. Vanessa had gotten a bit tipsy that night and Dennis had taken her to the boathouse. She was giggly and vulnerable, but Dennis did not take advantage and pressure her to sleep with him. For this, she was grateful. Dennis held her all night long, and that was just what she needed. She noticed too, that night and on subsequent meetings, that his sarcasm and teasing, especially where the school was concerned, had given way to a more understanding attitude. With that change came Vanessa's resolve not to talk to Dennis anymore about the school. And strangely enough, once she made up her mind to do that, the visions and unusual noises which had terrified her lessened to a point where they were barely noticeable. Vanessa felt very close to Dennis these days, though her attraction for Matthew Hanley continued to grow, and that was another subject she would not bring up in conversation. Instead, she would keep it to herself.

Her thoughts about "The Dark," now in its final stages of rehearsal, also remained private. Vanessa was struggling with the role of Emily, the young witch, and Karin Sayers, who seemed to have leveled off at an advanced state of disorder, was no help at all. More and more, Vanessa turned to Bobby Cannon for help with her part, and he proved very patient with her, going over her lines and encouraging her to explore the character. Vanessa knew she should be doing this with Dennis but felt embarrassed to ask him. Acting came so effortlessly to Dennis that Vanessa doubted he would understand her difficulties with the role. Besides, the subject matter of "The Dark," with its concentration on witchcraft and evil, was dangerously close to Vanessa's conflict with the school, the very topic she was reluctant to broach with him.

One afternoon, Vanessa was sitting with Bobby at the back of the auditorium. Onstage, Karin was running lines with some of the other actors. Vanessa was following along in her copy of the play, but suddenly she put her script down and listened to the dialogue coming from the stage. Its talk of midnight rituals and devil worship seemed so incongruous coming from the mouths of teenaged kids, who should have been acting in something much lighter. Racing around the stage, trying to imitate witches and warlocks, her classmates looked like children playing an ominous grown-ups' game—Karin

Sayers' game. Since there was so much evil at the school already, by throwing themselves into this play as though it were just a lark, weren't the kids actually perpetuating that very evil?

The thought disturbed Vanessa. "Bobby, what do you think of this play?"

"Well, opening night's just around the corner and I think I don't know my lines."

"Be serious, Bobby. I think this play has something to do with the school. I think a long time ago there were witches here. You know, we're not that far from Salem, and this place could have been a witches' training grounds."

Bobby had put down his script and was looking at her attentively. "Like in the play, huh?"

"Exactly," Vanessa said, then paused. What she was getting into here was pretty much speculation. Did she really want to share it with Bobby? She looked him in the eye. He was such a trusted friend that she felt she had to go on. Once she spoke, the words poured out in a flood. "You know, Bobby, I finally told Dennis I think the school is evil. Well, I think this play is evil, too. Beautiful, but evil. I wonder if the play and the school aren't connected. I mean, I don't know why I'm doing this part. Why am I playing a witch after all the shit that's happened to me? It's like we've all just been lured into something. I should know better, Bobby. I've seen what this school is all about. For me to be in this play is a contradiction, and I feel like a hypocrite. What if I'm contributing to the evil? Why are we doing 'The Dark' in the first place? Why aren't we doing 'Twelfth Night'? Because 'Twelfth Night' is a Shakespearean play that isn't going to change anything. It isn't going to make this place more horrible. I think we're being used, Bobby. Something we can't explain is using us."

Bobby sighed. "Holy shit, Vanessa. That's a lot to think about. Okay, if something's using us, what's the reason? We're just a bunch of kids."

"I don't know, Bobby. The school is using us for something. And we're playing right into its hands by doing 'The Dark.' What if this once was a witches' training ground? I'm talking about before Hanley was built. What if that's the reason nothing would grow here? Do you think it's a good idea for us to be doing a play based on that kind of history? If you believe in ghosts or spirits from the past, that's got to be just what they would want."

"Jesus," Bobby said. "I see what you mean. But what can we do?"

"We can leave."

Bobby nodded. "That's true."

"Dennis wants me to stay, but I think I should get out of here. What do you think?"

Bobby studied her for a minute. "I think you should go."

Vanessa looked hopeful. "You do?"

"If the school is making you crazy, Vanessa, leave."

"What about you?"

"I'm okay for now. I don't go to Hanley. I go to Abbott. I just come here for rehearsals. I don't like the play either, but in another week it's going to be over. I think I can get through it. If things get too nutsy, I can always drop out."

"Have you got a quarter? I'm going to call my father."

While Karin was looking the other way, Vanessa slipped out of the auditorium. She rushed upstairs to the second floor phone booth. Bobby Cannon had told her exactly what she had wanted to hear, that it was okay for her to leave Hanley. Now she knew what had made her pour out everything so suddenly to him at rehearsal. Her fingers trembled as she dialed her father's number in California. A busy signal. Shit! She got out her address book and looked up Evelyn Forbes' new number in Boston and dialed it. A recording. "I'm sorry. The number you have reached is not in service at this time." Vanessa slammed down the receiver in frustration. That was impossible. The phone had rung there just the other day, and her mother was not the type to go a day without a working telephone. Angry now, Vanessa redialed her father. Still busy. Goddamn it! Defeated for the moment, Vanessa hung up.

There was a clinking in the coin slot—her quarter—but a coin was not what Vanessa retrieved when, distractedly, she reached into the slot. Her fingers came away with thick red globules of blood. Oh, God, it was starting again. Vanessa was on the verge of screaming, but stopped herself. Somehow she knew that if she closed her eyes for just a second, the droplets of blood would be gone. She squeezed her eyes shut. This time, she knew it was the school playing tricks on her. By now, she was familiar with its evil little routine. Confidently, she opened her eyes. Blood was pouring from the coin slot in a torrent.

"You told her what?"

Dennis stopped in his tracks on the walk back to Abbott. He fixed Bobby with a cold glare.

"Jesus, Dennis, back off. What are you getting so pissed off about? She's already made up her mind. Vanessa thinks 'The Dark' was written about The Hanley School. She's been seeing things, she's scared and she thinks there's something evil about the school." Bobby's voice lowered. "I'm not so sure she's wrong."

Moving swiftly, catching Bobby off guard, Dennis grabbed him. He threw him up against a tree.

"Nobody cares what you think," Dennis barked. "Why don't you mind your own fucking business?"

Bobby was stunned by the fury in Dennis' voice. A sharp pain shot across his shoulder blades from the impact of the tree trunk. Bobby bit his lip and stared back at Dennis icily. "I thought you loved her."

"I *do* love her."

Bobby didn't believe him, not for a second. "Yeah, well how come you don't see what's happening to her?

She's flipping out, Dennis, and you don't give a good goddamn."

Dennis made a move toward the smaller boy. Bobby tensed and made a fist, believing Dennis was going to hit him. Instead, Dennis jabbed an angry finger in his face.

"Stay out of this, Bobby. I'm warning you. Vanessa's not leaving Hanley. You stay away from her, understand?"

"Are you threatening me?"

"No, I'm telling you. It's for your own good. There's a lot of things you don't know about. You're just a kid, Bobby. Don't try to act like a man."

Bobby's pain was giving way to a dull rage. "Don't give me that shit. You're the same age as I am. Vanessa's walking out on you and your ego can't handle it. That's what this is all about, right?"

A thin smile of superiority creased Dennis' lips. "She's not going anywhere. And you're not giving her any more advice."

"I'll decide that," Bobby said, defiantly. With a show of strength that surprised even him, Bobby pushed Dennis away. He stalked off across the lawn, leaving Dennis to look after him menacingly.

Rounding the lake, Bobby still shook with anger. He should have followed up that shove with a right to the jaw. He might have been able to knock Dennis down and put him in his place. But who was he kidding? Dennis would have just got up and flattened him. It looked like he had just lost his best friend—his roommate, for Christ's sake. No matter how much Dennis apologized—and Bobby guessed that he would—it couldn't change the way he had turned on him, the way he exploded. It couldn't change something else either. Dennis was lying—he didn't love Vanessa at all and probably never had. Then what was all that crap about Vanessa being his one and only, the perfect girl for him? He remembered how Dennis had flared up that time when Bobby had innocently suggested she was not his type. Bobby felt betrayed. In the past, Dennis had always leveled with him about his girl friends. They were nothing more than harmless flings. But, for some reason, he had tried to convince Bobby that Vanessa was different. But that was bullshit. If she was perfect for him, how come he didn't care about how she felt? How come he wouldn't let her leave Hanley? Bobby had been right. Vanessa wasn't Dennis' type of girl, so what was he doing with her? What did he want from her? Dennis was used to getting any girl he went after, and it was none of Bobby's business if he lied to them—sometimes that was just the way the game was played. But something was wrong here. If Dennis couldn't be straight with him, his own roommate, there must be something he was holding back, some secret about his motivations concerning Vanessa. But what could it be? Just now, he had spoken darkly of "things you don't know about." What were those things? Did anyone else know about them? Something in the way Dennis had just behaved made Bobby feel creepy. It was as though Dennis had shifted his allegiance from Bobby to someone—or something—else. Bobby glanced across the lake. He could still see Dennis, standing stock still on the lawn, a solitary figure, his face lifted upward, staring at The Hanley School.

Two days later, black, rolling clouds from the north invaded the skies over Hanley. By midafternoon, a nighttime darkness curtained the land. During rehearsal of "The Dark," thunder pounded the walls and a freak hailstorm hammered ice pellets into the building like nails. The flicker of lightning outside the windows of the auditorium outlined the students' reenactment of witchcraft rituals with a stroboscopic intensity that was thrilling at first but soon became unsettling. Karin Sayers seemed to draw energy from each lightning bolt as she whirled around the stage, shouting directions and orchestrating the actors' movements with manic detetmination. Finally, the relentless roar of the storm proved too much even for her—it was becoming impossible for the dialogue to be heard—and she sank down at the side of the stage, dismissing the group for the day.

The Abbott boys lingered in the foyer, hoping that the downpour would let up. Dennis and Bobby stood at opposite ends of the lobby, having not spoken to each other since the altercation near the lake. A few of the Hanley actresses clustered outside the auditorium for awhile, but most of the girls headed upstairs right away, preferring to be alone in their rooms for the duration of the storm. This was unusual in itself. Generally, in the past, when there had been similar cloudbursts, the girls had gathered together nervously, bolstering one another by nervously giggling at the fierce onslaught outside. But today the girls retreated to their own solitude, each one dealing with the freak storm in her own fashion.

Ingrid Strummer went to her narrow room at the end of the second floor corridor, bolted the door and cracked open a pint-sized bottle of Jack Daniels. Hail drummed against the window. Ingrid looked at it philosophically—it was perfect weather for a drink.

Marie Kronofsky, in her room down the hall, sat on the edge of her bed, feeling melancholy. She looked over at the other bunk, the one where Rickie Webster used to sleep. Rickie had been terrified by thunderstorms. Marie thought back to those nights when she had comforted her roommate, who had trembled in her arms as lightning crackled outside. Now Rickie was gone. Her bed, neatly made with fresh linen, waited there for some other girl, perhaps a future transfer student, but so far, to Marie's regret, no one had claimed it. Marie had a room all to herself now, but Rickie's empty bunk was like a silent accusation. What happened to Rickie had been so unfair. She'd never hurt anyone in her life. But as her roommate, shouldn't Marie have noticed the signs of distress? Marie had wrestled with her guilt. On more than one night since Rickie's suicide, she had cried herself to sleep. But there hadn't been any signs of distress. This was one of the things that worried Marie. What if something happened to her like what had happened to Rickie? How would she be able to recognize what was going on? Those nights she cried into her pillow, Marie had been troubled by something else. Her sobs seemed to be echoed in the walls by bursts of distorted laughter. Lately, when she'd had the urge to cry under the covers, Marie had fought back the tears, almost as if she didn't want the school to know about her grief.

Down the corridor, Laura Nash was closeted in the phone booth, having an argument with Matthew Hanley. Laura was furious. She'd been looking forward to an evening at the cottage, envisioning a lazy dinner before a roaring fireplace while the storm raged outside. But Matthew was being evasive. He might have to go into town to meet with one of the trustees. Or, if that appointment was canceled due to the weather, he might have to catch up on some correspondence he'd been putting off for some time. Laura didn't like the sound of it. She had the distinct impression she was being put off, lied to—Matthew just didn't want to see her tonight. Why didn't the son of a bitch come out and admit it? Matthew just laughed at her anger. Laura bit her tongue. She wanted to tell Matthew off, but that was not the way to get to him. Instead, she would give him a little preview of what she would do to him later that night. Laura looked through the glass of the phone booth, making sure none of the Hanley girls was waiting in the hall. This was going to take some time and it would be pretty hot. Laura could be quite persuasive when she wanted to be.

A finger of lightning pointed accusingly at Vanessa through the stained-glass window. Room Six sighed with a mournful wail as the sleet pelted the wall. Vanessa's ears perked up at the sound. She listened for a moment.

No, this wasn't the whispers. She could tell. The creaking was just an old building protesting against the elements.

Vanessa looked over the letter she had begun writing to her mother. At once, she crumpled the page, threw it in the waste basket and took another piece of stationery. It was hard choosing the right words. She was desperate to get out of Hanley, but she didn't want to sound like some crazy kid. How could she ever explain to her mother what was going on around here? No, the objective simply was to get Mrs. Forbes to pick up Vanessa and take her home. She would keep the note short and to the point. The rest of her fears about Hanley could be put on hold until she was in Boston, where she was safe.

"Dear Mom," Vanessa wrote in a firm hand. "I can't explain what's happening here but you've got to help me. I don't want to scare you and I don't think I'm in any physical danger, but I've got to get out of Hanley. I've been calling your number but they tell me it's out of service. I finally got through to Daddy's office. He's out of town on business and can't be reached. I'll tell you everything when I see you. Please, Mom, come and get me right away." She studied the letter for a moment, then signed it: "Love, Vanessa." Tears came to Vanessa's eyes. Hurriedly, she scrawled a postscript. "P.S. I haven't told you this in a long time, but I love you very much." She folded the note and sealed it in an envelope.

As Vanessa affixed the postage stamp, the heavy darkness outside seemed to seep into her room, turning it shadowy and surrealistic. The angry howling of the wind against the casement appeared aimed directly at Vanessa. She looked through the glass and in the distance could see the lake. Its one lamppost was ringed by a halo of mist.

Vanessa went downstairs to the mail slot near Matthew Hanley's office. When she reached it, she turned the letter over and over in her hand hesitantly.

From above, stained glass, streaked with rain, cast an unearthly glow on her face.

Vanessa felt indecisive. What was the point of sending this letter? If she really wanted to leave Hanley, there was probably a bus to Boston that night. She even had enough money to call a cab to take her all the way to her mother's, but it was doubtful whether she'd even get a cab in this weather.

She noticed a poster that someone must have hung on the bulletin board after rehearsal. In bold block letters it proclaimed "The Dark." The performance of "The Dark" was only a few nights away, and Evelyn Forbes had never missed seeing Vanessa in a school play. In fact, the last time they had spoken on the phone, Evelyn had told her she had already circled the date on her calendar. Vanessa's mother would be here soon, so why was she sending her this letter? It could alarm Mrs. Forbes, and God knows how she might react. But if she didn't mail the letter, her mother wouldn't be prepared, and Vanessa would have to spring the news of her departure on the night of the performance. Vanessa had enough problems playing a witch and didn't need extra anxiety like that.

Vanessa's mind reeled from the confusion. She wondered if the school itself was contributing to her indecision. But, except for the incident in the phone booth, the school had not been particularly threatening of late. And Vanessa had to admit she didn't feel in any physical danger. As for any visions or tricks that the school might play on her in the remaining few days, Vanessa felt she could handle them. She'd certainly had enough experience, going back to the first day of the semester. She glanced up once more at the poster. Everyone was depending on her to play the lead part of Emily. How could she have even considered letting them all down? Vanessa made up her mind. She would mail the letter. By the weekend, her mother would be here, the play would be over, and Vanessa would be in

Mrs. Forbes' Mercedes heading back to Boston for good.

She slid the envelope into the mail slot.

Sometime after midnight, the lightning bolts which had pierced the skies over Hanley since midafternoon zigzagged off toward the ocean like angular phantoms in search of new horizons to terrorize. As if to make up for the diminished rumble of thunder, the downpour rose to a crescendo as the heavens unleashed a sheet of teeming rain.

On the ground floor, a figure emerged from the shadows. In the meager light of the foyer, the staunch woman plodded along the marble floor toward the headmaster's office. Under her breath, she hummed a ragged, unmelodic tune. When she reached the postal box, Blanche Trousdale unhooked a brass ring of keys from the belt of her floral housedress. She gave a quick glance over her beefy shoulder to make sure no one was watching, then inserted the key in the mailbox. There were a few envelopes inside. It only took the old woman a moment to pick out Vanessa's letter. She scowled at it, then tucked it in her pocket. She returned the other envelopes to the box, relocked it, and trudged off down the hall. "Smartass little bitch," she muttered as she returned to the shadows.

That stormy night, as Vanessa lay sleeping alone in Room Six, her decision to wait until after the performance of "The Dark" before leaving The Hanley School would undergo a change. Once Vanessa had mailed the letter to her mother, she had felt a sense of accomplishment. That had been the right move. It would be silly to leave before the show; a few more days would not hurt her. It was the nights she hadn't taken into consideration.

About one a.m., Vanessa's eyes had finally grown heavy with sleep. Occasional light from the moon gleamed ineffectually through the falling rain. It did nothing to make Room Six less dark. Vanessa had installed a small night light across the room, near Laura's empty bed. It had helped reveal whatever lurked in the shadowy corners of the room. With the sounds of the storm muted, the rhythm of the rain had lulled Vanessa to sleep. At 1:15, the slithering noises began.

At first, Vanessa thought that the sounds were part of an unremembered dream she'd been having or a tree branch, heavy with moisture, slapping at her window. She forced herself to open her eyes. She was no longer dreaming and there was no tree branch close enough to her window to have made the noise. Puzzled, she looked over at the burning night light, then quickly scanned the room. She could discern nothing that could be responsible for such a sound.

And then the light went out.

In the few seconds before Vanessa's eyes could adjust to the dark, she knew a blackness so all encompassing, so terrifying in its density, that it threatened to smother her. Slowly, she began to make out the familiar objects in her room and that was when she screamed.

Standing at a lopsided angle at the foot of Vanessa's bed, her hair matted with slime and dried blood, her spindly arms held out palms-up, her swollen, mangled flesh there rotted and crawling with vermin, was the corpse of Rickie Webster. The dead thing's eyes protruded from her sunken face, the flesh peeled away to expose hordes of maggots. Steam seemed to rise from the body in putrescent waves, foul-smelling fumes from the grave. Scraps of the dead girl's skin dripped to the floor, leaving a slippery trail of cankered flesh that the corpse's bony feet sloshed around in noisily.

"Rickie. Oh, my God. Rickie." Vanessa choked on the words. At the sound of her voice, the corpse drew back its lips, exposing a pustuled mouth, cavernous and infested with wormy decay. Oh Jesus, dear God, it was trying to smile at Vanessa. Surely, it couldn't recognize her. The festered lips were moving slightly, and Vanessa had the awful feeling that Rickie was struggling to speak to her.

The initial shock had driven Vanessa backward against the headboard, but now she leaned closer to the rotting figure that had somehow broken through from the grave. Vanessa sensed a remarkable perseverance, an urgency about Rickie that had brought her here tonight. Vanessa couldn't entirely dismiss the possibility that Rickie was an apparition of the school, its latest assault in a constant campaign of terror, but somehow she felt this was different.

Words gurgled in Rickie's throat. Vanessa leaned even closer. She could see the corpse's half-eaten tongue flapping against stumps of teeth, trying to articulate.

"*Don't be scared.*" The words were unmistakable. "*Just get out. Leave the school now. Don't wait, Vanessa. Go.*"

Even as the words were being spoken, the image of Rickie Webster was shriveling drastically, melting away like blistered wax. In a matter of moments, the corpse had dissipated into nothing more than a seething, bubbling pool of lava-like residue. Seconds later, this too disappeared and Vanessa was left only with the faint scent of a musty tomb.

Vanessa sat in a chair by the window, with all the lights on, for the remainder of the night. There were no more disturbances, and by three a.m. the rain had finally ceased. Vanessa concentrated her gaze on the horizon as if by this action she could will the morning sun to appear, but the day dawned grudgingly, slate gray and with the scent of still more rain in the air.

When 7:30 came, Vanessa began to hear sounds from the nearby rooms. The other girls were getting up. It wasn't too early for her to make the phone call.

Vanessa started toward the phone booth at the end of the corridor, but she made a detour at the stairs and went on up to the third floor. In the phone booth there, she quickly dialed a number. The switchboard operator at The Abbott School answered in a sleepy voice. Vanessa asked for Bobby Cannon. There was the usual delay, then the operator came back on the line. Bobby had not responded to the paging on the school's P.A. system. Would Vanessa like to leave a message? Yes. Bobby should meet Vanessa Forbes at the boathouse in half an hour.

Last night's heavy rainfall had turned the gentle slope of the lawn leading to the boathouse into a boggy surface, pocketed with muddy puddles and treacherous underfoot. A red maple tree was bowed down over the boathouse like a drooping umbrella. The roof of the building itself was strewn with dead leaves and branches that had blown there during the storm. The lake had overflowed, and Vanessa was ankle-deep in water by the time she reached the door.

She had barely sat down on the cushions inside when the door opened. She looked up expectantly, but it wasn't Bobby who stood there—it was Dennis. For the briefest moment, Vanessa felt gulty, as if she'd been caught doing something wrong. The feeling passed when Dennis spoke.

"I was worried about you, Vanessa. The operator said you sounded really shaky on the phone."

"Where's Bobby?"

"Bobby's still sleeping. I took the message. What's wrong?" Dennis sprawled on the floor next to Vanessa. He looked concerned.

Vanessa turned away. "I really wanted to talk to Bobby. Something happened to me last night, something I'll never forget as long as I live, something so fucking incredible . . ." Vanessa's voice broke. "I have to talk to Bobby."

"Well, Bobby's not here," Dennis said softly. "Why don't you tell me about it?"

"I can't."

"Why not?"

Vanessa twisted a strand of hair. She turned back to Dennis. "It has to do with the school, and I promised myself I'd never talk to you about the school again. Anyway, I don't think you'd understand."

"Did you see something?" Dennis asked. "Was it like a hallucination? Were you hurt?"

"No, I'm okay, Dennis. Please don't ask me any more questions."

"Vanessa, you're shaking. I want to know what happened." Dennis squeezed her hand. "Forget what I thought before. I believe you. I can tell you're not imagining things. I want to help."

Vanessa hesitated. "No, you'll think I'm crazy."

"I swear to you, I won't," Dennis said solemnly.

Something made Vanessa believe him. For the next ten minutes she recounted in vivid detail the ordeal she had gone through the night before. Dennis listened attentively, not once taking his eyes from her face. When she finished he gave a low whistle.

"Christ, you must have been scared to death. Are you sure you're alright?"

"Dennis, I'm getting out of here. I'm going to be on the next bus to Boston. Rickie said to leave—and I'm going."

"Okay, Vanessa," Dennis said calmly. "Let's take this one step at a time. First of all, I believe you. I believe you saw Rickie. I believe she told you to get out. But do you think that's the answer? Is it really that simple? Now other girls at the school have noticed that the place is weird. We know this."

"Not just weird, Dennis. Evil."

"Fine. But you're the one who thinks that. You're calling it evil because, for some reason, you're the one who's been singled out. What's happening to you is frightening and, because you don't understand it, you're building the whole thing up to some evil force that lives in the school. Suppose the visions you saw had been beautiful . . ."

"They weren't, Dennis. They were awful."

"Yeah, but just suppose. If instead of blood and dead people, you'd seen, say, beautiful clouds and flowers, then would you think those visions were evil even if they were coming from some kind of mystical or occult presence that existed in the school?"

Vanessa looked confused. "No, I guess not," she conceded.

"Okay, then," Dennis went on, "assuming that the visions are coming from the school, and assuming you were chosen to receive those visions, then obviously the school is trying to tell you something. The visions are grisly because that's the only way the school can get through to you. You know what I think, Vanessa? This isn't just a case of you being terrorized by visions. I think you've been selected as the person who can unravel a mystery."

"I have?"

"Think about it, Vanessa. You've already guessed that much. You know you've been chosen. Otherwise, you'd have cleared out of here when this shit first started coming down. Are you going to solve anything by going to Boston? How can you unravel a mystery from there?"

"Rickie didn't say anything about a mystery. She just said, 'Get out.' I think I ought to take that advice."

"Why?" Dennis asked with a wave of his hand. "You didn't even listen to Rickie when she was alive."

"Dennis, she was a corpse standing at the foot of my bed. She told me to leave."

"And that happened in the school, right?"

"What are you getting at?"

"You told me yourself the school played tricks on you. What if Rickie was a trick? What if the school was telling you to go?"

"But why would it do that?"

"So you can't get to the bottom of things. Ever since you've been here, the school has been doing things to you to scare you away. Isn't that proof that the school doesn't want you here? Are you going to run just when you're on the verge of figuring everything out?"

Vanessa sighed. "I don't know, Dennis. Sometimes I just feel so alone."

"You don't have to be alone. Let me ask you something. Where was Laura last night when all this was going on?"

"Come on, Dennis. Laura's never around. She was at Matthew Hanley's."

"If she had been there—if someone had been there with you—do you think this would have happened?"

Vanessa thought for several seconds. "Probably not."

"Okay, I've got an idea. How would you feel if I stayed in Laura's bed on the nights when she isn't around? That way, if something happens, I'll be there to help. Maybe we can solve the mystery together. And if nothing happens, at least you'll get some sleep. I'll even sit up during the night if you want me to. What do you think? Would you like that?"

"Yes, I would. But I need time to think."

"Fine. I'm here when you need me," Dennis said. "But promise me this—you won't leave without telling me."

Vanessa put her arms around Dennis and hugged him for a moment. "I promise."

Vanessa went to all her regular classes that day, but she wasn't really there. Though she took notes and feigned interest in what her teachers were saying, her mind kept wandering back to her conversation with Dennis in the boathouse. His argument for Vanessa to stay at the school was quite logical and made sense, but Vanessa had rejected most of it until he had raised the possibility that the school itself might want her to leave. This had given Vanessa pause for thought. If somehow Vanessa had tapped into a psychic vein that ran through the school, perhaps the force that lived there, whether evil or not, wanted her out, lest she discover some awful secret.

Vanessa had a more disturbing thought. All along, she'd been assuming that the strange apparitions were confined to a specific locale—the school grounds. What if that weren't the case? What if Vanessa went to Boston and the visions followed her there? What made her think she could escape this madness by getting away from Hanley? Maybe Dennis was right. Maybe Vanessa should stay and puzzle it all out.

It wasn't fair, thought Vanessa. Why should all of this be happening to her? She was only a 17 year old girl who should be enjoying one of the best years of her life. Instead, she was a nervous wreck who was doubting her own grip on reality.

Vanessa had seen something in Dennis this morning that had eluded her up till now—a genuine concern for her welfare. Dennis was certainly no stranger to Room Six, having spent many a night there last year with Laura. But it took courage for him to put himself on the line, volunteering to stand watch, for God knows what, while Vanessa slept. Besides, if he got caught in her room he could be expelled from Abbott. Vanessa felt guilty. In a way, it was her fault that Bobby and Dennis were no longer speaking to each other. Maybe she should talk to the two of them and try to patch things up.

By the time the bell rang at the end of the last class, Vanessa felt better. She thought about her mother. By this time tomorrow, Evelyn Forbes would have read Vanessa's letter. That would pretty much decide things, Vanessa realized. Her mother would never let her stay at Hanley after reading that kind of plea for help. The matter would be out of Vanessa's hands, thank God—unless the horror of Hanley traveled with her. She could only pray that it wouldn't.

Coming out of world history class, Vanessa spotted Matthew Hanley, and all the logic of Dennis' persuasive argument crumbled into dust. Vanessa felt a fluttering of electricity in her stomach and her legs grew weak. The attraction to the headmaster was stronger than ever.

almost overpowering. This was no hallucination. This was no trick of the school. She was drawn like a magnet to a man she didn't even care for. This was painfully real.

Vanessa leaned against the wall, trying to compose herself. Only when Matthew disappeared out the front door of the building did she regain control. Vanessa tucked her books under her arm and started down the corridor. Now she knew what she had to do.

14

For the next two days, the skies over Hanley seemed to go mad. Vicious electric storms shot through the heavens that turned day to night and night back again to day. The temperature rose and fell by as much as 40 degrees, as rain gave way to hail, then snow. The lawns were bathed in dew, which by nightfall hardened to a slick frost nearly impossible to maneuver on. The freak weather became the main topic of conversation, almost an obsession, for the Hanley students who closely followed the local radio and TV reports to learn of flash floods which took out many of the roads in the area, mud slides which buried several houses, and crop failures involving vast quantities of produce. The Abbott boys who had to trudge over to Hanley for rehearsals assembled each afternoon in the foyer of their school with a jumbled assortment of umbrellas, raincoats, galoshes and even sun glasses to combat the blinding brightness that came intermittently through the bluish-black clouds in splashes of preternatural fury.

On the afternoon of the play's technical rehearsal, Dennis and Bobby walked over to Hanley on opposite sides of the lake from each other. The two boys still weren't speaking, and each cast a long, solitary shadow that jutted out like an intimidating spear. A slight drizzle was falling, and Bobby felt distressed. There was something sad about the way the sun hung half-hidden in the sky, as though it were being mocked by the sinister banks of pitch black clouds that threatened it on all sides. The sun had been a prisoner for the past two days and only was released for brief respites with a teasing cruelty that made its appearances that much more degrading.

As Bobby came up the incline of the lawn, he batted with his hand at a thick cluster of iridescent greenish flies that hovered in the damp air. How strange, Bobby thought, to see so many flies bunched together while it was raining. Involuntarily, Bobby's eyes went up toward the most reprehensible part of The School. He stopped dead in his tracks. Swarming around the monstrous gargoyles at the edge of the roof was a colony of darning needles, more of them in one pack than Bobby had ever seen in his life. Bobby shuddered. It was an insect that had always terrified him. He watched, his feet planted in the muddy grass, as the insects hummed and flitted about, their slender bodies abnormally magnified in the late afternoon blur of sunlight. Bobby couldn't imagine why but he seemed to be able to focus in on the flying insects' strong jaws and finely veined wings. Bobby hated darning needles. He'd hated them ever since he was a little boy. *Devil's darning needle*. The full name of the insect only added to his terror.

Inside the foyer, Bobby spotted Vanessa standing near the auditorium door. He went over to her. "Have you told Dennis yet?" he asked.

"You mean about me going home after the show?" Vanessa shook her head. "No, not yet. I just haven't found the right opportunity."

Bobby laughed. "How come? He's been sleeping in your room for two nights."

"Well, it's not that easy, Bobby. Dennis would like me to stay for the rest of the term. He thinks he's found a way to keep me here. But he's been so sweet the last couple of nights, staying up with me, talking to me, standing watch . . ."

"Oh, is that what he's been doing?"

"Sure, Bobby. Standing watch is what this is all about. It was really great that Dennis offered to do that."

"Well, is it working? Have you seen anything? Any visions?"

"No, but I've been up half the night with all this lightning and thunder. I'm glad Dennis was there. It was pretty scary. You'd think if the school was up to any more tricks, they would have happened while all that crap was going on outside. I was a bundle of nerves, Bobby, but, except for the weather, it's been pretty normal."

"Nothing's normal around here, Vanessa. You know that."

Vanessa nodded. "That's true enough. If I've learned nothing else about the school, I've learned this much—it sneaks up on you. Just when you think it's safe, Bobby, it pounces on you like a wild animal."

The other students were filing into the auditorium now. It was nearly time for the tech rehearsal to begin. Bobby looked around. There was still no sign of Dennis.

"Well," Bobby said, "I already told you my advice. I think you should get out of here as soon as possible. Just go."

"I can't just go."

"Why not?"

"That's not like me, Bobby. I stuck it out this long. Besides, I don't like letting people down."

"Like who? Karin Sayers? Do you really think she'd care? She's so fucking nuts these days she probably wouldn't even notice you were gone."

"No, you're wrong. She's obsessed with this play, and I'm her leading lady."

"Yeah, the chief witch," Bobby said with a smile. "I've got news for you, Vanessa. Marie was telling me last night she knows every line in this play. If you stepped down, she could play Emily in a second."

Vanessa punched him playfully on the arm. "Thanks a lot, Bobby. I've worked hard on this role. I'm not about to give it up just so I can leave two days earlier. My Mom's going to call me tonight. I'm sure of it. Marie may know the lines but she can't possibly play the part on such short notice. No, Bobby, I'm going to do it, and I'll be out of here the second that curtain goes down."

Dennis Bellivin slipped into the foyer and was only a few feet away, concealed by a marble pillar, unseen by Vanessa and Bobby.

"Well, Vanessa," Bobby said, "I still think you ought to leave now, but if you want to wait until after the performance, fine. It's still the right decision. And you know something? Whether you realize it or not, I think you did the right thing by not telling Dennis. I don't think you should tell him at all."

Still behind the column, Dennis clenched his fists. His mouth set in a thin, angry line, he started to take a step toward the unsuspecting couple, but then drew back. Better to wait. He looked around at the comforting walls of the school. Better to leave things in the hands of a higher power.

Bobby and Vanessa went into the auditorium, which was abuzz with activity. The technical staff was scurrying about, rigging lights and lifting scenery into place under the supervision of Ingrid, the stage manager. Karin Sayers, center stage, was shouting orders to the crew. Wearing a form-fitting black leotard and a pair of tight black shorts, she managed to look frenzied and funereal at the same time.

"Jesus, look at Sayers," Bobby said to Vanessa as the two of them hung back at the rear of the theater. "I've never seen her this wired."

"Are you kidding? She's been like this for days. I think

this weird weather really turns her on."

"But there's something about her face . . ."

"It's the eyes, Bobby. It's all that black eye shadow. She looks like a skeleton."

Just then, they felt a pair of arms encircling their shoulders from behind. They turned to see Dennis, a broad smile on his face. He made a sweeping gesture to take in the auditorium and ended by pointing to Karin.

"Welcome to Make-Believe-Land," Dennis whispered.

Down the hall from the auditorium, in the school kitchen, Blanche Trousdale sat at a gleaming chrome counter, polishing silverware. Occasionally, she glanced up at a five inch black and white television, which was tuned to a Bugs Bunny cartoon. The door of the kitchen swung open and Desmond glided in.

"I just talked to our friend," he announced. "The Forbes girl is getting out after the play."

Blanche turned a butter knife over with her stubby fingers. "That's time enough," she said. "Is he sure?"

Desmond lowered his bony frame onto a stool. "What do you mean, is he sure?"

"What are you, deaf? The girl keeps changing her mind. How does he knew what she's going to do? How do we know we can trust him?"

Desmond scowled at Bugs Bunny as he stepped off a cliff. "This is a fine time to be asking that, Blanche."

"He was always your choice—not mine."

"Yes, but you gave him your approval."

"Desmond, he's just a kid," Blanche said sourly.

"They're all kids when they first get here. He's done a lot of growing up."

"What are you talking about? He's had it easy. Star football player. Straight A's in class. Any girl he wants. But this is the payoff, Desmond. I just don't know if he's going to be up to it."

"If you're talking about loyalty, Blanche, he's got it. He knows goddamn well what made it easy for him. He also knows it doesn't stop here. You mark my words—that boy will run for President some day."

"Not in our lifetime," Blanche grumbled.

Desmond ran his palm lovingly along the tiled wall of the kitchen. "You shouldn't say that, Blanche. The school's been good to us for many years now. It's kept us young. If you ask me, anything's possible."

Blanche shoved a Western Union envelope across the counter. "This just came. It's for the Forbes girl."

Desmond took the message from the already opened envelope. He read the telegram aloud.

" 'Dear Vanessa. Save opening night ticket for me. Break a leg. Hope you're enjoying Hanley. See you soon. Love, Mom.' " Desmond passed the telegram back to his wife. "Perfect. It's just as good as the one we were going to send. Saves us the trouble."

"What about that line 'Hope you're enjoying Hanley'? The kid's going to know we didn't send the letter."

Desmond looked at her with a superior air. "Don't be stupid, Blanche. In this weather, she'll just think it didn't get there. I don't know what's wrong with you today. You're not thinking straight. What's the matter? Are you nervous?"

Blanche put her head down on the counter. "Of course I'm nervous," she said quietly. "We've waited a long time for all the elements to be in place. We're so close now. What if something goes wrong?"

Desmond patted the wall again. "You have to trust," he said tenderly. "The school has never let us down before."

The tech rehearsal was not going well. It had long been apparent to Ingrid and the other members of the crew that "The Dark" was a difficult show, with a seemingly endless procession of light and sound cues. The tech staff had prepared for the rehearsal, but before an hour was up, the students were becoming resigned to the realization that it was going to be a very long evening.

Not so Karin Sayers. She greeted each technical failure with an impatient wave of her arm, demanding that whatever was wrong be fixed immediately even when the tech staff protested that they would need time to resolve the problem. Karin herself had a workmanlike knowledge of light boards and sound equipment, but she was so fidgety and restless to keep things moving at all costs that she didn't take the time to help the students remedy the trouble. Instead, she merely raced about the auditorium, making random criticisms and snapping orders like a frayed drill sergeant.

At the core of Karin's being—in the vortex of what was left of her rational mind—was a determination to see this production through in a professional manner, but outside forces, unnatural elements, seemed to be waging war on all of her senses. As she struggled to retain a grip on what really had to be done today in the auditorium, she felt her equilibrium fluctuating dangerously. Her vision blurred as commonplace objects seemed to grow magnified while others appeared to shoot off into the distance as if Karin were viewing them through the wrong end of a telescope. Her hearing was occasionally jolted by sharp detonations of sound that exploded in her brain, tapering off to a low rumble. The air in the theatre seemed acrid and heavy, and a flinty taste, as of gunpowder, coated Karin's tongue. Her skin prickled, as objects in the auditorium met her touch with a touch of their own. The grip of the unnatural elements was slowly twisting Karin into submission.

Though the complete costume wardrobe would not be ready until dress rehearsal the following night, some of the outfits had already arrived. Several of the students were excitedly opening boxes and changing into 17th century clothing. Laura, in her high priestess garb, sat on a piano bench next to Marie, who was dressed as a peasant girl. Laura mopped her brow.

"I'm dying in this outfit. There's no pockets. I don't know what to do with my drugs."

"Maybe you should give them to Sayers," Marie said dryly. "She looks like she could use them."

Laura watched as Karin bobbed around the stage. "Are you kidding? The woman's stark raving mad. She doesn't need drugs."

"What do you suppose went wrong with her this year? She used to be so normal. You know, this is a really hard show to put on. Do you think it's the play that's making her crazy?"

"No," Laura said. "I think she got crazy first. And that's why we're doing this play."

"That's not funny, Laura."

"I know. I didn't mean it to be."

Freddy Cooper, a senior at Abbott, wandered over to them, his warlock's hat perched precariously on his head.

"Anyone selling tickets for opening night?" he asked.

"I am," Laura said. "You buyng? Ten bucks apiece. Ten bucks or three Quaaludes."

Freddy laughed, rolled his eyes and continued down the row of seats. Marie turned to Laura. "You selling your comps? Aren't your folks coming?"

Laura shrugged. "My dad's putting up condos in Saudi Arabia and my mom's at a clinic in Switzerland getting injected with sheep urine."

"Ugh, gross!"

"Yeah," Laura muttered, "and they say I'm putting shit into my body."

She reached under the lid of the piano and took out a small cocaine vial. Attached to it by a chain was a small silver spoon. Laura looked around and, satisfied that no one was paying attention, scooped some of the white powder onto the spoon and held it under her nose for two quick snorts. She passed the vial to Marie who also inhaled the drug.

"Sure beats sheep's piss," Laura said with a laugh.

Marie handed back the cocaine. "Wouldn't it be safer to keep this in your purse?"

"Nah, my purse is backstage. I'd have to keep running back to the dressing room. The piano's real convenient." Laura lifted the piano lid again and returned the vial to its hiding place. "I've got a pack of cigarettes in here, too."

Up on the stage, Vanessa was sitting with Bobby, going over some lines. Above them, Ingrid scampered along the catwalk, checking out the scrims and the curtain.

"Where's Dennis?" Bobby asked.

Vanessa looked up from her script. "I don't know. Last time I saw him, he was backstage with the wardrobe girl. His shirt popped a couple of buttons when he put it on. I guess they forgot he's a football player. He's such a jock sometimes—probably doesn't know his own strength."

"Oh, I think he does," Bobby said cryptically. He was silent for a moment. "I still can't believe he spoke to me."

"Well, Bobby, he was bound to sooner or later. You guys have been pretty good friends for a long time."

Bobby shook his head. "I don't like the way he put his arm around me, the way he hugged us."

"What do you mean?"

"It was phony. It wasn't like Dennis. Couldn't you feel it?"

"Yes, it did feel awkward, but maybe he felt funny about making up with you. And that was the easiest way to do it."

"You know, Vanessa, I'm not sure he made up with me at all."

Vanessa looked out into the auditorium and watched as a formidable figure came down the aisle. The intense glare from a technician's lamp projected the shadow of Mrs. Trousdale's huge head so that it covered one entire wall of the theater. Vanessa had the suspicion at once that the old caretaker was headed directly for her. Mrs.

Trousdale came to the apron of the stage and drummed her fingers impatiently on the floor boards. Vanessa went over to her and the old woman gave her a baleful stare as she handed her the telegram.

"Here," she said in a steely voice, "I signed for this. I hope it's not bad news."

Mrs. Trousdale turned on her heel and marched off. On her way back up the aisle, she nearly collided with Karin Sayers, who was running back from the light booth. Mrs. Trousdale patted Karin encouragingly on the shoulder and went on.

"Charming, isn't she?" Bobby quipped. Vanessa tore open the Western Union envelope and read the message inside. She showed it to Bobby.

"My mom's coming."

Bobby folded the telegram. "I guess she didn't get your letter."

"Probably the storm. The important thing is that she's coming. I can't wait to see her. I guess I can put up with the school for two more days."

"Maybe," Bobby conceded, his voice growing tense. "But what about Dennis?"

Bobby gestured toward the other side of the stage. Dennis was watching them, his arms folded arrogantly. His casual camaraderie from before had vanished, and he fixed Vanessa with a cruel, hard gaze that seethed with resentment.

By nightfall, jet black strips of clouds had positioned themselves around the moon, a sliver of light, ribboned and packaged like some giant gift that was waiting to be presented to The Hanley School. This mist spun a gossamer landscape that changed patterns as the north wind blew without mercy, whistling an ethereal melody for the night's creatures. The school seemed swollen this evening, puffed up and proud, insolent and waiting.

Deep underneath the building's foundation, in the very soil that it was built on, a pulsating, ritualistic rhythm had begun. On this ground, the particular circumstances of its origins too clouded to be remembered, the evil had started. Perhaps it had stemmed from a senseless killing in nature like one animal devouring another for purposes other than nourishment. Or perhaps, as a single flame carelessly lit multiplies to consume an entire forest in an inevitable conflagration, the evil had simply grown, burrowing its way toward its fated outcome. The syncopated rhythm, minutely louder with each beat, was the unstoppable cadence that nurtured each step of the relentless evolution.

Blood from helpless, unsuspecting victims had run into this earth, filling the cracks and crevices like a life-sustaining glue, holding the evil together and binding it to the structure that now stood on its Satanic soil. Under the skillful guidance of the school's founder, Malcolm Hanley, a shrine had been constructed. As Malcolm directed his workers, something infinitely more powerful and cunning directed Malcolm. What had begun with a trickle of blood or a wisp of flame was about to be renewed, ripening to a more advanced species of malignancy.

The setting was the same and would always be the same, but a new cast of players was on the stage. Now, before the thin wafer of moon would swell to its next phase, the ancient rhythm that coursed beneath the school would intensify, rising to a peak more shrill than the cry of a mutilated beast or the roar of a once verdant forest ravaged by a blazing inferno.

"But what about Dennis?"

The question that Bobby Cannon had asked two hours ago was still echoing in his brain. Dennis had been staring at him for nearly all of that time, and Bobby had gone from being mildly uncomfortable at finding himself the object of Dennis' unblinking scrutiny to being downright frightened at the sheer malice that his roommate made no effort to disguise.

Even now, while Dennis was enacting a love scene with Vanessa, his eyes never left Bobby. The stilted language of "The Dark," which had long-since lost its magic for the students, had never sounded more remote, especially since Dennis' eyes seemed to have no connection with the words that were coming from his mouth. Bobby wondered if anyone had noticed the way Dennis was behaving, how he seemed to be focusing all his attention on Bobby for God knows what reason. Vanessa was caught up in the scene, while Karin Sayers was following every line, looking transfixed, almost fervent. Next to Bobby, Laura was tapping her toes and fingers a mile a minute. She was gone, thought Bobby. As long as the coke held up, she wouldn't notice much of anything. Laura had been absolutely brazen about going to the piano for her stash and had even done it once when an Abbott student was hammering on the keys, playing a song during a break. But there had been very few breaks tonight—Karin Sayers had seen to that. This was a bitch of a production, and they would be lucky to get out of there by midnight.

Bobby watched as Ingrid climbed down a rope ladder from the catwalk, looking pretty steady on her feet. Bobby was relieved. He'd been worried about Ingrid lately, but she'd promised him she'd lay off the booze. Except for a few quick nips from her flask, she'd been true to her word. Bobby couldn't really blame her for those few lapses. The tech rehearsal was Ingrid's responsibility, and Karin had been on her case since this afternoon. Bobby caught a movement on one of the pipes near the catwalk. Something was stirring there in the shadows, black and furry. Bobby nudged Laura and pointed. She laughed. Jesus Christ, thought Bobby, only at The Hanley School would a tarantula named Baby be walking around during a drama rehearsal.

"Fuck," Laura said under her breath. "This goddamn place is like the Twilight Zone."

"I know," Bobby said. "Look at the way Dennis is staring at me."

"Is he?" Laura said, sounding surprised. "I thought he was staring at me."

"God, you're getting paranoid, Laura. You'd better lay off that coke."

"No chance of that, Bobby. Coke may make me paranoid but that's a good way to be around here. You can't be too careful in this place."

Ingrid hurried past them toward some ropes that were fastened at the side of the stage near the lightboard. Bobby was beginning to grow restless. The constant drone of dialogue between Dennis and Vanessa, with its references to evil, witchcraft and flowers of darkness, was getting on his nerves. His leg muscles felt a little cramped from all the time he'd been sitting on a hard bench. Bobby stood up and stretched, then wandered over to where a couple of stagehands were trying to build a witches' pyre out of construction board and two-by-fours. Dennis followed him with his gaze; his eyes were almost mesmerizing now.

Bobby turned away from Dennis. He knelt down with the stagehands and held a piece of board in place so that it could be affixed to a strip of wood. At least this would keep him occupied for a while and alleviate his boredom. The tedious murmur of the rehearsal hummed on, while directly above Bobby Cannon, a heavy rope, securely tied up near the catwalk, began to unravel like a deadly cobra writhing from a basket to the hypnotic melody of a snake charmer's flute. Free of its moorings, the rope shot upward sending a 50 pound sandbag plummeting down toward the stage.

"Look out!" Dennis shouted.

It was too late for Bobby to completely get out of the sandbag's path, but Dennis' cry of warning caused Bobby to duck his head slightly. The heavy sandbag missed Bobby's head by inches, slamming into his shoulder and driving him brutally to the floor. There was a stunned silence.

Bobby's conscious mind struggled through a maze of confusion. He couldn't fathom why he was suddenly sprawled on the floor of the stage, but an excruciating pain, beginning at his neck and running down the full length of his spine, was clamoring for his attention. Then as quickly as the sharp knife of pain ripped through him, it subsided as if his body was flooded with a comforting wave that washed away all the hurt. *I'm going into shock*, Bobby knew. An instant later he was there.

The stillness was shattered by a scream from Laura Nash. There was the heavy thud of running footsteps, and quickly Bobby was surrounded. One of the stage-hands rolled Bobby onto his back and he saw the face of Karin Sayers swim before his eyes.

Karin looked dazed, unable to help. Dennis pushed his way through the crowd. "Don't move him," he ordered. "Call an ambulance." Dennis seemed calm, in control.

Marie took one look at Bobby's crumpled body. *Thank God*, she thought, *at least there's no blood*. But Bobby's eyes were staring, unfocused, at the ceiling. Laura put her arm around Marie consolingly and led her away. One of the students charged down the aisle in search of a telephone. Bobby continued to lie motionless at center stage. Next to him, sand poured from the bag onto the floorboards like time running through an hour-glass.

At the edge of the circle, Ingrid was weeping into her hands. "Oh, God," she moaned, "I tied that bag myself!" Karin, her eyes glazed over, stared at her curiously. "Miss Sayers, I tied that bag. N*othing* could make it come loose!"

Alone, off to the side of the stage, Vanessa stood watching the proceedings as if in a dream. She felt oddly detached, like she was viewing a highway car accident that had happened to complete strangers. Bobby immobile on the floor, the halo of concerned students around him, the deflated sandbag—none of it seemed real, just play-acting. Vanessa half-expected Bobby at any moment to leap to his feet, a wide grin on his face, and take an exaggerated bow while the others applauded appreciatively. It's the school, she knew. It plays tricks on you. But in the corner of Bobby's eye a single tear had formed, wet and glistening, telling her that wasn't so.

A half hour later, an ambulance from the county medical center was parked in the drizzling rain on the gravel driveway at the front entrance of the school. Bobby Cannon, anesthetized now from the pain that had assaulted him as soon as the initial shock had worn off, was being wheeled out on a stretcher. The students milled about in the rain, except for Laura, who had wandered aimlessly over toward the side lawn. Laura wanted to avoid Matthew Hanley, who had been summoned from his cottage. She just wasn't in the mood for his take-charge persona, and she had seen just about enough of Karin Sayers, who was acting as if nothing unusual had even happened.

One of the hospital attendants turned to Matthew Hanley. "Looks like a fractured shoulder, sir."

Matthew nodded soberly. Beside him, Ingrid was still crying quietly. Bobby looked so fragile, engulfed in the pale white covers of the stretcher. As he was about to be lifted into the vehicle, Ingrid took Bobby's hand, squeezing it for just a moment.

"It wasn't your fault, Ingrid," Bobby said with conviction. His head moved slightly on the pillow so that he could look directly at Vanessa. He took a deep, wheezing breath and slowly exhaled it. "And it was no accident. Leave tonight, Vanessa. You might be next."

Vanessa couldn't watch as Bobby was loaded into the ambulance. As the vehicle drove slowly down the winding path toward the front gate, Ingrid came up behind Vanessa.

" 'You might be next?' What does that mean?"

Vanessa turned to face her squarely. "I'm leaving. I'm going home tonight."

Matthew had heard her from a few yards away on the lawn. He came over to Vanessa, his arm encircling her waist.

"What's this talk about leaving?" the headmaster asked. "Bobby's going to be fine. You're the leading lady, Vanessa. The school needs you."

Matthew brushed a strand of hair from Vanessa's forehead. Against her will, she leaned her body into his. Uncomfortable, Ingrid drifted away. The sexual attraction Vanessa had felt before for Matthew was heightened as she pressed her breasts against his chest. Matthew's strong, masculine smell fused with the smoky scent of rain-drenched autumn leaves, and Vanessa felt dizzy as if she had sampled some forbidden potion. Almost imperceptibly, Matthew's hold on her was tightening.

Laura was a silent witness from the side lawn. She felt a quick twinge of jealousy—what was Matthew trying to pull this time?—but the feeling passed almost right away. Matthew was up to something all right. He never did anything without an ulterior motive. If he was hugging Vanessa like this, in full view of everybody, it couldn't just be because he was consoling her or because he wanted to sleep with her. No, it was something more insidious. Vanessa was vulnerable and Matthew knew it. Vanessa was swaying in Matthew's arms like a starstruck kid. That was not like Vanessa, but it was sure as hell just like Matthew to take advantage of her for whatever devious purpose he had in mind. Laura was puzzled—and a little scared. What frightened her most was the figure of Dennis Bellivin, calmly leaning against an oak tree several feet away from Vanessa and Matthew, smiling at them with an unmistakable air of approval.

The siren on the ambulance bearing Bobby Cannon away wailed forlornly in the distance. As it faded, it was replaced by an even more compelling sound. The thunder was back. It came over the assembled group swiftly and drowned out the siren that cried out to the night. An arrow of lightning speared the sky and the bloated clouds rolled over Hanley like a huge brush painting the heavens and smearing out the moon. Under the cacophony of thunder was another sound, a snarling noise, almost metallic, an ancient creak like a sealed tomb's leaden door being pried open after a century. Though all who were at Hanley could hear it, only a few recognized it for what it was—the sound of unadulterated fury, primal and pristine. The pure anger of the school was keening into the dark. Those who knew what the sound was also knew that the Cannon boy had escaped with his life. He had not been supposed to live, but an instinctive warning, shouted in his direction, had prevented his death. Long after the storm had finally passed, the school screamed wordless obscenities into the night.

"Do you believe Sayers wanted to go on with rehearsal?" Marie asked, as she took a sip of her Margarita.

Following Bobby Cannon's departure, Laura had suggested that Marie, Ingrid and Vanessa join her for a bull session, the drunker the better. They had pooled their resources. Marie had a blender. Ingrid supplied the tequila and triple sec. Vanessa and Laura went to the kitchen and swiped the salt and some limes. After preparing two gigantic pitchers of Margaritas in Ingrid's room, the girls had been about to start drinking but had come to a unanimous conclusion. Being in the school was depressing. They would take their chances with the chilly, damp boathouse just to get out of the building. Besides, as Ingrid had pointed out, after a couple stiff belts, they'd warm up soon enough.

"What about Sayers out by the ambulance?" Ingrid asked. "She acted like nothing happened."

Laura licked the salt from the rim of her glass. "Maybe she couldn't see. She had so much mascara on, it probably blinded her."

"The woman's brain is gone."

The kerosene lamp in the boathouse window was lit, its wick turned up all the way. None of the girls wanted to sit in darkness surrounded by gloom. There had been too much off that lately. They huddled on the floor, wrapped in blankets, seated around the communal pitchers.

"I still don't understand why we couldn't go to the hospital," Marie said.

"Yeah, I really wanted to be with him," Ingrid said, her eyes still red from crying.

"No," Laura said, "the paramedic was right. Bobby's got to go in for X-rays, and we wouldn't be able to see him anyway. We'd just be hanging around the lobby. He's so drugged he wouldn't even know we were there. Better we should be here toasting to his quick recovery. We can see him tomorrow."

There was a thoughtful silence. Marie held up her drink, and the four girls clinked glasses.

Ingrid gulped down the liquor. "Did you hear what Bobby said? Vanessa might be next."

Laura grinned mischievously. "Well, Ingrid, that's up to you. Tie up another sandbag and see what happens."

"That's not funny," Ingrid said.

Marie giggled into her Margarita. "So how come I'm laughing?"

"Bobby said it wasn't my fault." Ingrid's voice rose defensively.

"He also told me it was no accident," Vanessa said. The others looked at her in surprise.

"Yeah?" Laura looked surprised. "No shit. You mean someone did it on purpose?"

"I tied the bag," Ingrid interjected. "Anybody could have untied it. Could've been just a joke. If it had just landed on the stage, we all would've laughed."

"No accident," Vanessa said and paused. "But that doesn't mean it was done by a person."

"What do you mean?" Marie asked. "If it wasn't done by a person, what are you talking about—a thing?" Her words were a little slurred. She was already feeling the effects of the alcohol, but the other girls weren't far behind her.

"I know what you're thinking, Vanessa," Ingrid said. "The school did it. Well, it wouldn't surprise me."

Laura refilled the glasses. "Fuck the school. We didn't come out here to freeze our tits off to talk about that goddamn place. We're out here to get away from it."

"No," Marie said stubbornly, "I want to hear what Vanessa means."

"Oh, great," Laura said, "we'll all sit around here telling ghost stories, scaring the shit out of each other, and then we've got to go back to the House Of Wax to try and go to sleep."

"Who's going back?" Ingrid said. "I may just pass out right here tonight."

"Actually, if you want to hear my theory about the sandbag," Laura said, "I think Walter Cox did it. Nobody's seen him for a long time. I think he climbs around the rafters in the auditorium like the Phantom of the Opera."

Ingrid managed a laugh. "I think your brain is climbing around the rafters."

The girls clinked glasses. This time they all drank greedily. Laura reached for the second pitcher and passed around the lime and the salt. Soon the quartet had fresh Margaritas.

Marie looked out the window sadly. "Poor Bobby."

"He'll be okay," Laura said. "Now he doesn't have to do this fucking play." She considered this for a moment, then looked over at Vanessa. "Neither do you."

"She's not going to," Ingrid said. "She's leaving tonight."

"Oh?"

Vanessa shook her head. "No, I'm not. I changed my mind. I'm staying."

"But out on the lawn . . . you said . . ."

Vanessa's voice was testy. "I told you I've changed my mind. I'm staying."

"You mean for the whole term?" Laura asked.

"No. Just till after the play. Then I'm going back to Boston with my mother."

"What was it that made you change your mind?" Laura asked. "Was it that little talk you had with Matthew? Could that have something to do with it?"

"I don't have to answer that." There was a trace of anger in Vanessa's tone.

Laura smiled knowingly. She had been right. Matthew Hanley had done something strange to Vanessa while they were pressed together on the lawn—something powerful and unnatural. She knew Vanessa desperately wanted to leave. She also knew her roommate did not want to do "The Dark." Yet the mere touch of Matthew had overridden all Vanessa's resolve. Where did this hold over Vanessa come from? Was it Matthew? Was it the school? And where did Dennis Bellivin, that silently watching figure by the oak tree, fit in?

An hour later, Laura pounded drunkenly on the door to Matthew Hanley's cottage. She had some questions for him and was determined to get the answers tonight. Laura knew she'd had too much to drink and she wasn't particularly interested in sleeping with Matthew, but staying the night at the cottage with him was preferable to being in the school. As a matter of fact, sleeping on a bed of nails was preferable to being in the school. Though Laura had spoken to Vanessa and a few of the other girls about the creepiness of the place, she'd never confessed to them the true extent of her fear at being there, a fear that was growing stronger each day. Laura knew if she weren't graduating this year, she would never stay for another term. It wouldn't be worth the price she'd have to pay—her sanity.

Matthew Hanley opened the cottage door. Laura eyed his look of surprise with indifference and elbowed her way into his living room. Suddenly, her demanding questions seemed a jumble. Her determination in the boathouse to get to the bottom of this Matthew/Vanessa thing had faded—it all seemed so silly now. What was it to Laura that Matthew was manipulative? She'd known that when she'd started her relationship with him. "Relationship." Even the word made her laugh. Matthew had never been more than a diversion to Laura. Now Vanessa would have to deal with him. None of these problems seemed as interesting to Laura as the pillow on the couch in Matthew's living room. Matthew still hadn't spoken a word of greeting. He just watched from the doorway as Laura sank onto the sofa cushions, rested her head on the pillow and closed her eyes.

"Can't sleep in that goddamn nuthouse," Laura mumbled. A minute later, she had passed out.

Marie and Ingrid tiptoed stealthily down the second floor corridor. Marie opened the door to her room, then turned to Ingrid. "I got a favor to ask you."

Ingrid clutched the triple sec bottle in one hand. She knew immediately what Marie wanted. "Uh-uh, Marie. No way. I ain't sleeping in Rickie's bed."

"Come on. It's just for one night. I'm scared. I don't want to sleep alone."

"Good. You can bunk with me. I'll put some blankets on the floor."

They continued along to Ingrid's tiny room at the end of the hallway. Inside, the floor shimmered in a faint red glow from the diminished moon which forced its meager light through the stained-glass window. Quickly, the girls constructed a makeshift bed for Marie, then Ingrid poured out the remains of the triple sec into a couple of mugs. "Sweet dreams, Marie," she said in a toast.

Marie looked around at the gloomy shadows. "Yeah,

fat chance of that."

Karin Sayers, naked and tangled in her sweat-soaked sheets, was in the throes of a feverish nightmare. The murmurs in the walls of her room had lulled her to sleep hours ago, but now they created a raspy soundtrack for her troubled dreams. Karin writhed on the bed, her fingers opening and closing in silent panic. With lips pulled back, baring her teeth, she seemed on the verge of a terrified scream. Behind her closed lids, Karin's eyes darted back and forth frantically, seeking a way to escape whatever monstrous, predatory demon was threatening her. There was no release. The scream kept catching in her throat, reducing itself to a helpless gurgle. Perspiration beaded her face, her corn silk hair, wet now, was like a twisted mass of straw on the pillow. There would be no let-up for Karin Sayers tonight. Her mind and body would be tortured like this until dawn.

At The Hanley Medical Center, Bobby Cannon drifted in and out of sleep all night. The painkillers worked only intermittently, and he was too excited to relax in any case. Hours earlier, when he had come out of X-ray, he had spoken to his parents long distance. They were driving up from New York first thing in the morning. Bobby had made a decision. He would transfer out of Abbott, hopefully to a private school in Manhattan. The alternative would have been to stay on at Abbott and disassociate himself entirely from The Hanley School, but that would mean giving up drama and all his female friends. Besides, he wouldn't really be getting away from the school, not even then. He would still have to look at it from the other side of the lake every day, and he doubted whether that small body of water was enough to keep the evil at bay.

Over the phone, Bobby could only hint to his parents of the supernatural-like events that had taken place. The evil was too fantastic to be summed up in a five minute conversation. Tomorrow, during the car ride back to New York, he would fill them in completely on what had happened and why he felt that The Hanley School should be closed forever. He knew that his mother and father would believe him, but he also realized that shutting down a place like Hanley would take time. Meanwhile, he still had friends there—very good friends. He had warned Vanessa to get out, and he could only hope that she and Marie and Ingrid and Laura would take that warning to heart. He would do everything he could to convince their parents that The Hanley School For Girls was a threat to their lives, to their very souls, but he would do all of that from the safety of New York. He had an overwhelming sense of relief. Tomorrow, he would be putting this place behind him and would never have to see The Hanley School again.

But what about Dennis? Again, he was asking himself that question. Dennis had saved his life. If he hadn't cried out a warning, Bobby would be dead now. But curiously, he felt no gratitude. Instead, he could only remember Dennis' cold, unwavering stare at rehearsal and how he hadn't even comforted him on the lawn after the accident. Bobby felt no compulsion to rescue Dennis. Something told him that Dennis was exactly where he wanted to be. Good, thought Bobby as he slipped back into sleep. Let Dennis stay there—but, God, let the others get out.

Dennis Belivin sat on the window seat in Room Six of the school. He looked at the clock. Two a.m. It had been unusually noisy this evening. First, there had been the thunder, deafening in its power. Then, there had been the obscene shrieks like quick slashes in the night. Dennis was certain he was the only one who could hear them. Around midnight, Ingrid and Marie had made a horrendous racket, giggling and lurching drunkenly down the hall. Even Vanessa's breathing as she slept, which had been soft and even for the past few nights, sounded rough, almost asthmatic. Dennis knew she'd had too much to drink, and that was probably the reason, but her coarse snoring only added to his discomfort. The school's timeworn plumbing, rattling and clanging in the walls, was a rusty symphony, loud and off-key. But it wasn't the disturbing sounds that had kept Dennis awake all night. He was scared!

The school was angry with Dennis, and he knew it. The wrath he had feared ever since the first day he had sealed a pact with the school had been unleashed tonight. Dennis remembered a dog he'd had when he was ten years old, a loyal, serving creature, who had one day turned rabid, coming after Dennis and turning on him with a vicious impulse to kill. That animal had once been Dennis' friend, but he could recall its foaming mouth, its jagged glistening teeth, its ferocious growl. It had turned into a killer, an enemy. It had forgotten every loving gesture he had ever shown it. Now, as he sat upright in Room Six of the school, he felt like he was trapped in the jaws of just such a wild, unforgiving beast.

Dennis heard a noise. Quickly, he glanced over at Vanessa who seemed in a deep sleep. There, once again was a moist sound, raw and dripping. He heard a faint snap like the sound of a small bone cracking—or worse, the clicking of sharp teeth. Dennis tried to relax. He squinted into the dark to convince himself that the shadows held no danger. He looked up at the ceiling. The red glow from the stained-glass window cast phantom shapes that elongated and danced down the walls. He looked down at the floor and saw the severed head, the disembodied arms, the fragments of flesh, literally torn to pieces. A thick pool of blood surrounded the dismembered body like oil, clinging to the meat one moment, pulling away the next. The entire, throbbing mass looked like it was alive.

Dennis brought his feet up under him on the window seat. He inhaled the tinny smell of blood—and something else. Musk. An unclean, furry scent swelled in his nostrils. Canine. Hungry. Dennis saw the beast then. It skulked along the far wall of the room. Virulent, red eyes were set deep in its skull. Clotted, dirty hair hung from its body like wet wool. Its face was covered with a viscous, white, foamy substance. Dennis steeled himself. He knew that what he was seeing was nothing more than a hallucination. He realized it would disappear in a few more seconds. Still, it all looked so real. So this was what Vanessa had had to cope with in Room Six. No wonder she was a nervous wreck. No wonder she wanted to get out of here.

Dennis had no doubt about why this vision was being shown to him. It was twofold—a reprimand for shouting a warning to Bobby and a threatening reminder to Dennis that the school could delve into his very thoughts, pick out his deepest fears and amplify them to an exaggerated degree of horror. Gingerly, Dennis got to his feet. He hoped that what he thought was true, that the visions would vanish as soon as he started across the room toward the door. He raised one leg. The rabid dog by the wall lifted himself on his haunches as though ready to pounce. The rancid flesh on the carpet continued to pulsate. Suddenly, Dennis wasn't sure what to do, but then he knew he had no choice. With one athletic lunge, like a quarterback diving into the end zone, he hurled his body across the room, stopping just short of crashing into the door. Hesitantly, he looked back. The malignant exaggeration of a pet he had once loved was gone. The disjointed remains of a ten year old Dennis Bellivin had disappeared from the floor.

One hand on the doorknob, Dennis exhaled heavily. He hadn't even realized he'd been holding his breath. He opened the door and hurried along the corridor to the side stairway, leading to the Trousdales' rooms. Dennis needed answers. He needed to be reassured. But more than anything, he needed to be told that he was forgiven.

15

Even before she realized that she was alone in her room, Vanessa was aware of the sun. She watched through the window as the clouds played tag with the bright yellow orb; these clouds were white puffy billows, not the coal gray ones she had been seeing for the past several days. The storms that had shadowed Hanley were gone; the air smelled fresh, as if it had been cleansed with a strong disinfectant.

Vanessa stretched. At once she was wide awake. She jumped from the bed. Of course Dennis wasn't still with her, she thought, as she looked at the clock. She had just ten minutes till her first class. Vanessa had overslept, and for some reason Dennis hadn't tried to wake her. Trying to ignore the slight, drilling pain in her head, like fingers drumming at her brain, Vanessa dressed quickly. She swallowed a couple of aspirins and raced out the door just as the sun was smothered by a fresh bank of playful clouds.

As Vanessa sped along the first floor corridor, the nine o'clock class bell rang. Good, she would be only a few seconds late. Even though Vanessa knew she would not finish the term at Hanley, she didn't want to leave with a bad record. She liked Barbara Price, her first period teacher, and didn't want to disrupt her class once it started. But arriving while the bell was still echoing in the hallway. Vanessa wouldn't even be noticed. She started to turn the doorknob to the classroom but something made her pause to look through the glass partition of the door. A burst of hysterical laughter lodged in her throat.

Something stood at the front of the classroom, pointing to the blackboard. Dressed in clothing from the 1930's, the skeletal, rotted figure pulled its blackened lips apart, exposing a thin, slimy cord of meat which darted in and out of its mouth like a reptile's tongue searching for food. Though the students' backs were turned toward her, Vanessa could tell from their hairstyles and what she could see of their garments that they too were wearing old-fashioned clothing. It's like the auditorium, she thought. I've walked into a different time. The corpse-like teacher smiled invitingly at her. "*Come innnn, Vanessssa, come innnn,*" it hissed from the front of the classroom.

Vanessa fell back a step, her hand still on the doorknob. She wanted to turn away but was held in place by the corpse's pleasantly malicious glare. Vanessa counted to three. All of this would soon disappear—she just had to hold onto her sanity and wait—then things would return to normal. But then the students swiveled as one to face her and slowly rose from their desks, laughing. Vanessa could see that many of them were missing limbs—some had no eyes, while others had large, raw, red holes where their mouths were supposed to be. A few of them began to dance in the aisles between the desks. It was like watching some mutilated carnival.

Vanessa took another small step back. Her hand slipped from the doorknob, as she gagged at the smell that wafted out to her. It was the stench of the undead that she had smelled before. Vanessa forced herself to look around the room for Rickie Webster. She wasn't there. Somehow Vanessa knew that she wouldn't be. Rickie had come back to try to warn her. What was happening now was no warning. This horror on the other side of the glass was mocking her, playing with her. The scent of things long dead was like an obscene perfume, intoxicating and revolting at the same time. As the fear traveled down Vanessa's spine, she was still somehow able to hold onto the realization that this was all a fabrication, nothing that could really do her any harm. And then one of the festering things smashed the glass partition and grabbed Vanessa's hair. She could feel its bony, little dirty fingers balling her hair into a knot, trying to get a grasp on her. My God, thought Vanessa in terror, it's trying to pull me through the glass.

Using all the strength that she had, Vanessa jerked away from the thing, feeling her hair being yanked out by the roots. Vanessa tore herself away, falling against the far wall of the corridor, only to feel more hands at her, this time catching her in their grip. Blindly, Vanessa smacked at whatever was holding her, trying to get free of its tight embrace.

"What the fuck are you doing?" Laura cried from behind her.

Vanessa froze. She blinked. Uttering a crazed half-cackle, she turned to see Laura's concerned face. Gently, Laura disengaged herself from her hold on Vanessa.

"They're dead," Vanessa shouted, pointing into the classroom. "Only, now when you look, they won't be. But I know. I know what I saw."

Laura went over to the classroom door. She peered through the glass. Barbara Price was pointing to the blackboard, explaining something to the students.

Vanessa looked down at the floor. No smashed glass. She lingered at the far side of the hall. "It's just a normal classroom now, isn't it? Nothing wrong in there, right?

But that's not how they were. I saw how they were. Dead. Rotting. I could even smell them. They changed back now, because you're here. They always change back. But you can't fool me anymore." Vanessa made a fist and punched the wall of the corridor. "You hear that, you fucking evil shit? You can't fool me anymore!"

Laura was scared. Vanessa had acted strangely before, but this was bad, even for her. Laura was scared for herself, too, because deep down she was afraid to ask what Vanessa had seen. She was fearful that she too would begin to see those things. And no matter how weird it sounded, Laura knew that whatever Vanessa said she saw was probably the truth.

Vanessa was still pounding the wall and muttering under her breath. "Who are you talking to?" Laura asked quietly.

"The school, Laura. I'm talking to the fucking school. It goes back and forth." Vanessa stopped to wipe tears and spittle from her face. "First it's the past. Then it's the present. Oh, I know what it's doing now. I know."

Laura's skin prickled, but she couldn't give in to Vanessa. She had to quiet her roommate and make her stop saying these things. Before she knew it, they'd both wind up in a loony bin somewhere. "Come on, Vanessa, relax. I'm here now. Everything is okay."

Vanessa was still mumbling. Laura shook her head. "Jesus, no more Margaritas for you. Can't you just have a hangover like everybody else?" she teased, hoping to get Vanessa's mind off whatever had happened.

"Back and forth, back and forth. But I know now. I know all about its tricks."

Laura peeked into the classroom once more. "Listen, they're going to come out here in a minute. We're both late for class. So cool it, Vanessa," she said a bit more forcefully.

Vanessa stopped muttering and began to giggle. "Cool it?"

"Yeah, get it together." There was a trace of anger in

Laura's voice now.

Vanessa looked at her friend for a minute. Laura just was trying to be helpful and Vanessa was grateful for that. But it wasn't help from someone else that she needed for the next two days before she could leave the school forever. No, she had to draw on her own stamina and her ability to distinguish between tricks and reality. The tricks of the school she could deal with as long as she saw them for what they were. She would just have to brace herself for the spontaneity of their attack. And now they weren't merely visions. They had broken through a dimension to actually touch her violently, to hurt her. Vanessa reached up to pat her hair where the thing from the classroom had grabbed it, but there was nothing to unravel. Her hair was perfectly in place, as it had been before. Untouched, of course. The school must be laughing at her right now.

Vanessa adjusted her shoulder bag decisively and turned to Laura. "It's okay. I'm fine now."

"You sure?"

Vanessa just pushed past her and walked into the classroom.

There had been no further visions that morning. Nothing had reached out to threaten Vanessa. When the bell rang for lunch, Laura had invited Vanessa to join her in the cafeteria, but Vanessa had politely refused. She wanted to be alone.

Out on the front steps, the warm sunshine, so welcome after the depressing days of rain, was complemented by a crisp autumn breeze that rustled through the accumulation of dead leaves strewn about the lawn like so much yellow and orange confetti. Vanessa had a fleeting thought about Walter Cox. The school still hadn't hired a replacement for the handyman, and the dried foliage was piling up. Not that Vanessa minded. She rather liked the wildness of New England color layered across the grounds, so different from the clipped, tailored symmetry that usually marked the building.

Huddled in a down coat—she didn't want to catch a chill before tomorrow night's performance—Vanessa scanned through the script of "The Dark." She had long since committed her part to memory. Now, with what she considered a cool professionalism, she went over the dialogue looking for nuances and added subtleties she could bring to the role. Vanessa was determined to give a great performance as Emily. She wanted her mother to be proud of her and to leave The Hanley School in triumph. But reading over the play one last time, she had the same aversion for it she had felt from the very beginning. There was something about the frantic pace of "The Dark," its jumble of morose metaphors piled one on top of another, that made Vanessa suspect its author had been deeply troubled and driven to complete the play under strange circumstances. Who was this anonymous playwright? Vanessa had often wondered. Was this writer still alive today? Whoever the writer was, Vanessa knew she could not identify with him in any way.

She felt a strong hand clutch her shoulder.

"I was hoping I'd see that."

Vanessa spun around and looked up at Matthew Hanley. "What?"

"You. Going over your lines. I'm glad you changed your mind."

"So am I," Vanessa said. "I'm going to be a terrific leading lady."

Matthew's long, tapered fingers softly stroked her neck. Vanessa frowned. She could feel the underlying sexual insinuation in Matthew's touch, but she felt little inclination to ask him to stop.

"Incidentally," the headmaster continued, "I spoke to the hospital this morning. The Cannon boy is on his way back to New York."

"Oh?" Vanessa said, surprised. "Some of us were

going to visit him after class."

Matthew smiled. His fingers were still massaging the nape of her neck. "That won't be necessary now. It was only a slight shoulder separation anyway. Nothing more."

"Thank God."

"Yes, well, he was a lucky boy."

"Mr. Hanley, did they say whether he would be coming back to Abbott?"

"I don't know, Vanessa. I assume so. Why wouldn't he?"

Vanessa lowered her eyes. "I don't think you'll see Bobby Cannon around here ever again."

"You sound sad, Vanessa. Did you two have something special between you?"

"Oh, no," Vanessa said quickly, jerking back her head. Matthew's hand, caught by her sudden movement, slipped down, brushing her breast. He let it linger there for a second. Even through her heavy down coat, Vanessa felt an electric charge. "Bobby and I were just friends," she stammered.

"Oh, of course," Matthew said. "You go with the Bellivin boy, don't you?"

"Not really," Vanessa admitted. "Not any more."

Matthew's voice took on a slightly patronizing tone. "These student romances can be so temporary. Sometimes a mature girl like you, Vanessa, needs a man who's a bit older, a little more stable."

"Really?" Vanessa said with a glint of amusement. "Where am I going to find that around here?"

Matthew brought his hand back to her shoulder. "You'd be surprised," he said huskily.

Vanessa was growing uncomfortable, but she enjoyed the sensation. She was on the front steps of the school and Matthew Hanley was coming on to her. There was something deliciously exciting about this, even dangerous, and it wasn't like last night when everyone's attention had been on Bobby. Now she was in full view of the other girls on the lawn and anyone who might look out a window. It made her feel special and wanted. Vanessa wished Matthew would just grab her, throw her down on some dead leaves and make violent love to her right there.

"How's the play coming along?" Matthew asked, breaking her fantasy.

"Okay, I guess."

"Is your mother coming?"

Vanessa looked at him warily. "Why?"

"She's a very charming lady. I'm sure she's very proud of you."

"She's coming. She'll be here tomorrow night."

Matthew brought his face down even with hers. His eyes were searching, confident.

"A charming lady," he said breathily, "and a charming daughter, too."

He tasted her mouth, briefly, firmly, yet playfully. It was so unexpected that it took Vanessa a moment even to realize he had kissed her.

"I'll leave you alone now," Matthew said. "I know what it's like learning lines."

Matthew started off across the lawn while Vanessa stared after him, breathless. "Mr. Hanley?" she called. Matthew turned. "Thanks for last night. Thanks for not letting me go."

Matthew looked back at her pointedly. He smiled. "Thanks for staying."

Vanessa followed him with her eyes as he headed down the lawn toward his cottage. She noticed Ingrid Strummer coming up from the direction of the lake. Also noticing her, Matthew made a slight detour and went over to Ingrid. Vanessa could see the two of them talking. Probably a harmless conversation about the play, Vanessa told herself, but she could feel anger rising inside her. Suddenly, Matthew threw back his head in a hearty laugh that came to her across the lawn like a sharp needle pricking her flesh. Vanessa watched sullenly as the headmaster wrapped his arms around Ingrid, giving her a friendly bear hug. He hurried off down the slope.

Irrationally, the jealous rage burned through Vanessa's body as though a hot stake had been driven into her heart.

For most of her waking hours, Karin Sayers, herself a dedicated teacher, spent her time under the tutelage of a much stronger mentor—The Hanley School. The nighttime was reserved for rewards from the school. Dreams would come to her, far more tantalizing than anything she had ever experienced in life, but those dreams could turn on her, revolving into gruesome nightmares. It was just the school's way of reminding Karin who the teacher was in this case, who held the learning stick, who could strike her down at any moment.

Most of the time, Karin found herself in this twilight of terror and bizarre pleasure. During the remaining hours, she would be frozen in total, unconditional fear of what was happening to her. It was just such a time now.

The midafternoon sunshine poured through the red stained-glass windows of the auditorium, drenching it in a fool's tranquility. It touched even the farthest corners of the room, exposing last night's shadows, quite harmless now in the glow of the sun but not to the unschooled eye. The golden sun charmed its way into the auditorium and bathed the room in a protective filter. Nothing could go wrong on an afternoon such as this one.

Karin Sayers sat like a puppet, limbs dangling, on the edge of the stage. The thin strings of reason that were holding her together, both in body and mind, had long since frayed. She tilted back her head, straining to absorb the warm rays which met her like an old companion. Eyes closed, she basked in the red glow of reality, but she could not completely dismiss her fears even in this peaceful setting. Fear had lodged itself deeply within Karin's brain, building an impenetrable nest there that could never be unraveled.

If it weren't for the dark semicircles under Karin's eyes and the recently formed strain lines on either side of her mouth, dressed as she was in blue jeans and a rock 'n' roll T-shirt, she might have been mistaken for one of the teenaged drama students. But the tension on her face gave her age far beyond her years. Later, when she unveiled her dress rehearsal outfit, chosen according to specifications, her image would be dramatically changed.

Karin looked out at the empty seats which would be filled tomorrow night with anxious, proud parents. "The Dark" was going to be a sensational triumph. Karin would stake her life on that. She lay back, pressing her shoulder blades against the freshly polished floorboards of the stage. A slight murmur of a breeze came from the wings, bearing with it the sound of expectant breathing. Karin drew her legs up, then flattened them out. She was prone now, staring up into the rafters above the stage, and felt an inexorable peace float over her. Her muscles relaxed. She unwound. In hours to come, if she were rational at all, Karin would recognize this was the final peaceful moment she would ever have.

It didn't last long. Something pale and ghostly was moving up in the rafters.

The young girl's bulbous tongue hung from her mouth in a twisted coil. Her eyes bulged from their sockets. She swung slowly in a floorless dance, her frail neck throbbing from the thick cord of rope that was wrapped around it, slicing into her jugular vein.

In the millisecond before the scream bubbled from Karin's lips, she had the awful impression that the young girl dangling from the noose above her was Vanessa Forbes. But that thought evaporated and the scream echoed through the empty theater. The girl in the blood-spattered, torn nightgown was not Vanessa at all but someone from another time. Karin couldn't be sure how she knew that, but as she sat bolt upright on the stage, startled by her own shriek of terror which was still ringing off the walls, it didn't matter. What smiled up at her from the front row of the auditorium was infinitely more grisly and demanding. She knew at once who it was. She had seen his portrait often enough in the headmaster's office.

Sitting benignly on the aisle, sporting a stylish black tuxedo and a lopsided, maniacal grin, a folded theater program on his lap, Malcolm Hanley looked the picture of 1930's elegance—except for the luminous meat cleaver wedged solidly in his skull.

Karin crawled backward on the stage defensively. Curled into a ball, as if that would protect her, she shielded her eyes. After a moment, she couldn't resist the temptation to look upward. A catwalk. A complex of theatrical lighting. Harmless ropes. No young girl suspended lifelessly from a hangman's noose. Now, the audience. Empty. No Malcolm Hanley, head cleft in two.

Karin Sayers' descent into madness was so complete she failed to realize that, having now seen the horror, as well as heard it, she and Vanessa Forbes were sisters in a nightmare of endless proportion. The noises she had heard earlier coalesced into a jeering gale of laughter—and Karin Sayers laughed too, hesitantly at first, but then with a hysterical heartiness she had never displayed before in a lifetime of rigid discipline and shattered illusions.

Nothing could go wrong on an afternoon such as this one. But it had.

"This dress is too tight," Marie complained, struggling to buckle herself into a medieval bodice.

"Maybe you grew since the fitting," Laura cracked.

It was early evening, and the girls were crowded into a backstage area which had been converted into a dressing room, separated by a canvas curtain from the boys' quarters.

"Very funny," Marie said. "Give me a hand, okay?"

Laura put down her cigarette and zipped up Marie's brocade dress with an effort. With mock strain, she squeezed Marie's ample breasts into the material.

"Jesus, don't take a deep breath. If those tits fall out, you're liable to kill somebody in the first row."

The other girls in the dressing area giggled, except for Vanessa, who sat regal and detached in front of her mirror. She was a vision of Emily in her floor-length, emerald-green, velvet gown.

The curtain rustled. "Can I come in?" Dennis called out from the other side.

Laura smoothed the wrinkles in her high priestess outfit. "I have all my clothes off, Dennis. Come on in."

Dennis pulled back the canvas and stepped inside. His eyes went immediately to the image of Vanessa in the mirror. She looked away. Dennis turned to Laura. "Sayers is here," he announced with a flourish.

Laura jabbed out her cigarette in an ashtray. "What's she wearing? A cellophane jumpsuit?"

Dennis shook his head and rolled his eyes. "You won't believe it."

Vanessa watched with a slightly superior air as her classmates rushed out of the dressing area in an excited flurry, leaving Dennis behind. They were alone now, just the two of them.

"You look beautiful," Dennis said. The compliment sounded false to Vanessa's ears. Dennis' athletic body, outlined in a maroon tunic and formfitting leotards, looked ridiculously musclebound. God, thought Vanessa, by the way he's preening over there, he probably things he looks pretty good. But he's only a boy. Even his voice sounds thin and reedy. As high school football players go, he's not too bad, but he sure isn't a man—and he sure is no Matthew Hanley.

"I'm glad you're staying," Dennis said, adjusting his collar in Laura's mirror.

"It's not because of you."

"I know."

"Yes, Dennis, I think you do know."

"I saw you and Matthew on the lawn last night. Did you know that?"

"No," Vanessa admitted, "but it doesn't change anything."

"You were going to leave, weren't you?"

"What if I was?"

"But Matthew changed your mind. Does that mean you're staying for the whole term?"

Vanessa was getting tired of the whiny, immature sound of his voice. "No, I'm leaving tomorrow night. My mother's taking me out of here. There's no way I'm staying."

Dennis gave her a sly smile. "You can't change what's preordained," he said.

"What's that supposed to mean?"

"Some things are just supposed to happen. They're meant to be."

Vanessa turned away. "Well, I'm not meant to stay at the school—not past tomorrow."

Dennis' eyes followed her in the mirror. "Maybe that's all that's needed."

Vanessa swung back to look at him. "Dennis, I don't want to hear about fate and destiny—not now. This play is heavy enough without listening to all that shit."

"I'm sorry. I'll leave."

"Yes, I think you'd better."

Dennis started for the curtain. Vanessa reached out and touched him gently on the shoulder.

"It's not you, Dennis. It's the school . . . it's the play . . . it's everything."

Dennis studied her for a moment, then nodded. There was a certain satisfaction in his eyes. He turned abruptly and disappeared through the curtain.

Alone now in the dressing area, Vanessa completed her makeup. She could hear muted noises from the stage area, but, for the time being, they didn't concern her. She felt distanced. Vanessa inspected herself in the mirror. Still too pale. There were some final touches she had to add. Vanessa fumbled in her bag for the dark pink lip gloss. Suddenly, she blanched. The mouth that she applied lipstick to was no longer her own. It belonged to a young girl with a porcelain complexion and a dreamy eyed look from long ago. Vanessa didn't even blink an eye, looking at the sad reflection knowingly. The communication was there again. They had shared it once before in this very auditorium. But then the girl had been writhing, hanging from a noose, an instant away from death. Now she stood here calmly, as if she belonged in this room. Vanessa felt the same compelling warning issue from her opaque eyes like a blurred beacon of brightness from an offshore lighthouse.

The lips in the mirror moved. "I know who you are now." The words fell softly in the room like flowers on dark silk. Vanessa couldn't be sure whether she spoke those words or whether they were uttered by this girl from long ago.

"Vanessa." The voice was loud and insistent. "Vanessa Forbes."

In response to Ingrid's paging her on the P.A. system, Vanessa emerged from the curtained backstage area. There was a cluster of students around Karin Sayers, and Vanessa could not see the drama teacher clearly. But then as each girl stepped aside, after getting last minute instructions from Karin, Vanessa was able to get an eyeful of the young woman and could barely suppress a smile at what she saw.

Karin was totaly devoid of makeup. Her long, thick hair fell naturally in cascades to her shoulders, like newly-spun corn silk. Her dress, sheer, white and belted with a sash at the waist, clung to her body sensuously but with no hint of sexuality. Karin gave off an innocence that was completely at variance with the provocative image she had cultivated at previous rehearsals. As Vanessa came closer, she felt as though she were approaching a little girl dressed in her First Communion clothes and playing at being grown-up. There was no doubt that Karin looked beautiful, even virginal, but Vanessa felt a knot of fear tighten in her stomach. Karin's persona effused such a pure vulnerability, such an innocent willingness to comply, that she resembled some kind of sacrificial creature ready, even anxious, to yield herself to a greater power. She was like some exquisite white sand sculpture that would crumble if Vanessa so much as reached out to touch her.

"There you are, Vanessa," Karin said, her voice like wind brushing against crystal. "We've been waiting for you. We can begin now."

The Hanley School had never known the conventional barriers of time, so it could wait. It had waited. It was used to waiting. The core of earth on which the building stood for centuries had learned to possess its malignant soul in patience. Time was on its side, since for most of its existence there had been no other side to oppose it. The soil at Hanley tolerated the concept of good, since without good there could be no evil, but for so many years now evil had held the upper hand, keeping the good at bay. It was really no contest. Still, there had been only isolated instances when evil had risen to total domination, smothering the good, however briefly, and replenishing itself many times over in the process. But for that to happen, all the necessary components had to be in place. All the players, on both sides of the balancing scales, had to be in position. Now one of those rare instances was approaching, and the players—both the ones who knew and the unsuspecting victims so vital to the fray—were poised on the threshold of an ancient struggle, the oldest one known to man. The school stood ready to revitalize itself, and this time it would nurture its corruption undisturbed for generations to come.

The dress rehearsal of "The Dark" was now in full progress. Unlike last night, when Karin Sayers had attempted to turn the tech rehearsal into a breakneck marathon, the mood was low-key and, considering this was the last run-through before tomorrow night's performance, even somewhat casual. Not too surprisingly, the Hanley and Abbott students responded to the drama teacher's more subdued approach by concentrating intently on the business of rehearsing, once they knew that the panic and fear of the previous night would not be repeated. Karin, for her part, reigned over the proceedings like a ministering angel.

Ingrid was feeling relaxed, and it wasn't just from the couple of drinks she'd had before the dress rehearsal. She had checked the rigging above the stage at least five times. She had firmly fastened the lights and especially had secured the sandbags. Though she still believed that last night's accident had nothing to do with human error, tonight she had tied the bags so firmly that, short of an earthquake, nothing could make them fall.

Ingrid missed Bobby Cannon. Not only was he a close friend, but he was always such a joy to have around at rehearsals, making Ingrid laugh and sharing wisecracks with her in the wings. She hoped he would get well soon and come back to school, but somehow she doubted that she would ever see him around Hanley again. Ingrid was still troubled by Bobby's remark outside the ambulance. He had told her that Vanessa might be next. What did that mean? Throughout the evening, Ingrid couldn't help following Vanessa's every movement, as if that would prevent some accident that could be waiting to happen. But that sort of thinking was ridiculous. Bobby had only been guessing. An accident could happen at any time to anyone. Last night had been just a fluke. Why did Ingrid think that there would be another accident at all? The answer to that question was obvious. This was The Hanley School—weird noises at night, whispering in the walls, sandbags that became mysteriously untied. It was certainly enough to make everybody accident-prone.

Marie also was thinking about Bobby. She had just gone through an Act One scene opposite Freddy Cooper with her mind a blur, still preoccupied with Bobby's misfortune. This afternoon Marie had tried calling him in New York, but Mrs. Cannon had told her that Bobby was resting and could not be disturbed. She would try him again in the morning. Marie rubbed her shoulders, still aching from sleeping on the floor of Ingrid's room last night. That had been a silly idea. The night before dress rehearsal she would have been better off getting a good night's sleep. Also plagued by a brutal hangover all day, she had to admire Ingrid's stamina. She did this sort of thing regularly, seemingly without any repercussions.

Marie cursed The Hanley School. If it didn't frighten her so, she would have been in her own bed last night, and she wouldn't have needed all those Margaritas to calm down after Bobby's accident. She cursed the school again. If it weren't for this place, Bobby wouldn't have had the accident in the first place. Marie knew she should be depressed about the way things were going—with Bobby laid up in New York, with Karin Sayers acting so nuts, with everyone being so edgy—but right now her overriding emotion was pure fear. Marie felt a basic dread of the school that had become a constant, but what troubled her most of all was that she couldn't specifically name the cause of her terror.

On the apron of the stage, Karin Sayers watched with contented pride as her charges, Dennis and Vanessa, rehearsed their big love scene. She was so pleased with her casting; the two of them were so perfect together, made for each other. Dennis looked so masculine and commanding in his medieval attire, Vanessa so lovely and alluring in crushed velvet. Karin felt perfect just watching them. Her skin tingled as the white folds of her dress swayed to the natural rhythms of her body in time with the lilting cadences of Lisa King's poetry. Finding this dress tucked away in the back of her closet had been a beautiful surprise. Karin didn't even remember buying it, but wearing it tonight had been an inspiration. The soft white of the fabric matched the way Karin felt inside—purged, cleansed of all harmful emotions, unstained. A girl didn't even need makeup when wearing a dress like this. Why bother with cosmetics? They would just soil her. Karin was composed and unruffled and knew that her appearance had something to do with it. Earlier when she had first put the dress on she had felt an immediate change come over her. Gone was the tension from last night when she had looked like such a slob in black. The kids had noticed it, too. At tech rehearsal Karin had been a real bitch, but tonight was different. Tonight her children were giving birth to a play. And, thought Karin, whenever new life is brought into the world, you ought to have a fairy godmother, a guardian angel. Karin ran her hand lightly along the soft, white contours of her breast. She knew who that angel was.

All eyes were on center stage, where Dennis and Vanessa were concluding their love scene. Dennis kissed his leading lady firmly on the lips. He sensed that their embrace must look wonderful from out front, but he had kissed Vanessa too many times in the last month to think that her warm response was genuine, that it was anything more than just clever acting. Dennis headed for the wings, not bothered in the slightest. He knew his part in Vanessa's life was almost over, and Dennis felt relieved. He had taken her to where she had to be. That had been his assignment, and he had done what was required. Now she was being turned over to a stronger entity which would look after her from now on. That was the way things went at the school. You did your job and you got your reward. It was as simple as that. Not that there hadn't been a few anxious moments last night. But with the promise of rewards also came the threat of punishment if you fucked up—and Dennis knew he had fucked up badly last night. But the sin of calling out a warning to Bobby had been washed away in the cool dampness of the Trousdales' rooms last night. Dennis had gotten what he was after—forgiveness. The vision in Room Six had convinced him never to let his feelings, however accidental, get in the way again.

Her scene over, Vanessa drifted to the wings on the opposite side of the stage from Dennis. She looked at the clock. Dress rehearsal would be over soon, then it would be a matter of just one more day to get through. Tonight, when she was in her room, she would decide what to tell her mother. There was no chance she would sleep anyway—not with the excitement of leaving, not with the pressure of the play. Vanessa had made another decison. Dennis Bellivin would not be spending the night in Room Six. He would only make her nervous. Besides, he wasn't needed. Tonight, Vanessa would be her own lookout. For the past two months, The Hanley School had been a formidable adversary. It was only fitting that on her last night at the school, Vanessa should face it alone. *Do What You Fear*. It had been good advice. Tonight, Vanessa would truly make it her motto.

She went through her remaining scenes almost by rote. The words of the play came mechanically to her now. Her movements onstage, which she had resisted while Karin was originally blocking them, were carried out automatically. All at once, getting through "The Dark" was absurdly easy. What made it all the more exhilarating was that even though Vanessa knew she was merely walking through her part, she could tell by the reactions of Karin Sayers and the other students that she was giving an impressive performance. Maybe that was what great acting was all about in the first place. Perhaps she was really learning something tonight. Certainly, she was basking in the glow of appreciative attention from Karin, Marie, Ingrid, Freddy and—Vanessa's sweeping glance out into the theater stopped short at the aisle seat in the first row. The school had her in its grip again. Malcolm Hanley, the hatchet blade buried in his forehead, stared up at Vanessa, grinning sweetly.

It took Vanessa only a moment to regain her composure. Except for a quick, panicky blinking of her eyes, she gave no evidence of what she had just seen. She didn't even lose the line of dialogue she had begun seconds earlier—not until she swerved slightly at the end of the sentence and spotted a stunned Karin Sayers gaping out at the same seat. Vanessa put her hand to her mouth and bit down hard to stifle a scream. Oh, my God, Karin sees it, too. The hallucinations that the school had terrified her with were no longer just for her. The look on Karin's face told her they were now being shared—and at the very same instant. But Vanessa caught herself. How could she be sure of that? Maybe Karin was gazing at another vision of horror. There was only one way to find out.

Following the scene, Vanessa approached the drama teacher who seemed to move back from her warily. Vanessa nodded out to where the apparition had been. The aisle seat was now empty.

"You saw him too," she said, almost casually. "I mean Malcolm."

Karin's look of shocked disbelief told her everything she wanted to know.

Somehow, Vanessa got through the remainder of dress rehearsal. Just before Karin dismissed the students for the night, Matthew Hanley slipped into the auditorium. Vanessa noticed him immediately. Without the familiar three-piece suit, dressed in tight jeans and a turtleneck, Matthew looked like he could almost be one of the boys from Abbott. But Vanessa knew he was so much more than that.

As the students filed down the aisle toward the exit, Vanessa had the feeling the headmaster was waiting just for her, and she was right. As she drew near him, her heart began thumping in her chest, and she was certain that her legs were wobbling. Vanessa couldn't believe it. No close embrace with a boy, even in the most intimate situation, could produce the instantaneous sexual excitement that Matthew could generate merely by standing in the theater aisle, looking at her with an appreciative smile.

"Congratulations, Vanessa," he said in a voice loud enough for only her to hear. "You should be very proud."

Vanessa felt awkward and cast her eyes down at the carpet. "Thank you," she mumbled.

Matthew's hand, strong and sinewy, tipped her chin upwards so that their eyes met. "There, that's better. Don't be so bashful, Vanessa—not with me. Don't ever be afraid to look me in the eye. You're so very pretty. You must be very tired. You've worked so hard. Go and rest now, Vanessa." He stroked the side of her face; the touch of his fingers against her cool skin was hot and persuasive. "Have beautiful dreams."

Vanessa muttered her thanks and stumbled through the exit into the corridor outside. She felt flustered. That brush with Matthew, coming on the heels of everything that had happened at rehearsal, was nearly too much for her. Her emotions were in conflict. She wanted so much to be with Matthew right now, yet she felt relief at having just escaped his alluring web.

Thank God, she thought, none of the other kids had seen that little exchange. As they gathered around her in the hallway, their minds were obviously on something else.

"Ingrid has a little Wild Turkey in her room," Laura said. "Want to join us?"

"No, I'm kind of tired."

"I got some real good coke. That'll wake you right the fuck up."

"No thanks, I'm just going to go upstairs."

Vanessa started up the steps and saw Dennis leaning against the bannister. "You were a great Emily tonight," he said. "If I were you, I wouldn't change anything. You were perfect."

Vanessa gave Dennis a blank stare. "There is something I'm going to change. I won't need you in my room tonight. I think I'd rather be alone."

"Oh, that's rather brave. Not scared of the school anymore?"

"No, Dennis, I'm over that. The school isn't what scares me now."

Vanessa was already hurrying up the stairs. She barely heard Dennis as he called after her. "What's that supposed to mean? Hey, I thought we were going to talk . . ."

Karin stood alone in the theater at center stage. The soft glow of the moon did little to penetrate the brittle darkness of the auditorium. She stared out at the empty house. She stared especially hard at the seat where, just a short time ago, she had seen Malcolm Hanley, dead for more than 50 years, sitting serenly, a gleaming axe splitting his skull in two. There were no visions now. The seats resembled tombstones in an ancient, neglected graveyard. Karin's reflexes were slow. She felt disengaged from reality.

There was a slight shifting in the room—a slick tremor. A scent, acrid and old, made its way up to Karin and clung to her like a slippery tendril, making her swoon for a moment. The dizziness past, Karin moved gingerly to the lightboard at the side of the stage. Like a blind person reading Braille, she slid her fingers over the knobs on the machine. She counted wordlessly and flipped the third switch. A circle of light danced to life, center stage. Karin glided over to it and stepped inside like a nocturnal swimmer testing the water. She fit into the circle of illumination perfectly. Her white, sheer dress shimmered with delicacy, like a million moths hovering around a flame.

Karin felt two pinpoints of pain shoot through her eyes, needle-like and precise. Her heartbeat, strained and irregular, sounded like a muted drumbeat in her head. And just as suddenly as the assault began, it stopped. There was more shifting in the theater, this time a faint rustle of decades-old material. An expectant sigh lingered in the air, as if an audience of phantoms from another time leaned forward in excited anticipation.

Karin accepted that sigh as her cue. "I am a flower among thorns. I am a servant of the Dark Powers." She recited from memory in a clear, rounded voice. Her speech was becoming impassioned. "I am the life giver. I am the love among your daughters. I am a girlchild who stands before your wisdom. I wait to be judged, poised to renounce my very soul to answer truly your demands. I am your sacrifice. The blood flows in my veins as you breathe fire into my heart. Speak and I will hear. Command and I will follow."

It was from memory, yet Karin had never heard or read these words before. Now the invocation swam through her mind along familiar currents. She recited it again, perspiration lining her brow, her hands balled into small fists. Outside, the dim, pale eye of the moon peered in at her sadly.

As the words rang out in the vastness of the theater, hitting against the walls and bouncing back at her like invisible blows, Karin became aware of the two figures cloaked in shadows advancing toward the stage. Still, she kept reciting. It wasn't until Desmond and Blanche Trousdale joined her in the small circle of light that Karin finally fell silent.

"That was excellent, Karin," Desmond Trousdale said approvingly. "Excellent."

Karin couldn't respond. Her tongue was thick and coated. She felt as if she'd been drugged. Though there was some small, slinking beast gnawing at her nerves, she remained calm and still. The silence hardened around Karin like an impenetrable crust.

Desmond reached for Karin's hand and broke through the dense layer of quiet. "Come, my child. Soon you will be one of us. Come."

Karin and the old man clasped hands, he the practiced participant, she the willing partner. The sensation for Karin was like a jolt of electricity. Desmond's palm, rough with age, felt like scorched parchment. Blanche Trousdale, her customary frown replaced by a saintly smile, put her large, veined hand over theirs, as if sealing a pact.

16

In Room Six, the clock on Vanessa's night table was inching toward 11:00 p.m. Wearing just a T-shirt, bra and bikini panties, Vanessa stood in front of the dresser mirror, vigorously brushing her hair. It was refreshing to be alone after several nights of having Dennis with her, slouched over in the corner chair, his eyes roaming—a sentry, waiting for something unknown to pop out of the dark. She liked lounging around nearly naked, something her naturally shy nature had made impossible during Dennis' tenure despite their relationship. Besides, she hadn't wanted to encourage him sexually. Each night she had overdressed for bed, not wanting to be a tease. Tonight, she could just be herself.

Vanessa felt good about the way she had handled Dennis after dress rehearsal. She had to admit to herself that she'd enjoyed the look of bewilderment on his face as she'd marched up the stairs. Dennis wanted to talk, but there was nothing more for them to say to each other. Vanessa no longer had any feeling for Dennis. Even the gratitude she'd felt initially toward him for volunteering to stand watch in her room had disappeared. It had been sweet and generous of Dennis to give up his comfortable bed in order for Vanessa to feel relaxed and unafraid, but now, looking back on his offer, Vanessa suspected that there might have been another motivation. She couldn't put her finger on just what that might have been, but now she guessed it hadn't been so altruistic. Vanessa continued brushing her hair. It wasn't worth speculating on. None of that mattered anymore. Dennis thought that he was so adult, but a lot of his behavior had been plain juvenile.

In the space of just a few minutes following rehearsal, Vanessa had had conversations with both Matthew Hanley and Dennis. She could never imagine Dennis, with his fumbling macho ways and his immature teasing, having the quiet self-assurance that Matthew had exhibited in the auditorium. But then, of course, Dennis could never make her go weak at the knees the way Matthew could either. At times, just a chance encounter with the headmaster could be quite unsettling.

Vanessa suddenly heard a noise. The telegram from her mother which she had tucked into the corner of the dresser mirror was flapping. It was then that Vanessa noticed the strange heat in her room. It was coming from a sudden sultry breeze, almost tropical, that had whirled up out of nowhere outside. Vanessa went to the window and put her head out. She had been mistaken. The wind outside was cool and autumnal. The room had heated up by itself; in fact, it was beginning to get stifling. Vanessa opened the casement even further, hoping that the refreshing air outside could penetrate the room's turgid stuffiness. She was wrong. Inexplicably, the room grew hotter.

Vanessa needed to slip out of her bra. It was tight and restraining. She wanted to feel the cool touch of silk on her skin. In her closet she found a thin, silky nightgown she had never worn before. It was one of the presents her mother had brought from Paris. No sooner had she slipped the garment over her body than she felt sensuous and revived. She admired herself in the closet mirror. The white, diaphanous gown clung to her firm, young breasts, outlining the hardened nipples beneath. God, Vanessa thought, too bad she was just going to bed. If Matthew Hanley could see her in this outfit, he would drool.

Someone was watching her.

She could feel cold, lifeless eyes boring into the back of her neck. Must be tricks again. Even before she turned around, she sensed that the school had prepared a vicious little surprise for her on the bed. Then she turned.

Vanessa thought she had sufficiently braced herself, but the sight of the two girls in her bed, under the blood-splattered covers, sent her reeling. The girl on the left, buxom and blonde, was missing her right arm. At her elbow, blood spurted uselessly out into the steamy air of the room. Her companion, petite and wide-eyed, was struggling hopelessly to cram her writhing entrails back into her meager abdomen, but the gaping cavity that had opened there was far too wide ever to be closed. Vanessa continued to edge backward but stopped just short of screaming.

Suddenly, the twitching figures on the bed grew still. Slowly, very slowly, they sat up against the pillows. Vanessa steeled herself. The girls' lips parted into infested, malicious grins. Though their mouths were smeared in smiles, their eyes were filled with accusation, and strangely enough Vanessa felt an overwhemling sense of guilt.

Vanessa forced herself to take a step forward toward the bloody visitors on her bed. "You're not real," she charged in a choked whisper. "You don't exist." The room felt like a sweltering box all around her.

The girls' grins widened. The scent of blood spilled years ago, sickeningly sweet with decay, invaded Vanessa's nostrils. Vanessa felt as if she were walking haltingly through an ocean of noxious fumes.

"You don't exist," Vanessa repeated, but she knew the words were only half-true. They did exist—a long time ago. These two mortally wounded girls, her own age, had once been as alive, even as vulnerable, as Vanessa now was herself. Charlotte Feren and Helene Ronson were students at The Hanley School a half century ago, two victims who had been dead all these years, two girls Vanessa could never have known—yet why were they so disturbingly familiar? And why did Vanessa feel she somehow had had a hand in their violent deaths?

Vanessa sank to the carpet and began to weep tears of remorse. Like a veil being lifted, the obscenely warm air filtered from the room, taking with it the vision of the brutally slaughtered girls from long ago. Vanessa felt bone-tired. More than anything, she just wanted to sleep. The sheets on her bed looked spotless, cool and inviting. She drew back the covers, then paused. She glanced across the room. It would be better not to tempt the school, she decided. Vanessa would sleep in Laura Nash's bed tonight.

Ingrid's room at the end of the hall was crowded enough when its solitary tenant was there alone, but now, with a couple of guests, it was positively constricting. That was precisely why the girls had chosen it as their late night party setting.

Laura, Marie and Ingrid had thought about gathering for drinks down at the boathouse, their usual sanctuary, but the coziness of Ingrid's room, with its small confines and comforting familiarity, promised to be an especially soothing haven. Unlike the boathouse, with its dim lighting and hidden alcoves, Ingrid's room would be bright and predictable. No surprises or dark shadows here. Things that went bump in the night would do so somewhere else. At least, that was what the girls hoped.

Once Ingrid had closed the door and propped a chair under the doorknob as an added security precaution, the girls instinctively took up positions on the floor, their backs against the bed. Over the past two months, the school had instilled certain apprehensions in them, and each wanted to be situated in the room in such a way as to keep an eye on the door and window at all times. Behind them was only the wall, and surely nothing could get at them from there. Seeing that all three of them had tacitly assumed the same defensive posture, the girls had giggled with nervous recognition mixed with relief.

The trio's initial conversation had centered on the smoothness of the dress rehearsal, something none of them had been expecting in the light of Karin Sayers' recent behavior. Naturally, there had been the expected snide comments about Karin's white dress—Laura kept referring to her as "the marshmallow with tits"—but soon the girls got down to the business at hand. Getting high.

The "little White Turkey" Ingrid had promised turned out to be an unopened half gallon bottle. Not standing on ceremony, the girls drank straight from the jug, hefting it to their lips, precariously at first but with greater ease as the contents of the bottle diminished. Laura opened her purse and took out her drug kit; with a grand flourish, she laid out the cocaine paraphernalia on the floor. After snorting several substantial lines of the drug, the girls were in an animated mood.

"God," Marie said, "I'm going to be up all night."

Laura waved the Wild Turkey in the air. "Nah, this will offset it. You drink enough of this stuff, puts you right to sleep."

"I'd better go easy on that, too," Marie said. "I had a vicious hangover this morning. I don't want to go through that again tomorrow."

"Don't tell me." Laura laughed. "You want to be fresh for tomorrow night's show."

"Well, yeah, I do," Marie admitted.

"What the hell for? Nobody's going to understand this fucking play anyway. What's the difference whether you're good or bad?"

Marie nodded. "You do have a point."

"Have another drink," Ingrid said.

"Maybe a small one," Marie answered, taking the bottle. "You know, it isn't so much the performance. I don't really care that much about the play. It's just that my parents will be there. I'm going to have to spend time with them. They make me nervous enough as it is. I don't want to be all wired from not sleeping."

"You won't be," Ingrid said, mysteriously. "I've got a little surprise here, far superior to alcohol for calming a young lady down."

Laura leaned forward excitedly. "Oh, I love surprises. Come on, Strummer. What have you got? Fork it over."

"I thought I'd save it for later."

"Fuck later. In this goddamn school, there may not be a later."

"Don't say that," Marie said. "I don't want to talk about this place. Not after what happened to Bobby."

Laura shook her head in agreement. "Now *you* have a point."

"I've got a great idea," Ingrid said. "Let's call Bobby."

"Uh-uh," Laura protested, putting out her hand. "First the drugs, Ingrid. Then the phone call."

Ingrid reached under her bed and retrieved a small, plastic bag. She unzipped it, relishing the suspense she was creating with Laura. With a sly grin, she handed her a cellophane packet. "Bet you haven't seen these babies in a long time," Ingrid said, proudly.

Laura examined the pills and smiled at Ingrid respectfully. "Jesus Christ, where did you ever find pharmaceutical Quaaludes? You can't get these anywhere. I don't believe it."

Ingrid leaned back against the side of the bed with satisfaction. "You forget. My father's a doctor. I stole a whole bunch of these years ago. This is all that's left. I've been saving them for a special occasion."

Laura eased the pills out of the packet. She looked at

the other two girls. "Well, this feels pretty special to me."

"Go ahead."

Reverently, Laura swallowed one of the large, round pills, washing it down with a mouthful of Wild Turkey. She shook out a pill for Marie.

"No thanks. That would put me right on the floor."

"You're already on the floor," Laura reminded her.

"No, I think I'm going to turn in. Let's call Bobby and then I'm going to go to my room."

Ingrid took the pill from Laura and swallowed it. She looked at her watch. "No, it's probably too late. Bobby will be sleeping. Let's call him at lunchtime tomorrow."

Marie got to her feet unsteadily. She started toward the door, then stopped. She went over to each girl and hugged her. "Thanks for the party. It was fun. Don't get too wasted, you guys. Tomorrow's going to be a big day."

Five minutes later, with Marie gone and the chair jammed back against the doorknob, Laura and Ingrid were sprawled on the floor. They had taken down the pillows and blankets from Ingrid's bed and fashioned a cozy area for themselves there. The girls listened in silence to the occasional rustle of dried leaves on the trees outside. The room had grown chilly with the night air, but Laura and Ingrid huddled in their blankets with no thought of closing the window. Smoke from their cigarettes curled out into the night.

"You feel anything?" Laura asked.

"Yeah, my legs are getting numb."

"I was thirteen years old when I took my first Quaalude," Laura said. "I was with my friend, Dave. Boy, did we play doctor that day."

"I can imagine. Quaaludes make you feel so good. I always get tingly. Kind of sexy. Uninhibited. Sensuous."

"Horny, I think you're looking for the word horny."

Ingrid giggled. "That's the word alright. Not that I've done much about it in the past. I don't exactly have a lot of experience with boys. I took some ludes a few times with guys but we didn't really do it. Not completely. We did just about everything else but . . ."

"Hey, Ingrid, it's no big deal," Laura interjected, kindly. "You're just *technically* a virgin."

"Yeah, I guess so," Ingrid admitted. She took another swig of Wild Turkey. "Maybe we shouldn't be drinking on top of the Quaaludes. Can't you die or something?"

"If anyone dies, it'll be me. I did so much coke at rehearsal."

Ingrid suddenly burst out laughing. Surprised, Laura watched her for a moment, then cracked up herself. Both girls continued laughing giddily, kicking their legs in the air. Finally, Laura threw a pillow at Ingrid, which only made the two of them laugh all the harder until their sides hurt. They struggled to catch their breath.

"Hey," Laura gasped, "what are we laughing at?"

"Karin Sayers. That white dress of hers. She looked like a giant line of cocaine. It's a wonder you didn't snort her up, too." Ingrid wiped tears from her eyes.

"I think I liked her better last night when she was dressed as The Happy Hooker."

"I wonder what she'll wear tomorrow."

Laura puffed on her cigarette, giving Ingrid's question considerable thought. "Maybe something in black leather—like a nun's habit."

Their peals of laughter reached no further than the window and door of Ingrid's room. It was as though the school was restricting all evidence of mirth that night.

Karin Sayers heard the scream in her head seconds before it ripped its way through her parched lips. When, finally, the scream tore itself free, it sounded choked and feeble. Karin was thirsty. Her mouth tasted of exotic herbs. Her energy ebbed and soon her strength was just a dim memory. Karin could barely turn her head to look at the small, cave-like room that appeared to have no angles or defined corners, just an airless, curved cubicle from which shadows sprang out at her then crouched back among the few objects, hiding and primitive. A seemingly endless row of flickering votive candles gave off the smooth, sweet odor of melting wax, tinged with the more demanding smell of decay. Karin was reminded of her father's makeshift church, and like Henry Sayers' domain, this place of worship had little to do with God.

Swellings and discolorations of a grayish lumpy matter seemed to grow from the clay-like walls. The sight of the protrusions made Karin want to gag, but her mouth was too dry even for that. Patches of a deeper darkness stained the stone slab on which Karin sat, upright and unnaturally rigid. I've been drugged, thought Karin almost casually. Her eyes went to the tarnished silver goblet next to her, and the smell from the brownish liquid rose up to her. It was medicinal, like the taste she had in her mouth. Still, it was wet, and Karin was so thirsty. No, don't drink it, she cautioned herself, pushing the goblet away. Karin's thinking was becoming less clouded. She rubbed the back of her neck and felt the coarse, unfamiliar material there. She stared down at her arms, at the flowing sleeves of the black gown she was wearing. The garment was almost like a nun's habit in appearance. Karin felt the scratchy burlap stinging her sensitive skin and realized she was naked beneath the robe.

What was she doing dressed like this? Who had taken her clothes? What had happened to her beautiful white dress? And what was she doing drugged in this strange room? The questions whirled in Karin's brain, but no answers would come. She tried to backtrack over the events of this evening, but couldn't remember anything that had happened after she'd dismissed the students from dress rehearsal. Karin looked up at a sudden noise. Something furry and black was scuttling above her. Karin felt her perspiration, thick as oil, under the heavy gown. Fascinated, she watched the nimble limbs of the tarantula as it gracefully tormented her from within its lacy web, but the spider, only a creature of nature, wasn't what made Karin's heart begin to race inside her chest. It was the pair of legs coming down the rope ladder into the tiny, curved chamber. Desmond Trousdale was followed by his wife, Blanche, and a young man. It was the handsome, boyish face of Dennis Bellivin that startled Karin the most. The old couple merely looked resigned, but Dennis looked eager and feverish.

Desmond indicated the goblet, his brow creasing into frown lines. "That's not empty, Karin," he scolded. "You're very thirsty now. Why don't you take a nice long drink?"

Karin didn't move.

"Well, child," the caretaker said, in a voice that was kind but edged with steel, "take your time, but you know if you don't drink it, we'll force you. You've always been an exceptionally bright girl, Karin, and you've done what you've been told. That's one of the reasons you're here with us now."

Desmond stared pointedly at Karin, who made no reply. She licked at her cracked lips, trying to work up more saliva. The goblet next to her was tempting; Karin had to clench her fist to keep from reaching for it.

"Look at us, Karin," Desmond continued. "What do you see?" He gestured at Blanche Trousdale. "A man and a woman. Two old people. Caretakers who have watched over The Hanley School since the day it was built. That's a long time, Karin. Blanche and I need to rest now. We need another caretaker. The school needs new blood. You've been selected, Karin. The school has chosen you."

Teetering on a thin line between comprehension and a drugged vagueness, Karin was aware that Desmond was saying something significant about her future, but she was having difficulty pinpointing exactly what it was. She stared back at the gaunt old man. Her eyes took in his sunken skull-like face. Next to him, in marked contrast, Blanche Trousdale loomed in massive serenity. Karin's eyes finally came to rest on Dennis Bellivin, who was scrutinizing her with a kind of cocky amusement. For the first time, Karin noticed all three of them were wearing somber ceremonial robes like the one that she had on. Finally, when Karin could stop her heart from pounding, when at last she could moisten her lips to speak, it was to Dennis she addressed her question.

"You're one of them?"

Dennis, looking much older than his years in his severe, black garment, spoke in a low, rough voice. "Yes, Karin, I was honored several years ago."

Blanche spoke for the first time in her growling, staccato voice. "You're standing on holy ground right now, Karin. The Master chose this place himself."

"The Master?"

"The Lord God Satan," Desmond said solemnly. "We serve Him. These grounds are His domain. Once they trained witches here, and the blood of virgins flowed in the earth's veins."

"A witches' training ground," Karin said slowly. That much had sunk in. "Like in 'Flowers of Darkness.' "

"It was no accident you found that play," Blanche pointed out.

"You wanted me to find it?"

"The school wanted you to find it," Desmond corrected.

"The Master wanted you to find it," Blanche added.

Dennis reached out and took a handful of Karin's hair and twirled it around his finger possessively. "Lisa King was one of us, too," he said, his voice barely above a whisper.

"Oh, my God."

"The school chooses carefully," Desmond said. "She did as she was instructed. She was summoned and she carried out her orders perfectly."

"But Lisa King was weak," Dennis reminded the old

man. "Once she committed the murders, she could have embraced The Master forever. But she lost faith. She was a coward. If she hadn't hanged herself, she would have had a lasting reward. The school would have seen to it that she was exonerated and she'd be alive today, looking as young and beautiful as she was back in 1931."

The drugged veil had lifted somewhat from Karin's mind during Dennis' explanation, and she found herself able to focus on what he was saying. Though Dennis spoke with conviction, he reminded her of a schoolboy, reciting his lessons by rote before a pair of approving mentors.

"We can't change what happened in 1931," Blanche said, "but this time there will be no slip-ups, no weaknesses. The school has made sure of that. Even as we speak tonight, the events of 1931 have been set in motion once again."

"But with a new cast of characters," Dennis said, "just like in the theater. Surely, you can appreciate the irony of that, Karin."

Karin was suddenly fearful. "What are you going to do to me?"

"Do *to* you?" Desmond repeated soothingly. "We're not going to do anything *to* you. It's what we're going to do *for* you. We're going to allow you to be one of us, my child. You can join us in worshipping The Master."

Blanche laid her meaty hand on Karin's shoulder. "As a minister's daughter, you'll be especially welcome."

Desmond reached across to the stone altar where the votive lights were burning. He selected a large black candle and handed it to Karin. "Let the ceremony begin," he said gravely.

Ingrid and Laura were splayed on the floor like a couple of rag dolls. The bottle of Wild Turkey was half-empty. Ingrid had put her hair up in a ponytail, strands of which stuck out at odd angles. Laura's makeup was hopelessly smeared from tears of laughter. Under one eye, a deposit of mascara gave her a slightly off-kilter look. Despite the ravages of their late night bull session, the girls looked peculiarly young and very vulnerable. They resembled a pair of startled, battle-weary rabbits nestled in a hutch after a hard day in the forest.

"God, I shouldn't have taken that other half a lude," Ingrid said, her tongue slurring the words.

"Why? You look fine to me."

"Oh, yeah, gorgeous. I always wear my hair like this."

Laura took a deep drag from her cigarette. She strained to blow a smoke ring into the air, but the smoke merely came out of her mouth in disconnected wisps. "Shit, I never could get this right," she complained, batting at the smoke. "It used to drive Dennis crazy."

Ingrid weighed Laura's words and nodded thoughtfully. "Dennis was pretty intense tonight. Did he break up with Vanessa or something?"

"Sure looked that way, didn't it? They acted pretty weird with each other on the stairs." Laura played with the cap of the liquor bottle. "I think it's good for Dennis. It'll humble him up a little bit. He thinks he can get anything he wants."

"He usually does."

"Well, not this time. Fuck him."

An impish smile spread across Ingrid's face. "I know something Vanessa wants," she said, almost in a singsong.

"Yeah? What's that?"

Ingrid's grin widened. "Matthew Hanley."

"You think so?"

"Of course, Vanessa did say he wasn't her type—right after she wanted to rip his clothes off."

"Vanessa? She told you that?"

Ingrid nodded her head, suddenly serious. "She did. She said she never wanted Matthew to have any other woman but her."

Laura threw back her head and laughed. "That's a

rather extreme statement, even for Vanessa. Does she realize who she's talking about? Matthew Hanley would fuck a spruce tree if it was young enough."

"God, you've got a great attitude," Ingrid said with admiration. "Matthew doesn't seem to bother you at all."

"Are you kidding? He's a lot of fun. He's terrific in bed, but I don't care if he screws around. I'm not going to change him. Why should I want to? If Vanessa's got the hots for him, she ought to go for it."

"I don't know. Not everybody's as gutsy as you are."

Laura tipped back the Wild Turkey bottle and let the bracing liquor flow down her throat. She handed the jug to Ingrid, who took a polite sip.

"Uh-uh, not fair," Laura reprimanded. "We're taking full swallows here, kiddo."

A bit reluctantly, Ingrid took another gulp. "God, I'm going to choke," she protested.

Laura pointed to the bottle. "That is what will give you guts, Ingrid." She watched with satisfaction as Ingrid wiped her mouth free of alcohol.

"Jesus, Laura, I think we'd better stop soon."

Laura was lost in thought for a moment, then she cleared her throat. "Let me ask you something, Ingrid. Promise you'll tell me the truth?"

"I promise."

"What would you do if you could get your hands on Matthew Hanley right now?"

"I don't know. Probably pass out on his chest."

"Not a chance. I know what you'd do. I know what I'd do, too."

Laura looked at Ingrid with scheming glee. At once, the two girls broke into a chorus of giggles.

"Are you saying what I think you're saying?" Ingrid asked between spasms of laughter.

"I'm saying it's time for you to get gutsy."

The school knew. It crouched in the darkness, waiting,

lurking. Outlined in the night, it was an abhorrent black blotch against the sky, getting stronger. Nature knew, too. Leaves fell from silent rows of huddled trees as if in a macabre ticker-tape parade. There was a lonely, frightened rustling carried on the sad wind to creatures of nature, warning them to stay away. The horror that had slept for half a century was about to awaken.

A breeze whipped the autumn foliage into a frenzy, like multicolored confetti long forgotten after a celebration. The pond rippled, liquid shivers on the glass-like surface. The old boathouse, its planks seeped through with age and moisture, leaned out from its moorings. The massive iron gate that proudly bore the plaque, "The Hanley School For Girls," creaked with a weight almost beyond its endurance as its spiky bars seemed to meld into a single barrier, momentarily cordoning off the evil within.

Overhead, their stone visages silhouetted against the night sky, the gargoyles, primitive caricatures of the wary beasts that were already scurrying for the protection of their lairs, seemed to tense their stone haunches as if ready to prowl in search of prey. The deep red of the building's facade, still rain-splattered from the recent deluge, sparkled coolly in the moonlight. The metal drainpipes, hanging at intervals from roof to gutter, rattled an intermittent complaint against the bricks.

Inside, the foyer was deserted. The moonlight, through the opaque stained windows, cast a scarlet glow on the mosaic floor. In the deep textures of the gloomy floor-to-ceiling tapestries, gray and blue forms appeared to undulate, their feral eyes seeming to shift cunningly in watchful exhilaration. On the poster for "The Dark," which hung nearby, a likeness of the character Emily vibrated with a resemblance to Vanessa Forbes. Near the front entrance, the minute hand on the bronze clock inched toward midnight.

Dirty and bruised, on the verge of mental collapse,

Karin Sayers sat in her room, rocking slowly on the white wicker chair where just a few weeks ago she had first read "Flowers Of Darkness." But now, she wasn't reading. She was sobbing. Karin wished that the memory of the last few hours would vanish but she recalled everything in all its corrupt and lurid detail.

Through tears, Karin surveyed herself in the mirror across the room. She was back in her white dress. Though it was torn and stained, Karin felt absurdly clean in it, in contrast to the way she had felt while wrapped in that awful black robe—filthy, soiled, and ultimately damned.

All too clearly, Karin remembered the horrible, little claustrophobic room in the subbasement—and Dennis with his rough hands all over her. But first, there had been the ceremony. Desmond Trousdale had draped a satin stole around her neck, then she was made to kneel on the cold stone floor, while Desmond, his voice cracked and phlegmy, invoked the blessings of Lucifer. The black and blue bruises on Karin's sensitive knees were a painful reminder of just how long she had knelt there in that clammy damp cellar.

The Trousdales' giddy laughter had twittered nastily in the small chamber. Now, the taunting echoes of it pealed in Karin's ears. The old couple had seen everything and had delighted in the act Karin had been forced to perform on the stone slab altar, the act Karin had approached with reluctance, even revulsion. But those feelings hadn't lasted very long. Karin became a willing partner only moments after Dennis' first expert embrace. Their black robes slipped to the floor, and Karin had welcomed the feeling of pure lust as he had pushed himself into her. She had met his rhythm, clinging to him as if her very life had depended on it. Maybe it had. But performing the sex act with the young boy wasn't what was sickening or even frightening. She could run away from tonight's indiscretion and start over. She could begin a new life away from Hanley. But what about Karin's soul?

The Trousdales had told her that the school was a living, breathing entity, and, of course, Karin knew they spoke the truth. As Karin lay under Dennis on the altar, she had become aware of the hungry sounds coming from the walls of that tiny room. And the panting. An unseen voyeur was matching her rhythm with its own. Karin had heard that sound many times before. It was the school itself. She knew that now. Maybe she had always known it. The building housed unspeakable evil. It thrived on corruption and chaos. Karin would rather die than become involved in the Trousdales' pact. The old couple had told her she would be the school's new caretaker, but how could she agree to that and ever hope to save her immortal soul? Her father hypocritically had hid behind his religion, using God as an excuse to do evil. And now the Trousdales and the school also had a religion—the worship of Satan. Karin couldn't accept that. She might die, but she would die with a clean soul.

Karin stopped the motion of her rocking chair. A warm breeze had crept into her room. She felt a little nauseous and was terribly thirsty. Karin had only pretended to drink the last of the liquid in the goblet, but she had gotten enough of the unknown drug in her system to make her still feel dizzy and still taste the sting of the drink on her tongue. She wondered how long the narcotic's effect would last. Karin would have to clear her head before she could take any action. She had to get away tonight.

And then, like a practiced, familiar ritual, the breathing began in her room—first softly, filling only the corners, then more urgent, spreading like a shroud of sound, insisting that Karin take notice.

She stood and met it head on.

"No, you can't have me," she whispered through clenched teeth. "I know what you are. Go ahead and kill me. I'd rather die than be like you."

For an imperceptible amount of time, the room grew still, then something damp and oily seemed to press against Karin's face, only for an instant. With the slick, invisible intrusion came a mocking exhalation of laughter, bringing with it a fetid stink of decay and contamination.

Karin felt a powerful oppressiveness, as though a heavy weight of futility was being hammered into her mind. She staggered backward, clasping a hand over her mouth so as not to gag from the stench. The laughter and torturous breathing joined in an effusion of defeaning dimension. Karin's hands flew to her ears to silence the bombardment of noise and she began to choke on the malodorous fumes.

"Stop it!" she shrieked. "Oh, God, help me!"

The Bible. Of course. Her father's Bible was under the bed, locked in a suitcase where Karin had placed it so many weeks ago. The School was evil—Satin ruled here—and she had to combat the evil with good. But who was Karin Sayers to stand up against evil? She was a fornicator, a blasphemer, a murderess. She had killed Henry Sayers, had lit the match that had set fire to his church. She had stood outside and watched his flesh burn and melt until all that remained was a pile of ashes. How could she cry out to God for help? Why should He listen to her? But Jesus was all-forgiving. Hadn't He washed away the sins of Mary Magdalene and the thief who hung beside Him on the cross? His Word would be her salvation, and the Bible was His Word.

In a rush of inspired frenzy, Karin threw herself down on the floor and tugged the heavy valise out into the middle of the room. Hysterically, she rummaged through sweaters and blouses for the familiar wine-colored volume. Finding it, she rose to her knees. Tears running down her face, she clutched the Bible to her breast, and the words to her first childhood prayer came readily to her lips. "Our Father," she blurted, "who art in heaven, hallowed be thy name . . ."

The laughter was demonic now. The odor of sulphur and feces was overwhelming, permeating the room. Karin felt the Bible in her tight grip grow fiery. She stared in horror as a column of smoke curled up before her eyes. The book burned to her touch, and Karin felt something come away in her hand. The cover of the Bible was crumbling in her fingers, while the skin on Karin's palm was becoming scorched. The Bible was being reduced to ashes in her hand.

Karin recoiled and flung the remains of the Bible across the room. Like a burning comet, it arched through the air, crashing into the far wall in an explosion of smoke and fiery debris. Its charred remains fluttered down to the carpet like a shower of black snow.

Utterly defeated, Karin could scarcely feel herself moving backward as she retreated toward the door. Like the Bible, the words of The Lord's Prayer had turned to ashes on her lips. More frightening than the barrage of sound—that guttural laughter mingled with raspy breathing—was the sudden enveloping quiet that descended upon the room like a weighted curtain. Stranded for an instant in a curious pocket of normalcy, Karin could detect natural sounds filtering in from the outside—crickets, a loose shutter rapping against the side of the building, a village clock chiming across the farmland from far away.

Squeeeak. Whooooosh. Had she just seen the walls move?

Karin couldn't take any more of this. She had to get out of this room now. She had to leave The School forever. The walls moved again. Karin was sure she'd heard some kind of suction noise from nearby. She couldn't stay another minute and reached for the doorknob. It came away in her hand. And then the door disappeared.

It bubbled. The oozing substance that was squeezing its way through the seams of the door was like a thick, colorless putty, sealing off Karin's exit, filling the cracks and creating a smooth surface, molding what had once been a door into a mere continuation of the wall. In just a matter of seconds, Karin's escape hatch was transformed into an impenetrable extension of the room itself.

Squeeeak.

Whooooosh.

Hesitantly, Karin extended her arm, letting her fingers explore the newly formed wall. It pushed back against her fingertips, and Karin jerked away. The wall began to contract and expand as if a massive, pumping heart were enclosed within it. All the walls of the room were beating now in syncopation with the crude suction noises that were coming from everywhere at once. *Pssshh.* Soft and spongy now, the walls sprang forward. Karin drew back. Another leap. It was as though the walls were toying with her, acting out some deadly version of a child's game of tag, and Karin knew what her role was. She was *It*. Another jump. *Creeeek.* Already, the room was one-third of its former size.

There was another way out.

The casement window across the room was fastened shut, but it glowed before Karin's eyes like a summoning exit sign in a darkened movie theatre. Karin quickly moved toward it, stopping just short of the window seat. She half-expected the jelly-like substance to ooze from the window sill and the cracks around the glass, sealing off her last hope for deliverance, but nothing happened. Even the walls had paused in their relentless pursuit. The next move in the game was Karin's.

Through the glass panes, in the dim moonlight, the fire escape's metal frame beckoned to her. Karin reached for the casement handle, swiveled it to the right and felt the cold, night air of freedom filling her lungs. At once, the dank, rotting odor that had seized the room evaporated. Behind her in the room, the walls seemed to squat, as if tensing for a bolder leap forward. The heart-like pounding and the awful suction noises had sunk to a low murmur, almost as if they emanated from some ravenous beast that had somehow just been satisfied. With one last, fearful look over her shoulder, Karin squeezed through the window. She stood uncertainly on the spindly fire escape as the autumn wind whipped the folds of her dress.

Karin started down the metal staircase, her heels clattering on the steps. She didn't get very far. Halfway down to the next floor, she felt it. Something hot, searing and leathery, had latched onto her ankle. Karin kicked free of it, then looked down. In the last hour, Karin Sayers had experienced a concentration of horror unlike anything she had ever known before, a constant assault on her senses that was enough to make anyone stark raving mad. But nothing—not the obscene ceremony, not the Bible that had exploded into cinders, not even her room that had shrunk into a tomblike enclosure—could compare with the thing that was ascending the fire escape, grinning maniacally, its charred hand held out in greeting, meeting her again after all these years. *It's lesson time, Karin. Thwaack!* The crack of The Discipliner lashed out against the spidery metal railing. *You've been a very bad girl, Karin—just like your mother.*

Karin stood paralyzed. The acrid smell of gasoline, smoke and burning flesh came off in waves from the advancing figure that was once Henry Sayers. Karin stared in slack-jawed terror as his scarecrow-like, twisted body, still draped in the scorched rags of his minister's black suit, mounted the stairs. Her father's stumpy legs, ravaged by the fire, protruded from his threadbare trousers. Again Henry Sayers cracked the menacing strap against the side railing, his misshapen arms, caked with ashes and strips of parched flesh, flailing about in skeletal wrath. But it was his face, hoary and grotesquely distorted, that held her immobilized. The skin on his forehead and cheeks had peeled away, leaving his eyeballs bulging in their sockets in fanatical piety. His nose had disappeared, swallowed up by the contours of his face. His thin-lipped mouth was just a jagged line, dripping seared flesh down the remains of his chin. His singed hair stood out from his skull like burned electrical wire. And that smile, grim and corroded, never left his face as he hurtled upward.

The roof. If Karin could climb to the roof she could make it to the fire escape on the side of the building and then could race down to safety. The sheer terror of seeing the corpse that had been her father dissipated the remaining effects of the drug she had taken earlier. Karin calculated that she could easily outdistance the decrepit remains of Henry Sayers, who could only lurch at her in feeble fits and starts. Before she knew it, Karin was clambering up the remaining flights to the mansard roof above. The strange world up there which suddenly loomed before her eyes looked medieval—a moonlit landscape of oddly angled slate gables and sprawling cupolas. Resting her hand on a stone outcropping that jutted out from the roof, Karin turned her head slightly. She dared to look back down. Her pursuer was gone. Henry Sayers had vanished from the fire escape.

Suddenly, an excruciating bolt of pain tore through Karin's right arm. The piece of masonry that Karin was holding on to had just bitten her. Shocked, she stared at the stream of warm blood that spurted from the sharp punctures on her fingers, flowing rapidly down her arm to meet the smudged white sleeve of her dress. Karin's agonized scream bellowed out into the night as she ripped her fingers away from the stone creature that was gnashing at them. With her other hand, she quickly hoisted herself onto the roof. She inspected her fingers. The gargoyle's bite had left vicious gashes. The reality of what had happened was just beyond her grasp, and Karin peered at the snaring mongrel almost casually. Had it really sunk its fangs into the flesh of her hand? The beast's jaws ground together eagerly. Saliva and bits of Karin's skin dripped from its voracious mouth, its beady eyes narrowing into cunning slits. It's watching me, thought Karin. It's going to go for me again. It wants to rip me to shreds. Weary now, Karin looked around. The rows of stone animals—canines, wolves, cats—were glowering at her, ready to pounce. Overhead, another row of creatures—hawks, falcons, pterodactyls—stretched their talons and extended their wingspans, poised to swoop down on her. Karin had come to the rooftop for safety, but now she found herself trapped in a stone menagerie of carnivorous beasts that the school had brought to life.

And then the sound started—stone against stone, grinding and meshing. The creatures stretched, moving languidly at first, then with the graceful confidence of animals on the prowl. The moonlight, almost conspiratorial now, caught their glistening eyes and flickered in an evil gleam. Karin knew she should run—but where?

Instead, Karin let her eyes drift out over the school grounds. The trees seen from above were a quivering maze of light and shadow. The lake, rippled by the chilly wind, mirrored the sky's glittering panoply of stars. Directly below, the lawns and paths fanned out in a precise pattern leading to a world where life went on without the ever-present terrors of The Hanley School. Karin winced at the grating sound of concrete in motion as the predatory creatures continued to stir. Her eyes zeroed in on a thick bed of dried autumn leaves straight down from the edge of the roof where she stood. The cushion of foliage was so far below. Karin knew she could never survive the leap, but she could never survive the rooftop either. The creatures who lived there would see to that. Karin knew that if she shouted out her acquiescence, submitting to her caretaker's role, that there was a chance the vicious gargoyles would retreat back to their perches, reverting to stone once again. But she could never do that. And besides, the bed the leaves looked so inviting. On a cushion like that, in the soft moonlight, Karin could sleep forever.

And in those days men will seek death and will not find it; they will long to die and death will fly from them . . .

Death did not fly from Karin Sayers. Stepping off the parapet of The Hanley School for Girls in her soiled Communion dress, she flew to meet death like a frail angel of the night.

The sound outside Vanessa's window made her instantly awake. She sat up in Laura Nash's bed, her eyes quickly scanning the room. Everything was as it should be. There were no tricks from the school, not in the room anyway. Vanessa scrambled out from under the blankets, hurried over to the window and unlatched the casement.

The lawn below was a study in tranquility. The bracing night breeze swept across the grounds, transporting the clean scent of newly mowed grass. The lake, with its gentle ruffles, looked comforting and serene. Across the way, The Abbott School was entirely dark, a peaceful presence. From somewhere down below Vanessa's window, where heaps of dried leaves were gathered, a strip of white material had been caught by the wind and was blowing out over the lawn. Probably one of the girls lost her scarf, Vanessa thought, and would be looking for it in the morning.

Vanessa was just about to close the window and climb back into bed when she heard a tittering noise. Curious, she glanced out over the grounds. Vanessa thought she heard the closing of a heavy door at the side of the building. She waited. The giggles grew louder. With their girlish high pitch, they seemed an intrusion on the quiet beauty of the night.

In another moment, the source of the laughter came into view as Laura and Ingrid, dressed in skimpy, sheer nighties, sweaters thrown over their shoulders to protect them from the chill, appeared at the corner of the building. Vanessa was puzzled at first, then smiled as she noticed that the two girls seemed to be holding each other up. They're really drunk, Vanessa thought, as she watched Ingrid stumble and Laura practically fall over her. Where were they going at this time of night? Probably the boathouse. No. The boathouse was in the other direction. They were veering off toward the other side of the lawn, moving on clumsy tiptoe, moving toward Matthew Hanley's cottage. Vanessa followed them with her eyes as the pair shambled down the gentle slope of the lawn. As they grew smaller, going off into the night, they reminded Vanessa of two gangly scarecrows; from this distance, their bunched-up clothing and unkempt hair looked like bits of straw spilling out of their bodies. As the girls disappeared from Vanessa's view, taking their adoescent giggling with them, the night became still once more.

A sharp, exact pain bore through Vanessa's head. For a split second, she thought she might have been shot. Her hand flew to her head to check for a wound but there was no blood, not even a scratch. Surely, a pain so precise had to be orchestrated by someone or something. Vanessa stumbled back from the window. The ache was making her dizzy.

And then the pain was replaced by an emotion that was much more overpowering—hatred!

Even as she felt the white hot, blinding rage, Vanessa was surprised, almost ashamed, of her emotion. She recognized the jealousy that was at the heart of the hatred, pumping inside her and growing stronger with each beat.

The school had been a patient observer for more than half a century, ever since the scenario for what was to be enacted was first written. It was time now. The players were in place. For the next hour, consumed by an inflamed coil of hatred that twisted through her very being, Vanessa would be guided by something infinitely more powerful than anything she had ever felt in her short life. She had always wanted to be a great actress. Tonight she would play a role which had been created especially for her by The Hanley School For Girls. It would be a tour de force performance—the role of a lifetime—and the school would direct.

Vanessa first could feel the beads of perspiration on her forehead, then her armpits grew moist. She smelled the foul odor of her own body. Lurking just underneath the salty aroma was a scent of animal musk, the smell of the hunt. The silk nightgown that had felt so cool and sensuous against her skin now damply clung to her and irritated the V of her crotch. Vanessa mopped her brow with the back of her hand. The icy breeze outside stopped just short of her window, as if a heavy veil of sweltering air hung at the casement, sealing off Room Six from the night chill. Vanessa staggered back toward the bed. The sheets felt rough and charged with heat. Vanessa drew her hand away from the covers and tiny silver sparks jumped at her fingers. Was the panting her own breath she heard, or was it coming from the room itself? She stood absolutely still in the center of the room and held her breath. The panting continued. And something else—murmurs and irresistible commands as sultry as the room itself. Vanessa could not make out the exact words that were being uttered, but the school's intentions were clear. Vanessa turned and started toward the door.

She startled herself as she glanced at her reflection in the mirror—a haunted predator. Then she saw her face change into the face of someone else—a young girl she had seen before, dangling from a noose in the auditorium. The girl once had tried to communicate with her, sharing a special bond. Deep within the ghostly face, desperate eyes peered back into Vanessa's. The lips in the mirror began to move, and Vanessa strained to hear the eerie visitor's words. Just then, what seemed like a blue streak of lightning flared near the ceiling of the room, slicing the image in two. The girl's fragile features shattered like a piece of china. Then she was gone. Vanessa's own face stared back at her from the mirror—the hunter, yet submissive and obedient.

Vanessa glided to the door. For the last time, she left Room Six. Her next stop would be the pantry where the rows of sharp, gleaming knives were hanging in the moonlight, waiting.

It had taken Laura and Ingrid nearly ten minutes to weave their way to Matthew Hanley's cottage. They had collapsed in fits of giggles several times on the lawn below the slope, with Ingrid expressing misgivings about their midnight venture and Laura playfully coaxing her on. Finally, at the door of Matthew's darkened house, Ingrid lost all nerve. She grabbed Laura's hand before she could ring the bell and dragged her friend away from the cottage.

"I'm not going in there," Ingrid mumbled. "Not tonight. Not tomorrow. No way. No how."

Laura looked at her companion in exasperation. "I thought you were over that."

"I'm not going in there," Ingrid repeated. She made a stern face. "And neither are you."

"I always knew you were a chicken."

Ingrid put her hands on her hips, and her voice rose indignantly. "I am not a chicken."

A light came on in Matthew's window, and the girls blinked from the sudden glare. "Oh, shit." Ingrid said under her breath. "I'm getting the fuck out of here."

"It's too late," Laura said wickedly.

The door of the cottage was opening, bathing the girls in an even brighter glow. Matthew Hanley, in a bulky blue bathrobe, stood in the doorway, looking disheveled and slightly amused. "Too late for what?" he asked sleepily.

Vanessa ran her index finger along the razor sharp edge of the meat cleaver. She smiled with satisfaction as a dark droplet of blood bubbled up through her skin. In the bright vermilion of the stained-glass window overhead, the bead of blood shone briefly, then trickled down Vanessa's finger. The grim steel of the blade blinked its steely eye of consent.

More than 50 years ago, this small pantry had served as an unnatural isolation chamber, a strange little haven providing an interlude before an act of unspeakable violence. It had been here that Lisa King was purged of whatever shreds of decency still clung to her young soul. Now the school seemed to be bulging through the walls, the floor, the ceiling, swelling up with pride, watching and eavesdropping on its nearly cleansed pupil, waiting for her next move. Vanessa nodded determindly. Her small, delicate hand, which in all of her 17 years had never been raised in violence, closed into an angry vengeful fist around the handle of the murderous blade. She went to the door of the pantry and paused. An unholy halo of crimson light sprang up above her head, lingering there for an instant like a fiery circle of benediction, a last blessing before the school sent her out into the night.

The side door stood open, and Vanessa passed through the exit, scarcely noticing the large rock that was wedged at the threshold. In their drunken giddiness, Laura and Ingrid had slammed the side door earlier, but someone else had inserted the stone as a doorstop so that, later on, Vanessa would have easy access back into the school.

As Vanessa drifted across the lawn, moving purposefully despite her dreamy air, she was being observed by a trio of monitors who huddled together at a basement window. The watchful eyes of Blanche and Desmond Trousdale were timeworn and reconciled, while Dennis Bellivin looked through the glass with fearful fascination.

Vanessa was nearly at Matthew's cottage, the meat cleaver flashing like a sliver of moonlight in her hand. Short-circuited, her mind and nerve endings were like raw fibers twitching with electrical spasms. Incomplete thoughts and loose sentences writhed in her brain like squirming serpents. *Matthew's house. The grass is so soft he'll hear me coming. I'm cold inside and I'm dead. The moon is watching me. Good. I don't care. I'm watching the moon. The hedge. It needs clipping. That's okay. I'll cut it on the way back. Mother's coming tomorrow. I can't wait to see her. Maybe I'll cut her hair. I have so much cutting to do. Laura and Ingrid. Cold. Dead. I'm going to spoil their party. My finger hurts. It was bleeding. Matthew's going to bleed too. Do What You Fear. I'm not afraid now.*

Vanessa arrived at the window of the headmaster's cottage and could see right into his bedroom. Everything was as she had expected. The school had warned her in advance. Seeing Matthew and the two girls sprawled obscenely on the bed wound the coil of hatred inside Vanessa even tighter. Laura was a whore. Ingrid was a common drunkard. Those were their pathetic excuses. Matthew, the wise, sensitive headmaster, could have no excuse. He was supposed to set an example, supposed to know better. The leering, half-naked pig whose hands were all over those two girls was the real Matthew Hanley. All the stories Vanessa had heard about him were true. How could she ever have thought otherwise?

Inside, the threesome on the bed were unaware that they were being watched. Matthew waved a bottle of cognac, filling up the girls' glasses, while Laura tried to wrestle him completely out of his robe. Both girls had discarded their sweaters, and Ingrid, for all her girlish fears and shyness, had already stripped off her nighty, lounging in front of Matthew in just a pair of white bikini panties.

As still as death, Vanessa lingered at the windowpane, unable to look away from the degrading, almost comic tableau. Her eyes felt salty as if she were going to cry, but no tears would come. Matthew and the two girls seemed to fade in and out of focus as if she were watching them through great mists of heat. *Move, Vanessa. Go inside.* She was listening to a quiet command, urging her into the action. Still, she remained transfixed.

On the bed, Laura had succeeded in disrobing Matthew. The trio was completely naked now, splayed on a bundle of blankets and pillows. Even Matthew was giggling now, his laughter coming in machine-gun-like spurts—high-pitched yet bestial, jolting Vanessa with each round. Laura and Ingrid wound their limbs around Matthew, forming a grotesque three-headed beast that throbbed and grunted loudly on the bed. *Go inside, Vanessa.* But she was already moving and needed no further command.

Vanessa floated to the door of the cottage. Her fingers closed around the doorknob, and she twisted it clockwise in the moonlight. Locked. A smile twisted the corners of her mouth as a torpedo of blistering air was blasted from the direction of the school. It left her fingers singed and the door slightly ajar.

She entered—into the parlor, past the sofa, across the carpet, drawn on inexorably by the rectangle of light coming from Matthew's bedroom.

"Mr. Hanley."

The threesome on the bed whirled around to see Vanessa standing in the doorway, her hands behind her back.

"Vanessa." The headmaster looked pleased. He made no effort to cover his nakedness.

Vanessa locked eyes with him. "You made a mistake," she said, her voice a ghostly trill. "You should have let me go home."

Ingrid was closest to Vanessa on the bed. Seeing her friend, she had erupted in embarrassed, bubbling laughter. Vanessa advanced on her.

"Hello, Helene."

Vanessa's right arm shot out. Ingrid heard the whirr of steel slicing air before her suddenly frightened eyes spotted the shining meat cleaver in Vanessa's hand. By then it was too late. The blade severed Ingrid's chest just above the heart, chopping half of her breast off. Thick red blood shot out, splattering the walls and celings as if some mad sprinkler system had gone awry. Ingrid pitched forward onto the floor and was dead before she landed. Laura's mouth opened in a silent scream. Vanessa hefted the meat cleaver in both hands now.

"Nice to see you, Charlotte."

Again, the razor-sharp weapon hummed through the air. Expertly, Vanessa buried the blade deep in Laura's midriff, nearly halving the girl. Laura's eyes rolled back dully in her head as what was left of her naked body twitched in its final convulsions. Her blood joined Ingrid's, drenching the bed covers and pouring down the walls in slippery trails of death.

The man was next and he knew it. The rigid fear that had rendered him immobile with the first appearance of the blade gave way to a frenzied instinct, primitive and all-consuming, to survive at any cost. Matthew Hanley hurled himself from the bed, a bellow of horror rising in his chest. Landing on the inert form of Ingrid, he squirmed away in revulsion, crawling toward the door. With a force that shook the entire cottage, the door slammed itself in his face.

He slid backward toward a corner of the room, his knees and buttocks sloshing in the newly pooled blood. Kicking Ingrid aside, Vanessa moved toward him, then glanced at the blade for a second, puzzled. She wiped the sticky gore—red rivulets and shreds of dead flesh—onto her nightgown.

"Please. Oh, God, Vanessa, please," Matthew begged on his knees, cowering in the corner.

"Malcolm," Vanessa intoned, her voice sounding like a cannon in the room. Words that had been penned by Lisa King in a drama society notebook back in 1931 came to her lips.

"Warm seed, warm heart; let us never be apart."

A hand stronger than her own guided Vanessa as she swung the meat cleaver in a clean, level motion, sinking it into the throat of Matthew Hanley. The pure power of the blade's whistling curve butchered Matthew's head neatly off his shoulders. His eyes still stared in an uncomprehending plea as the head thumped onto the carpet. The remainder of his body, topped by a tangle of spurting veins and arteries, pumped currents of blood uselessly upward toward the ceiling.

Vanessa stepped back. Her body ached, her veins felt as if they were hardening, and her bones seemed brittle. The meat cleaver was growing heavy in her hand. She could barely keep it in her grasp. Vanessa looked down at her fingers. They were gnarled, almost arthritic. Suddenly, she had to get out of here. She had to leave this cottage. She would go back to the school and await further instructions.

As Vanessa shuffled wearily to the door, she was oblivious of the scene of carnage she was leaving behind. The hacked corpses on the bed and on the floor looked like misshapen, life-sized dolls that had been wrenched apart, then casually discarded. The wall behind Matthew's bed was a gruesome mural, a vast canvas of blood red that was almost festive in appearance.

Outside in the pale moonlight, Vanessa measured the distance to the dark bulk of the school. The building seemed so far away, the path up the slope of the lawn so steep and arduous. The muscles in her calves protested as she trudged up the incline. Tears coursed down Vanessa's face, pausing in wrinkles that weren't there moments earlier. Her hair, once a deep auburn, had lost its youthful luster, fading into a bristly nest of gray and white coils.

Coming out from the shadows of the low-lying trees Vanessa saw three figures clustered at the side entrance to the school. Even in her blank state of mind, she could recognize Dennis Bellivin and the Trousdales. They were motioning to her. Obediently, Vanessa moved toward them. The cleaver felt like a leaden weight in her hand. She wanted to drop it onto the grass, but her fingers were wrapped around it too tightly.

The Trousdales embraced her at the entrance. Blanche pried the cleaver loose from her grip, nearly snapping her skeleton-like fingers to get it free. The old woman tucked the blade under her cloak and took Vanessa by the arm. Desmond supported her on the other side. As Vanessa was led into the school, Dennis hung back, too shocked to follow. He had been expecting the 17 year old Vanessa Forbes he had held in his arms just a few days ago. Instead he was staring at a girl who, in the course of a single evening, had aged into a stooped and withered woman no less than 70 years old.

The night The Hanley School For Girls had awaited for more than half a century was drawing to a close. The school had failed with Karin Sayers. Her leap from the rooftop had thwarted its malicious plans—but only briefly. Vanessa Forbes had come through. She would receive a passing grade—and the school would have its new caretaker.

EPILOGUE

At 7:30 the next morning, the body of Karin Sayers was found in a bed of autumn leaves a few yards from the building. The discovery was made by Jon Waller, a 23 year old ex-G.I., who was reporting for his first day's work as replacement for Walter Cox, the school's former maintenance man.

A few minutes later, Joyce Stewart, a 52 year old Haitian housekeeper in the United States illegally, knocked on the door of Matthew Hanley's cottage. Receiving no response, she assumed her employer had gone to work early. Using her key, she let herself into his cottage, where she came upon the mutilated bodies of Matthew, Laura and Ingrid.

The police arrived shortly after 8 a.m. and officials from the local coroner's office were on the grounds soon afterwards. A general roll call of students and teachers revealed that only one person was missing—Vanessa Forbes. It was feared that she too had been a victim.

A horde of media reporters flocked to the school. In television and press interviews, Hanley Chief of Police

Clarence Sears theorized that a maniac had somehow gotten into Karin Sayers room, dragging her up to the roof in order to attack her. She had broken away from him and plunged to her death. Sears further speculated that Vanessa, in the room directly below Karin's, was awakened by the noise and went to investigate. She also had been killed, though her body was still missing. The murderer then had gone down the side lawn and, perhaps seeing a light in the headmaster's window, had completed his night of senseless violence.

After extensive questioning at Hanley, the police put out an All Points Bulletin for Walter Cox, known to be a disgruntled employee with a vicious streak, who, because of his former position, had a set of passkeys and was a familiar figure on the grounds. This would explain, according to Sears, why there had been no signs of forcible entry at either of the crime scenes. Cox had not been seen for weeks but, due to the evidence, he had to be considered a prime suspect, though the police were following up on other leads.

Early the next week, the Hanley town council held an emergency meeting. As in 1931, a motion was made to close down the school, but the motion was voted down. It was decided instead to recommend increased security on the Hanley grounds. Though the Hanley family name was once again dragged through the mud, and there could be no excuse for the headmaster's behavior with two of his own students, the council felt it best to adopt a wait-and-see attitude. After the furor had died down, the parents of students would make the decision regarding the school's future. The Hanley name still carried a lot of weight in the area, and the school contributed more than its share of taxes to the city. In the aftermath of the tragedy, only five girls withdrew from the school, while the list of applicants for the next semester actually grew longer.

Vanessa liked her new room. It was true it had no

windows, but by now her eyesight was so poor she barely minded. It was quiet here in the subbasement of The School, and she appreciated that. There were no loud noises to disturb her timeworn, sensitive ears and frail nerves. The time passed easily. Vanessa couldn't tell whether it was day or night. It didn't matter. She spent most of her time staring at the walls—at peace and preparing. The length of time she would spend here in this room was going to be short. Blanche and Desmond had told her that. The Trousdales had been so kind to her, looking after her every need. They even shared their meals with her—fresh food from town, never anything from the cafeteria. And with every meal, there was a newly cut flower—a blood red rose. There was nothing wrong with Vanessa's scent of smell; the aging hadn't affected that. The school had been good to her, too—protecting her and providing a place of refuge while outside they searched for the 17 year old Vanessa Forbes. They would never find her. She no longer fit their description. Sometimes, of course, Vanessa did get lonely. Dennis hardly ever stopped by to visit, and the Trousdales had their chores and couldn't be with her all the time. But everything would change soon. She'd been promised. Her caretaking role would begin. Yes, Vanessa liked her new room, and soon she'd be permitted to leave it.

Bobby Cannon sat alone on a long marble bench in the main lobby of The Museum Of Natural History in New York City, dwarfed by the gigantic skeleton of a tyrannosaurus rex that towered over him. It had taken him weeks to summon up the courage to step inside this vast hall, overcoming his childhood fear of cavernous rooms and prehistoric beasts. It had been a necessary first step for what Bobby knew was still to come.

It had been so great seeing Marie all this week, and now that she was transferring to a private school here in Manhattan, they'd be together all the time. Marie had filled him in on everything that had happened up at Hanley. The details had been graphic, but it was a welcome relief to get the truth from someone who was there, someone who really cared. It was such a contrast from the lurid sensationalism about the murders that had been assaulting him from the TV set and the tabloids. Together, he and Marie had sifted through the facts, assembling the pieces with the help of their own impressions and beliefs. Neither of them thought for a moment that Walter Cox had anything to do with the grisly killings. Neither of them believed that Vanessa was dead or—and this was the latest media speculation—that she had been kidnapped. Bobby and Marie were convinced that the real culprit was the school itself.

Bobby had tried repeatedly to reach Dennis Bellivin by phone. This morning, he had finally gotten through. Dennis had been weird, abrupt and evasive. He had told Bobby he didn't want to talk about the murders. Vanessa was dead and they would find her body soon enough. He had other things on his mind. The Abbott School football team was still unbeaten and, with Dennis as the quarterback, they were going to stay that way. How could he have gone on like that about a stupid sport? So uncaring. There hadn't been even a trace of emotion in his voice when he'd spoken Vanessa's name. Dennis could be a selfish bastard but this was going too far. When Bobby had hung up the phone, he'd broken into a cold sweat, racked by an overwhelming feeling of dread.

He'd be seeing Marie again tomorrow night and would take her to a small, family-owned Italian restaurant in the neighborhood where he grew up. At a time like this, familiar settings were so comforting. And in the restaurant, they could talk and maybe work out some kind of plan. At least they could try. But, Bobby thought with a sinking feeling, would it really do any good? What could they hope to accomplish? No matter what they said, who would ever believe them? How could they convince anyone that a building, a mere pile of bricks and cement, could breed evil in the first place? Maybe he and Marie were just being foolish. They were safe here and had a new life together. Maybe they should just stay away.

But Bobby knew that others would die.

He glanced up at the ivory-colored jaws of the dinosaur skeleton. His eyes moved further up to the ornate domed ceiling. It had been 13 years since he had been in this massive room with its long-dead creatures that had terrorized him in his nightmares. Earlier this morning, he had trembled on the steps of the museum before venturing in. It all seemed so silly now. It was just a big old harmless room. But The Hanley School was different. He certainly had reason to fear that place. Suddenly, with a stab of conviction, Bobby knew that one day he would go back there and get to the bottom of what had happened. He would tell everyone. He would blow the whistle on The Hanley School and close down that goddamned place for good.

Feeling better now, Bobby stood up. As he strode to the exit, he never saw the huge dinosaur's jaw click open, grinding slowly; its unseeing, hollow eyes deep within its ancient skull followed his every movement with contempt and disapproval.

THE END

ELECTRIFYING HORROR AND OCCULT

2343-1	**THE WERELING**	$3.50 US, $3.95 Can
2341-5	**THE ONI**	$3.95 US, $4.50 Can
2334-2	**PREMONITION**	$3.50 US, $3.95 Can
2331-8	**RESURREXIT**	$3.95 US, $4.50 Can
2302-4	**WORSHIP THE NIGHT**	$3.95 US, $3.95 Can
2289-3	**THE WITCHING**	$3.50 US, $3.95 Can
2281-8	**THE FREAK**	$2.50 US, $2.95 Can
2251-6	**THE HOUSE**	$2.50
2206-0	**CHILD OF DEMONS**	$3.75 US, $4.50 Can
2142-0	**THE FELLOWSHIP**	$3.75 US, $4.50 Can

MORE BLOOD-CHILLERS FROM LEISURE BOOKS